ABOUT TO HAPPEN . . .

"My name keeps coming up. It's Mercy this, and Mercy that. Why? Because I'm the one who is the magnet. I do all the attracting to this house.

He waits, and peeps. *Thing* is getting ready to spring. *Monsters* are everywhere. But good things are in the world. Stephen comes here to see me and takes me out. Oh, I am growing tall and fair by the minute, that much I know, but there is something else to all this, something more. Even a girl wants to undress me, a girl, and stare at my jewels. She hides steel instruments with which to sample me further.

It's pretty scary all this, but—well—kind of thrilling. And it will not go away."

MERCY

A NOVEL BY

JOYCE MACIVER

AVON
PUBLISHERS OF BARD, CAMELOT, DISCUS, EQUINOX AND FLARE BOOKS

TO W. W. SCOTT
Merciless editor, but man of mercy

MERCY is an original publication of Avon Books. This
work has never before appeared in any form.

AVON BOOKS
A division of
The Hearst Corporation
959 Eighth Avenue
New York, New York 10019

Copyright © 1977 by Georgette Scott.
Published by arrangement with the author.
Library of Congress Catalog Card Number: 76-49707
ISBN: 0-380-00843-2

First Avon Printing, January, 1977

Printed in the U.S.A.

PART ONE

1917-1925

HIM. He was all over the place back when I was dressed in that soft white blue-ribboned stuff all girl babies wore in those days. As soon as I could understand words, I was introduced to Him, and after that, as I told you, He was everywhere.

He was powerful and mysterious and exciting as all hell, but peculiar, definitely peculiar. You could never tell when He would come or go. They were always talking about Him. No matter what else they were talking about, He somehow got into the conversation.

Who was He? Hell, who is He? Because He's still around, in a manner of speaking. Hold on. He could make anything happen to me, well, mainly to me. He had singled me out, that is, this Big Man. He was in fact my waiting bridegroom.

My mother explained, tenderly and carefully, how it was with Him, this watcher, and how to keep in with Him. She seemed to think it was very easy: just don't do anything you want to do. Anything that comes naturally is *wrong*, He won't like it, He's watching and adding up the score.

I had a picture of Him wearing a stiff shirt and me wearing a long, white dress. The picture was pretty foggy, but included ice cream and cake, and music, and lots of expensive presents; that was about as far

2

as I could imagine, except that the presents would keep on pouring in.

He was in my mind, in kindergarten, on the streets, during meals. They saw to it that no matter where I went or what I did, I would always have to return to Him and say a few words, which I began to do rather mechanically, the way a whole lot of people do.

As I grew older and began to face school, I also began to have a concept of my own about Him, and this concept had two sides, one good and one pretty bad. I heard that not only was He my bridegroom but He was also my father, an interesting if confusing pair of facts to put together, especially interesting, as He had all this *wealth* which was all for *me*.

I also heard He had some feminine characteristics, being capable of tender love, such as protection and maternal feelings, but was also a man. Now this has a strong sexual appeal for a child, combining love and touching from both, mother and father. You get that, and with money, you've hit the jackpot! With a person as famous as He, with all He had going for Him, and me His kid and future bride, things were looking up, and I was prepared to do His bidding.

Then I heard His name was Jesus Christ. It was of course a very famous name, but I didn't particularly like it. Being a run-of-the-mill, middle-class, Wasp kid, I would much rather He had been called Thomas Wells Harrington III or something like that. I heard He was Jewish, or *had been* Jewish, and that was peculiar on both counts, as was the news He had been killed for some reason, but had come back, risen from the dead, that kind of thing. He was still around, anyway, and was waiting for me.

He had this Father called God, who was joined on to him, somehow, at least they were one, sort of Siamese twins. And there was a third person, the Holy Ghost, who joined the team. Altogether there were three heads, but this was beyond me, so I settled for Him, figuring to get to His family, such as it was, when I had to, as

3

they were kind of peculiar, if you want to know the truth.

Those pictures of Him in a nightgown and on His knees were pretty disappointing. Of course Rudolph Valentino wore nightgowns, but only when he kidnapped people! Besides, he was on horseback and the nightgowns became flowing robes.

I noticed that *I* did all the talking whereas He was pretty damned quiet. But He was there, oh was He there, and watching me! No matter, Jew or Gentile, dead or alive or resurrected, whatever the hell it was He did, He either reached, or was pushed into me. He cut a pattern of love right out of the first clear paper of my being, damn His hide. He doomed me to a fearsome sense of respect for the unattainable, forced me to go looking for Him in the room that never was.

Now, the unattainable was pretty fashionable at that time, glorified by Joan Crawford and Lillian Gish and other sad, silent-movie beauties. It wasn't much fun, of course. No wonder we kids were stirred by galloping horses and bad men involved in a good hot kidnapping. At least the bad men were not just waiting around in the wings and peeping like old Jesus.

That He was watching was emphasized at home and in Sunday school, whither I was deposited every week, dressed to the nines and singing, "I'll be a sunbeam for Je-sus, And shine for Him each day." He was watching closely, particularly when I was naked. He knew all about me, down to the small mole on my left hip which "Aunt" Rose, my black nurse, said was a beauty spot.

Images of His wonders *took,* much as a picture is impressed on film by the camera lens. My future husband, this man, had magic powers, and was mine, all mine. I didn't even have to sit rubbing a lamp like Aladdin had to do. Now I'm up. But He was dead, nailed to a nasty wooden cross with the blood dripping off like water. Now I'm down. *But* He had risen, He was still *alive,* possibly located in a balloon nearby, or

4

in my house, wearing some kind of invisible cloak or skin. He is dead *and* alive, and I am up *and* down.

It was the Reverend Dr. Robert Lyons who informed me about my future husband in a sing-song style, with endless anecdotes from the Bible I took to be scientific data. While much of this was totally beyond my comprehension at this time, and I squirmed on stiff church pews, dreaming of chicken with gravy and pie with ice cream, some of it, notably the story of the loaves and fishes, made very good sense.

It was right up there with all the magic stories we kids were fed and devoured whole—Santa Claus, Cinderella and Aladdin, all the great rewarders. Then came the non-rewarders, the punishers, the I'll-get-yous, giants and dragons, cruel stepmothers, a parade of monsters, running neck and neck with old Jesus and God for our attention, and one day, all of this was rudely interrupted by a genuine live monster, the Kaiser, complete with sharp-pointed helmet and gnashing teeth. Alive, in the world, not dead like Jesus, and in the business of tearing off skin by the yard.

We sat at the table listening to our mama thanking Our Lord for the food, and we waited impatiently for the atrocity stories going the rounds. The "woah" was coming on apace. "Little pitchers have big ears," my Aunt Jenny admonished Mamma, who sat at the end of the dining table reading the nightmare news stories, letting her eggs grow cold as she devoured the headlines, but Mamma, youngest, prettiest and the only married one of three sisters, was not to be silenced. I heard how German soldiers, called Huns, had cut the breasts off Belgian women, and the hands off babies. She read how London hospital cots held Belgian children, innocent little girls like me, with no hands!

The word "crucified" brought to mind my old friend Jesus, waiting in the wings, remember, and peeping in on me like mad. I heard how the Huns had "crucified" Canadian soldiers. Canadians were practically Americans like us! They could be reached by train and anybody who could be reached by train was a neighbor.

5

The Huns had stuck bayonets through their hands and feet. After bedtime my sister Virginia Anne and I would creep down the stairs and listen intently as the evening papers were read aloud.

We heard how the Kaiser's men had bundled corpses and sent them back to Germany to be made into grease and soap, and after hearing this, my washings of face and hands took on a certain grim aspect, containing as it did at least half a dozen dead people. For all that my uncles bravely denied or pooh-poohed the crucifixion stories, we kids took a dim view of old Kirkman's Borax soap on kitchen sinks and those round chunks of Yardley's on bathtubs.

I spent a great deal of time loving and hating my parents with unbridled passion and trying to figure out just what in hell they were up to. Didn't He eavesdrop? Hadn't He spent nineteen hundred years doing just that? What, for instance, was my Daddy going on about as he sat of a morning devouring sausages and pancakes, guzzling coffee by the gallon?

"That gumshoe Bill Stone," he would start, "been at it again. He's a German spy—that pacifist! He's trying to cripple the country. We've got to get in there and stop him. Every time he opens his mouth—playing Germany's game. Friend of the Kaiser—ever since the woah began!"

Mamma, anxious to get upstairs and fit the dress she was having made for the night of her concert, would try to quiet him down. "But he did try to warn Americans, dear."

"What?"

"Warned them not to go on belligerent ships."

Daddy shook his head. "Oh, well, yes. Ever since the woah began he's been doing that. Even said our citizens had no right to be *on* the *Lusitania*. Only, we *did* have the right to be on the *Lusitania*. He was on their side! He opposes us every time we turn around. He's pro-German, anti-British, all the way down the line. He's a German agent, that's what he is!"

Mamma tapped her foot under the table, watching

6

the telephone as she tried to listen. We waited impatiently to hear more about the Kaiser cutting people up.

But Daddy fixed her with a beady eye. "Living idol of the Germans—that's what this Stone is! Wants unrestricted submarine warfare. Why, I'd swear he wants it more than Von Tirpitz, maybe even more than Hindenburg."

"Nobody seems to be sure of anything," said Mamma.

"The Germans are. They're sure of him. He's their man, that's what he is. I'd like to see him shot through the head, and so would every other American in his right senses. Head of the Foreign Relations Committee. Him! No wonder we're helpless."

Mamma tried again. "But there's been a break between him and President Wilson. I was just reading about it." The minute we heard President Wilson's name we knew it was going to be boring.

Oh, there were things going on "over there" and they supplied another kind of thrill, different and less benign than the Jesus one, but better because it was happening now. Wherever you turned, the Kaiser could be seen in posters large as life, his evil cape flowing after him, a monster, current and active.

It was a while before he came real close, a while before the war, like some great flying dragon, cast its giant shadow directly over Baltimore's Hollins Street.

One day in the spring of 1917 a number of newsboys descended and began calling "Ex-ter, pa-par, Exter, Ex-ter."

"It's the Kaiser!" announced my sister Virginia Anne, who dropped the doll's house we were repairing in the backyard and tore through the house.

"That's Johnsy Dowse, he's somewhere down the street," said Mamma. Johnsy's voice, for once, was distinguished in the medley. "Well, I guess it's come," Mamma said to Rose.

"Yes, Miz Bassford," Rose agreed. "We're in it now. Yes, ma'am."

"We'll wait for Johnsy," said Mamma, as we all

four went down the vestibule steps and stood in a group on the top step.

Johnsy was considered "backward." Sometimes you could hardly hear him, but today his voice was loud and wild. I could make out the words, *"Press Wilson."* Other newsboys were screaming their lungs out. People were running into the street to buy their papers. A newsboy came around the lawn near the big, gray stone house on the corner where the rich Farrars lived, and another was hollering down the block, *"Press Wilson duck-layered woah, Press Wilson duck-layered woah against Germany!"*

"We won't buy any papers till Johnsy comes, no matter how long he takes," Mamma told Rose. The newsboys nearest us were almost sold out. Then, just as another boy appeared, Johnsy came running into our block, yelling, "Pressed Wilson duck-layered woah! Getcher ex-ter papar!"

Rose bought the three papers left and Johnsy began to jump up and down, hollering, "Hey, Mercy, I'm goin' to jawn up," and we all laughed at the eight-year-old capering on our steps.

Things began happening. President Wilson had indeed duck-layered woah. A whole new rhythm entered our lives. Suddenly everybody had a part to play, no matter how small. Women, and even some men, were busy knitting socks, rolling bandages and, later, wrapping packages and driving out to Camp Meade or further to visit the soldiers and giving parties and dances for them.

Aunt Rose, now turned house servant, let me hold the ball of khaki-colored wool, as she let fly with the needles for soldiers' socks.

Rose was a part of me. Warmth seemed to seep out from under her dark dresses and surround her enormous black lap; she grew in the house as a tree grows in a garden. While the white adults came and went, she stayed in one place, and, unlike them, she was cool and collected and never surprised or fooled.

8

We were never certain of her family name, and Rose herself was magnificently uncertain. "Ah-ve got some real nice names, haven't I?" she would say, on those rare occasions when letters or packages were delivered in care of us, addressed at various times to Rose Hicks, Rose Jackson, Rose Gaines, Rose Jones and Rose Calhoun. "My mammy's name is mostly Hicks, but my pappy's name was Jones and Gaines. My grandpappy's name was Calhoun. He was born down to Mista Calhoun's place. That's a pretty name, Calhoun, but mostly I'm called Rose Jackson."

One day I was standing in a crowd beside my Uncle Clinton. We were going to join Mamma and Daddy at a downtown restaurant for lunch, but Uncle Clinton had to stop and wait to see if his number had been drawn. He was holding my hand so I wouldn't get lost in the crowd. I entertained myself looking at the posters of the Kaiser biting into a globe of the earth. Then I stared at other posters of naked, starving Armenians. I listened to talk about the draft and felt tired and hungry.

Meanwhile Uncle Clinton's hand was getting sweaty. He was not my favorite uncle; he never brought presents or candy, and I didn't like being left with him, especially in this loud hot crush. He had gray hair when he was only twenty-three and he always took us to restaurants where there were more napkins and tablecloths than food and he would sit opposite us telling jokes he thought appropriate for young people.

I was contemplating these matters when he suddenly let go of me. I heard him say, "No-o-o-o! No-o-o-o-o!" His voice was low and he was angry, too. He moved away from me, leaving me to fend for myself as he made tracks through the crowd toward the front to read the numbers more clearly.

I followed him, staking out a place just behind him. "Goddamn it to hell and gone!" It wasn't at all what I'd heard people were supposed to feel when they were drafted. Some men down front were throwing their hats in the air and shouting, "Hip, hip, hooray," "Atta-boy!" and "See ya in the army."

I grabbed his hand, but he did something I can only describe as throwing it away, as he turned, cursing softly but continuously and saying "shit," a word I had never heard before. Meantime, he was taking large steps and forcing his way back out through the crowd.

"Are you in the war, Uncle Clinton?" I asked, as soon as I came abreast of him, and we were both out in the clear.

"What?"

"Are you going to war?"

"That's what it looks like," he said. He dropped the words flat.

"Gee," I said. "That's wonderful." He gave no sign of having heard.

A few weeks later we began to see soldiers in khaki in and around the red brick houses in the neighborhood, in groups and singly, day and night, and usually laughing. The civilians were more worried than they. A general mien of seriousness crept into conversations around the table and in the parlor when the soldiers were not present.

Soldiers were invited to dinners and honored at parties where tableloads of especially good food were served with rich, expensive desserts. It was as if it were some soldier's birthday every day at my Cousin Louise's house across the street. Honey, not yet turned sixteen, but a beauty and a popular belle, seemed to know hundreds of soldiers—corporals, majors, colonels and privates, and they flocked to her like bees.

Everybody was for the war, and why shouldn't they be? Hadn't the Germans sunk our ships, sent spies into our factories and now weren't they putting germs into our water supply that could kill people by the thousands?

It was all thrilling! Especially that stuff about cutting people up! It beat the Jesus and giant stories hands down.

One day my Aunt Jenny came home and reported that she had, with her own eyes, seen Stephen Farrar III, the tall handsome rich boy who lived in the gray stone house across the street, walking in a parade of anti-war demonstrators.

"There he was, big as life, walking with about a thousand boys, and *men*," said Aunt Jenny. "Went right past the Academy of Music."

"What!" exclaimed Mamma. "You mean he was with those demonstrators?" My parents were horrified that Mrs. Farrar, a beauty and a lady of great wealth and social prominence, would allow her son to march with "those evil slackers," those people who not only were *not* doing their bit but were proud of it to boot, daring to parade in protest, a nasty piece of business, broken up by the police.

This Stephen Farrar was an exceptional young man, tall, with broad shoulders, an attractive smile and a speaking voice of almost hypnotic charm. He had picked me up from a tumble in the snow and carried me home upon more than one occasion, and afterward he always brought me delightful gifts—picture books or boxes of expensive chocolates; memories of these incidents lingered.

I was disturbed that Stephen was one of the protesters. We got the idea that they favored the Kaiser, condoned his slaughtering of Belgians, and the slashing off of breasts and tearing off of skin to make soap. They ought to be punished by law, we heard, and meantime certainly should not be received in our homes.

The Kaiser was clearly a genuine, hot, exciting villain, but this business of the slackers confused me, especially when they mentioned Stephen, who reminded me of all the rewarders I had ever heard of. Who would believe this handsome boy of sixteen, who lived in the stone castle on the corner with the lawn *all around it*, was *bad*? How could anyone who spoke with a faintly foreign or British accent, not at all Southern, who picked people up when they fell in the snow, be bad?

11

Why, he was running neck and neck with Jesus and was one hell of a lot more reliable.

Daddy usually arose about nine, took an hour to dress, then came downstairs and sat for a good hour and a half, devouring an enormous breakfast. First a dish of fruit—figs, a baked apple with cream, fresh peaches or a melon in season. Then, eggs with sausages or bacon, cakes with maple syrup, a whole potful of coffee with cream, and often, fried tripe or hominy grits. At intervals, while devouring, he would let forth his opinions of the woah, the Presidency, the state of "mah properties," which, to hear him, were always going into decline and likely to fall down in a good storm.

These properties kept him busy finding repair men who would do the work without eating into his profits, and now that the woah had come and factories were opening up, getting workers was harder than ever.

I imagined he had built the properties himself and they all belonged to him down to the last brick, and that he needed all these piles of pancakes to go on erecting more and more properties until he had a great empire stretching from one end of the city to the other. It took me a deal of time to discover that they belonged to my paternal grandmother, and wouldn't become his until her demise.

Meantime, he was the overseer, collecting weekly rents, mostly from blacks who, when not working, paid off "later on." The properties were small dark houses or shanties, heated with coal stoves and without basements but with remarkable woodsheds in the yards into which strayed all the discarded "white pets" from the neighborhood.

My father liked to have at least one woman listening to his opinions and occasionally asking questions such as, "What was that, sir?" or "How interesting," or "You don't say!" My mother sat there doing this too, no matter how long it took, stopping only occasionally to wink at my Aunt Jenny, who was also given to asking these brilliant questions.

12

No wonder. Their mother, my grandma, had told them, "When he returns home of an afternoon, a man should be received at the door by the servant and handed a change of coat and soft shoes. Then he should be kissed by his wife and served a cup of hot broth or a short glass with a biscuit."

These rules of life were handed down to me along with those of Jesus' mastery and benevolence.

When Mamma asked me to tell her what I had done that day in kindergarten, I knew all the answers without thinking. Complete passivity and strict obedience *only* were required of little brides of Christ, and I reeled off the story of what an angel I had been, then took leave and ran off to fairer pastures.

Aunt Rose was waiting in the kitchen to tell me what was really going on. "Your Cousin Louise wants you to get over there *right away* the minute you gets home," she whispered one afternoon. "You better go on now and don't stop to eat. She's in a hurry."

I rushed across the street to see her, the youngest and only remaining daughter of my Aunt Gus and maternal Uncle Tom, and a beauty. We called her Honey; sixteen and already popular with men, she had two special beaus whom she ran on alternate nights, Raymond and Clarence, both now happily in the army, and now a whole slew of soldiers had found their way to her house.

Honey had a dimpled round face and perfect teeth. Her body was pretty, but not in the sense of the look on Fifth Avenue today; but then she was a belle, and what a belle! She had small breasts, a tiny waist and a fat behind. I remember her dainty, expressive hands and small ankles, and her great piles of curly brown hair which she wore up. She had big hazel eyes and long black lashes and a perfect complexion. As I see it now, every part of her body was either small to breaking or fat to bursting but she was pretty as a picture just the same, merry on the surface and fun to be with.

My Uncle Tom, Louise's father, and my Aunt Augusta lived in the big old red brick house across the street, with the green lawn and poplar trees and pots of ivy and geraniums.

Nobody knew for sure where the Masons got the money to keep their house going, with the two servants, Goldie down in the kitchen, who lived in the back room, and Harrison living back in the alley but showing up most every morning for cleaning and ready to be called for parties or for "carrying-in" when my Uncle George got drunk and decided to pay a visit, often settling on the front steps with pals and shouting family secrets.

The Jewish neighbors, the Zieglers and the Whitestones, ran candy and stationery stores and sold underwear right out in the open. They talked about their businesses, so a person knew where they got their money, but the Masons were secretive. The family knew, but nobody mentioned it. Aunt Gus was busy with dressmaking. She didn't admit that she did any at all. She said she sometimes "fixed things" for friends or for "charity," for the church in particular, but we knew she did it for money.

Uncle Tom worked at something or other downtown. He got up early and returned home late, coming down the back alley and entering the house through the back yard. Whatever he did, he had to change his clothes and bathe before sitting down to dinner or addressing his wife, whom he called "Mrs. Mason," but that was all we knew, besides, of course, that he was a professional churchman and constant pallbearer. I noticed early on Uncle Tom was kind of crazy. He talked to himself and was always quoting from the Bible, often getting it wrong.

He was fond of saying, *"Blessed are the defiled,"* and other gala inaccuracies. The greatest trial was to have to sit at the table with the delicious odor of hot bread and baking ham in the nostrils, and be forced to wait and listen, more or less, as he read his favorite passages from Proverbs.

His most favorite of all was about "the strange woman," the "stranger which flattereth with her words." I heard about this damnable woman so often I could practically recite what she did, "in the twilight, in the evening, in the dark night." I knew all about how she would wait at the corner in the streets for the innocent young man, to lure him to her home where she had decked her bed with coverings of tapestry and carved works, and made said bed odorous as all hell with myrrh and cinnamon. I heard all about how her husband was away and she practically forced the innocent young man "as an ox to the slaughter." Then when Uncle Tom read how she had "cast down many wounded," and how "many strong men had been slain by her," I concluded I had heard another murder story and wondered why the woman had chosen to commit her crimes in such an uncomfortable and smelly bed.

Altogether, my Uncle Tom, Honey's daddy, was an overly serious and exceptionally boring man. How he had ever managed to sire such a lovely and wanton piece as my Cousin Honey I will never know. I adored Honey and hurried across to her house whenever Aunt Rose gave me the high sign.

This time I found her sitting in her big rocker, knitting brown wool socks as if her life depended upon it. I could tell what was on her mind from the animated way she started talking the minute I entered the back sitting room, just off the big porch where Aunt Gus and Honey could usually be found either sewing or, these days, making up packages for soldiers. "Mercy, darling, I've got something for you. Oh, have I got something for *you!*"

Aunt Gus looked up from the box she was packing long enough to ask, "What are you two up to, *Lou*-ise?" I knew from the way Honey dropped the socks she was folding like a hot potato we were going upstairs fast where we would soon be involved in a very private matter.

"I'm going to get out my little blue dress and try it on Mercy, Mamma. I declare that dress would fit a child, it's tiny and tight and all it needs is to be taken up and in."

The last words were being said as she hurried me out

15

of the room and up the stairs and I knew she had much more than any blue dress on her mind. She wanted me to go with her to the bathroom, which she was somehow unable to do alone. She couldn't bring herself to admit to her mamma or anybody except me and her dog Screamer that was how it was. As a young child I had earned a constant supply of pennies and nickles by simply being present whenever Honey needed to do her "binnie" and couldn't seem to do it alone.

"I declare I get so lonesome," was the way Honey explained it to me. No explanation was really necessary, as I accepted Honey as I accepted myself, though I loved her much more. The chore was sometimes uncomfortable and uninteresting for me, especially when it took time, but I loved her and even sitting there watching her with her skirts pulled up straining, didn't bother me.

Later on, she moved in a special chair for me so I could sit and talk to her while in action, so to speak. She had put a rubber pillow and mat in the tub those times when she took a bath, so she could lie back and talk. This setup was useful during those periods when I was in school and she was caught short, because then Screamer, the half-collie, half German shepherd, was a stand-in for me. She would take him by his collar and drag him up the stairs to the bathroom where she would hold him locked in, a captive audience, until she was finished, either bathing or sitting, or both. Old Screamer didn't mind coming up but after a while he wanted to leave. In time he caught on that he couldn't and then he would try to resist going along altogether.

"I just can't have a good operation all alone by myself," Honey would say, by way of explanation for her peculiar requirements for companionship. "But the minute you come sit by me, Mercy, I declare everything loosens up."

Honey also liked to have me sleep by her side at night. On many a summer's night I hiked across the street with my little suitcase containing my night clothes and toothbrush to save her from her terrible fate. "It's so hot and lonesome up there, Mercy darling," she would say in the summertime, even when the overhead, hanging-from-the-ceiling fan was going full blast. "A person all by theirselves could just die." And in the winter, when I came with my flannels, she'd say, "I'll freeze to death if I have to sleep by myself. I declare I'll be found dead as an old stone."

On this particular day Honey was in seventh heaven because both Screamer and I followed her up the stairs. The front doorbell rang as we three, led by Honey, made our way up the dark, carpeted stairs to the hall leading to the upstairs bathroom. Honey stopped at the first ring and leaned over the banister to see who had come in. "That's old Miz deVaughn," she whispered. "Mamma's having her in to tea and that'll take a heap of time, thank the Lord." Since Miz deVaughn was one of the people who regularly paid Aunt Gus for dressmaking, and since the entire matter was covered up by the ritual of a pretended visit with tea served in the parlor, I knew what Honey meant.

We made our way on upstairs and were soon ensconced in our regular places in the bathroom, me on chair and Screamer on the mat in the tub, while Honey, having bolted the door and pulled up her dress, was proceeding on the pot.

"I've missed you so, Mercy," she began, gradually emitting small groans of joy. "Waited all morning for you. I tell you what . . ." she went on, as she concentrated with her entire personality and energy on the movements going on in her colon, "you stay awhile with me, after my operation, and I'm going to give you—" followed by a long "Ahhh" of undiluted joy, "the rest of the money I owe you. You can stay now, can't you, Mercy? You've got to. *Promise?*"

I said I could, I had no errands to run that afternoon, and, having finished her work, she pulled up her pretty embroidered drawers, pulled down her skirts and began washing her hands as if her life depended upon it. Next she dried and powdered them, straightened up and, turning to me, smiled one of those incredibly bright, dimpled smiles.

"Let's go now, Mercy darling, and you wait, you just *wait* till you see what I've got."

I came away with nearly fifty cents in nickels and pennies, half a box of chewy caramels, a blue silk dress pinned up and taken in, and endless promises of parties, more money and enduring love that would go on forever and ever. I had to promise to come by in the morning before school and stay awhile with her, which I said I would. All of this took some time and it was nearly dark when I left at the precise moment soldier Clarence came in. He was Louise's favorite beau, tall and laughing, whereas Raymond, to whom she was engaged, was serious, and he always escorted me home, either piggy-back or on his shoulders, a highly pleasant experience.

Womenfolk those days were soft as butter, warm as toast. As I look back upon them, the lot of them, it feels like falling into a mess of cotton taffy, an experience I could do with a bit of right now. They all had roots and a place; even the rootless were taken in and *placed*, a mighty act in any culture. My Cousin Maria, for instance, fat, aging and deaf as a post from birth, came to each member of the family one day a week, had breakfast, lunch, tea and dinner, late supper before bed, of course, and was put into her own soft bed at night which was cleaned up and turned down for her.

In return she did a bit of mending, minded the children, played the piano of an evening and sang, those awful hymns mostly, with only an occasional popular song thrown in, such as "I'm Afraid to Go Home in the Dark," and even those had some kind of a moral, at least that was how we kids interpreted it.

Cousin Maria had seven homes she visited regularly, five in the city, in each of which she had a room and a bath of her own, and two in the country, my Aunt Grace's and my Aunt Mandy's, one at the seashore and one in the mountains. She divided her time between

18

them in the summer and she stayed till the first frost, giving the rest of her time to her city relatives.

They were, as I say, a mighty soft parcel of women. I can tell you that, having crawled all over them as a child. And they all had menfolk protecting them. Not only this, but they were asked in marriage by men without being pretty. Without *having* to be pretty, slim, rich, or important, men seemed to want them and to actually like them. My beloved Aunt Jenny bore a faint resemblance to a buffalo. But a buffalo you love is unquestionably something special. My mother was the only pretty sister in her family.

They all kept house, baked tons of muffins, roasted herds of cattle, brought up children and entertained in the evening with and often without benefit of servants, but I don't believe a one of them ever felt victimized.

The average middle-class or even richer women still had their talents, as did many of the poor. They could play the piano and sing, give piano lessons, design clothes, sew, dance, converse, paint, throw a party for fifty people without neglecting a single detail and keep it going for hours.

I had aunts and cousins who did paintings that were shown in museums, sang or played at concerts, some of which were well received by critics, without any of them making much of a fuss about it.

A good many of them knew about as much about the sexual details of life as they did about raising a building from the ground up. They came to their marriage beds in a state of determination combined with utter terror. "Whatever happens, just let him do it and say nothing," my grandma advised. The general idea was that, at worst, friend husband would turn into twelve kinds of a fiend and demand their lives. At best he would tear them into shreds and leave them exhausted, bleeding and in need of a doctor; but if they went through with it and managed somehow to get to their feet in the morning and put their clothes back on, eventually he'd quiet down and somehow or other life would go on.

After that, of course, they would be murdered again and again.

What a man actually did and how on earth he did it was never mentioned, and anything that was never mentioned had to be pretty terrible. The beautiful things that were mentioned constantly, presents from Jesus and the like, often didn't materialize, but you could be sure a husband, if he didn't actually kill his wife on the wedding night, would sure as hell take a crack at it.

Women went to college, music school, teaching school as they pleased, or the economy permitted. Mostly, men went on to become doctors, lawyers or just plain rich. My Cousin Honey had "been through" high school, but no diploma was ever in evidence. As I look back on her talents, they were not minimal by any means. She could toe it on the ballet stage with the best of them. The Chopin études that floated from Aunt Gus's parlor had more feeling, or surely as much, as those of my mother, who had given recitals that were well reviewed in the papers, and when Honey went out to sell Liberty Bonds she hit the highest number in our block. And men flocked to her by the hundreds.

With all of today's competition for careers and media coverage, and people going naked on lighted stages and in the streets, no wonder a body can be pardoned a sigh of longing for the time when a big girl could be happy and fat, make pans of caramels, batches of muffins and cocoanut cookies, play a hot game of Parcheesi or Lotto nights and still get a man to love her. And her almighty ignorance of what he might have a mind to do to her, far from being held against her, was considered a veritable asset in the market of men's favor, in a world where innocence was hot.

So there I was, my friends. A little goodie, middle-class Wasp kid, scared half to death of old Jesus who spied on me continually and knew everything I did; I was furious underneath, right underneath, too. You don't have to plunge deep to see that one. A person who is constantly watched rebels. I was going for instance, to

20

feel myself and see what it was I had; let Him peep His eyes out. Feel I did, but not without paying a price. When I came down with scarlet fever so mild Dr. Hardwick called it scarlatina, I was certain He had struck back, and that my skin was about to fall off. After this I would go through life just like those skinned rabbits piled up at Heinzer's butcher stall in Hollins Market. Cold winds would blow on me, even at home in a warm house, because with no skin I could never put any clothes on. Eventually my family would have to hide me in the attic the way folks did with those crazy people who weren't in the asylum, and I'd stay up there peering through the shutters till the end.

And when I came home from kindergarten with lice in my hair I simply assumed He was crawling around in my brain, peeping down there to straighten things out. He had put all those nasty bugs in my hair. He had thousands of them in jars, and I'd never have any hair after this!

Because who was it, waiting, watching from the ceiling as I sat at the long table in the sunshiny preschool room, drawing a house with red and blue crayons? And who was it hanging over the table like a damned bird when I went home to lunch, waiting as my mother thanked Him for the food and I, too, had to wait to grab the sandwiches and gulp down the milk? Him, of course. The Eternal Peeping Tom.

One Sunday, right after Sunday school, I went over to Aunt Gus's to deliver a package and found my Uncle Tom reading to his wife from the Bible, and Aunt Gus staring off into space, no doubt where the saints and prophets were playing about in her mind. They both insisted I have chocolate cake, which I accepted, but later I was sorry I did because Honey was nowhere to be found and Uncle Tom went on and on.

This time it was all about curses being put on people whenever they didn't obey the commandments of the "Lawyud," especially if they went after "other gods" and, oh, it was awful. I waited impatiently for the very

21

first interruption and took to my heels, right after the Lawyud had done in the armies of Egypt, including their horses and chariots, and made the water of the Red Sea to overflow them and drown them like flies.

I was so eager to be out of earshot of Uncle Tom, a depressing personality if I ever saw one and a very slow speaker—the words came out of his thin mouth like lead, and in my eagerness to be out of the front door, I went through the parlor.

I began walking hastily across the heavy Brussels carpet. The place was in semi-darkness, the dark green draperies pulled nearly together over the windows, but I could see at once from the fading light filtering in across the carpet that something was wrong! There were *feet* sticking out from under the piano, the most peculiar kind of feet I had ever seen. I stopped dead still and looked. There lay two girl's black-stockinged feet, and right over them, slightly to the sides, two of the biggest feet and legs I'd ever seen, in laced leather boots and turned backwards, or upside down. There was more to it, there were long khaki-covered thighs just above the boots and what strangely resembled a man's behind in the same kind of khaki, moving in and out in the most peculiar but fascinating way.

I started to walk quietly and carefully around this array of parts, but, in my desire not to miss anything, I kept my head turned toward the moving object, and, as I did, knocked into the piano, and my arm banged down on the keys. I knew I'd done something wrong but I didn't know quite what or why, so I stopped dead and began picking up Honey's sheet music and trying to put it back on the piano. It took only a few seconds, but next thing I knew, there stood my Cousin Honey herself, side by side together with Lieutenant Clarence Jarvis! "Why, hello there, Mercy," said Lieutenant Jarvis, offering me his hand, "Glad to see you." I let him shake my hand, then Honey came up from around the other side of the piano.

"We lost a ring," she said, by way of explanation, "I

guess it dropped behind the piano—and—we were looking for it."

Honey was having trouble with her skirts but then she was always having trouble with her skirts, making them come down over her hips, and she was always laughing, showing her dimples and shaking her piles of curls, so there was nothing new in her appearance. But the way those two stood there, trying to stop me from going behind the piano, the way they spoke in chorus, "Never mind, Mercy, dear," and giving me all that literal explanation, "We're not sure it's back there," and "Don't bother now, it's too dark, we'll find it later on!" That was confusing.

There was something going on all right, but meantime I went on behind the piano just the same and it wasn't dark back there to me. The ring was there all right, *and* a black silk stocking, and of all things, a brassiere! I wouldn't show that to Lieutenant Jarvis and embarrass Honey, I decided as I crawled out from under the piano, handing Honey the ring but folding the stocking and brassiere which I hid quickly under the Spanish shawl which served as a piano cover. "Thank you, Mercy, darling," said Honey, showing her dimples. "Now Clarence is going to see you home."

The lieutenant put his arm around me and helped me across the street. He had such a big arm which he placed gently around my shoulders and he kept talking to me as if I was a grownup person. "You're real pretty, you know, Mercy? I'm going to write to you from overseas, and you write back, you hear? And when I get to Paris I'm going to get you a real French present. You write and tell me what you want." I was glad I'd broken in on them and helped them find the ring. At the vestibule he pressed a coin into my hand and kissed me on the cheek. I didn't even realize I had the coin until I got inside and saw it was a silver dollar. Watching him hurry back across the street to Honey, I thought, what a wonderful man!

Nevertheless this was not a good day. There was something funny about this day. Something hard to get

23

hold of. Whenever you didn't know just what to do or who to talk to, you could hear the kitchen calling, *Come on in here, come to me. I'm big and bright and warm, I am, and ready and waiting,* and that's where I headed. My sister had a fever and was being kept in bed and watched over; there had been an epidemic of measles. Rose, between cooking and singing hymns, was burning some plants in the corner, an activity purported to bring magical results She found time to say, "How's you, baby?" and I started to tell her. First about the feet sticking out from under the piano. "You ought not to interrupt peoples that're courting," she said.

"But they weren't courting. They were looking for Honey's ring."

"Maybe so. Maybe they were hiding back there and kissing each others good-bye."

That was just plain crazy, and I told her so. I tried to tell her the rest of what was on my mind, but it didn't come out right, as I didn't know what it was that really was on my mind.

Now the average grand piano those days was really quite a thing, covered with a plentiful embroidered Spanish shawl with long silk fringe dripping down, and with the standing lamp in the corner throwing a loving puddle of soft light back there. Why, it was a great place for anything. It usually had on top a silver platter containing cards and bills and letters, a cut-glass vase of flowers, most often dead with only the dried ferns left, silver framed photographs of family and relatives, a box of cigars and odd presents and ornaments—china slippers or Japanese dolls. This one had framed diplomas from Aunt Gus's three daughters' graduations—Honey's wasn't there, and the inevitable Chinese vase with the covered top, containing dried rose leaves that smelled like eternal life.

Aunt Gus's parlor, along with most other parlors, had the usual long, gold-framed Pierglass mirror between the windows, two horsehair sofas facing each other, with tiny lamps beside them, big overstuffed chairs, fringed lamps and heavy draperies over the lace curtains at the

24

windows. The parlor had two doorways, each kept covered with those dark green velvet portieres so heavy you could barely move them.

Those parlors weren't usually used for passageways, but kept for receiving company. Family members entering or leaving the house did so by way of the hall which ran beside the parlor at right angles. Therefore anyone who just happened to be under the piano could easily up and leave without being spotted by simply crawling around behind the ample Spanish shawl. Come to think of it, it would be nice to be courting and kissing back there. And if one person could crawl out, why not two people? With its heavy Brussels carpets and almost complete darkness, I began to see it was just about the perfect place for Honey to kiss Lieutenant Jarvis good-bye. Maybe they'd been kissing when she lost her ring. "But when did she lose her brassiere?"

"What's that?" Rose stared hard.

"Honey's *brassiere!* I found it in back of the piano." I was trying to keep my patience. "And a stocking."

Rose chuckled. "Times like that, all kinds of things drops back of furnitures. Ain't nobody's business going around picking up other peoples' underwear and talking about it. No little lady does things as that kind."

"What do you do then?"

"Just picks up quietly and folds 'em nice and lays 'em down where the party's that lost 'em can find 'em. And that's *all* you does."

One thing about Aunt Rose, she seldom quoted the Good Lawyud. A relief in itself. I never heard the name Jesus on her big pale lips except, on the rarest occasions, as a kind of swear word, an exclamation of delight or horror or thanksgiving. "Holy Jesus, them plants is burning up this kitchen. Everything's going to be all right."

Rose was free, but I was foresworn. I had to pray to Jesus at night, "Now I lay me down to sleep," out loud, a long old Bible-belt prayer, and then, having kissed both parents good-night and jumped into bed, you think my thing with Him was finished? Oh no, I was told, while lying there in the dark, to think about Him, to commune with Him. I was encouraged to talk to Him, tell Him what I wanted.

"He's right there," they would say. Both my parents seemed to believe what they were saying. Often their last words were, "He's right there in the room with you, you're not alone." A spooky business, if you ask me, especially now that I was beginning to think about my naked body and might have enjoyed being alone. "He loves you, He waits for you."

I tried to think about Him loving me and waiting up there for me but to save my life all I could think of was Him staring from the ceiling or the transom over the door, wearing that womanish white gown He wore in His pictures. There He was, more peeper than lover; more like a detective, a regular Dick Deadeye of a chap, only *half woman*. Tie that! Truth to tell, I had continued to feel myself for some time now, nights before I went to sleep. Most children do, thinking they're the only ones in all the world who have discovered this big, awful secret. I marveled at the silky smoothness of my skin, the softness of my small goodies. Him up there put kind of a crimp in the proceedings until I discovered the covers!

Aha, now all I had to do was to pull up the sheets and comforter and let Him peep His eyes out. I imagined Him staring down hard at the covers, wondering what on earth was that moving around in there? But He just couldn't see what I was doing. I was ahead of Him for once.

As this matter became more interesting with each passing month, low clouds of guilt set in, but I was not about to stop. Come to think of it, once started you can't stop. Nobody stops. I kept on talking to Him and thinking about Him as I had been told to do, of course, but more mechanically, because as time went by, He and His promises became as some far-off music you can't help hearing. Always there.

A hell of an important man in our street, the Lawyud was on everybody's lips. The Lawyud, the Good

Lawyud, He was going to fix everything. Gave us all we had and took it all away, too. Dear Lawyud Jesus, we thank Thee for this our evening meal. We thank Thee, Deah Lawyud, for the remarkable privilege of having been born. We thank Thee, dear Lawyud, we beg Thy forgiveness for our sins, including those murderous thoughts; we beseech Thee, forgive us our trespasses— anything that was fun was a trespass—as we forgive those who trespass against us.

This was how it went. The Methodists and the Presbyterians and the Baptists and the Episcopalians went on like this, white and black alike. Of a Sunday, in the gray stone churches where dressed-up whites congregated, and down the alleys where dressed-up black folk who didn't make it to church sat in groups on the steps of shanties, listening to the preacher tell them all about the wonders and the terrors of the Lawyud.

The Catholics thought so highly of the Lawyud they used an intermediary, a middleman, or in this case— first of the liberationists—a middlewoman, to get in touch with Him. They said, "Hail Mary Mother of God, Blessed art Thou amongst women, Blessed is Thy son Jesus." Now, if Mary was the mother of God, well, the whole business of who was who became even more confusing.

My Uncle George, who worked for the *Baltimore Sun,* told me some years later that Jesus Christ, *the* Jesus Christ of ceiling-peeping, the Lawyud himself, wasn't all that important, not by a long shot. "He is just one of many prophets. Interesting, lyrical in some of his presentations, but simply one of many." He mentioned a few of the others. "There's Mohammed, for instance, and Buddha, Zoroaster, Moses, John the Baptist—he's the wild-eyed man in the big painting at the museum downtown. Jesus is just one of many," said Uncle George.

The Jews called their God Jehovah, and, from what I could see, they were pretty scared of Him, too, or at least held Him in awe, but forgot about Him more

27

quickly than the others. At least they weren't always talking to Him.

The Catholics went to mass and confession, and that was that, but with us He was a hidden manipulator who had to be spoken to with soft, flattering words and obeyed, because of all He could do. He could stop the woah today, if He'd a mind to, but meantime people were being slaughtered by the thousands. He could make anybody richer than Croesus, but meantime people were starving, and even we ourselves were being rationed with puffy pancakes and peculiar-tasting muffins. This was His will, they said, but I had no need to worry because He loved *me* and was waiting.

Of a Sunday, singing about how I'd be a sunbeam for Jesus and shine for Him each day was one thing. But at nights I began to notice Stephen Farrar's features covering up old Jesus' more and more clearly. Stephen didn't peep and promise, either. He was there. Stephen, tall and beautiful, who spoke with the faintly British accent, and who knew everything, could give you information of all kinds at a moment's notice and talk with the tongues of "men and angels," ah, now, this way was easier, Stephen-over-Jesus, I welcomed them both, especially under the covers at night where I could revel and dream, the first, fresh dream of love.

It is morning. Lights are on in the kitchen. A dark, rainy day out there in the yard. Mamma and Aunt Rose are both up early. The great black stove is red-hot on top, a person daren't go near it. Rose is beating up batter while Mamma runs around picking up objects from plates and putting them back on other plates. She doesn't seem to know quite what she is doing, but she's trying to help. "Give him a big breakfast, Rose, you hear?" Rose makes that Ummhmm sound, living essence of the positive, it says yes to everything. "Here, make him some fried tomatoes. He loves them."

"Ummhmm." Rose starts to slice the tomatoes, lays them out on a plate, then forks each one into the bowl

28

of batter. "Tomatoes fixes him, Miz Bassford, even when he's fit to be tied."

Mamma is worried about Daddy who is so worried about the woah he's practically unable to run his business. "The way he sassed that poor plumber yesterday. And all just because he brought the wrong tools."

"Ummhmm, that Mista Hochner won't be waiting around so much on Mista Bassford ferm now on."

"How do you know that?"

"He's going to work in a plaint."

This worries Mamma the worse yet. "He *is?*"

Rose beats batter and talks on. "When he come by the kitchen fer coffee and cake he tole me so, that's how I knows."

Mamma goes on, as if her speech can stop things from happening. "I know Mr. Bassford didn't mean to insult Mr. Hochner. He's a good plumber, Mr. Hochner, and when Mr. Bassford can't get that other one, or the one before him, he always calls Mr. Hochner in. Right now he has to have a plumber. And Oh Lordy, he needs bricklayers and painters and just about everything."

"Ummhmm. Shanty right next to mine needs fixin' this minute. Whole top went sidewise week before last. Like'ta bashed Mary Kimball's head in."

I ate my breakfast and listened to how the whole world was changing. The wheel was turning so fast the black stream that ran behind the white streets might run dry. It must be true because Mamma was agreeing, as she went about carefully setting the breakfast table for Daddy, running back and forth into the kitchen.

Mamma and Rose were like girl friends, working together, comparing notes, revealing themselves to each other without fear of reprisals, as they worked together on my father.

The two women talked about Daddy as if he were some large animal that didn't rightly belong in the house but had been left in their charge and responded when stroked, fed and spoken to softly. When Animal entered House the atmosphere changed; Animal growled, and soft lights and soft voices appeared, sometimes music, and always, food and attention, and Animal would soon settle down and purr. It was no wonder, considering the problems Daddy had to face, the high cost of living, "with no ceiling in sight."

Grandma had repeated to Mamma, "Remember, when a man comes in, no matter what he says or does, you should give him tea or a short drink with a biscuit, and another if he don't seem right. Then, if you look pretty and you listen real well, he'll soon go on upstairs to his desk and smoke cigars."

I heard these words, "No ceiling in sight, no end to it" and imagined the ceiling on our house lifting up to let in the snow. Eventually the snowstorm would take over the house, and we would have to go down to the basement and wait it out.

The woah going on overseas entered the house and was waged every morning at the breakfast table. The workers painting walls and laying floors had to be paid off in something called Inflated Currency; materials were costing double, everywhere people were taking advantage of the shortages. Those long hours Daddy spent at his club, he was exchanging piles of money for this other "inflated" or "swollen" money, at least that was how I imagined it. I saw him making impassioned talks about conditions, wearing himself out trying to get things more normal, poor Daddy.

One day Mamma took us by the club to pick him up, and arriving early, imagine my surprise to find him sitting in a big leather chair in front of a long window, idly drinking something in a tall glass and smoking a long cigar, smiling and talking to some other men who were all doing the exact same thing, exchanging funny stories and laughing.

After much going on between Mamma and Rose, footsteps were heard overhead. "Those new men are coming in today," Mamma whispered.

"Don't you worry, Miz Bassford, foods I'm fixin' gonna make things look real pretty."

Half an hour later, with only the first pile of pancakes downed, Daddy threw figures at Mamma while she sat, impatient but smiling, scurrying between telephone calls, scribbling notes hastily in her big engagement book and running back to the table to listen. "Had to pay six dollars a barrel for those apples I bought yesterday," Daddy announced. "Apples, plain apples. Why, that's a cent and a fifth an apple, Susie May, counting three, five hundred apples to the barrel."

Mamma kept saying, "Tch-tch, tch," or "I know, I know," indicating deep sympathy, words designed to slip in softly, to soothe and leave uninterrupted the stream of Daddy's resentment, words made of cotton and sugar and medicinal water. Nothing words.

There was a great Industrial Disease going on in the United States, aimed at Daddy and all the other men endeavouring to do business, and he had evidence to prove it. As he pounded home the fearsome facts and filled his stomach, his breathing would quicken as if there wasn't enough air in the dining room, and here the wet cottony words came in handy. "Tch-tch, tch-tch, I know, dear, I know," from Mamma, and "Ummhmm, Ummhmm, Ummhmm," from Rose were like oxygen, and, soothed, Daddy would continue his litany, making it sound as if the ground was being pulled from under his feet, as if we were all in danger from this rising tidal wave coming straight from the Kaiser and right on up over the buildings across the street. Any day, tomorrow, maybe today, even Mamma's stream of love, and Rose's standing in the wings with the cakes and sausages, wouldn't be enough to stop it from coming in and drowning us all.

Meantime, Mamma would wink, and Rose would wink back. Two kinds of winks, one came with a bit of a smile. "He's quieting down," but the other was quicker, it was done with eyes alone, and this one said, "More food, quick!" Whereupon they would both work at it again.

I assumed my Daddy had only a few dollars left in the world, that he must be working on the thinnest economic margin, that, of course, the money was his own, special and precious as his blood. But, instead, it was his mother's, a good bit of which he'd already inherited.

He knew the amount to a dollar. He had already inherited his twenty money, his twenty-five money and his thirty money, and was forever adding it up aloud, together with profit and interest—he expected dollar for dollar—interrupted by goings-on about the economic persecutors. "Club charges fifteen cents for two apples. Two cans of vegetables cost a quarter. Boxes of cereal —shrunk down to nothing, aren't they, Rose?"

"Ummhmm," Rose, waiting for the signal from Mamma to deliver a third pile of pancakes, agreed with Daddy about the food shortchangers. " 'Nuff papers start a fire stuck in them boxes. Ummhmm."

Mamma began the changing-the-subject ploy. "Up north they're having diet squads, dear, to see how little they can live on."

But Daddy went on eating. "Diet squads lead to sick people," he finally commented, and "I'll permit no diet squads in my house," just as the doorbell rang, and Rose announced the arrival of Mr. Hochner, who was shown into the parlor. Mamma told Rose to take Mr. Hochner some coffee and was just about to run off, but Daddy stopped her with an aside, "Just a minute, Susie May," and to Rose, "I'll have a few more of those cakes —if they're good and hot."

One day Aunt Rose was in the kitchen mumbling over her slowly burning plants. "Soft now, low-down, that's right, that's good, *that's good!*" It was noon and Good Friday. I was helping whip cream for strawberry shortcake. Relatives from Virginia were coming for lunch and Mamma was busily fixing flowers in the dining room.

"What's good?" I asked Rose.

"Plants is burning low and sweet, that's what's good." She'd close her eyes when she came near the burning plants; sometimes she'd put her hands over the big iron pot in which they were placed and smile to herself, with a look of waiting on her face, of listening for someone to answer. Then, "All right, all right," she'd say.

"What's all right?"

Smiling, opening her eyes, "Spirit don't want no more worry, Spirit is working it all out. Just look how them plants is burning."

I leaned over and saw they were burning smoothly, a soft white ash was forming. I was always attracted to the plants. "What's the Spirit, anyway, Rose? I bet you don't even know, you're just imagining."

"Don't never ask peoples about that," replied Rose with cool dignity. "Peoples all knows what the Spirit is."

"Well, what?"

"Everything you is, that's what. Everything you ever going to be, or have, or got now." A full order.

"Then, if it's everything, what're you burning plants for?"

She shook her head, as if everybody knew about that. "Spirit's speakin' when the plants burns. Plant picks Him up and passes on what He says. Anybody can see that if they half looks."

One Monday morning in November, a day almost like spring, I heard that kid down the block, that awful Thiele boy with the loud bossy voice and the harelip, screaming in the streets.

ARMS was the word I heard, as I came downstairs, but from the way Mamma and Rose were running to the door I knew it was something pretty important.

EXTER PAPER . . . ARMISTICE IS SIGNED . . . WAR IS OVAH . . . Another voice near our door told us more than Willie Thiele. FIGHTING ENDS AT 6 A.M. . . . KAISER FLEES.

Daddy came rushing in with three copies. He kissed Mamma and hugged Rose. Then Mamma and Rose hugged and kissed each other, then everybody hugged and kissed me, and Mamma dried her eyes with Daddy's handkerchief. Next thing, Virginia Anne came home from school, yelling, "We've gotta get ready for the parade," and there was more hugging and kissing. Everybody was laughing and crying. This went on a while before things quieted down enough for Daddy to read the newspaper, about how troops and workers were ruling Berlin. How the World Woah had ended at six o'clock Washington time and eleven o'clock Paris time.

We were most excited about how the Hohenzollerns and their aides, especially the Kaiser, had been beaten to a pulp, with all of them running off to Holland in armored cars. Nothing made sense. It was all so big, with millions of people dead. "The reincarnation of the monstrous Attila who led the Huns of an earlier day to the butchery of Europe," Daddy read. "The madness of the man from Potsdam who considered himself the chosen instrument of God, no such ever known in the world, evil and madness incarnate, now gone, beaten, fleeing in an armored car so people wouldn't surround him and kill him!"

I wondered what happened to his cape and helmet and the sword he used to slash off hands and breasts.

Walking down toward the parade, we ran into crowds everywhere. Schools and homes emptied out like upturned cans of hot running people, all laughing and crying and screaming, as streets flooded over with people of all sizes and colors. Blacks poured out of the side streets and the alleys and the big parade was black and white and so full you could hardly tell which was which. A sudden storm of torn paper fluttered everywhere, from windows and roofs and ledges, as a tremendous sound reverberated in the streets, of wild music of joy and relief. Love was everywhere, a new surge of life and, withal, a great permissiveness. In the restaurant where we finally went for our midday meal, Virginia Anne and I were told we could order anything we wanted, as this was officially "Anything You Want Day."

Virginia Anne ordered ice cream and cake to start with and was told she could have it, too, but she had to wait till after the crab cakes, because the ice cream was too hard. Then we all went to Grandma's and ate all over again and, when we finally fell into bed, we were asleep before we hit the sheets, with no thought except that all the trouble in the world was over forever and ever.

But there were calamities. Someone the grown-ups were talking about these days, a certain Millicent Harding, was now dying in a Baltimore hospital as a result of a "criminal operation." Something *they* did. Was it breast cutting-off?, we wondered, as we listened intently.

The man in the case was a leading merchant and church worker. Why, he was an active participant in Billy Sunday's revivals! One of the very men we'd seen "hitting the trail." But the criminal operation (that's what the newspaper called it and what my aunts repeated) was not exactly breast cutting-off, but something else, something caused by something a man's *thing* did to a woman, something even giants wouldn't stoop to do. What men did to women and how and why were matters totally unknown to us, but apparently it was pretty bad, always causing death and transfiguration.

Now a man, *every* man, had a thing, a cross between a crowbar and a tiger, which anybody knew could do a heap of damage. When with a man of unknown character, a young girl had to be in the company of her entire family, at least two brothers and a father, because if Thing got loose it was sure to go wild and commit a crime.

For some mysterious reason, Thing was after girls and women only. Thing never hurt men. A man had little or no control over his particular thing and sometimes just a look could get it out of hand.

When first I heard about Thing, I couldn't imagine where men kept theirs, but later, when I heard it was in their pants, I thought it must be in pockets, maybe one in each side, or in a cage of some kind.

I'd like you to meet Thing as I met him, as presented to us kids, one and all. Oh, he was terrible! Sired by a lead pipe and a wild ram, with smoke bombs for a face, Thing was an animal with a life of its own. Had to be, now didn't it, when the man who owned it had no control over it once it got up and out?

And dirty! Oh, was Thing ever dirty! We thought men must use their things to wipe up floors and clean out basements. We figured that must be when their things were docile, in the early mornings, say, or when asleep, or at least when they weren't up and running after poor, innocent women.

It was a long time before we found out, while not exactly what it was Thing did to women, at least something of the effect it had on them. And what it was called. Thing was simply called by his name, which anybody knew was just Thing. But what he did to women was *it*. This crime or murder or whatever was called *doing it*.

Now comes the clincher. Early on, I began committing some heinous crimes, of the kind you can never be forgiven, until after old Jesus comes and decides in your favor, if He has a mind to. By age five or six, like I said, I was aware of His peeping. And I wished, oh, very secretly, I never came right out and said it, but I wished He would die! Or, at least, go home, go back where He came from, Bethlehem or Jerusalem or wherever. Because everything I did was against His explicit instructions. At least, that's what *they* said He said.

"Don't listen to grown-ups' conversation!" "Don't steal!" and "Don't covet!" And, above all, "Don't feel yourself!" You'd turn black with leprosy if you felt yourself real good.

All the things that come naturally were strictly forbidden by Him, but He did them all Himself. Wasn't He eavesdropping like mad, which is a form of stealing and covetous as all hell? He was practically in the business.

He had said we weren't supposed to know anything more about Thing than that it was after women. The end result was fatal, death after some terrible disease. Everything would turn dark and drip through the floor.

All right, now at least we knew what effect Thing had, but how did he accomplish this crime? Ah, that was the question little ears were after hearing.

One bright summer's day six of us kids were playing in Thelma Hodges' big backyard down the street from us. A wonderful place, with trees and flowers, a big flagstone piazza under the back porch, with a swing on rollers that would hold eight, and tables with umbrellas where lemonade and ice cream and cake were the least to be expected.

Toward afternoon, when things were quieting down, Sara Lou Martindale, the oldest of the group who looked after us of an afternoon, brought up the subject of Miss Mamie Callendar's death. Now, Miss Mamie was one of those childless old maids who foolishly dote on children. Any child who just happened in to ask how she was feeling, presenting her with a four-leaf clover or a dandelion, could receive as much as three or four quarters and half a chocolate cake.

Needless to say, Miss Mamie was never lonesome in her big house, and her death was a matter of great interest and inconvenience to us all. She had contracted pneumonia and died after a few weeks, during which time no children were allowed in to see her. Two stern nieces from Atlanta came and supervised her and there was quite some talk of a mystery surrounding her death.

Sara Lou Martindale, aged fourteen and general supervisor of the summer's afternoon play and nap-taking, presently sitting in the best seat in the Hodges swing, waited for the proper moment of quiet during the consuming of lunch-time sandwiches to make a dramatic statement.

"I know how Miss Mamie died."

This announcement brought a hushed silence. Some of us even stopped eating. Thel was the first to gasp, *"How?"* But Sara Lou made us wait.

"It was from the plants they left in her bedroom. They murdered her cold with the plants. Can't never be traced when you kill somebody with plants."

Gasps of wonder and horror. Plants were generally recognized to be bad at times, and now the stories of Miss Mamie's death seemed more real and wonderful than ever before, especially as Sara Lou went on to explain the science of the matter.

37

"Plants sucked up all the air till Miss Mamie couldn't breathe and just suffocated."

She went on to explain about the plants of all sizes and kinds that were left in parlor windows, on mantles and in dining rooms, but particularly in bedrooms, where Miss Mamie slept. Wax plants and rhododendrons, frog plants and ferns and geraniums and baby's breath. Why, they were left all over the place, wherever the sunlight could get to them! I wondered how much precious life had already been sucked out of me.

Seeing the stir she had caused, Sara Lou, who knew a thing or two about these scientific and medical matters, went on in hushed tones.

"Those two nieces filled up her room with new plants every night. Every day they went and bought bigger and bigger plants. They knew all the time those plants were sucking out Miss Mamie's life."

"Johnsy Dowse told me those girls like to bought out that flower store he delivers for," I offered. Sara Lou must have thought highly of this because she nodded in my direction.

Then Thelma put her two cents in. "I see them in the market buying that stuff that climbs to the ceiling."

"They practically turned her bedroom into a greenhouse," said Sara Lou. "My papa says it's the cleverest murder job he's ever *seen*. Looked just like they loved their aunt, bringing her all those pretty green things, and all the time they were killing her dead." Somebody asked, "Did the doctor catch on?", but Sara Lou pushed that out with something about how the doctor didn't realize what they were doing, and besides they hid half the plants whenever he came in to pay his call.

From murder by plants it was a quick step to murder by Thing. The sun was crawling slowly up off the grass to the side of the house, leaving the swing in the marvelous light of early afternoon, before the real stuff started coming out. Helen Haines, the girl next in age to Sara Lou, started the ball rolling.

"That was a terrible thing happened to poor Alice Carver," she began.

Sara Lou was ready and waiting. "You mean because of what she did with that Chickie Hines?"

"Ummhmm," agreed Helen Haines. It was getting for nap time, but everybody was on the *qui vive;* besides, we had been promised the whole afternoon and meant to have it down to the last juicy second.

Questions of "What did Alice do?" came from everywhere. Sara sat up straight and cleared her throat.

"That dirty Chickie Hines went and did it to Alice," said Sara Lou. "Chickie did it to Alice right in her own parlor when her mother and father were out to Wednesday night prayer meeting."

There was more, but the words *did it* were the most fascinating. At last I was going to find out what Thing did and how he did it. Thing had to be involved in this deal. I knew something already. Chickie's had come loose and run for Alice.

"What did Chickie *do* to Alice?" asked Thelma.

"Why, I thought everybody knew *that*," said Sara Lou. "He had *sedshual indrakorz,* is what he did."

"What's *that?*" came in a chorus.

"That's *doing* it," said Helen Haines, this time with impatience and emphasis.

"Chickie and Alice thought they would finish up right then and there and clean up the place before her folks got back from church. But it didn't work out that way, oh, no sirree."

To demands of "What happened?" it took Sara Lou again to give the explanation, but this time at last things became clearer.

"Chickie's thing swelled up inside of Alice and wouldn't pull out!"

I began to see something. Chickie's thing had run after Alice, bitten into her neck or somewhere, and then swelled up so he couldn't pull it out.

"Gee whiz!" said Thel.

"That's terrible!" said Roberta Staunton. "Couldn't they do nothing to get loose?"

"You kids don't know the scientific facts about *indrakorz,*" said Sara Lou. "You don't know that sometimes a man's thing blows up like a balloon, five, six, ten times life-size. Women bust open and die."

"That's right," Helen Haines added in approval of Sara Lou's overall medical accuracy. "This Chickie just couldn't move his thing one way or the other. It was stuck in there like a rock. And Alice's parents were due home any minute."

"What'd they do?" came from six eager little mouths.

"Well, of course," began Sara Lou, "Chickie tried to pull out, to keep from busting her open, but he couldn't move, and there they were on the sofa or the chair or wherever it was they were doing it, just staring at each other. Now Chickie had an idea that if they waited it would go down and, well, he thought if he could just get hold of some cold water and pour it on, maybe that would do it. Anyway they tried that but it didn't work."

"How'd they ever get to the kitchen to get the water?"

"I don't know. Must have moved back awful slow stuck together like that."

"I heard they had a pitcher of water right there in the parlor on the piano. But it was hard to get to it—stuck together like glue."

"If a man does it to a woman before she's *ripe* why they just always stick together and it's terrible," Helen Haines instructed us. "It's just terrible!"

Ripe. That was the first time I'd heard *that* word. It was a while before the older girls could get through the questions. "If Alice busted she'd die, wouldn't she?"

"Umhmm. Chickie's thing kept growing and growing. Every minute it got an inch or two bigger, till poor Alice couldn't hardly breathe. Just as it was about to bust, they heard Alice's parents come in the door. Alice and Chickie managed to get behind the piano. They figured to hide there all night or maybe for days anyway until his thing went down."

"But how would they ever get anything to eat?"

"Oh, they couldn't eat. Or sleep. They couldn't get a wink of sleep with something like that going on. You can't eat when you're stuck together and standing up, unless somebody feeds you."

"I guess they just stood there and prayed."

"That was a good idea though, hiding behind the piano."

"Yeah, only it didn't work. Alice started to cry and she got hysterical and her parents heard her and they came rushing into the parlor and went round back of the piano and found them."

"Go on."

"Well, old man Carver saw what had happened right away and he was getting ready to shoot Chickie Hines, but Mrs. Carver said no, not to touch him because any move he made now would affect their daughter's life. Their only hope was to call a doctor. Well, they did, and the doctor came right over and he said to put a sheet over them and he would send for an ambulance and take them to the hospital. He wanted to get them to the hospital to give Chickie ether, because he said that was the one way that worked when people got stuck together this hard. Ether."

"That's right," said Helen Haines, "It's the only way to get a man's thing to go down to normal. I guess that's what they must have done when they got to the hospital."

"Do they go to sleep standing up?"

"Of course. And they had to go to the toilet standing up and everything."

"Until they start coming apart it's very dangerous and the woman can die at any minute."

"Anyway, the last thing was seen of Chickie and Alice was they was coming down the steps with him walking backwards covered in a sheet. People looking from the windows across the street saw their four legs sticking out from under the sheet. I hear they looked just like a Halloween donkey. They were helped into the ambulance, and then they closed the doors and took them to the hospital."

"My mamma says Alice is lucky to be alive," Helen Haines went on. "She says sometimes they can't get people apart and they just die that way and have to be buried together like those Siamese twins they have down

41

to the circus. She says it's better to be married three or four years before you try *sedshual indrakorz* and, then I guess maybe it's better to have a doctor there with some ether."

"That's right," said Sara Lou. "Just in case your husband's thing swells up and can't get out."

We had all to be dragged home and away from the fascinating Sara Lou and her helper Helen Haines to whom we listened till the end, leaving with glazed eyes and bated breath. My taste buds were fairly glazed, too: the fried chicken and the tapioca pudding I ate for my supper tasted exactly the same. But now at last I knew what Thing did and nobody could fool *me* again!

I was one up on my sister, who had been swimming during the conversation reported above, and I gloated over her ignorance. Virginia Anne listened wide-eyed, interrupting with the usual ahhs and ohhs as I described the horrors attending Miss Mamie's murder, but when I got to the near murder of Alice Carver by Chickie she just stared speechless.

Next I described how they had waited in the hospital for Chickie's evil thing to go down and how the couple had meantime to be fed standing up and go to the bathroom standing up and how finally Chickie had had to be given ether until the two of them came apart. At last I had her. She listened, admiring and horror-struck by my vast sophistication and medical accuracy.

I could hardly wait to get back to Thel's backyard the next day but Sara Lou and Helen Haines were not in attendance. Instead a prim black maid watched over us and wouldn't even tell us a story. Oh, well, we talked among ourselves about *sedshual indrakorz*. Name of a big, nasty giant. Had a huge head and no eyes, no nose, big mouth and was all black inside. Could spread disease and death and make you disappear in a flash.

One morning Thel appeared at breakfast and whispered, "Mercy, you come over and play, you hear? Sara Lou and Helen Haines are coming."

This time the conversation didn't start until late afternoon, just as lemonade and cake were being served, and the big girls were having coffee. As before, Sara Lou cleared her throat just as we gathered around and looked as if she had an announcement to make.

"Did you hear what happened to Francis Hollander?" She began by asking Helen Haines, just as if we weren't even present.

"Oh, yes," Helen Haines was quick to reply. "Wasn't it terrible?"

"Ummhmm." We asked and asked. It was a long time before Sara Lou would tell, but when she did it was worth it. "She done it with Ripper down on Gilmore Street and he got her maidenhead." This was a new word. Sounded like a summer resort.

"What's a maidenhead?" asked Thelma.

"You kids just don't know anything!" commented Sara Lou. "Who wants to tell these ignoramuses what a maidenhead is?"

"Oh, I'll tell," said Alicia Schmidt. She was older than we were but not as old as the other two oracles.

"Go ahead," said Sara Lou. "That is, if you know."

"Your maidenhead is a big ball hidden inside a woman."

We all thought that over, and it sounded all right. Then somebody asked, "Where is it?"

"It's way up beyond your navel, isn't that right, Sara Lou?" said Alicia, who was wise beyond her years.

"Ummhmm. Go on, Alicia."

"Now when a man hits it with his thing, why it falls down and comes out. Isn't that right, Sara Lou?"

"You bet it does," said Sara Lou. "Falls straight through your basket, just like the ball falls through in basketball."

"What's your *basket?*"

"Your basket's your stomach and veins and all that stuff up there."

"Well, what happens after a ball falls out? What do you do with it?" I asked that question. I thought it sounded pretty bright and I just had to know.

"Man just picks it up and keeps it," said Sara Lou, as if this kind of thing happened every five minutes. She

43

sounded indignant as she asked, "What do you think you do with it?"

I thought that over and admitted I didn't know, making things even worse by asking, "Well, *where?*"

"Where *what?*"

"Well, he has to hide it, don't he?"

Helen Haines said, "Just wraps it up and puts it in a closet or a drawer or someplace like that. Isn't that right, Sara Lou?"

"Ummhmm. Some real bad men must have hundreds of them big old balls hidden around."

We all sat still and nodded. We knew a thing or two now, all right. I remembered how the men were laughing when we went swimming in the bay the previous summer and one of them called out, "Watch out or the sharks'll get your balls!" Now at last I knew what they meant. It was all so obvious once you knew.

I liked everything about Grandma's house, where I was often left while Mamma pursued her music career. She had plans to be a concert pianist, which required continual practice on things called études and fugues, and she didn't especially like people setting up housekeeping with big blocks behind the piano. In fact, she seemed to resent being asked, in the midst of Bach or Chopin, "Mamma, when are you going to stop *banging* on the piano?"

One day a new face appeared at my grandmother's house, and I was introduced to Cousin Ruth, a girl of sixteen, about as old as my Cousin Honey. Now Ruth had been adopted by remote relatives over in Virginia after the death of her mother. She had only lately been reclaimed and was being harbored at my grandmother's.

Ruth turned out to be a tall, good-looking girl with green eyes, long black hair, perfect white teeth over painted lips and a smile that was so big and steady it was terrifying. She said "Hello, Mercy," and kissed me on the cheek, then asked immediately if she could take me for a walk, which everyone agreed was an excellent idea, as something had been mentioned about Ruth helping out with the children when Rose was busy in the kitchen.

Once outside the house, Cousin Ruth, as I was told to call her, held my hand hard and walked fast. I was barely able to keep up with her. But I managed, especially when I discovered she was heading for the candy store up the street, which carried confections of the very best kind. She went in and bought a quarter-of-a-pound box of chocolates which she put into her pocket, without even offering one to me, and walked on back home to Grandma's. The minute she got home she took the candy out of her pocket, right in the parlor. I saw she had not only the small white box of chocolates she had bought but five Hershey bars to boot! Turning to me she asked, "Well, wasn't that a nice walk?" as if that was all there was to it.

That very night Mother informed me in her sweetest voice, "Cousin Ruth is coming to stay with us for awhile."

My sister, Virginia Anne, asked "When?" But I asked "Why?"

"Very soon," said Mamma, deciding to answer only Virginia Anne. She was gathering up her sheets of music. "She just dotes on children, she's been so lonely and neglected. She's had no mother. Now at last she's going to have a family life." She waited for us to express interest, which eventually we did.

"How old is she?" Virginia Anne inquired, and when we heard she was sixteen, my sister commented, "Gee whiz. Why isn't she in school?"

"She's between schools," said Mamma. This explanation didn't sit very well. "We're trying to get her into Eastwood." I was relieved when I heard Cousin Ruth would be with us for only a short while. Inside of a few days, sure enough, my Cousin Ruth was sleeping in our house and taking care of the children.

"How long is she going to stay?" I asked Rose.

"What's that?"

"When's she going home?"

"What's the matter?" Rose asked when we were alone

45

together in the comforting kitchen. "Don'tcha like your own blood cousin?"

"No," I replied.

"You mean you don't want that poor girl to have no home?"

"No."

"Then what does you wants t' happen to her?"

I thought that over and arrived at the answer, which was that many potted plants should be put in her bedroom, but I took it all back the minute I heard the terrible truth, to wit, that she was going to sleep in the bed right next to mine—we would smother together.

Ruth arrived of a Friday and was escorted promptly to "her room," which was no longer my room. I watched her opening her suitcase and taking out clothes. Followed by pots of rouge, boxes of powder and lipsticks galore. She brushed her long hair with my hairbrush and pushed my private objects—pencils and crayons, combs and pictures and books, off to a small table beside the big bureau. She paid no attention to me whatever, a characteristic I noticed she had when no adults were present. I must say she moved with great efficiency. The very minute she finished emptying her suitcases she stood before the mirror painting and powdering her face within an inch of its life. This amazing task completed, she turned and addressed her sole remark to me, the only sign she had given she knew I was even alive, much less present in the same room. "Get out now. We're going downstairs and eat."

Downstairs at the table she put back on the big smile that showed all her teeth and to my mother's question, had she found everything she wanted, she replied in a soft voice that came on suddenly from nowhere, "Oh yes, Aunt Susie May. Mercy helped me with everything, didn't you, dear?"

The general attitude of goodwill extended toward my Cousin Ruth by my parents continued in spite of her behavior at the table, where, whenever the fried chicken was offered, she would shovel off half the platterful as if it was all intended for her, and she was

46

generously leaving some for the rest of us, causing poor Rose to have to go back and refill the platter again and again, no doubt leaving little or nothing for herself. Cousin Ruth ate fast and furious like a starving animal, then sat silent and smiled that terrible smile as if she expected praise for what she had done.

Here she was sitting at my table smiling and eating, like an anaconda, it is true, but then a great many relatives overate at our house. She had been "taken in" by my parents in her kind offer to "help out" with the children. All perfectly normal procedures, such as went on in hundreds of families every day of the week.

Between schools. From what I could gather she had spent the greater part of her sixteen years between schools, walking straight between them but seldom entering. She was quiet. Maybe she was too busy with that smile to speak many words. To have spoken would have meant dropping it and letting her large and shapely mouth go back to normal. Or possibly in those unknown places where she had lived, she just hadn't learned much in the way of family talk at table.

But there was something more, something else. She seemed to be waiting. She would eat, finish eating, and wait. She would answer any kindly inquiry Mamma put to her, "Oh, yes, Aunt Susie May, it's beautiful in the country," stop quickly at the precise end of the sentence, and wait. Between eating and speaking, she would sit with her hands held self-consciously in her lap—someone had obviously told her not to put her elbows on the table—staring at nothing with the big smile settled there like a cement fixture. Waiting.

During Ruth's first night in residence I felt kind of queasy when I heard she was going to see to my going to bed, but nothing much happened. She stole my book, an oldie inherited from my Aunt Margaret called *Girls of the True Blue*. Since I could already read, and had the book marked where I had left off reading, I thought she would lose my place but I wisely kept my counsel. When, after half an hour, I found her still staring at the first paragraph, I did tell her, "Please don't lose my place."

She turned to look at me; we were in the bedroom but not yet turning in for the night, and for the first time I saw her smile was gone. "Your *place?*"

"Ummhmm."

"What's that?"

"That's where it's marked, where I'm reading."

"You're lying," she said, as casually as if she'd said hello. "You can't read."

"Yes, I can."

"All right then, what's this book about?"

I told her the story of this boring book about these very boring goodie-good kids doing everything right, and during the entire recitation the smile stayed off her face. It was scary seeing her without it. It was like seeing her without her clothes. She waited till I had finished, then she nodded her head.

"I knew you were lying," she said. "You can fool your mother and father but you can't fool me."

Since my parents had gone out to a dance, and Rose was going home that night—my sister was already asleep in the playroom making those even-sleep sounds—I decided to take no chance with this creature by arguing with her, so I said nothing. She began getting undressed, dropping her clothes and letting them fall to the floor, then scooping them up and throwing them on the chair in a heap. When she was down to pants and brassiere, I stole a glance and saw all her underclothes were black, not white or pink like other peoples'. She was tall, about five eight or nine, with strong muscles, especially in her neck and back and upper arms, and she had big, strong hands with extra long fingers. All aspects of her body were oddly developed and hard by comparison with the soft backsides, rounded breasts and dimpled cheeks I'd seen around. I didn't know what to make of her, standing there with her long, rich black hair in her black undies and without her smile. She was quiet, as usual, but I noticed as she undressed she kept the book open on the bureau and when she had got down to her shoes she turned to me.

"Come here," she said. I got up from my side of the room and came over. "There!" She pointed to the first paragraph of the book. "Read that."

"I've already read it, Cousin Ruth," I said.

"Read it out loud," she commanded. "Read it to me."

I stood by the bureau and began reading the first paragraph out loud. When I finished she gave me a straight hard look. "You're lying," she said. "You can't read at your age. You made that all up." I tried to tell her I hadn't, but meantime she had moved over to the mantle on which were other books including one, Holy Bible, which she selected and brought back to the bureau. "There. Find the twenty-third Psalm, since you're so smart."

I turned the pages and found it. "Read that." I began reading, "The Lord is my shepherd," stumbling only at words like "restoreth" and "preparest" but getting to the end in pretty good time. "Your mother made you learn it by heart," she said. "I'm going to ask her tomorrow and if I catch you in a lie, we'll see about that." Smile was nowhere to be seen. I went promptly to bed, determined to get to Mamma first thing in the morning and report on Cousin Ruth's peculiar antics.

Nothing of the sort happened, however, for when I came downstairs for breakfast the following morning, Cousin Ruth had already gone out on errands of her own, my parents were still asleep, and it wasn't until midday lunch that I came face to face with her again. This time the smile was back on her face and in answer to questions about the previous night, Smile reported, "Oh, it's wonderful, the way Mercy can read." She went on to explain just what I had read, expecting denial, but Mamma proudly exclaimed over my marvelous learning capacities, telling how, even at the age of two, relatives had come hundreds of miles to hear me describe my picture book, *The Book of the Li—on*, pronouncing each word as if I had written it myself.

Smile took it straight and said nothing, but she did look at me through her smile. And I looked back. Things were different between us. She knew and I knew, and I knew that she knew, and she knew that I knew. Bad.

During the afternoons she walked me wildly through the streets, holding my hand as if it were made of paper that should be torn up and thrown away. It was the curbs that got me down, as she regarded them as objects to be leapt over in a gallop which she invariably did, using her long legs in two-yard swings and pulling me in mid-air behind her by one arm. I was always flabbergasted when I finally found my two feet on terra firma.

These walks were not without incident. I found her talking to all sorts of strange people in the parks and in stores, where she loved to browse. She said the most peculiar things to these strangers, such as that she was my governess, my French tutor, my dancing teacher. She said we lived on Calvert Street or Mount Vernon Place or any street she happened to fancy at the moment, and gave any old telephone number that happened to come to mind, but never the correct one.

During these walks I noticed she invariably wore her best clothes and was never without Smile, and what she said to me, though not voluble, was of a relatively more friendly nature, such as "Hurry up, slow poke!" or "What'sa matter, you paralyzed?" Occasionally she would give me chewy caramels or chocolate fingers or even a brand new handkerchief she had got from God knows where.

I never saw her steal anything, though she hung around in stores and talked to the owners as if they were brother and sister, and if she bought a nickel's worth of candy she was always given something else for me. Smile was in heavy evidence on these occasions, of course, and she was wise enough to let her adversaries do the talking, so things worked out in her favor.

One afternoon while flying through the park on our way home we ran into Stephen Farrar III, the beautiful young man from the big gray house on the corner. He stopped, said a cheery, "Hello, Mercy, where've you *been?*" and I introduced him to Cousin Ruth, who stepped up so near him he had to take a step back. Smile went into full service as he escorted us through the park. He had a special voice, faintly British, that went through you like a velvet knife.

However, since Ruth and Stephen Farrar had nothing much in common, she talked about me, but this time she was really talking. In fact, she spoke more words in those few blocks in the park than in the entire week I had known her. Now, Stephen always spoke to me as if it mattered, as if we two were the only people in the entire world.

Even his aside to Ruth when I introduced them, "How do you do?" was quickly relinquished in favor of me. "Tell me, Mercy, what have you been reading?" he began. But Cousin Ruth cut in by asking him some crazy thing—I've forgotten—and he answered her gently, but put her off.

Something was happening to her. I saw that. Another person seemed to have entered her skin, an animated person who spoke in a regular rhythm like a regular girl, with Smile coming and going, almost like other peoples'.

"How long have you known Mercy?" she asked.

"I really can't say, come to think of it. Seems like forever."

And again she asked if he knew how well I could read. He said yes, he did. She became so excited as we approached the exit to the park, she forgot to hold my hand in that awful pinch of hers, and before you could say Jack Robinson the two of them were walking ahead of me.

It was Stephen who quickly discovered the missing person and came back to claim me, taking my hand and smiling down at me. "Come along, Mercy, dear." He escorted me across the street all the way back to the side of my captor. "Here's your charge, Miss Hackett," he said. "You mustn't forget her. She's kind of precious, you know."

The smile dropped from Ruth's face as Stephen bade us good-bye. As he hurried to pick up his car, parked on Calhoun Street, she stood staring after him until the car was out of sight, then, recovering herself, she strode on without a single word the rest of the way, walking in those terrible strides, holding on to my hand as if to break the bones. Whenever I stole a sidewise glance I saw her chin was pulled up hard, making her large mouth look kind of funny. But the glance I'd caught of her as Stephen escorted me back to her side, admonishing her to take special care of me, lingered with me, for I saw that air of waiting was suddenly struck from her and in its place was a look that suggested what she had been waiting for had come to hand.

After supper that very night I came face to face with another facet of the personality of Cousin Ruth, one I was ill-prepared to meet. She was warming her feet in her favorite place which had been my favorite place in my bedroom, a big sofa placed conveniently before the heater, with another of my books open on her lap. I started to say, "That's my book. Could I have it, please?" Something stopped me, something in the way she was fingering it. I knew by now that she couldn't read, yet there she sat holding the book and staring at it. I had been watching her sidewise, and she couldn't see me, but suddenly she turned and stared.

"There's something written there in front." She pointed to the inscription. "What's that he wrote in front?"

"Who?" I asked, pretending not to know.

"You know who." She moved the book across the sofa so I could see it. "It's something he wrote, huh?"

"It's an inscription."

"Read it."

"I've already read it," I said.

"Read it out loud!" She pushed me so hard with

52

those awful fingers I began to read immediately. I tried to change the wording. I knew something was going on with her, but I couldn't think of any way of changing the words that quickly, and she was waiting with those iron hands.

"To my dear friend Mercy Bassford," I read.

"What else does it say?"

I had hoped to avoid reading the rest, but apparently she knew there was more, so I finished. "From your friend and admirer, Stephen Farrar," adding quickly, "That's all it says."

Cousin Ruth grabbed the book away again and turned back to warm her feet at the heater.

"How do *you* know that fellow?" She asked the question without even turning in my direction.

"Gee, I don't know."

"You do *so* know. You're *lying*." I didn't say anything. I knew she was mad from the way her words came out, hard and distinct, whereas she usually spoke rather mechanically but softly, running her words together.

"When did you meet him?"

"Seems like I've always known him."

"Listen! A kid like you, you can't fool me. You'd better tell me the truth. I'm supposed to take charge of you. Where did you meet him in the first place? You two seem like you know each other awful well. You picked him up in the park, didn't you?"

"Oh, no. I'm not allowed in the park except with Mamma or Rose."

"I know plenty of kids hang out in the park. There's something going on between you, him giving you presents and all."

"I met him in church, in Sunday school."

"I don't believe you. You're lying, but I'm going to get to the bottom of it."

She sat still after that, holding the book on her lap and fingering it for quite a long time.

"I'd like to have it back," I said. "I've been learning the poetry to recite."

I didn't expect to get it, but Cousin Ruth was never predictable. I had hardly got the words out of my mouth before she turned and flung the book across the room, hitting me hard in the elbow. I didn't say anything. I was afraid. My plan was to get into bed while she was busy at the heater, but once again she surprised me by turning back to tap me on my shoulder. "Time for the bath," she said.

I saw Smile was back. "I take my bath by myself," I said quickly. "I've been bathing and dressing myself for years."

"It's part of my job to see to you, Mercy. You wouldn't want me to get discharged now, would you?"

That was precisely what I did want to see happen to her and what I planned to ask Mamma to do first thing in the morning. But meanwhile Rose was at her home taking care of her old mother, Virginia Anne slept like a corpse, and I was alone with Smile and it seemed best to go along with her plan.

As time went by, in the peculiar, terrible way it does in childhood, now so fast and wonderful you just can't take it all in, then, suddenly slow and inexorable, interrupted with those long, white waits—somewhere along the line I had begun to sight the line of enemies. First came my bridegroom, Jesus, who punished those He loved the most, followed quickly by the Kaiser, retired from his empire but not from my memory, followed by Thing, the wild, waiting to spring from any man alive, and just as I was beginning to make my way, lifting my small light into the pitch black, along came Smile to take care of me, and at this very moment in time planning to bathe my naked body, in fact, gloating over her plan. "Look, I've got a nice, new bar of Yardley's soap, so go on, hurry up, get undressed and I'll be right in."

I could bear the hard hand-punching and the book-stealing and the dirty insinuations about Stephen, not fully understanding what she meant, but a bath by her was something else. Grabbing my blue flannel

54

robe, I tore out of the room, screaming, "I bathe myself!"

I ran into the bathroom, carefully locking the door behind me. As if that wasn't enough, I moved the shoe-shine stool, a heavy chair-like device, with four legs and full of all kinds of brushes and polishes, against the door, just as you do to keep out a burglar.

Then I waited, afraid to take off my clothes. I decided upon another plan. I would run the water, pretend I was taking a bath, then let the water run out and come on back to bed. I didn't want to take a bath with her so near. I didn't know what I was afraid of, but afraid I was, down to the marrow.

I was just scrubbing my teeth when I heard a sound at the door and I stopped in time to see the turning knob. She must have come down the hall in her stocking feet because I hadn't heard her. The knob stopped moving, and I began to feel better. Oh well, she hadn't gotten in. I finished cleaning my teeth and started the water running in the tub. The warm water looked kind of nice, and I thought of changing my plan and taking the bath; it would keep me away from her for awhile. Maybe she'd go to sleep and by the time I got back she'd be off, and there would be no more trouble with her until morning.

With these comforting thoughts in mind, I began undressing and was just testing the water with my toe when the door leading from the bathroom to the playroom where my sister slept, opened suddenly. I thought it was locked, as it usually was. There she was, Smile herself, holding the bar of soap she had mentioned. I almost knocked into her I was so surprised.

She promptly locked the playroom door from inside, and without a word, crossed the bathroom in one stride and sat down on the shoe-shine box, which she kicked into position with her foot. Next she put down the soap with one hand and with the other reached for my arm and pulled me to her. She stared at me, standing half naked before her. I had already taken off my robe and unbuttoned my drawers which had fallen

55

to my feet before she entered, so I stood before her in my undershirt, bare from the waist down and very embarrassed.

The way I was standing up, with Ruth holding both my hands in that awful hard one of hers, my face reached to the exact level of her face, my eyes were level and uncomfortably near to her eyes, which looked unnaturally big to me, at least the irises did. Smile was wider and more gleaming than I had seen it since first she glimpsed the big platters of fried chicken or roast beef arriving at the dinner table.

"Now, Mercy," she started, in a voice that was so soft that, if it hadn't been issuing from Smile, would have sounded almost kind, "you said you had a pain in your stomach, didn't you?" I had indeed said something of the kind right after supper, having nearly devoured two entire pieces of apple pie before they hit the plate. But that was hours ago.

"It's gone now, Cousin Ruth." I was trying to placate her. I was scared half to death.

"I have to examine you and see where it hurts." She pulled my shirt over my head before I realized what she was doing, but this task required both her hands, so I pulled loose and ran to the playroom door, knocking on it as loud as I knew how, but knowing at the same time nothing short of gunshots would awaken my sister. Meantime, Cousin Ruth got up and yanked me back across the bathroom by the arm, this time holding me by the hips with those big hands.

"You had a pain in your stomach." Smile was there again. "I have to see where it hurts, and maybe I'll have to give you an injection."

Injection, meaning enema, was enough to frighten me into doing anything to escape. Besides, I noticed she had her feet on my robe and underclothes.

"You let go of me!" I heard myself scream. "You give me back my clothes and let go of me. I'll tell my mamma and daddy! They'll put you in jail!"

"Now, Mercy. I'm not going to hurt you." The voice

went soft again, but Smile was growing wider with each move. "You just relax and lean over like I say. I'll see where it hurts."

Meantime she began pinning down both my arms with one of her big hands and, with the other, she began feeling down over my body, pressing first here and then there, holding me prostrate against her bare legs. I was so terrified I lost my voice. But then suddenly she turned me around and started feeling me in the back, sticking my head toward the floor, and, to my amazement, I got back my voice and let out a scream, "Help! Help! Rose, Rose, come on up! She's going to kill me!"

This must have worried Ruth. She let go of me, I got to my feet, and, giving me a hard push, she said, "Go ahead and take your bath!" When I looked around I saw she had opened and closed the door and gone out as silently as she had come in.

As everyone who has been a child remembers with acute horror, adults, even the best of them, operate in the limited area formed upon them by their needs. All those ambitions, such as my dear mother's to be a concert pianist and my dear father's to be a successful real-estate owner, lock them in the prison of their plans.

Now in one of these Mamma was deeply involved as I came downstairs for breakfast the following morning, fully prepared to tell her what had happened with Cousin Ruth. I looked quickly into the dining room and discovered my Cousin Ruth herself had got there first. She must have been on her third or fourth cup of coffee; she gulped coffee as she devoured food, as if she was squirreling it away somewhere inside her for fear it might be seized at any minute. The first thing I saw clearly was Smile and the first sounds I heard were her words coming out in the familiar music-box sound.

"Good morning, Mercy. You slept late, didn't you?" Sister looked at me sideways and winked, so I knew something was going on.

"Where's Mamma?"

"She's gone," said Cousin Ruth. She said the words, then came Smile, and then, waiting. Meantime, I heard my mother in the hall, gathering up sheets of music and shoving them into the long black case she carried daily to her piano lessons. I ran out just in time to see her opening the front door.

She stopped long enough to say, "Well, I heard about your playing doctor last night." She was actually smiling.

I managed to ask, "What?"

"Cousin Ruth told me—you two had yourselves a time." I gasped as I heard this last. "Well, good-bye," she added hastily. "See you this afternoon." Next thing I knew I was eating my breakfast, then watching Rose in the kitchen, just as if nothing had happened the night before.

The only sign I had before the day began was my sister whispering before she went off to school, "She's crazy" in pig Latin. "Eeshay's Azeecray." *She* was waiting, in coat, with Smile, to take sister off to school, so we had no chance for another word.

Watching Rose in the kitchen is no pleasure this morning. Rose's round, soft black face with the big, pink lips and the great red, white, and brown eyes are turned to those things in the corner she is now burning. She has a big iron pot brought from her own home, Shanty No. 3 in the alley off Gilmore, the bottom of which is covered with dark plants "got from the island" and kept in a sacred spot for just such a moment as this, when her mother, down with pneumonia, and returned from the hospital for convalescence, has been "took again," a genuine relapse.

Rose is burning the plants and going on in her singsong voice, and the smell in the kitchen is of a burning brush fire. Now and then small flames leap up out of the iron pot. Rose stands swaying from side to side as she sings and murmurs, words I can't understand, interrupted occasionally by her eyes closing, her hands folding, and her head leading her whole torso in circles

58

round and round. During this part of the ritual she is quiet, then she begins again with the singing and the murmuring. She stops after a while and sits down at the kitchen table, opens her eyes slowly and looks at me. "What you doin' bothering now when you knows I'm burning plants?"

"How long will you be burning plants?"

"Three days and three nights. Why'nt you walk on out with your Cousin Ruth? She'da taken you for a nice walk down to the market."

"I don't want to go to market with Cousin Ruth. I hate her!"

"Oh, that ain't nice." I try to tell her about what happened last night but I know from what she says she isn't listening. "That's just peoples' ways when they's getting used to a new fambly. You just wait few days and she's going to settle down and be real nice."

She gives me another muffin with butter, but I notice she put it in the dining room which means she is going back to those awful plants, leaving me alone. "Your Cousin Ruth's coming back for you right soon now. I heard your Mamma tell her to take you to the department store and get you some nice new shoes."

This time she closes the door to the kitchen but I can hear her the minute she begins again with those damned chanting sounds. Johnsy Dowse is playing ball in the yard next door, and there is something comforting in that clump, thud, clump, thud.

I could open the dining room window and call him. I could say anything to Johnsy, anything at all, tell him anything I felt like, a great luxury at any time in any place, but sometimes it was like talking to myself. Johnsy Dowse was three years older than I, and in a way, the closest friend I had in the world. He was supposed to be "backward."

He was slow, very slow, but he knew how to work. He swept the yard mornings, went on errands for his mother, cleaned all the rooms the widowed Mrs. Dowse rented out, and then delivered flowers much too heavy

59

for him to carry for Stearns Florists. What he said was always something you already knew yourself. But sometimes it's good to hear those things said out loud. I was thinking of calling him just as I heard the front door opening and, bang, there was Smile sitting down at the table and talking exactly as if nothing in the world had happened!

I was getting ready for bed one night. Smile was out somewhere, the family was downstairs at the dining room table, when I thought I heard light footsteps coming up the stairs. In a few seconds I heard taps on my bedroom door. A voice whispered, "Mercy, have you gone to bed?"

I said no, and opened the door immediately. There stood Honey, staring in at me. The light from the bedroom lamp shone smack on her pretty face which flashed some terrible message I couldn't quite read. "Come on in, Honey," I said, lowering my voice to a kindred whisper. She came in and stood by my bed. I offered her two whole chocolate marshmallows which she not only disdained to touch but hardly seemed to see.

"Can you come over?"

"I guess so," I said. I wasn't quite undressed and could easily put my clothes back on.

"Oh, Mercy," whispered Honey, "I'm in trouble and you'll have to come over right away."

Honey crept back down the steps, with me following close behind her, just about dying of curiosity to hear about her new trouble. What had happened, I wondered, wildly guessing as we crossed the street. Had Uncle Tom threatened her with the House of the Good Shepherd, a terrifying retreat for retarded or delinquent females, where it was said girls were tied to beds or laced into straight jackets when not being injected with needles to quiet them down, or else locked in black dungeons and fed stale bread and water for weeks on end?

It had to be something bad threatening my beloved

Honey. I knew from the way she held my hand as we scurried up the steps and into the bathroom with Screamer in hot pursuit behind us. This time we went straight up the two steps leading from the bathroom into Honey's bedroom, and, seeing how she ignored the pot, I knew it had to be something terrible. Screamer came tearing in behind us, his license plate tinkling loudly, his breath coming heavily as he grabbed Honey's blue bedroom slipper and began rushing under the bed, making chase-me sounds of happiness as he shook and tore at the slipper.

"Oh, Mercy, wait till you hear what happened! Just wait till you hear."

Now everybody in the world needs a confidant, I know that much, somebody you can tell everything to, no matter what, without fear of reprisal. One of the reasons people crack up and die early is because confidants of this kind are so hard to find. The older person has no better confidant than a loving and bright child. Honey had me. Indeed when she tapped on my door and whispered, "You've got to help me," I said, "Sure," and meant it with all my heart, for Honey represented womanhood, a situation I needed to examine as much as she needed to have her situation examined. A highly desirable exchange.

Tonight, as she turned on the soft bedroom lamp with the pink shade, I didn't see anything unusual. I watched as she took her stance beside her bureau. Her eyes were wide to bursting, her cheeks flushed and her lower lip, for once unpainted, was being bitten within an inch of its life by her pretty teeth.

"Look!" she burst out suddenly. I looked around but I couldn't see a thing. Then she pointed to her bureau. "There, Mercy. *There they are!*"

I looked and saw a brush and two large covered jars filled with something that looked like black shoe polish, or black cream of some kind. I said, "Well . . ." as she hurried me down the steps from the bedroom into her bathroom, Screamer quickly following with slipper in mouth.

"Sit down with me, Mercy, please, while I take my bath."

I had often done this but this time she looked so worried I couldn't figure out what was going on. Meantime she tore off her clothes and got stark naked very quickly. Only she *wasn't* naked. There were patches of white cotton cloth across her breasts and still larger ones on her backside. She usually sang as she got into the tub, but not this time.

"I've been bad, Mercy," she began, bursting into tears. "If Mamma or Papa found out what I've done they'd put me in the House of the Good Shepherd."

"What on earth happened?" I asked, stupidly trying to guess. "Look, if you've got smallpox they'll put you in the hospital, that's all."

"You see those big bandages?"

"Oh yes, they look awful. You hurt yourself, didn't you, Honey? Or have you got some disease?"

"No-o-o-o-o-," she sobbed. "It's worse than that, Mercy. It's more . . . permanent."

"What is it? What happened?" That seemed to worry her, so I changed it to, "You got hurt, didn't you? Somebody hit you, some big, dirty man!"

"No. It was this *woman*. She came from New York City. This Mrs. Elba. She had this cream, this Growing and Shrinking Cream. She was staying at the Hotel Rennert so I went to see her. Oh, Mercy, it cost me sixteen dollars just for those two jars." She pointed in the direction of the evil jars. "They're supposed to grow your breasts and shrink your behind." She turned off the water and cried so loud poor Screamer dropped the shoe and came over to see what could be done. "Only they weren't *marked*—because of *the law*."

She stood up and pointed to the bandages over her backside.

"Look what happened. I must have got them mixed! Oh, Mercy, I'll never be the same again."

"What is it?" Her backside did look swollen and red, but I wasn't going to tell her.

"I put the wrong stuff on each place. Made my

breasts shrink and my backside grow. Now I'm bigger than ever back there," she wailed, "and I've begun to shrink down to nothing up front. I'm turning into a freak."

Still crying, she motioned me to help her pull off the bandages, which I did. We started on her breasts and when we had them off there, well, to tell the truth, they did look small and extra red. She pointed first to her breasts then to the tape measure, which I went and got for her.

"Let's just measure them," she wailed. "Oh, Mercy, they're meaner and smaller than they were ever before. They're g-g-going *in*." She had written down thirty-four in big numerals in a copy book she kept. We began washing her breasts, then we applied the tape measure, and the tape came out to thirty-two. We measured again, and once again, sure enough, it was thirty-two again.

I said, "Maybe you got it wrong the first time," but she swore she hadn't.

"Two whole inches in just one day," she wailed, "And by tomorrow, oh, my God! And there's no way to stop the stuff from working, Madam Elba said that. It goes on its own, she said!"

"Oh well, Honey, maybe they're big enough. What do you want such big ones for?"

"You wouldn't understand, Mercy," she wailed. "If they keep on going in, I'll be deformed. Here, help me!"

I tore the rest of the bandages off her backside. She stood there biting her lower lip and wailing, and Screamer began to howl so loud I was afraid her parents would hear us. We got the tape measure and began measuring part number two. "Look in the book. It says forty," Honey instructed. I looked, and it did read forty. Then she held the tape and I measured and, if I read correctly, even pulled tight, it was forty-two. Honey looked down and read for herself. "Forty-two— and in just one day. Think what it'll be like tomorrow. And in a week I won't be able to sit in my chair!"

Now I didn't know what to say. The situation loomed terrible, with part of Honey going in and the other going out. Forever.

"Forty-two in twenty-four hours. Forty-four, maybe forty-six, this time tomorrow. And that terrible Madame Elba's gone back to that awful New York, and I don't know where to reach her. And even if I did she said it won't stop its action. She said it can't. Oh, Mercy, my whole life will be over."

"No, it won't, Honey. Maybe we measured it wrong. Here we'll try again . . ."

I grabbed the tape and this time I pulled it pretty tight. I was afraid to pull it any tighter for fear of hurting her, she was already so red and swollen. I looked and there it was: nearly forty-two.

"What does it say?" sobbed Honey.

"Forty-one," I lied. "Besides it's all swollen. Wait till it comes down."

"It'll just never come down. My whole life's finished."

"It is not, Honey. *It is not,* you hear? Men are just crazy about you, you know they are."

"What men?" But I noticed she had stopped wailing.

"Every man you see. Clarence and Raymond and that man who was at your party and that other fellow who was with him. Every man that sees you. Every man in the whole world."

"How do *you* know?"

"I know. Everybody says so. Uncle Johnnie says no man is safe around you. He says you turn their heads."

All this was true. My cousin Honey had been engaged a dozen times, and not one of the men with whom she had broken the engagement would ever take back the ring. Aunt Gus and Uncle Tom had had to force back the tokens. It wasn't that they were such gentlemen or so generous as that they were still involved with Honey and they wanted her to have some part of them.

"But suppose my breasts disappear and I'll be all f-f-anny. Then I'll be a fr-r-r-eak."

"No, you won't. And even if you are you'd find dozens of other freaks after you, Honey."

64

The idea made her cry as she pulled up the tape again, but this time it wasn't tight and read forty-two and a half.

"Come on, let's wash it off real good, Honey, and it won't grow you any more."

I hurried to the tub and turned on the spigots full blast. Now I was worried myself. I saw the cream which had caused the red welts on Honey and was afraid to touch the vile smelling stuff for fear of catching something. I, too, could shrink and grow, and having almost nothing to either shrink or grow, I'd as lief remain as I was. Maybe I'd lose my hands, I thought, as I sailed in and began scrubbing her with soap and water. Honey had been too good a friend to let her down at a time like this but every time I touched the black stuff I thought my fingers looked smaller.

"You take a good bath, now, just scrub it all off again and it'll go away," I kept saying, not knowing what was going to happen from minute to minute.

While she was bathing, the telephone started ringing as one, then another, of Honey's admirers cut in on her tragedy, and each time she hoisted herself out of the tub and began talking away. "Yay-us, yay-us, I do, deah," is what she mostly said, between long talks about plans. "Yay-us, oh, I most certainly do. Just you."

"A man must never see you sa-yud, Mercy," she announced, drying her tears with a towel. "Even after you're married, they have to think you're happy all the time. You just can't tell them anything, the dirty dogs."

"Why?"

"Because they'll just go to pieces, if they see you sa-yud. Didn't you know that? They'll go into *decline!*"

She climbed back into the tub and we continued once more with the scrubbing. Once settled, she seemed slightly more hopeful and began talking in a more normal vein.

"Ah get so lonesome, Mercy, going to the bathroom all by myself. It's all so awful. Oh, it's so awful lonesome. I just hate to take a bath all the way up here all by myself, and now with my body deformed, and you going to school and all, it's going to be worse than ever."

"You won't be deformed, Honey, and even if you are, like I said, you'll find other deformed people by the hundreds."

Honey's precious parts must have eventually gone back to normal, because by the time we all went down to John Clifford's for the Thanksgiving holiday, nothing more was said about deformity.

Besides, Clarence and Raymond were coming around, and Honey was too busy with parties and dances to think too much of the evil Madam Elba who had meantime left town in a hurry and, according to what Mamma read out loud in the paper, was being sought for questioning for some fake cosmetic she had peddled around town.

Sometime just before Christmas—Honey owed me nearly two dollars for pot sitting on a regular basis, a sum I was eager to add to my Christmas money—I received another frantic call and went over as usual.

"Mercy, darling," she began, the minute we passed through her bedroom door. "Wait a minute. Sit down, and look, just look at this."

She had pulled down her slip and was holding out her bosoms for me to inspect. I watched stupidly, not knowing what to say.

"Well, what do you *see?*"

"Nothing," I said. "I mean, just a couple of bosoms. That's about all."

"Look carefully, Mercy." She stood holding up first one bosom, then another, for me to inspect. She was waiting for a verdict, for all the world like a patient showing a malformation to the doctor. I stared uncomfortably at a round pink nipple surrounded with the usual white flesh, wondering what on earth was expected in the way of comment.

"It looks all right to me," I finally said. "I haven't seen too many of those things."

"Is it perfectly normal, Mercy?" "Sure," I said, but she went on. "Tell me the truth now."

"Well, it looks a lot like things I've seen in the doctor's book we have home." She kept hanging on to her bosom while staring at me. "Why don't you just let go of it?" I suggested.

"Well, because I saw Alicia May's when she was here last week and hers were brown."

"Gee whiz!"

"Dark brown, too. And hairy."

"For goodness sake!" It didn't seem right to have something dark brown and hairy, but I had no idea what Alicia May could do about it. I felt stupid as I finally dredged up a comment. "That don't sound right to me."

"That's just what I thought." I must have said the right words because this time Honey moved in close and dropped her bosoms at last.

Thus encouraged I went on, this time inspired. "Yours are the right color, Honey, and hers are just *wrong*. The idea, going off and turning brown and hairy, at her age. Alicia May had better have them fixed, that's all."

I knew I had hit the jackpot with this one because inside a very short time Honey had put her clothes back on and was jabbering away about her party Christmas Eve and how her mamma had said she could have the floor waxed downstairs and hire a band and how she was going to give me some more lessons before the party so I could dance with Cousin Russell Owen who was fourteen and knew every step there was.

At home began two weeks of what I can only call pseudo-normalcy in Cousin Ruth's behavior. She'd been hired to look after both my sister and myself, and we each noticed her peculiarities and talked together about her. One day she would be especially nice to me and ignore my sister; the following day she would be overly kind to sister and ignore me. But we didn't much mind. "Issthay issway oryay ayday," "This is your day,"

67

we'd say to one another. Occasionally Smile would hear us whispering together, and then we would notice a slight widening of the painted mouth and a more complete showing of long, white teeth with red tongue moving, resembling a caged wild animal. Whenever Mamma or Daddy would ask, "Well, how do you like Cousin Ruth?" we would burst out in a chorus, "We don't!"

"But you will in a short time," they would reassure us. "She's just new," Mamma kept on saying, in the infuriating conciliatory way she had. "She's been alone, you know."

Once Virginia Anne piped up, "She treats us funny. One of us is her favorite one day, and the other the next day." Virginia Anne was told she was imagining things, and she turned away disgusted.

"A poor homeless girl," Daddy put in, as if he expected us to cry over Cousin Ruth, as if there was something inhospitable in *not* snuggling up to her. "Someone going from school to school, she needs to be in a family and this is your opportunity to help her!"

During the two weeks of "normalcy" I mentioned, Cousin Ruth nipped about town with Virginia Anne and me, taking us to movies and ice cream stores, in and out of department stores, libraries and museums, holding both our hands as if to crack the bones, and striding as if a double-barreled shotgun was pointed at her head. She was something to see, her black hair flying behind her, her painted mouth and flashing eyes. Her long torso, with arms protruding, was sometimes a good yard and a half ahead of us. She moved as if she were after something, as if there was something or someone she was just about to catch; then, when she'd slow down, you knew she hadn't caught it or them or him, because she was still watching and waiting.

Meantime, as if drawn by a magnet, Stephen Farrar kept stopping by our house, leaving small but delightful presents, with messages inside for me. Once he called late in the afternoon with a beautiful new game of Parcheesi, and asked Rose if he might wait and deliver it in person. Since I was playing with Johnsy Dowse in his backyard that day, Rose said yes, and invited him into the parlor, and next thing Johnsy Dowse, Stephen and I were sitting under the big chandelier beside a crackling fire.

Cousin Ruth came home as we were playing. She was standing between the folding parlor doors staring directly at Stephen and not saying anything at all. Old Smile was there, the great wide one, but no words came. Stephen instantly got to his feet, and said, 'Good evening, Miss Hackett," then she stood and he stood and we stared up at him, waiting impatiently for her to go. "Well, if you'll excuse me," he managed, finally, "we're into a wild game here, don't you see?" He sat down and Cousin Ruth went off without saying a word.

My parents thoroughly approved of Stephen, who had been to Oxford and was teaching English literature at the Old Town Prep School for Boys. And when he asked permission to take Johnsy and me to see *The Hunchback of Notre Dame,* they gave it gladly.

It was marvelous, though Johnsy did have a cold and breathed so heavily he could be heard over the entire theater, especially during those terrible minutes when the monster was climbing up to the belfry tower.

We never mentioned a word of this expedition to Cousin Ruth. She had Saturdays off, anyway, and usually went out early in the morning, so I was amazed when, as we came out of the theater, she was sitting all by herself down front in the third aisle of the emptying theater. I thought she must have followed us. Yet she was staring straight ahead into the empty seats as if she had no idea we were there. But I knew that she knew.

Of course, I had written the engagement down in my diary, but I kept it hidden in my desk under lock and key. Besides, she couldn't read.

Stephen put his arms around us as we went through the park toward home. Johnsy, half a head taller than me, snuggled into his shoulder, I came just over his waist. They were talking man talk. "I can climb trees easy," Johnsy boasted, "but I don't know, going straight up like that, how'd the monster do that?" And Stephen explained about "sets" in movies and how it wasn't a "real steeple," and that Lon Chaney wasn't up anywhere near as far as it looked.

I listened, but I had the feeling Cousin Ruth might be somewhere in the park following us. Once when I turned around I thought I saw her black beaver hat in the distance outlined against one of the snowy bushes. She was not home when I got back. She did not return to eat her dinner and had not returned by the time I got ready for bed. I remember saying to Virginia Anne, "Maybe she's gone and will never come back," and my sister replying, "No such good luck."

It was real nice having my room to myself again and I went happily about rearranging crayons, drawing papers and books in the order I'd had them before Cousin Ruth's arrival. I was going through the nightly rituals in the bathroom obeying the continuous parental chorus, "Wash your face and hands and clean your teeth!" and planning to ask Mamma if I could have a certain blue velvet dress I had seen in a window downtown, when the bathroom door opened and closed so softly behind me I hardly noticed. I turned around and there was Cousin Ruth. I thought from the way she kicked the stool around she had already locked the door behind her. She strode across behind me and tried the door to Virginia Anne's bedroom.

I was too frightened to say anything. She wasn't talking, either. She was just standing there looking down at me. I could hear the water running, having forgotten to turn it off. She was holding her left hand in a fist. Then, as she moved back across the room, I thought I saw something gleam, but as I looked more closely she put her hand behind her back and smiled.

"You didn't go to the bathroom today, did you, Mercy?"

"I did so."

"When?"

"Twice. Once this morning and once tonight."

"When tonight?"

"Just now."

"You'll have to let me see."

I started to scream, "No-o-o-o-!" but she grabbed me with her free hand and pulled me toward her as she settled down on the boot-shine stool.

"Now if you're telling me the truth, I'll know right away." She put something down on the floor—was it the thing I'd seen flashing from her fist?—and began undressing me. She moved fast and deftly, and she had my robe and half my pajamas off before I could get back my voice and let out a piercing yell.

"You let go of me! Let go, let go!"

With the strength of panic I managed to get out of her clutches and run across the room where I stood near Virginia Anne's door, banging on it with all my might and screaming my lungs out.

"Wake up, stupid, and open the door. She's going to do something terrible!"

But there was nothing but silence from Virginia Anne's room. Cousin Ruth got slowly to her feet. I looked back once and saw she was standing up and smiling. That was when I noticed the object from her fist laying on the floor right where she had put it, catching the light. It looked like a small pencil made of steel with a round head.

"I have to examine you," she said softly, her fingers reaching down to the floor to locate the steel object. "You don't have to yell. It won't hurt. Come here, Mercy."

But I wasn't coming and, in my terror, I did and said everything wrong. "You're not supposed to examine me or give me an enema or anything!" I hollered. "You're not supposed to touch me!"

"Oh, yes, I am, and I'm going to."

"Don't come near me! You're just jealous because Stephen Farrar likes me," I said.

Cousin Ruth's smile, which had diminished slightly

71

during the fray, suddenly widened. I was in danger now, all right. Having gone so far, I couldn't stop. "You followed us to the movies. I saw you spying on us in the park, too."

I was about to bang louder on Virginia Anne's door, but Smile came across the room in one stride and grabbed me with both hands. This time she tore off my pajama top and held me in a strong vise in front of her as she sat on the bench pinning my arms and holding me down. It felt as if she were breaking my back.

But she didn't do anything. She sat there staring hard with her big green eyes. I never had anyone look at me naked before in this peculiar way, not even a doctor. She stared at my flesh as if it fascinated her, her eyes roaming from my bare shoulders to my stomach to my knees and then up again, as if undecided which part to attack first.

I let out another scream loud enough to wake the dead. Her grip tightened. Then she leaned over to pick up that thing on the floor. I thought I heard a sound in the hall, somebody moving behind the door, but it stopped. I tried to scream again but my voice had gone. Just then I heard a sound behind Virginia Anne's door. The smile disappeared from Cousin Ruth's face. She must have heard it, too. She eased her grip on me, grabbed the washrag and began wildly washing my face, just as Rose appeared in the bathroom, followed by my sleepy sister.

"What's going on here?" Rose demanded.

Cousin Ruth spoke very evenly. "Mercy hates getting cleaned up, Rose."

"Peoples ain't locking doors to wash up childrens."

With Rose there, my head came back, slowly at first. I grabbed the steel piece which had fallen to the floor in the excitement and handed it to Rose.

"She was going to do something terrible! She brought this thing with her." Cousin Ruth tried to grab it from me, but Rose took it at once and, seeing that Ruth was reaching frantically to get it, she threw it through the open window. I heard it fall down the roof of the porch, landing on the bricks in the backyard. Cousin Ruth backed away from the sink.

"Come awn, hurry up and put back on your clothes," said Rose.

"Never mind." Sister patted me on the arm. "Eeshay's awngay utsnay," she whispered. "She's *gone nuts.*"

My clothes were barely on my body when Ruth started pushing me toward the door. "I'll put her to bed," she said in one of her sudden soft voices, but Rose, a woman of few words when angry, stepped between us.

"You done enough puttin' for one night," she said. "You can go on to bed yourself, but this child's staying with me."

Cousin Ruth tried once more with the smile and soft talk. "Mercy always hates getting bathed," she said, but she saw it wasn't working on Aunt Rose and went quickly down the hall.

Rose put Virginia Anne back to bed, locking both of her doors, and took me downstairs to her room. I noticed she went immediately out into the yard, turned on the lights on the back porch and went searching for the steel object. When she finally came back, I could see she had something in her hand.

"What is it?" I wanted to know. I couldn't guess what it was or what it was for, but it interested me no end.

"I dunno," was all Rose would say. "Whatever it is, we got it now."

She put it carefully away in her bureau drawer. I heard her moving around, locking the door to her bedroom and putting things away, but it was difficult to stay awake after a night like this and before long I snuggled in beside her and was far, far away.

I knew about how Thing got loose from men, couldn't be controlled and ran around looking for women, bringing down on them all kinds of horrors. I knew a lot more, too, including how Thing broke through women's maidenheads and brought down balls by the thousands, and bad men kept the balls in their closets. And behind it all was Him, the peeper, my bridegroom! He was peeping particularly, in fact unilaterally, at me, a fixation of His.

I was too young and impressionable to figure out why He did this peculiar business, but He knew and I knew, and I knew that He knew. Dead over nineteen hundred years and still peeping *at me*. If ever He should come alive again, as He had in the past, He'd hot-foot it straight to me. In some way, I had brought this on myself, probably by not loving Him the way He said I should in the first place.

Meantime, He was magic and could be anywhere at any time, and I imagined other men possessed some of His sinister talents, my daddy, my uncles, and later, my teachers, and would wonder sometimes if this one or that one staring at me might be Him come to life, wearing a disguise so He could peep real good.

And a genuine *you-can-see* monster lived in my home, not by way of the imagination, or the chimney, but the front door. My own *cousin* and a girl! and who was not after Virginia or anybody else but me.

As time passed, I overheard Mamma talking to Aunt Jenny about the necessity of finding a new school for Cousin Ruth "as soon as possible," but nothing more was said of the events of the preceding Saturday night, although I knew Aunt Rose had told Mamma the entire story. Meantime, Cousin Ruth went on eating her way through a whole herd of cattle, panfuls of chickens and hams.

Aunt Rose told me Cousin Ruth was leaving soon, and one Saturday morning when I came down to breakfast I heard she had gone. I promptly went upstairs to my bedroom. Everything was exactly the same as it had been before, on the surface at least, and I dressed happily for a day of shopping downtown, museums, movies and lunch in a restaurant with Aunt Jenny and Virginia Anne.

It was not until the following night that I discovered certain precious possessions were missing from my room,

74

notably my Parcheesi game, the book of verse given me by Stephen and autographed for me, and my entire new paint set. As if this was not enough, when I lifted my piggy bank and shook it, there was not a solitary penny left inside.

She had cleaned out my entire savings, the whole dollar and ninety-seven cents earned by long half hours of pot-sitting for Honey and to be used for the seventeen Christmas presents on my list.

I was told by all the adults not to worry, that the lost presents would be supplied in one form or another. Mamma gave me four quarters to start a new account, and Honey gave me forty cents, eight nickels for one sitting. Mamma let us play in the parlor right beside the piano if we wanted. Aunt Rose brought in sandwiches, cake and tea, placed it right on the round rosewood table with the tapestry cloth and put the table in front of the fire. And Mamma stopped practicing to remind her, "Don't forget the chocolates for Mercy, she can have one now, and one before supper."

Something has happened. Something bad. *To me.* I know because they are all making amends. Virginia Anne is getting in on the act. Mamma is placating me, playing up to me. She knows the Chopin, Debussy and Ravel are over my head and boring to me, and she turns to something she says is humorous. "About an animal," she explains. "A dog. Listen now, Mercy!" I listen and watch her slender fingers moving precisely on the keys; it goes on and on, sounding like no dog I had ever heard. But I listen because I know she is doing it to please me.

Johnsy Dowse is invited to come in and stay to supper, and I can go over there and play darts in his backyard where he has a great wooden outhouse on which a marvelous dart board has been placed, and Stephen Farrar is encouraged to take us all out whenever he wants.

My name keeps coming up. It's Mercy this, and Mercy that. Why? Because I'm the one who is the magnet. I do all the attracting to this house.

He waits, and peeps. Thing is getting ready to spring. Monsters are everywhere. But good forces are in the world. Stephen comes here to see me and takes me out. Oh, I am growing tall and fair by the minute, that much I know, but there is something else to all this, something more. Even a girl wants to undress me, a girl, and stare at my jewels. She hides steel instruments with which to sample me further.

It's pretty scary all this, and kind of thrilling. And it will not go away.

PART TWO
✄(1925-1929)✄

I CAN see them all standing guard at the wall of my psyche. *Him* up there, God that is, too enormous for contemplation. Then J, for Jesus, the peeper, on the ceiling. Then Thing, that got loose in men and drove them crazy. Then That in my cousin, Ruth, of the green eyes. By the time I reached high school, becoming really wise, I knew what Thing did. *Indrakorz*. When Thing struck he committed *indrakorz*. From *indrakorz* you got *caught* and died slowly. For some unknown and medical reason, Thing acted quite different with married people. Became tame and kind of stung at them something like a wounded bee. As a result they got *pregnant* and produced children. They didn't die, or rarely did. But other people, unmarried and young, got *caught* and died in a slow, obscure way. They, too, had babies, but the babies grew to gigantic proportions and killed their bearers. Or they were mostly born dead and bright blue.

For example, there was Hope Curtis, a pretty girl with a round face like an apple, rosy cheeks and perfect skin. But she got *caught* in her sophomore year at aged fifteen. Poor Hope didn't know what was happening to her. She kept getting fatter and fatter. She and her family thought, maybe she had a tumor and ought to see a doctor. But Miss Weingard, an assistant principal of Wesleyan High School, sent for her mother. After that it went around the school that Hope was pregnant, and everybody knew except poor Hope herself. Another word came into being, another guardian arose. *Expelled.* If Thing got loose and *attacked,* you got caught and would be expelled. Your education would then stop. After being expelled you would drop to the very bottom of the black, leaky, social barrel and thenceforward slither further down into some nameless slime and death.

The day Hope was expelled, she came back to her home room with a pale color in her recently rosy cheeks, dried tears showed down to her mouth and there was no color at all in her lips, one of which she was biting with her upper teeth. She walked with her eyes staring straight forward and went to her desk.

The room went deadly silent, changing from the noisy routine of kids grabbing their books, hats and coats, and the general hullabaloo of the leavetaking, to sudden hush, then absolute stillness. Nobody spoke to Hope. She sat down at her desk for a while and did nothing, not even cry, as if she didn't understand what was happening to her or what she was supposed to do. There was some doubt as to whether she was even going to clean out her desk. The whole class stopped moving, and everyone watched. It was awful. Miss Talbacher was decent enough not to stare at her. She went on about her desk work, then got up, opened the windows from the top and came back to her desk, still taking no notice of Hope. Thel and I looked at each other, and shook our heads. We felt sorry for Hope but didn't know quite what to do.

After a few minutes of this awful staring, the kids all started moving again taking up their books and going to the cloakroom to get their hats and coats. A tide of conversation began. A minute or two, and bang! The entire room was cleared of all except Miss Talbacher, Hope Curtis, Thelma and me. Hope was still sitting there. She hadn't lifted the top of her desk when we came by, as if moved simultaneously by some unseen force, and sat at the desk beside her.

"We're walking through the park," said Thelma.

"Why don't we all walk home together? We can stop by Tobin's for coffee and cake," I suggested.

For the first time Hope raised her head and looked at us, first Thelma and then me, and a glint of recognition came into her eyes, as if now she knew where she was and who we were.

"Oh. Oh yes, thanks," she spoke very quickly. She looked as if she might cry again, but she didn't. She didn't do anything at all. She didn't even lift the top of her desk and take out her things, expensive reference books she had and a gold fountain pen.

"You go ahead now, Hope," Miss Talbacher said. "I think it's fine, you three girls going home together." Then she added, on second thought, "You can get your things some other time, or the girls can bring them to you." Hope looked at her, nodded and got up slowly, as if she could hardly make it up from the seat, and we followed at her side. During the ensuing weeks, as Hope's sorrow deepened, something seemed to draw her back to the school. She would show up at the cafeteria at lunchtime, quiet, restrained, and pale, but eager to get back to her familiar school situation, as if she hadn't been expelled. Thel and I would always come and sit with her, but usually we three were the only ones at the long table. She would speak to the other girls, but they would say hello very quickly and move away, as if afraid of contracting her disease. She was a fallen woman at fifteen. There was a reason for this grisly attitude in that Evelyn Marshall had got caught and expelled in her freshman year; Evie had tried to commit suicide, and the story of her tragedy was still rife in the school. She had been discovered in time and saved, but the legend lingered on.

In both these cases, and dozens of others, the male whose thing had got loose and Done It to the girl was an invisible man. His name was never mentioned.

About this time my Cousin Ruth, having been thrown out of six different schools for girls, had settled at Grandma's like one of the lost animals my aunts were forever taking in, only the animals were charming. Ruth now worked in an office downtown and was usually out of an evening with first one man, then another. Despite her good looks and bright conversation, none of her relationships seemed to come to anything, and at twenty-two she'd never been engaged.

My aunts always worried about her, and no wonder. Just as she had been sent home from first one school and then another, so she would leave one job after another, spending her in-between time hanging around the house, calling up people my aunts had never met, then disappearing suddenly and coming home at odd hours, sometimes late at night or early in the morning. Ever since she had been gently but firmly sent away from our house, she had treated me very coolly, but occasionally, especially if we were alone or with one or two of our aunts present, she would attack me all over again.

"You think you're pretty, dón't you?" she said to me one day, as I stood rearranging my hair before the Pier-glass mirror in Grandma's parlor.

"She is pretty, too," said my Aunt Jenny, who was sitting by the window reading and had, therefore, been overlooked by Ruth. "Mr. Hardy says Mercy's a beautiful girl and will make a beautiful woman."

Ruth flew up from her position on the piano stool as swiftly as a bird. I was frightened, finding her standing there behind me. "You say she's pretty, and old Mr. Hardy says she's pretty. Well, just let me show you something!" I tried to move, but she had hold of my hair. Aunt Jenny stood up. "Don't worry!" Ruth threw the words at my aunt. She was pulling my hair, taking it all up in her hands, holding it so tight I couldn't move.

"Let go of me!" I screamed. "If you touch me, you'll be sorry."

I saw her face in the mirror, Smile had returned, that awful shark's look.

"I'm not going to hurt you, Mercy," she said, her voice pouring into my ears. "I just want to show Aunt Jenny what you *really* look like."

I stood my ground, frightened. "What do you mean what I *really* look like? She can see what I *really* look like." Blood rushed to my face and neck, as Ruth pulled back my hair to the top of my head, tighter and tighter. "Now look at her, Jenny girl. Look at her without her hair. Is she pretty *now?*"

Aunt Jenny drew in her mouth. She was frightened but determined. "She's pretty all right. Now will you let go of her!"

Ruth smiled and pulled my hair even tighter until my mouth went dry and I knew I was going to be sick. When she did let go I fell over the sofa. The room trembled, with furniture, Jenny and Smile tumbling over each other.

At age thirteen and a sophomore in high school I would find myself dreaming nights of two men in a composite image bearing a shadowy resemblance to Stephen Farrar and Dr. Gardiner, the principal of the Wesleyan High School.

One night Uncle Clinton took Thelma and me and Cousin Elizabeth to the movies where Vilma Banky was being beautiful and damned. The picture had already started as our group entered the hot, dark theater. The piano player was working away down front, but there were few seats to be had and I found myself being pushed into the only one available to the side of the theater where it was dark but pleasant. I was at first relieved then delighted to find myself alone. I glanced around once, just once, to locate my group.

There was Uncle Clinton, just beginning to relax and smile. He was far away at the opposite side of the theater, removed from me by a deep, thick crowd of heads and faces, a sea of eyes drinking in the movements on the screen. Ah, now I could watch without being watched, drink in and dream.

This was a plush movie theater, blue-black carpeted, with an exceptionally large screen and a talented piano player who touched the keys softly, lovingly. As I settled into my seat, he was into a soft rendition of "Memories" as Vilma Banky stared out of the window of her expensive-looking, heavily-draperied apartment into the street below, staring at the limousine that was carrying her lover away, far into the distance of a long street shining with rain.

I moved into greater comfort, letting the heavy odor of cheap perfume mingled with talcum powder and sweat fill my nostrils. At length, after a few minutes of rarely enjoyed privacy and safety, I settled into a blessed numbness where I followed blindly the movements of Vilma, her bare shoulders, arms and back showing from just the right spots in her dark evening gown, as she fingered her pearls, bit her lips, shook her ringlets in sorrow and then began the sighing and walking the length of the long luxurious room like a caged lioness.

Then, suddenly, the telephone was ringing. Vilma stopped fingering her jewels and listened, biting her rouged lower lip. A Negro maid in a white uniform came into the room to answer it for her, but Vilma waved her aside. Slowly she advanced toward the instrument, and sank into a French chair at her desk. I sank, too, as the game was no longer up to me, and I gave up willingly. Now it was Vilma's fate that was being decided, and mine only indirectly, as I was, of course, a part of Vilma and she was partly me; we were from the same river, flowing into each other. We met at an unknown junction where the events we would undergo were slightly more safe.

A woman was sitting beside me, slumped down in her seat; I sensed immediately she was heavy and repulsive. She had huge thighs, behind which she kept moving her torso back and forth on the seat, making it difficult for her to get comfortable and causing her to emit low grunts and groans, and during Vilma's walk to the telephone she was sucking her teeth.

I moved to the far edge of my seat to escape. The place and the atmosphere were important for the dream. A new man, tall and elegant, had arrived at Vilma's apartment, with a smile I could not yet interpret, could only feel. He exuded male confidence and easygoing passion, so confident he could afford to be amused.

I had the last seat in the aisle, my favorite because

there one was assured of at least half-privacy, but I began to feel the woman in the next seat starting up, but this time she was gathering herself to get up, reaching noisily first for her bag of chocolates with paper coverings, then her hat and last her heavy, awful body. She made it, after bumping heavily against my knees and feet, but leaving the seat beside me mercifully empty.

I saw all this through the window in the side of my left eye without once taking my glance from Vilma and the beautiful man. They had met once or twice before, but were just now beginning to discover one another, in the most perfect setting, sitting before an open fire and with drinks in their graceful hands.

In the dark movie house the man at the piano was playing "Something to Remember You By," playing it softly with just the right touch, and that was when through the same left-eye mirror I saw the stranger enter the aisle, my aisle, a tall man who came lightly over knees and feet and settled as quietly in the seat beside me as if it was his own personal chair in his very own sitting room. Vilma and her man were flirting now; ah, they liked one another, they were finding out they had both traveled to the same far city and they found amusing incidents and people they had in common.

My excitement was slightly vitiated by a reaction to the stranger in the next seat who exuded a remote but delicious odor of a lemony cologne combined with rich, fragrant tobacco. As he slipped out of his coat he had barely grazed my elbow, but he muttered softly in what sounded like a faintly foreign accent, "I beg your pardon." A tingling sensation started in my arm in the very spot he had touched and quickly spread to my thighs. I neither looked nor moved nor said a word in response. In the periphery of my vision, with my eyes riveted on Vilma as she and her visitor went on discovering each other, I felt the stranger move his long head ever so slightly to the right, just barely enough to glance in my direction. I felt glad he had seen my left profile which was better than my right.

Whatever he saw must have caught his attention, as

he did not turn back to the screen at once, but continued to watch me with what I could see was a slight opening of his mouth. I couldn't be absolutely certain of that, as I kept my eyes riveted on Vilma, but I could feel his pleased glance and was instantly alerted.

Truth to tell, I had had some slight contact with strangers who had sat beside me in movie theaters before, and had instantly rejected their attentions for various reasons, but this time the aroma, behavior, and general sense of the person beside me was curiously pleasing.

The first rule of the game in which I was now involved was never under any circumstances to glance in the direction of the stranger, or reveal by any move any interest or awareness of his presence, for fear of obtruding reality into the magnificent shadowy dream.

The average men and boys who contacted young girls like myself were bumblingly awkward and inept, and gave one no time by their pushing jumping ways, the awful quick kiss or feel, for a dream to even begin, much less develop. But here was a stranger who didn't approach, who was unknown but sending off secret signals and who was, perforce, kept at bay.

A dream had started now, and one could show one's receptivity by subtle innuendo. My face became instantly more appreciative of the movie. I smiled at the gay banter between Vilma and her tall friend and opened my big, expressive eyes, which, with their long lashes, showed up best when fully opened.

Somewhere along the line I thought I detected the faintest sound escaping from the shadow at my left, perhaps a faint "ah," and, when he turned back to Vilma, he moved about in his seat, and adjusted his overcoat over his lap. Now we were both watching the picture together, but a signal had been sent and received. The curtain had risen. The play had begun.

I imagined my behavior was so subtle and beyond reproach that myself and my secret desires were practically invisible. It must be Fate, in the form of some kind of ray that had quickened the wellsprings in the stranger and forced him to move in my direction, but only slightly. One more glance at the profile of the young girl beside him staring wide-eyed at the picture on the screen, the slightest thrust of the body sideways in my direction, and back we went to the dream. Only this time in the dark silence somewhere down there I could feel a long shoe barely touching the side of my pump as the side of a trousered leg delicately grazed my silk stocking.

Electric current shot through my body, flashing up my legs and thighs, vibrating up from the point on my leg the stranger had so delicately touched. Now it was happening fast. In a matter of minutes his overcoat had moved again, up and down, a delicate accident, of course, but it had fallen in precisely the right place, covering his hands and knees.

How was it my own hand had fallen to my side, to be claimed by delicate but large fingers that immediately began gently stroking, and, opening and covering my whole, small, bare hand and softly rubbing it in his large one?

His foot moved, his leg touched my instep, then, some delicate maneuver, and his leg moved my entire leg nearer to his, and his hand crept daringly up toward my knee, but touching it gently, rubbing, caressing, and then taking it away.

Before I realized what was happening, suddenly in one adroit move, the stranger's knee was locking with mine and he began pressing and rubbing harder and harder. Deeper and deeper went the pressure, just as Vilma was seized, but gently, by the man in the tuxedo. Good God, they, too, were locking, but in a kiss. We were all four locked now.

The piano player switched to "The Chariot Race," as Vilma tore away from her lover and stared before her, biting her lower lip in passion and shame, and the stranger next to me, leg locked to leg, rubbed as hard and fast as the horses in "The Chariot Race" were running, harder and harder, higher and higher, on and on and up, off the ground. I was getting wet, then limp. I kept my eyes riveted to the screen. I could, of course, see the stranger watching me, an extra thrill never to return his glance.

I was just sliding down into a world of soft rose petals. The music was rising higher. I could see the stranger's mouth opening, and barely audible groans began to escape his beautiful lips. The high peak of the thrill coming on burst over and under us both at once. Control was giving way. I went down further into the dark, sweet seat and was drowned.

Just then I felt a nudge on my shoulder. Some terrible person had moved into the seat behind me. I turned at the precise second as the stranger, he from the great world of lemon and tobacco scent and God knows what else, withdrew hand and leg in a tense but magnificent move, gracefully, if a bit precipitously. I turned and looked over my shoulder into the unwelcome face of my Cousin Elizabeth, who was offering me, of all things, a chewy caramel from a paper bag.

"Isn't it wonderful?" she whispered. "Here, you can have two, I got a whole bag."

I barely muttered, "Thanks," and, turning, I saw to my dismay that she and Uncle Clinton had moved into some seats almost directly behind my unknown love, fortunately somewhat to the left. I pulled myself together, as the saying is, and so did Lemonscent.

You can see how adroit I was at age thirteen, already a woman of the world, crafty and passionate and deceitful, but capable of deep fulfillment even on these quixotic terms. Old Lemonscent was crafty, too. The event of Elizabeth with the caramel caused him to withdraw into himself and look at Vilma Banky as if she were the only woman in the theater.

Some time later, by the time the movie let out, he rose and disappeared into the thin air to which I had already relegated him by the law of the secret ray I sent out. This was the perfect place for him, as far as I was concerned. I had not seen him, neither his face nor his body, a most important matter, this not seeing, but I had smelled him, his marvelous masculine odor, and felt his sure touch, and somehow I conjured up a picture of him that was all my own, a figure and a face, a pair of eyes, a nose and mouth, forehead and brows. Oh yes, there was someone behind that lemon and tobacco odor, someone brilliant and subtle, having the energy and the imagination to cause those remarkably cool, clever hands, those hard legs, to move as if by magic.

Unmistakable assets were his, to bring about the joy he had shared with me, for which vague fears were beginning to stir, and by the time I reached the street they were jumping around inside me like crazy frogs fighting for supremacy in the fiery pond inside.

The prayers I had been taught from infancy were now mechanical and depressing, like lifting the receiver on the telephone and finding no voice at the other end. "Almighty God" was the way the Victrola record began. No answer from Him, none whatsoever.

But another voice started inside, and another, more conclusive recording began. "I don't believe you are Almighty. I don't know who in hell you are or where you are. You sure don't show yourself, you like to keep hiding. A person doesn't even know if you exist, if you, for instance, even hear all that crazy praise that goes on, flattering you almost beyond endurance. I mean, if people kept kneeling down to me and giving me all that junky flattery, I'd be embarrassed, I really would. And maybe that's what you are, if you're up there at all, which I doubt, maybe you're embarrassed. Or you're laughing. If you exist, why all this awful stuff going on? People killing each other, that man down the street who actually kills other peoples' pets—why don't you do something to him? Why don't you stop all this awfulness? Why . . . ?"

Virginia Anne had diphtheria. We were quarantined. The doctor came in the mornings and went up to see her, accompanied by Mamma and Aunt Rose, who was there to receive directions as to what food to cook. I wasn't allowed to come into her room for fear of catching the dread disease. Mr. Roten, the butter and eggs man who came in from the country each week, was instructed to leave butter, eggs, milk and ham in the vestibule but not to ring the bell or enter the house.

I amused myself talking on the telephone, writing and rewriting my poems, doing English compositions and a play, and when tired, I went into the kitchen to help Rose. She was glad to have me beating up the eggs and stirring the soup as this allowed her the time and concentration required to burn the plants in the familiar big iron pot she kept on a discarded geranium holder in a corner of the kitchen.

The burning went on in every crisis and illness in the house, and there was one now. Knowing the fire from the plants sometimes went higher than was safe, she had surrounded the entire corner with asbestos and there she stood, muttering soft words to unseen beings and apparently receiving softer answers. At least I couldn't hear a word from them.

When she turned around at last to face the preparation of the food I asked her, "Is Ginny Anne going to be all right? That's what you're praying for, isn't it?"

"Ummhmm, that sure is what I'm working for. Why you always watching and question peoples for? Peoples your age shouldn't be always questioning other peoples."

"What should people my age do?"

"Peoples your age should be more 'ceptin' things. Fixing their hairs pretty and painting and studying their lessons."

"This is one of my lessons," I said. I had noticed the new phrase she said, that's what she was *working* for. Not praying over, not supplicating God to do, not peering up there into the empty distances, not calling a number that never answered. *Working for*. The plants didn't make sense to me, but the words sounded more sensible.

"Well, how's it going? Is she going to be all right?"

"Ummhmm—Look, you stop beating that batter, it don't need no more beating, just you stir and stir with the spoon now while I'm working, you hear?"

"All right, but tell me, first. How do you know she's going to be all right?"

"I knows 'cause it comes over me head to foot, Miss Question, that's how I knows."

"*What* comes over you?"

"This here knowledge comes over me, that's what comes over me. If you know something, you knows it."

"What do you do then? I mean, after you find out, what do you do?"

"Then you don't do nothing. You just goes on 'bout you business."

"Well, I guess you have faith or something?" I sighed; I always felt gloomy when I thought about that faith stuff I kept hearing about.

"*Faith?*" She looked at me with her big, bloodshot, cotton eyes and I knew at once she didn't even know what the word meant. Oh, how I loved her in that minute. Here was the most honest person in the whole house.

"Faith? That thing you said, what I got hasn't got nothing to do with nothing like that. Nothing at all to do with working my work."

How many people in my own family, Uncle Tom, for instance, and Uncle Clinton to name just two, were religious as all hell and kept showing off their faith, but they were both kind of crazy. Uncle Tom outright crazy as a loon, muttering and going on aloud and proud of it, so to speak. Uncle Clinton, secretive and nasty, with his long, pale face and his awful talking to himself, was a hiding-it crazy like a secret drunk. They both had faith and shouted it at you.

I stirred the batter with the spoon, as she had instructed, and kept at her. I was very much impressed with what she had said. Maybe, just possibly, it wasn't the ancient African voodoo of which my parents were contemptuous. Maybe it was something else, something neither I nor they understood. They, with their empty religion that couldn't bear up under any strain or questioning whatever, might just be wrong.

"Then what is it, if it isn't faith?"

"What are you talking about now, Mercy Bassford? What is *what?*"

"What is it you know?"

"What?"

"Well, I mean, how do you *get* this knowledge?"

"I hears it and I sees it and I smells it. That's how I gets it. Like I tole you I feels it all over me."

"Well, then if you know so much, the doctor said Virginia Anne was worse this morning."

"I don't go round listening too much to no doctors. I does what they says, to give medicines and cooking things, but I don't listen to them more'n that. People is worse today gets better tomorrow."

"What about praying?"

"Who to?"

"Jesus," I said.

"Him? He went to lunch whenever Rose Jackson came calling. I usedta pray to Jesus Christ. I did a whole lotta praying, but he didn't do much answering. Now, I got a whole lot better'n Jesus."

"Is that what you've got against Jesus?"

"I got plenty against Jesus."

"What? Tell me."

"Well, first he's white. Second, he's dead."

"So what've you got that's better than Jesus? I'd really like to know."

"That's my business, Miss Curiosity. Now go on stir up that batter some more, it's got lumps all over it."

It wouldn't have happened if I hadn't seen Miss Gaither at just that particular minute as I left school. I looked at her. I had to find her eyes behind the fallen lids, thin lines of washed-out eyeballs, before I could speak. I had to speak to someone, but in a few seconds of searching I began to think there was just no one in there behind those eyes. I began searching again in there, this time for some *thing*. I found it, the tiny spark of fading life, and spoke fast.

"Can I help you down the steps?" Her head moved slightly. It said "No."

Then after a wait, "It's just the cold." I offered her my arm but I could see she didn't want to take it. She wanted to stand by herself, to leave under her own steam. It was not cold, it was rather a mild, soft day. As I looked once again at her face I had the sense I had seen something in those old eyes. I had seen life hovering in the wings, all right, but I had also seen it leave and come back.

I guess it wouldn't have happened if I hadn't told a "story." I still don't consider it a lie. Edie, that's Edythe Burton, had been home sick with a cold. She was always getting colds and staying out four or five days and looking at me to cover for her, damn her hide. I was way up there in English Lit. I could write and speak and do anything with words, including remember them. A double-plus in English Lit, and A double-plus in French and Art and History.

Anyway, old Edie phoned me and asked me in her desperate voice, "What happened at school, Merce?" She wanted me to go over the assignments, and I did. I went out of my way to give a rundown the way you do when people want so desperately to fill up on news. All about the gorgeous Dr. Mannheim who told us about theory of music at Wednesday morning assembly. I was in third year high, going on fifteen. I described his eyes, "Oh, very large and bright. Young and knowing." Edie said, "Aw, come on Mercy, all eyes are alike."

Patiently I explained, "Not his, not Dr. David Mannheim's. His eyes are dark brown and they come out to you and take you in." Oh, how wonderful, to be taken in, included, *surrounded,* even by somebody's eyes, only of course I didn't tell her that. Nor did I tell her I had waited to speak to Dr. Mannheim.

He was hurrying off surrounded by his cohorts, two young men and an older woman, but I caught him just as he was coming down the steps from the assembly hall. "Doctor Mannheim," I called. He turned and said, "Yes, Miss." The two young men tried to keep him going, but he had already stopped.

I heard him say sotto voce, "Wait, boys, what have we here?" The boys and the woman waited impatiently, while we stood there a full five minutes discussing his lecture. Dr. Mannheim explained, among other things, how people were not really born with an innate sense of music.

His big eyes poured all over and into me. I went away feeling damp and full, the way a young girl does at age fourteen, when eyes coming out and getting your eyes are enough and the world is closed off.

Edie said, "Ugh," as if she might be going to vomit. Girls who live in houses with circular drives, and whose fathers are doctors, very often react like this to the suggestion of anything sexual, and eyes are sexual as all hell, especially eyes that come out like old Dr. Mannheim's.

I neglected to mention he was about a hundred and had warts, but I didn't really see much of that at the time. I sort of fixed him up in my mind as handsome and knowing and stopped there. I changed his long-winded stuff about music into something more pleasing.

"Did you know music has great social significance?" I asked Edie. She kept saying "No," and "Go on." "Did you know how music can change people?" She wanted to know more about Dr. Mannheim, but I closed up like a clam. I switched to the gym class and the basketball scores. I told her how she'd get another chance playing side center and I practically repeated the entire French lesson. I said "Mam'sell" Elfreth inquired about her health.

Well, she took it all in. Now you've got to remember Edythe's one of those girls who, when she talks to you, why she's drinking all your water, so you get dried out. She kept saying "Really," and "Go on, Mercy," and "Please don't stop." As if she's milking a cow. She just never gets enough. Well, anyway, then we reached the point where I just couldn't think of any more to tell her.

I'd done my good deed and now I wanted to run. The telephone was in the dining room. I was sitting on a chair the perfect size for an elf. Besides, the dining room is right off the kitchen, where the smells of Rose's bread baking in the late afternoon can drive you wild, but Edie would not let me go. "Tell me more, Merce, didn't anything happen, anything particular?"

That was when I remembered about Miss Gaither. I could see her leaning against the red brick wall of the building with her eyes closed and her cheeks like gray old apples and her small open mouth and the feeling I had that she had gone off somewhere and was trying to call herself back. Meantime I kept smelling the fresh bread baking and I kept hearing Edythe saying, "Something must have happened, I just know it did. You are holding out on me." That's when I told her kind of soft and casual the way I did sometimes when pressed hard, "Miss Gaither died."

"No-o-o!" I had her, I knew that she was taking time out for that one. Now she'd let me go. Then suddenly she screamed, "But she's got my floral painting!"

What a fine, compassionate, unselfish girl Edie is! Not a word about poor Miss Gaither, just her horrible floral painting. She hoped that would bring up her grade. "You think she marked us before this happened?"

"Oh, sure. She'd never die without giving you a mark, no matter how low."

"Well, uh, what do you think she did with the paintings?"

"I think she took yours straight to the grave." Edie must have recovered; I could tell that from the nature of her questions.

"Well, go on, Merce, for heaven's sake. You've just begun. What did she die of?"

"Of a heart attack," I said quickly.

"In *class?*"

"Ummhmm. Of course in class. Right in front of my eyes."

"Oh, Lord! I wish I'd been there." Then Edie started wailing, "Oh, that's terrible, I wonder who'll be next."

"Next to go? Maybe you."

"No, stupid, next teacher. I hope she's old and easy. Go on now, Mercy, tell me the rest, tell me everything."

"Well, Miss Gaither went very red and then she turned very white, and then she wheeled around almost

94

like she was going to dance, and then she just keeled over on the floor."

"Oh Lordie, I wish I'd seen it."

I knew I had her now, she was getting kind of respectful, so I went on. "She hit Mary Levine's desk as she went down and scared Mary's pants off!" I know it wasn't nice but by this time I was kind of interested in this matter. This description of a death scene was pretty good.

"Oh, my God, what did Mary do?"

"She upped and ran out of the room. The funeral is tomorrow."

I could hear somebody talking in the background. I thought I heard Edie repeating what I'd said about Miss Gaither's being dead and the funeral being scheduled for the next day, but I didn't think much about it. To tell the truth, I haven't thought much about it since. Oh, I know it wasn't exactly right to say Miss Gaither was dead when she wasn't, but I didn't really mean it. And, she was ninety-two. I mean, it's not like saying a teacher like Miss Kellogg was dead—she's thirty-six—not by fifty-six years it isn't.

But Miss Gaither was a very old lady and she was swaying. She had these long, thin, hanging breasts, like dish towels let out to dry, and you could see them outlined under her sweater, and it's sad to see something like that under people's sweaters, it really is. And she wore these long skirts and men's shoes because her feet hurt, I guess, and when she moved near you she smelled like a whale.

But she was still there. I mean she was not dead at all, that was obvious, and what's more she could still teach drawing and painting, even though the chalk fell out of her fingers and we all had to keep picking it up.

I guess it was that people didn't retire so early. I guess it also meant Miss Gaither was almost dead, but of course that's different from being entirely dead, it's really quite different.

Anyway, Edythe took it big, and it made her day.

"Oh, thank you, Merce, I'll do something for you

95

sometime." She kept saying what a fine, true friend I was, stuff like that. By the time I hung up I'd begun to think I was a fine, true friend.

I guess a person never knows the effects of his acts. I didn't know I was going to tell Edie Miss Gaither was dead until I heard myself saying it. And then as I went on about the heart attack and her going red and white and falling over and all, as I listened to myself in amazement, someone else had entered my body and was talking on, and I had to go on and I did, till the end, the very end.

I didn't think Edie would blurt it out to her mother, and her mother would start calling up around the neighborhood, that the Burtons would run out and order a wreath. I know this because Johnsy Dowse delivers for Stearn's Flower Shop and he told me about it. I guess this was on account of Edie's being bum at art. Edythe was small with big lips and flat feet. She was always bringing presents and flattering people, especially teachers, and Dr. Burton, her daddy, was a well-known general practitioner, and the family had a big shingled house with all the grounds and the tennis courts and all, over an acre right in town.

But Edie couldn't draw a straight line with a ruler. I guess that's why she and her family were so interested in Miss Gaither's going to her reward. Anyhow Johnsy had already delivered those darned flowers to Miss Gaither at her home the next day!

He said they were addressed to Miss Gaither's nephew, but Miss Gaither came to the door herself, big as life. I guess she must have been kind of surprised but she signed for them. Maybe she figured they were just a sudden flood of presents or something.

"Course, there were other flowers," Johnsy Dowse informed me.

"What other flowers?"

"Oh, wreaths and stuff, from other people."

"Not for Miss Gaither?"

"Sure, for Miss Gaither. She looked awful funny, like I said, when she first seen them. After that, when more came, it looked like she got mad and she sent her nephew down and the two of them went on something awful."

"Well, what did they say, the cards I mean?"

"I don't know, just sympathy about somebody popping off. Only, like I say, it got her pretty mad."

I was scared now and didn't want to hear any more.

I had this conversation with Johnsy on Friday. All weekend I tried not to think about what I'd done and sometimes I succeeded. But at two-thirty the following Monday when I went to drawing class in Miss Gaither's room, I ran into a group of fourteen juniors standing clustered outside of room 203. A few of the girls had apparently gone in, but Edythe must have stopped the others with the terrible news. The girls standing around outside talked excitedly in lowered voices. Edythe was the center of the gathering.

"Hello, Mercy," Edie said, patting my hand in such a comfortable way I thought nothing much could be wrong.

Then came, "Mercy told me first." Then Mary Levine came forward to comfort me. "Poor Mercy, it must have been awful for you." I saw I was kind of a heroine for finding out first. I worried a bit about that, but not much. I did not have time to worry much.

It was raining cats and dogs outside, and it was dark in the school corridor. Suddenly a loud clap of thunder came through. Everybody jumped. You know how those school halls are, long and kind of depressing with big windows at both ends, that's all the light you get except for occasional doors opening out of classrooms. Just then someone closed Miss Gaither's door gently from inside and after that it was quite dark in this part of the corridor.

It would happen that at this very time a great flash of lightning lit up the entire hall, and we all saw two figures coming out of Dr. Gardiner's office. One of the girls let out a scream. There was a scuffle as she fell down to the floor, and two other girls tried to pick her up. The lightning flashed again and this time, as the two figures began moving slowly down the corridor in our direction, we all saw one figure was that of an elderly lady who bore a hell of a resemblance to Miss Gaither. The other looked exactly like the principal, Dr. Gardiner, who was escorting her to her room.

They moved very slowly, I was happy to see, and just as they were fading into the completely dark part of the hall, there was a louder clap of thunder, and then a great nasty flash of lightning and you could see them illuminated real bright. It was eerie as anything, and this time everybody saw them. You should have seen the girls' expressions, standing with their mouths open like a pack of baby birds. Who was this spook, this ghost, if Miss Gaither was dead? There was a terrible silence and then some peculiar exclamations. "Ohs" followed by "Wha-a-t's tha-at?" Some of the girls stood their ground, but others took to their heels and went tearing down the hall.

Those Newly girls, twins, always did things together. They were the first to run. Then came Sarah Linton and, seeing them tearing down the stairway toward the basement, I followed close behind. I was in a suggestive mood. Reaching the end of the corridor, I stood at the top of the stairs for one brief second watching Dr. Gardiner and Miss Gaither and the group of girls all standing still and staring at them in horror. No matter what I had done, I wasn't going to miss the third act.

Some kind of conference was going on just outside Miss Gaither's room, with Dr. Gardiner nodding his head toward the girls. He seemed to be making some kind of speech, his voice carried, but the only word I could make out was "mistake," and from that I knew what he was talking about. Then Dr. Gardiner escorted Miss Gaither to the door of her room. She looked very grim as she walked in. The girls traipsed in behind them one by one.

I got back to my homeroom at quarter to three, after drinking quarts of coffee in the cafeteria. As I entered I noted the usual smell of chalk and girls' skins, face powder and sweat and that other unknown smell coming from armpits and behinds. Merle and Hallie Olender walked in behind me. I noticed they went straight to their desks without looking at me. Some of the other kids looked up but not one of them smiled the way they usually did. There was a quiet spell going on, all right. Everybody was waiting for the bell to ring, but nobody was talking.

I walked to my seat and that was when I saw the note from the principal's office on my desk. I opened it and as I read it I could feel eyes watching me. It was from Dr. Gardiner's secretary asking me to come to his office immediately after school and I knew then I was in for it. They had all seen the note, the bastards, and they knew what was in it, too, and that's why they were looking the other way. I walked unconcernedly into the coatroom to pick up my sweater when I found Helen MacDonald waiting for me. I had promised to lend her my Golden Treasury for the weekend, and she was waiting to claim it. "Mother says I can buy it from you, Mercy," she announced happily.

"It's not for sale. Why should you want to buy it, anyway?"

"Well, in case you are, umm, *expelled,* you wouldn't want to keep all those books, that set of Dickens you have and all those other books, would you?" Good Lord, it was all over the school in two hours.

"Next thing you'll be asking to buy my clothes," I said haughtily. They're mean devils, girls are. The rest of them came out and grabbed their things without looking at me. I was just thinking, what am I, a leper or something, when I saw Thelma looking in my direction and winking. She was waiting beside the door. "They all saw the note, the scums, that's why they stared," she whispered. Even Miss Talbacher looked up from her old feet, where she'd taken off her shoes under the desk, nodding, more briefly than usual, a nod of dismissal.

I'm mentioning all this to show you how mean people act when something bad happens to a person. I mean, when I see somebody in trouble, I don't care what they've done, I feel like helping them.

Suddenly, groups of kids were talking to each other without noticing me, including that glassy-eyed snob Edythe Burton. I could tell she was off me for life.

I was combing my hair to go downstairs to face the principal, when Thelma came up beside me and whispered, "Don't worry, Merce, he can't expel you." I hadn't thought of that, even when that horrible Helen MacDonald asked to buy my books, but now I did.

"Why can't he?"

"Because your grades are too high. And you've been in the magazine so often. And you wrote that piece in the paper."

Nevertheless, as I went downstairs I was beginning to feel really scared for the first time. I began to realize just what I'd done in saying Miss Gaither was dead.

It came over me more and more fully as I walked toward the principal's office with Thelma beside me. She even said she would wait, but I told her no, she'd better go. To tell you the truth, I was at least fixed up, my hair was combed properly and I had on these expensive pure silk hose I got for Christmas for $1.95, whereas Thelma was wearing soiled white socks.

Teachers are pretty ornery about kids' clothes and I guess principals are no exception, being just teachers once removed. I know they are supposed to be high-class and compassionate and all like that, but most of them prefer rich kids, "normal," truth-telling kids to "abnormal," making-things-up types of kids like me. With all of this in mind I went on into the principal's outer office.

I waited a long time for Dr. Gardiner. I remember sitting on the bench in the outer office beside a little fat man with glasses, probably the parent of some freshman who was flunking out for truancy. A lot of them played hooky and couldn't pass the exams. He would stare at my legs, then he'd look at my face and smile. I looked at him once, and by accident our eyes met. I noticed him moving his little ass around in the seat, trying to get nearer to me. Kids kept coming in and out to get their things from the Lost and Found and to sign registers.

I began to feel depressed, especially with this sweaty man sitting there all horny about my legs. I thought of getting up and moving away, but both the benches were taken. I could go stand near the door, of course, but I decided not to, for fear of missing my call. That would be pretty insulting to Mr. Sweaty if I did that. He looked so poor. His shoes were run down at the heels, and his black pants looked shiny and thin.

I was thinking, it must be sad to be horny *and* poor.

I listened to the singing coming from the music room where Miss Bonner was leading a hundred girls in choral practice. Bonner has a great big voice, actually she's something of a giantess. She was six foot four in her flat shoes and, with her small head, fair hair cut short, large lips, and long, stretched-out arms, she looks like a beautiful insect. I knew this song she was singing by heart and it always pleased me because of its exuberance.

"Love divine, all loves excelling, Pure unbounded love thou art. Something, something, humble dwelling, Enter every trembling heart."

My thoughts were rudely interrupted by the "parent" at my right.

" 'Sa pretty song, huh, girlie?" was the fascinating opening. I nodded politely. " 'Sallabout love, huh, girlie?"

I nodded and sat still. Thus encouraged, he went on. "I could drive you home in my car. It's nogooda walk if you can ride, huh?" He roared laughing. I was just deciding, maybe I would get up. Hearing his behind scraping against the leather seat made my blood run cold.

Just then the door to Dr. Gardiner's office opened, a young girl I'd never seen before came out followed by an older woman, her mother no doubt, and after them came Miss Heflin, Dr. Gardiner's secretary. She came straight to the wooden rail and said softly, "Miss Bassford, Dr. Gardiner will see you now."

I got up and walked toward my doom. Miss Heflin has loose hair around her large round face and big, bulging eyes, and with her head shaking slightly the way it does, she looks something like a Pekinese. Her face is one of those faces that's more like a disguise, almost like a regular Halloween mask. I mean, it's almost as if there's another face back there behind the first one, a face that says something because the one you see says nothing at all. Most faces are saying something. And here's what's funny: neither does her voice!

When she said, "Step right this way, Miss Bassford," it was the sound of something automatic, say, a foot walking across boards, something like that. If she had a shoe in her mouth and it moved up and down at that particular moment, that's more what it would have sounded like.

Once quite by accident I saw her in the teacher's room downstairs and she was eating a chocolate éclair. It was the first time in my two long years at Wesleyan I ever saw any expression on her face, and she looked eager and her face was saying, *"Yes! Oh, yes!"*

Well, I came on in and sat down beside Dr. Gardiner's desk. Dr. Gardiner was not there, so I waited. I was sitting there feeling kind of depressed and scared. I thought about the sweating parent out there. I heard again his profound crack, "It's nogooda walk if you can ride, huh?"

I was wondering which was worse, which was more repulsive, as a group in their dealings with the young girls, boys who try to kiss you with the sides of their damp chins, or middle-aged men with their smirky, depressing questions? And I was thinking, how different it all was from what you read and dream about love and what you see in the movies. And I was wondering, didn't *they* ever read or think about what they were doing, for heaven's sake? And I was just thinking, *maybe they don't,* maybe they just did all of this without thinking or feeling, when in came Dr. Gardiner.

He was sort of nodding and sort of smiling, a tentative kind of smile in my direction. I must tell you right away Dr. Gardiner is tall and quite handsome, entirely different from the squat, bald-headed principal who preceded him. I knew immediately he wasn't entirely happy with what he had in his mind, but still that half-grin was there and it was comforting.

Dr. Gardiner is about six foot two or three, with a long, pink, oval-shaped face, nice, keen blue eyes with black brows and eyelashes, very long white teeth, and interesting, shiny, black and white hair. Even the lines in his face are sort of right: they're mostly dimples that have lengthened with time and continuous smiling. He looks more like a middle-aged tennis player than an academician. He had his hand out as he came in and he shook hands with me, almost as if he was going to congratulate me for some accomplishment.

"Well, you're Miss Bassford, aren't you? Mercy Bassford, I believe?" I said, "Yes, Dr. Gardiner." My hand was damp and cold. It felt small and silly in his big warm one, and I stood up so fast it made me feel foolish.

"Sit down now, please, and be comfortable, Mercy, so we can have our visit."

Our visit, *our visit*. I love the word visit. The way he was smiling I figured he might have mixed me up with somebody else, some student who really had done something brilliant to add credit to Wesleyan. He certainly wasn't acting as if he were going to deal with the Gaither matter, not right away, anyway. Maybe he didn't even know yet I was the culprit. But he knew my name, all right, and called it, *Mercy Bassford*.

I remembered Thelma mentioning that Dr. Gardiner and Miss Gaither called Edythe Burton up to Miss Gaither's desk to talk it all over with her. The question was, did Edythe tell it the way it was? Did she say right away that Mercy Bassford was the one who said Miss Gaither was dead? But this was one of those questions that come with the answers ready-made. I mean, it hardly needs to be asked.

"Miss Heflin." Dr. Gardiner called out across the room, "Would you bring me those Bassford papers?" Then he was leaning back in his chair and cupping his hands together, so the fingertips all met in a circle. He wasn't looking at me any more, which wasn't good. When principals make cups of their hands and call their secretaries to get certain papers, it is not good. Besides he was quiet, which is the way adults get when they're going to give it to you.

I just wished he'd get it over with. Miss Heflin appeared with a blue folder of papers and said, "Here it is, Dr. Gardiner," in that expressionless voice, and he said, "Thank you, Miss Heflin." Now he was leaning back in his chair and he began riffling through the papers. Things were bad.

He's reading about me, I thought as I watched him peruse the papers in the file. He was making a hmm . . . hmm sound as he studied the typewritten sheets. While waiting for the axe to fall, I studied him more closely. His face was clean-shaven, no bristles showing anywhere, and he had a nice mouth. His lips were too thin, though, something like the ones kids draw when they make a man with crayons. Next thing, he put down the folder. He took off his glasses and cupped his hands again.

"This is a pretty fine record, Mercy," he said, "something to be proud of." I said, "Thank you, Dr. Gardiner," or something like that, and he continued, "These contributions to *The Wesleyana,* they're the best things in the entire magazine. Very good poems. And this short story, and the play you wrote! This is most surprising. I'm sure you can develop the theme into something that might be published elsewhere."

I listened with a kind of numbed joy. Instead of talking about expulsion, he spoke as if he were about to give me some kind of promotion. "There's a great potential here, Mercy," he said.

I knew the word *potential.* A whole lot of adults use it when they don't know what else to say; they tell you you have potential. But this time it was as if I'd never heard the word before. I heard a sweet girl suddenly speak in a soft, interesting voice full of expression and a kind of suppressed exuberance. "Why, thank you, Dr.

Gardiner." And then, of all things, the voice, by now not only exuberant but also faintly British, came out with, "I hadn't thought of it quite that way."

"Well, you ought to think about it from now on," Dr. Gardiner was saying. "There's talent here."

Potential, talent. They fell on my ears like virgin words, I swear to God. He had the school magazine in his hands, a crummy publication, the issue which he had was full of the most third-rate stuff by half-baked kids you ever saw, including that magnificent poem by yours truly. He was actually reading the damned thing, no fooling. I could see his eyes following the lines. He was reading *my poem,* and it was like he was holding me in his arms.

> How doth the bee
>   know which flower
> to enter?
> The firefly when to
>   flash his cone?
> Whereas I must wander
>   and wait at center.
> Why are you silent,
>   Mysterious One?

Can you imagine my writing down a word like *doth?* I gave birth to this beaut one summer's night watching the fireflies in the backyard. This was the first time I'd thought about it, after the thrill of seeing my name in print, that is. But now I was reading it in my mind with Dr. Gardiner. To have yourself read for the first time by someone who really knows is quite an experience. You meet people and you talk, and they talk, but nothing happens. But here, now, *something was happening.* My heart was being visited, and I felt it quicken.

"This is a fine poem, Mercy." Then he put it down. I felt my flesh draw back. "But I must talk to you now." He cleared his throat. "About the, well, the story you told about Miss Gaither." He waited a decent interval, then he drew himself forward, coming nearer to me. "I guess we've all told stories now and then. I did, myself, when I was young. Do it even now occasionally. If I don't watch myself."

He smiled, yes, he actually smiled at me. Suddenly, I heard that girl's voice again, coming from somewhere where the world was clear, open and free as the waters of a new stream. What was it saying? "It's true, I told a story and it was wrong."

"Very wrong. And most painful to Miss Gaither."

"I see that now, Dr. Gardiner. Poor Miss Gaither must have been hurt. I didn't mean to hurt her, sir. I really didn't."

"How did you come to tell the story, Mercy?"

I heard my voice again, describing the telephone call from Edythe Burton. Telling how she kept pressing me for news, anything at all. "Well, there wasn't more news, so I—guess I must have made something up. I planned to call back Edie that night to tell her I was only fooling, but I didn't get around to it. And then the weekend came up. And then by Monday it was too late."

"Much too late," Dr. Gardiner agreed.

"But, well, as you said, sir, everybody tells stories."

"Yes, they do, Mercy. Why don't we talk a bit about that?"

"Yessir. A lot of times people tell stories about themselves, to make themselves sound more interesting or more important than they really are. Older people do it, too, sir."

"I agree with you, Mercy. Some of the lies a person hears give you the creeps. Now, you tell me something about what you hear, and I'll tell you some of the things I hear. And we'll stack them up together and see how we come out."

Suddenly we were talking away like two people the same age, two friends, say, desperately reaching to know one another. First I'd open a door and show him a piece of myself, an observation, an anguish. Then he'd open a door into himself and show me a person, an incident, something or other that had either amused or troubled him, or both, something that showed up in glaring colors the inadequacies and little meannesses of people. I hardly know what all we said to one another. It went so fast. People, *people!* They said they were rich when they were poor and they said they were poor when they were rich, and lots of other things that weren't true at all. "And what's so awful is, nobody asks them to tell these lies, sir," the sweet, well-modulated voice was saying. "They just do it. At least in my case, Edythe kept begging me to tell her something, and it was like asking me to give her something, *anything*. And I did!"

I felt that he understood every word I was saying, the way he smiled. Now just about this time, listening to this dialogue, something funny began to happen. You see, the first impression I'd got of Dr. Gardiner from the past wasn't any too great. I remembered seeing him once in the park outside Wesleyan standing in the sunlight and I'd noticed he had a layer of flesh protruding from under his chin and a wart, rather a large wart, near his ear. I'd noticed some other things, too. In fact, I had the impression that he wore long drawers. The way his socks were so thick over his ankles, I was sure he had on woollies.

Well, now all of that had faded out, exactly as if an eraser had moved over him rubbing off signs of age, leaving him clean and handsome and young. His skin wasn't wrinkled or dry, it was sunburned. Russet was the word. His voice was masculine, yet melodious, of a rich timbre. And his eyes, I swear to God, his eyes were young, beautiful and melancholy. Yearning. And he was brilliant beyond compare.

I have to admit I'm apt to get these ideas about people, especially men, if they show the slightest interest in me. If they have any kind of good looks, I imagine them more handsome than movie actors, and, if they're not complete dolts and can converse at all, I'm likely to think they're presidential material. If they say something *to* you instead of making remarks *at* you, it's wonderful! I know it's just plain decent behavior, but it's so unusual it has some special magic.

Also, I'm likely to think these rare people are sad or lonesome, and they need me, just me, to fix all that. My

107

company, my charming company, they're not going to find it anyplace else in the whole wide world. Half the time the sons of bitches are not sad or lonesome at all. I know that, and, if they are, I'm not the only one who can solve their problems, but that's what I *think* anyway.

Things with Dr. Gardiner went from interesting to confusing to wonderful and back again in rapid succession. Something was happening, all right. His face seemed to move backwards and forwards. I forgot where I was. I hardly heard what he was saying. I felt something coming over me, all over me, if you know what I mean. It was like waking up naked on a warm summer's day and walking on soft grass toward the sun. Only it wasn't the sun; it was a pair of eyes drawing me into them, and the principal's eyes, at that. A stranger, Dr. Gardiner, Dr. *Hilary* Gardiner. It was kind of crazy, like going on a trip.

Meanwhile, he was talking on. "I should say it'd be a very bad thing to let a, well, prank, get in the way of this work you're going to do." He went on to say something about accuracy and honesty. "It wasn't *accurate* for you to say Miss Gaither was dead when she was still alive."

I said, "No, sir, of course not. Only, as I was leaving school that Friday afternoon I met her on the steps." I went on to tell him my experience with Miss Gaither, seeing the life-force going out of her eyes and coming back.

"So you built your story about those few seconds when the life-force seemed—absent?"

I said, "Yessir, I'm sorry to say that's just what I did."

Then suddenly, I was pierced through by those blue irises and the blue rings surrounding them, and that's all I could see. It hit me in a flash. *I love you, Dr. Gardiner.* I must have swayed closer to him. I know I was on the edge of the chair. I was so afraid I was going to say something or do something, I could hardly hear him. Then I heard something new. I heard his silence. I noticed him blink just as he turned his head away from me. He picked up the big pencil he had and began tapping it on his desk. He must have moved around in his chair. I heard it squeak once or twice. "Well, now, Mercy," he finally said—I could tell he was stalling for time—"We've talked this over now, haven't we?"

"Yessir, I guess we have," the voice not quite as British as before. We both fidgeted. It felt very hot in the office, and, for some reason, I began to feel embarrassed. I don't know how it happened, but in the next minute or two we both began laughing. It began first with a kind of giggle, then it went up, and there we were guffawing. I remember seeing Miss Heflin staring from over her typewriter. It must have been plenty loud, but neither of us could stop for a while. I think I stopped first. Next thing, he started talking again. "Yes, well, now, Mercy, you should perhaps write a note of apology to Miss Gaither."

I said, "Yessir, I certainly will." Only it busted me up again and I started to giggle again, too. I don't honestly know how I got out of there. I know I did, because I practically fell over Thelma. She was standing right outside the door waiting for me.

"Are you expelled?" she stage-whispered.

The corridor was empty. The word had the effect of waking me up. "No." I said. "No, not at all."

"You mean not even two weeks' absence?"

"No."

"Well, then what?"

As we walked toward the school exit I told her. "I have to write a note of apology to Miss Gaither."

"And that's all?"

"Ummhmm."

Thelma looked away as we walked on toward the park. "There's something funny going on," she said, as we crossed the street and entered the park. As we walked on, Thel was at first quiet, then she became curious and nosy, not satisfied with finding out I wasn't going to be expelled, and somehow suspicious, wanting to know more and more.

Now Thel's mental or psychic age is different from mine. I'm an older soul, as you might say, and stuck here on this earth with all these young, young souls, like Edie Burton and Thelma Hodges, who always want to know what you're hiding. There was my friend Thelma asking, "What happened, Mercy?"

"Oh, nothing much. We just talked, and Dr. Gardiner decided on the letter to Miss Gaither."

I wanted to be alone with Dr. Gardiner, truly alone, without his eyes, but with my own thoughts about him. I wanted to relive the entire interview and make it mine. I thought of all kinds of things connected with him I had never thought of before. For instance, his first name happens to be Hilary. Now I'd never even heard of anyone named Hilary before and I began thinking about that. Hilary, I thought, Dr. Hilary Gardiner.

I thought of him coming toward me, say to meet me and take me somewhere, and I heard myself saying in that faintly British voice, "Oh, hello, Hilary, my dear," and him saying, looking down from those big blues, "Mercy, my dear, how are you?" I had heard his wife wasn't too attractive, an extraordinarily large woman who wore small spectacles and walked fast in long strides, and they had one daughter of about eighteen, also large and plain but smart. She was away at Barnard College in New York, home only on weekends. Hilary must be lonesome, I decided.

He sometimes had groups of girls to his house. He liked fun, he liked to laugh. I wished fervently I was in his Shakespeare class so I could see him and study him at first hand. Now, at least, I had a pretty clear picture of him physically. The eyes and the smile, the way he was cracking up there on his office chair, the way the two of us kept bursting out laughing. And that hair, that fuzz on his hands going up under his cuffs, reddish hair with freckles interspersed, the whole business began to look pretty nice. I was now absolutely sure he was attracted to me. I could hear it. Everybody knows that sound, the sound of the click. I heard it there back in the office, sure as shooting, and now I wanted to hear it again.

110

"You haven't told me what happened," Thelma was saying.

I said, "What?" and she repeated it, and this time I heard. What did happen? I wondered, besides the click.

"Really, nothing much," I began. "He said I had potential."

Thel muttered, "Sure, sure," so I asked her, "What makes you think anything happened?"

"Aw, come on, Merce," Thelma looked disgusted. "When I see that look on your face it's just like a flag going up. It's a signal something's happened, more than the principal saying you had potential. That's like saying it's a nice day. Now what was it? What did you do?"

I had just begun to research Hilary Gardiner, his life and works and I didn't like being interrupted but I decided I might as well tell Thelma. I wanted to try it out on someone and, besides, maybe that way I'd find something out.

"Well, we got to talking and we burst out laughing."

"You wha-at?"

"We cracked up. Got the giggles."

"You and Dr. Gardiner got the giggles over the matter of Miss Gaither's *premature* death?"

"Ummhmm." We were just passing the men's toilet in the park. It was dark there, even on a sunny day, and we'd been warned never to go near the place. To hear my parents talk you'd think nobody but child molesters and murderers ever urinated. But we didn't need the instructions; the smell of the disinfectant was enough to drive anybody away. This time it had the effect of waking me up from my dream. We turned quickly in a new direction away from the urinals, and I barked at Thelma, "Why not? Why shouldn't people laugh together when something is funny?"

"Because," said Thelma, "principals and juniors are not *people,* not at Wesleyan High, they're not! And if they are, there sure is something funny going on. And what's more, I bet I know what it is."

"Well, what is it, Miss Brains?"

She raised her eyebrows and smiled. "New crush,

huh?" Crush. The word rankled. "How about him?" she went on. "Did he return your interest?"

"Maybe."

"You needn't be so mysterious, Merce. Quite a few girls have crushes on Dr. Gardiner. He's pretty good-looking when he's fixed up and his long drawers aren't showing. I was at his house last Christmas when the Gardiners had that party so I know quite a lot about him."

Well, now Thelma had another use. I could extract information from her on the home life of the Gardiners. I, too, had been invited to their Christmas tea, but I had had a cold and couldn't go. But old Thelma had gone and now I craved to hear everything she knew about the Gardiners. The first thing was to put her off the track. "I wish I did have a crush on Dr. Gardiner," I sighed, just as we approached Tobin's Ice Cream Parlor and made for the last booth. "I wish I had a crush on somebody, instead of—"

"Instead of what?"

"Instead of just nothing," I sighed again, as we settled into the comforting leather benches where we could look out the windows and watch without being seen. It was a faintly British sigh. A waitress approached to take our order. We both ordered coffee and ice cream cake and the conversation picked up where it had left off.

"If you're just feeling nothing, what're you looking so soft around the eyes for, Merce?"

"Oh, I'm just kind of gloomy about the Gaither business, I guess."

"But you got off. Say, what'd it take you so long in there for?"

"Was it long?"

"I'll say. Nearly three-quarters of an hour. I went down to the cafeteria and then down to the gym and both times when I came back you were still in there."

"He didn't show up right away."

The food came and we fell to as if we hadn't eaten all day. Thel had two Melachrinos and gave me one.

112

Before we finished the coffee I had spied out Hilary Gardiner's home life from the facts she let drop. All about how *he* was dominated by *her*. "She calls *Bar*nard College *Ber*nard." How there wasn't enough to eat at the Christmas party. How stingy she was. "At first there were those plates of little sandwiches they always have, ham and cheese and chicken salad, stuff like that, but they went like wild."

"Wasn't there a maid even, bringing in the seconds?"

"I don't think so, seems to me the old girl did it all herself. There was tea, of course, and cocoa and cake, but it was all gobbled up real quick. For a long time, with all those kids milling around and talking to Dr. Gardiner and the few other guys there, well, there was just nothing but cake and water."

"You mean that's all? The second half of the party with nothing but *cake* and *water?*" Thel nodded.

"Well, that's funny."

"I think she's stingy. I don't think he's stingy. I know when she finally went upstairs, he went into the kitchen himself and made some more cocoa and brought in a whole new cake. I bet she was saving it, too. It went in five minutes."

"How did he seem, Thel?"

"What!"

"Happy? Did he seem like he was happy?"

"Uh-uh. Nice and talkative, keeps smiling and telling stories. He's kind of interesting."

"Was he dressed nice?"

"Not very." She thought about it, bless her. "He doesn't seem to care any more. It's like somebody's done something to him, I don't know. He looks real good when he'd dressed neat, but he just doesn't care any more."

Ah. Now I knew. Hilary, I thought. Hilary Gardiner, he just doesn't care any more. "Sometimes you can see his long drawers showing," Thelma went on, and I nodded. I hated to admit, even to myself, he wore longies that showed and weren't always white, either, but now that we both knew I wanted to forget it as soon as possible.

"I guess it's because of her with all that money."

"How much d'you think she's got?"

"Bucketsfull. Her daddy's got cotton plantations and horse farms all over the place. I guess that's what makes her so *bossy*."

"How do you know she's bossy?"

"Oh, the way she talks, kind of jumps on you when she says something. She's rich is what it is. She wears ground-gripper shoes and those bifocal glasses and she's dirty rich."

"You don't wear bifocals because you have money. They're actually worn to correct eyesight."

"Yeah. Well, anyway, they say she just lives for her daughter, that Millicent. I wonder why people call ugly girls these beautiful names."

"Yeah, it only makes them seem uglier. *Is* she so ugly?"

"She's got his eyes and they're real nice, but somehow she looks like her mother. Now take you and me, Merce. We're both pretty. But our parents call us plain names. Thelma Vaughn Hodges and Mercy Blaise Bassford. Plain as all hell. But they make us prettier."

"Yes, I guess. But what's he like? What's Hilary like to talk to at a party like that?"

"Well, he kept poking the fire. He loves fireplaces, Dr. Gardiner does. He loves to read out loud with the fire going. He told us about all the fireplaces he's ever had in all his life, and he showed us a book on old fireplaces going way back. He's nice, he really is."

"What else?"

"Oh, he asked us all what we wanted to do when we left school. The usual!" She stopped talking and stared at me. "That stuff is pretty boring, but after all, a man wears gray drawers, what can you expect?"

"He does not wear gray drawers. Only now and then. Because he doesn't care any more and maybe he's lonesome."

114

Thelma asked in a soft voice, "I mean, did it just happen today?"

"What?"

"Did you fall just now, I mean just then, over the Gaither death story? Come on, I won't tell, I swear I won't!"

"Yes."

"That's what I thought."

"How'd you know?"

"The way you fought over the gray drawers." She laughed out loud. "You should have seen your face! Well, how about him?"

"What about him?"

"I know he's not going to expel you. He's not even going to give you the usual two weeks away from school. Did he show any special liking for you?"

I tried to explain to Thelma, a naive girl who knew nothing about love. "Yes," I began.

"What did he do?"

"When a man's attracted to you, there's something you *feel.*"

"Oh, sure, of course. What else?"

I tried to tell. "You see, there's also something moving in the grass, moving softly but hastily, covering more and more grass all the time. And it's sort of like a sound of water hurrying, hurrying to break somewhere. Yes, that's it, only it's coming from inside, sort of as if a motor way down inside is turning faster and faster, spreading this warm water. And it was turning in him at just the same time it was turning in me. Spreading this warm water across the grass inside us . . ."

"Holy God!" said Thelma. Then, "How did you know this motor and this water thing was running *in him?*"

"Because it clicked. His and mine at just the same time."

"How do you *know?* He didn't stop and say, *'Pardon me,* Miss Bassford, but my motor just clicked and I'll just have to mop up the old water?' "

"No, of course not, we were both absolutely quiet and we were sort of going into each other."

115

"Jesus!"

"And after that, well, we sighed and then we began breathing again, normally. That was when we busted out laughing."

After the interview in Dr. Gardiner's office, time passed and very little happened. But something *was* happening. I kept thinking about him. Whatever I was doing, having my breakfast, writing in my diary, painting, working on my essay on Dickens, even explaining pentameter to Miss Kellogg's class, yes, even standing up there staring all those kids in the eye and talking out loud—I was thinking about him. Maybe he would just be walking down the hall as he often did and peep in the class and see me. Hilary, I would think, and the name would make that lovely sound in my mind.

I had few friends in school since the trouble with Miss Gaither. I was not punished at all; in fact I was sent right back to her drawing class exactly as if nothing had happened. Edythe Burton hardly spoke to me, naturally, but after a few days the rest of the kids began talking to me again, and of course I had Thelma and Marian Swoboda.

My parents disapproved of my spending time with Marian Swoboda, but you wouldn't. Now you've just got to know Marian, and once you do, well, she'll become a part of you, maybe like some secret place you have where you can dip your wounds and get them fixed. Say, like that deep black mud place we have in our backyard where it's always damp, where I'd dip my hand after a bee-sting. A girl like Marian does something for you. I'm not sure how it works, but it does. A girl like that, gee-whiz! And so in spite of my parents' disapproval, I saw Marian to my heart's content.

"You got a case on the old man, huh?" Marian said to me once when we were eating the rest of her left-over lunch in the park near Wesleyan. "Lots of girls like old men, Merce. Don't worry none, Hon, old men are good luck, I swear to God!"

By now I had written my note of apology to Miss

116

Gaither and left it on her desk. She must have opened it and read it, and maybe she had reported back to Dr. Gardiner. It wasn't a very good note. In fact, I considered it feeble. But what can you say to somebody you've accused of being dead? You can't say I'm sorry I pushed you into the grave prematurely. You've got to get around it, and I can tell you it wasn't easy.

It took me over an hour, and even then it turned out bum. Still, it was a composition and it was mine. I remembered Dr. Gardiner saying he would see it and talk it over with Miss Gaither, so now I had them both to contend with. Maybe he was right now holding my note in those nice long hands with the reddish fuzz and the freckles going up his arms.

It's crazy, but I found the idea of him holding my note exciting. I kept seeing him, tall, and a big wheel in the educational system, peering at me with those piercing blue eyes, at the piece of me that was not in the note. Maybe the note wasn't as bad as I thought. Hell, maybe it was pretty good, but whatever it was I felt warm thinking about his hands on it, and it's fun to feel warm and thrilled, anybody knows that.

"I betcha like a lotta men, don'tcha, Merce?" Marian asked, as she bit into her ham-on-rye. I didn't answer. "I like a lotta men, too. Somelikeaback and somedoanlikeaback. S'good like that, huh?"

Marian always went further than I could follow, but I could see where she was leading. I *am* a little bit interested in every man I see, come to think of it. That is, I was then and I have been straight through my life, in varying degrees or moods and with selectivity.

"You're supposed to wait till they're interested in you," I told Marian.

"Yeah, that goddamned thing, that there waiting—but nobody doan do nothing like that."

"What do they do?"

"You just jump on 'em is all, an' they love it."

I never completely understood what Marian was saying. She got to the point too fast, but I had a hunch the parts I didn't get might be pretty good. Sometimes

I wondered just what she did in those long afternoons she spent playing hooky. I imagined her going around jumping at men like a frog, but then Marian was in another, quite different world from mine. I was interested in how men looked and spoke and what their attitude toward me was, and if it was good, as Dr. Hilary Gardiner's was, I could go into one of these lovely, warm dream sessions I just mentioned but that would be only for someone very interesting, and quite frankly, I was also slightly interested in all other men. Even that little character sitting beside me on the bench while I waited for Dr. Gardiner, illiterate and poorly dressed and sort of repulsive, I felt sorry for him.

In a sense I could see how an ugly, plain, middle-aged man like that could want to know a young girl like me. I didn't return the compliment, but I could *understand* him, and maybe that's my trouble.

One night I went to Thelma's house to spend the evening. The Hodges lived in the big, red brick house down the street, with the iron grill fence and the pots of ivy and geraniums. Thel and I often studied together, dressed to go to parties together, and sometimes spent the night at each other's houses. Well, after supper we went upstairs to the Hodges' upstairs sitting room. We played checkers and Old Maid and Parcheesi, and then when we were tired we looked over her daddy's books. He happened to have a full, unexpurgated set of *The Arabian Nights* which we had been carefully instructed not to touch, so we headed straight for the set and picked out one at random. We put the book on her daddy's teakwood desk, turned on his green student lamp, pulled up two chairs side by side and began reading together.

At first it was kind of hard going. I mean all that "Praise be to Allah, the Beneficent King is the Creator of the Universe, Lord of the Three Pillars in its Stead." Well, it was beautiful and poetic, but it wasn't exactly what we expected to find, and then when we got to all these people, these knights and braves, with their

118

different names, and all the letters they all wrote before they took their journeys on horses with saddles of gems —encrusted gold—stuff like that going on, it was still slightly disappointing and boring.

We kept turning the pages, until we came to a remarkable man called Shakik-al-Balkhi, something like that, and immediately things became very interesting. In a way, I guess you could say, a whole new world opened up with a bang.

Now you see this Al-Balkhi, after performing those miracles the people in Arabia perform all the time, well, he finally won the fifth daughter of the King. She was the great looker, Kut-al-kubub. I think that was her name. Thel and I called her Kute in discussing her, pronounced *cute*. Anyway, after Kute and Al-Balkhi were washed and bathed and fed bouillis and galangle water, the way they always are in the Arabian Nights, well, then this *thing* happens.

"Listen to how it happens," I said to Thel, and I read it all over again out loud, "And he drew forth his sword and swived her far into the night. And he found her an uncleft pearl."

Something moved down in my stomach just below my navel and turned over like a snake uncurling. I heard Thel whisper, "Jesus!"

I said, "Yeah," very slowly. We read on, then turned back and read the same story all over again.

That night when I went home I could feel the tall, marvelous man on the white horse, with the great sword, this Al-Balkhi, and there he was drawing forth his sword like anything, only this time it was I who was present, not Kute. I was the uncleft pearl.

Swive! It was a wonderful foreign word. Maybe he held his sword a certain way and kissed her at the same time. Being unsure of the word swive—it wasn't in the dictionary—I would arrive at the word and go off into vague but thrilling pictures and feelings as I lay in bed. Up to this point I didn't know just *what* it was men did to women after they were married or before, or *how* they did it. I thought some men had a thing, like I told you, the killer, and some men didn't have a thing, or they had a very tame and docile thing that couldn't get loose and kill. Now all that confusion was over. Al-Balkhi had arrived on his white horse beside my bed with his sword and and he was going to swive.

He did, too, I know, because I was tired the next day.

All those nights toward spring I would go to bed and think vaguely but beautifully of Al-Balkhi. I would see him coming into my bedroom on his white horse with his sword in its sheath, which he was going to draw forth and swive me "far into the night."

I would see Al-Balkhi dismount, stand beside my bed, pull the long, gleaming sword slowly from its sheath, take his stance leaning over the bed and kiss me passionately. I was swived and swived and I would melt with delight.

Al-Balkhi wore a long, flowing garment; black locks drooped from under his turban and he had long, fierce, black mustaches, flashing, beautiful black eyes and large white teeth. We would kiss long and passionately, he standing there with his great, raised, flashing sword, me lying there receiving and melting till all hours, delighted but kind of scared and, at times, exhausted.

Once, in the shadows, I thought I saw another face coming over the Arabian's, and next thing I knew, when I looked again, I recognized another set of features. Hello, a new mouth and *blue eyes*. It was Hilary holding the sword this time, my own Hilary Gardiner! And after that it was Hilary riding the white horse, Hilary leaning over the bed delivering the *swive!*

The essay I was writing for Miss Kellogg's English Lit II was moving at a snail's pace, and, often as not, I just couldn't remember my sides for the role of Julia in *The Seagull* which we were doing for the Easter vacation. I knew this ineptitude was because of Dr. Gardiner, Al-Balkhi, and our nightly meetings, but I knew of no way of stopping the revelries, nor wanted to, to put it mildly. Anybody would find it difficult to contrast the technique of Robert Louis Stevenson with that of Theodore Dreiser when people on horses came into their bedrooms at night.

No wonder I nearly jumped out of my skin when I ran smack into Dr. Gardiner of a Wednesday afternoon. I was just bolting out of the reading room at the far end of the corridor when I saw him standing near the window. I felt a sharp prick of interest in the figure standing there. He wasn't looking at me, he was looking down the hall, but I felt, somehow, he was waiting for me. He had a book in his hand. A ring he was wearing caught glints from the light coming through the window.

I noticed his long legs and his hands and his long, narrow feet. I was, in fact, sort of measuring him quickly, while he wasn't looking, taking a mental photograph, so next time I came abreast of him at night I'd have a few more details. By now he had turned, and all was forgotten in those piercing blue eyes, as he said, "Why, hello, Mercy."

"Good afternoon, Dr. Gardiner. How are you?"

"Why, just fine, Mercy, thank you." He took a step or two toward me. I could hear his breath coming and going. "I wanted to speak to you about the letter you sent to Miss Gaither. Suppose we come into my office, shall we, and have a visit?"

He touched my elbow gently to direct me down the corridor toward the door marked "Principal's Office," opening it for me to pass through. As I walked in, with him following close behind, I could still feel the spot on my elbow his hand had touched.

The office was empty. He pulled the chair beside his desk forward, said, "Sit down, won't you, Mercy," and settled in his own big chair, tilting back slightly. "Now about the note," he began. He spoke exactly as if nothing was happening between us, as if he was merely a principal of a high school talking to a student about some misdemeanor.

What's coming now? I wondered, is he really going to give me two weeks enforced absence after all? Al-Balkhi had fled into the shadows, and here I was up

121

with my fate. He moved about in his chair, then he began speaking, as if he had been thinking it all over carefully and was ready at last.

"It was a fine letter, an honest letter. I must congratulate you, Mercy."

"Ah—thank you, Dr. Gardiner. That's very kind of you, sir."

I hardly knew what I was saying, I was so relieved. And, once again, there it was, the close feeling; as if we were the only two people alive in the whole world, left there talking into the fading light of the late afternoon. Everybody else dead, gone, washed up. Just us two left. I began wondering what would be coming next.

I often think, when something wonderful is happening, what's coming next. It's like a river flowing through you all the time, but you can feel it only *sometimes,* and still other times you can almost *see* it bringing things from wherever it starts. Sometimes, stuff that's pretty rotten. It's kind of eerie watching one damned minute flowing into the next, and catching it as it comes, but you've got to do it.

"You know, Mercy, I've read your things in the school magazine. You might say I'm a fan of yours."

"Thank you, sir." I felt glad Mamma had taught me not to say "Aw" when receiving a compliment.

"But, frankly, I liked the letter to Miss Gaither because it told everything."

"Did it? I didn't think . . ." I stopped, seeing he was ready.

"That's what was so good. You didn't think. You just told everything, the way it must have happened. And I think Miss Gaither believed it, too, I know *I* did."

I hardly remembered what I'd said in the old letter by now, and I certainly didn't know how Miss Gaither felt about it. I just assumed she'd read it, but she hadn't said a word to me. Now I knew. She had shown it to him, maybe left it with him. Had he come and asked for it? And, if he had, well, it was like asking to see some more of me, wasn't it?

He must have read my mind, the way he filled me in. "I asked Miss Gaither if she'd heard from you, and she said she'd received this note of apology, and then I asked her if she'd mind my having a look. I've kept it in my desk ever since."

He had it in his desk. He was keeping it, this little piece of me. The minutes were flowing now, bringing me nice presents. Most of the time nothing much comes down the river but guck. Maybe that's why when something good comes, you're over-ready.

Something was trying to happen between us. I remember saying, "I hope Miss Gaither wasn't displeased," something like that. I guess I must have smiled as I said it, anyway, he smiled back and then—Jesus—we both began to laugh, just as we had before.

We sat there chuckling and trying not to; he was starting to guffaw, but he did manage to say, "Well, I don't know as she was exactly *pleased*." But he burst out laughing on the last word. He pulled himself together and said, "But I was pleased, let's put it that way."

He looked at me, and I looked straight back at him, and it took about a minute, and then things sort of slowed down, or maybe they went in another direction. Anyway, from then on Dr. Gardiner began trying to carry on a conversation with me, and I was ready to help him along, indeed I was.

He talked about the President and asked me what I thought about his statement in the papers yesterday. I was glad I remembered Daddy reading the headline, and what college I was planning for and which subject I was going to major in, and everything I said seemed to meet with his approval.

There for a while, during the minute we had been quiet, staring and sort of encountering each other, I had seen Al-Balkhi coming out of the shadows, drawing closer, at one point covering Dr. Gardiner with his flowing robe. But then, as Hilary began speaking in the more normal principal-to-student manner, he stopped being even half Al-Balkhi; the sword was completely

123

withdrawn. Then he'd go quiet and look at me again, hard, and bang!, the metamorphosis would begin again, from Hilary to Al-Balkhi and back again, sometimes in rather rapid succession.

At one point it was Hilary's eyes, blue and piercing, and Hilary's face, but Al-Balkhi's white robe and the barest outline of his sword.

Hilary began patting my hand with his hand and it felt large and hot at first and slightly damp. He patted and patted as he went on probing into my future plans, but as time went by I knew it was more patting than probing that was on his mind because he would stop probing now and then and just pat. He had to remind himself to probe when he got going good with the patting.

He was not exactly adept. He would pat and stop, and then begin again harder and stop more suddenly. Once he moved his chair forward, I assumed to be nearer to me, and I could see his full body, no longer covered by the desk, and I noticed the edges of his long drawers peeping over his socks. At that very second Al-Balkhi disappeared completely, and I, Mercy Bassford, fourteen and depressed, was face to face with Hilary Gardiner, the aging principal of Wesleyan High School.

This reality flashed on and off my inside screen as quickly as the shadowy Al-Balkhi. My, how these people were coming and going, and meanwhile there was Dr. Gardiner more or less himself, asking me those stupid conventional questions adults ask adolescents, I don't know why.

His hand was kind of hanging there near mine. He didn't seem to know quite what to do with it. As a matter of fact, it began to resemble something separate, apart from his body, a large, pink animal with reddish fuzz. He was looking at me, a kind of pleading look, I'd say. Without thinking what I was doing, I reached out and took his hand and held it gently. He smiled down on me like a baby, then broke into a wide grin. "Mercy, I, I hope to see more of you sometime, maybe real soon." He had cheered up like anything. "I'm giving a class in Shakespeare. Do you think you'd be interested?"

I said, "Oh, yes, sir. I've heard about your class. I'd be very interested."

He grinned like a kid. "Then you just come in next Friday. It starts at three-thirty in the assembly hall. We're doing *Richard the Third*."

I got to my feet. I don't know why, but I did, and he stood towering above me, smiling happily. "This has been a fine visit, Mercy," he said softly. This time he held my hand in both of his. "I'll be looking forward to seeing you this Friday." I thought I heard him say something as I withdrew my hand, some kind of a low cry, a mixture of joy and surprise. "Ah-h-h . . . oh-h-h . . . ah-h-h . . ." It sounded like somebody seeing some wonderful place they'd heard about for a long time, say like the Grand Canyon or the Atlantic Ocean, some place they'd never actually believed they'd see, I mean ever in all their lives, and now there it was!

I don't know what I expected to find as I entered the assembly hall at three-thirty on Friday afternoon. The third bell was ringing as I came up the steps. I half expected I might be the first to arrive, but as I came in through the front doors, only one of which was open, and that only slightly, I saw to my amazement the group had already assembled and were in their places on the stage down front. Dr. Gardiner was sitting under a light at the right of the stage, and surrounding him in various positions, some sitting, some standing, were twelve of the best-known seniors of Wesleyan. I heard Dr. Gardiner speaking as I closed the door and came down the aisle.

"All right now, Doris. Cue us in, please."

"It's scene two, Dr. Gardiner. A room in the Duke of Lancaster's palace."

I saw Hilary look up from his book and peer down the aisle. I knew he was watching for me; in fact, his eyes caught mine as I came forward toward the stage.

"Come on up on the stage, Mercy," he instructed. The girls all stared at me. In the silence that followed, my shoes made a great clatter as I came up the steps and, as no one else acknowledged my presence by so much as a nod, I was glad to see Dr. Gardiner get up from his chair and bring me downstage.

"Ah, I see you have the play. Good. Here, we're on scene two. Who's on, Doris?"

"Gaunt and the Duchess of Gloucester."

"Good, Alice, you read Gaunt, and Mercy read the Duchess. All right, girls."

Alice Comegys began speaking in her affected Southern British accent.

> "Alas! The part I had in Woodstock's blood
> Doth more solicit me than your exclaims,
> To stir against the butchers of his life."

My cue was the word "life" and I was ready . . . "Finds brotherhood in thee no sharper spur?" I began. It was a long speech. I read it well, Hell, I'd been reading the damned play since he first mentioned it. But I had no idea what I would accomplish. I was forcing them all to watch and listen, something I suspected they hadn't been in the habit of doing. I could feel their eyes fastened to my face. Dr. Gardiner was watching me with a little smile on his lips. My, but I was having at it, and so quickly.

When I got to the last lines I had them! I could tell from the way that Alice Comegys came on, so slow she had to be cued in, and when she finally started reading, "God is the quarrel," her voice sounded dull and flat, it really did, by comparison to mine. We read through the scene, broke for discussion and then went back to read it again. The second time around I was even better than the first. And when I came to the last lines,

> "Desolate, desolate will I hence, and die:
> The last leave of thee takes my weeping eyes,"

126

I was standing only a few feet from Dr. Gardiner and again I heard that sound, that "Ah-h-h . . . oh-h-h . . . ah-h-h . . ." It sounded something like an animal about to be let out of a cage. The girls were all watching him; I, too, and you could see him straightening up and kind of going back into his skin. "Well, that was a good reading." But he said, "I'm afraid we'll have to quit now."

There was a chorus of "Yessirs" and "Good-bye, Dr. Gardiners" as the hall emptied out, with everyone hurrying off the stage and down the aisles toward the main door. I'd left my coat and books on a chair upstage and decided to go out the stage door, so as not to run into the crowd. I was just going through the short, dark hall that led to the downstairs exit when I heard a step behind me and, turning, almost ran into Hilary as he came toward the stairs. "Well, Mercy, running along home, are you?"

I said, "Yes, sir."

He looked down at me, staring. "I think it's going to be interesting from now on." It was dark and slightly cold in the hallway. It was usually overheated in the school, teachers always using those long sticks with the steel fixtures on the end to lift the windows up and freshen the air, but here in the hall, I felt slightly cold. It was dark in spots and shadowy, too. I was on the first step. I looked up at Hilary and in the shadow I saw Al-Balkhi in his robe coming over Dr. Gardiner; only this time I noticed his hand, Dr. Gardiner's, with the red fuzz, hanging over the black rail of the steps, and Al-Balkhi slowly faded. I was looking into Dr. Gardiner's face. He had that pleading look, especially in his eyes, and the excitement of Al-Balkhi, so strong and powerful, and recent, too, and the sweet thrill disappeared, as, for some reason, I don't know why, I felt sorry for Hilary Gardiner and wanted to get away.

"I—I thought we might—talk a little while . . ."

I didn't know what I was going to do but I knew I didn't want to stand there any more, nor did I want to go back to his office where I sensed he was heading. Meantime he moved forward and stepped down till he was standing on the step beside me. Then, to my surprise, he stepped down to the step beneath me and looked up at me, still with the same pleading look.

I did something real crazy then, something I should never have done. I leaned over and kissed him lightly on the cheek. It was awful, I mean, kissing an older man like that just because he was standing around. He must have been stunned. He didn't move and, again, as I hurried down the stairs, I heard that funny half-animal cry coming out of him and I thought, "Jesus," and ran like mad.

I don't know exactly how it happened. I guess it started with him that first time in his office when he seemed to know me. He knew why I had told that awful story about Miss Gaither; he was at one with me on it. Now that's a pretty great thing, that being at one with another person. Why, it actually *makes* you one for awhile. You are whole and full, being one. You start being two again awful damned soon, but for that short time you're one and it's something, it really is.

It was after that first reading. We were into the third act, that scene on the coast of Wales with the castle in view, with the drums and battle flags and the soldiers and bishops and dukes all over. I wasn't reading that day. Alice Comegys always read the Duke of Clumberle's part, Merle read Scroops with her Southern drawl, a dish mop's version of Sir Stephen. We had a hard time not to giggle when she read, "Ay, all of them at Bristol lost theah haids." But Alice came on with, "Where is the Duke, my father with his power?" She read well, and right then things picked up.

Hilary always read King Richard and he was marvelous, with a thrilling timbre to his voice. When he got to the part,

"And nothing can we call our own but death,
And that small model of the barren earth
    Which serves as paste and cover to our bones.
For God's sake, let us sit upon the ground
And tell sad stories of the death of kings."

he fell over on the bench at the side of the stage, exactly as an actor would do, and at the end, read with conviction, "I live with bread like you, feel want, taste grief, need friends: subjected thus, how can you say to me, I am a king?" And when Helen Ann Alberle started reading the Bishop's part, she read her lines all wrong and there was a catch in her voice. Hilary had made her cry.

It was a bright day, pushing for spring. We all left early and in a group, running out of the main doors just as the janitor came in to put out the lights and lock up the school for the night.

I walked along downstairs with the girls, most of them talking together, ignoring me the way they always did. I was used to it by now and I was just going out alone when I realized I'd left all my books upstairs. I thought maybe I'd better just leave them there, the third floor would be locked up by the time I made it back up. But I remembered I had to write a paper for Miss Kellogg and my notes were left inside with my books. So I ran quickly down the front stairs, through the hall and up the back stairs.

The door to the stage was open. The light was fading; it was shadowy on the stage, but I found my books just where I had left them on the chair near where I'd stood and I grabbed them up and was just going off when I heard something, or someone, move. I turned and saw him. He must have just gotten up from the bench where he'd been crouched reading the death of kings speech. I had the crazy idea of turning and sneaking out, pretending I hadn't seen him.

I already had my books, I could just walk on real fast and quiet and run like mad down the steps. He'd never be able to go as fast as I could, even if he tried. I was wearing my dark blue serge skirt, cut in those wonderful gores, wide at the bottom so you can walk like wild. I must have made my decision quickly, the skirt flashed and danced around my legs as I turned, hurrying toward the door.

"Mercy," he called so loud I had to stop.

"Yessir?" It was too late now. He crossed the stage pretty fast for a man just up from a bent position. I remember in my first quick glance he had seemed to be still crouched and brooding.

"Mercy, how nice to see you." He was at a loss for words. I could tell the way he was just standing there staring at me. In the small slant of reddish sunlight hitting him from the back his face looked dark. "I saw you'd left your books and—I was hoping maybe you'd come back."

Hoping I'd come back. *Hoping.* What a funny word! Al-Balkhi didn't crouch on seats in empty schools hoping people would come back.

"I wanted to talk to you. The way you're beginning to read, you've got quite an excellent set of vocal cords, young lady. As I keep telling my own daughter, a girl today, and boys, too, of course, all young people, should have more than one talent and develop them. You have more than one, you probably know that, and perhaps many more I know nothing about."

"Thank you, Dr. Gardiner."

"Sit down, won't you?"

I settled into the chair and dropped my books, as I saw him pulling up the bench to sit opposite me. I felt excited but confused and scared. I wasn't afraid of him exactly, even though I knew we were all alone in the empty school. It was something else. I was afraid of something that had almost nothing to do with him. All of this going on from minute to minute was so mysterious and liable to go any which way, whereas, in my dreams at night when Al-Balkhi arrived, it all went off into a wonderful rosy golden brilliance that was controlled by *him*.

"I know your parents give you good advice, but every young person needs a *mentor,* a guide, a guru. You know that word, Mercy?"

"Yessir. It's the Hindu for mentor."

"I keep forgetting your word sense. How much the young need *Vexata quaestio*. Ha, I'll bet you don't know that one."

130

"No, sir, I don't know Latin. I wish I did. It sounds like a *vexing question.*"

"That's right again. *Mooted question* is what it actually means."

Oh, well, at least he wasn't *hanging* the way he did the last time. This time he was hoping. And talking. A step up. I was just slightly afraid he might remember the last time, but he hadn't at all. He was back in his skin, masterful, at ease. I began to feel better. He would be an influence, the brilliant Older Man, giving me unity, coherence and emphasis. Which are the basic rules of English composition and a person's future, if it comes off all right, that is.

Midway in this conversation I felt myself lifted up from the too-bright pages of the book I'd been *living* back into the stream of life and I forgot the mole near his ear, the flap on his neck, the long drawers. Instead of being near-sighted, his eyes became piercing blue. He talked some more. I forget just what he said, something about "psychological positions," things like that.

Walking back through the park, with the twilight showing through the pink sunset, I knew Al-Balkhi was back. I was *in*. There was a ship that was always moving. A good many people were already on it, the lucky ones, and now I was getting on it. Back at home as I passed the open parlor doors, the chandelier was lit and I could see Martha Washington staring down, smug and disdainful, from the colored lithograph over the mantle. "You'll never make it!" That's what she said every time I passed. "You'll never get in! You're out and you'll *never, never* get in."

She was starting to say it again this very night, but I straightened up and stared her back. "I'm already in!" was what I was saying as I hurried past her nasty, cold eyes. "I'm already in, I have a mentor, and there's nothing you can do about it now."

- It was quite a long time really before something happened. We had read *Cymbeline.* I was Imogene, the king's daughter. Alice played the Queen to Dr. Gardiner's Cymbeline. It was fun saying all that silly "Good

131

morrow" and "No, no, alack! There's other work in hand." I thought it was a boring play and could hardly wait till Hilary got to the rhyme at the end, but, for some reason, he seemed to like the damned thing. We read *Troilus and Cressida* and were all the way back to old Richard II. And during all this time, all these long, full, exciting weeks he was being like he said, my mentor, reading my poems and telling me more about pentameter than I ever thought existed, and by night he was, of course, Al-Balkhi, and I was Kute.

One afternoon he left as soon as we finished reading. I was sitting on the floor finishing a piece I had to hand in to Miss Kellogg. I sat there working as the place closed up for the day and was just finishing up and putting my notebooks and pencils back into my carry-all when I saw him.

He had come back in and was waiting for me. He said, "Let me help you," and reached down to pull me to my feet, but the minute I was up and standing before him I knew it. He was hanging again, only this time it was his head instead of his hand. He kept staring at me. I started talking, pretending I didn't notice anything. When I stopped I saw him holding his lips in a funny position. When he spoke it was so sudden he almost barked the words. "Do it again, please," is what he said.

I started to say, "Do what?" I had the words all ready to go but I didn't say them. It seemed kind of mean when I knew exactly what he meant.

What to do now? What to say, if anything? I hadn't planned on anything like this. Why, just last night Al-Balkhi knew exactly what to do and say, bringing me up to the lovely, golden roses. Where had he gone, leaving this pleader in his place? "Just this once, Mercy." He was holding his hands and biting his lips, almost like somebody pleading for leniency at court. I moved to the side, but he moved, too, sort of covering me. "I know it's wrong of me to ask you, but just this once."

I leaned forward on my toes. I planned to kiss him just once lightly on the cheek and bolt, but he moved

132

again catching me unaware. This time he caught my lips with his hard, compressed little mouth, which he pressed and pressed on mine. It was a hard pressing. I thought he'd never let up. But it was not a kiss.

When I finally moved back I wasn't quite sure what he said. "Mercy . . . I . . . ah . . . I don't dare say it . . . and I won't . . ." I smiled, a false smile but kindly, as you might say, and, as I made for the door, I heard that cry again, that animal one I had heard before, only this time it continued longer and was somehow more poignant.

I went away feeling pretty depressed. I wished I could have helped him but I honestly didn't know what to do. It's awful, hearing a grownup man, standing around making those awful sounds. I can tell you that for a fact. I know a whole lot of girls and women, too, hear a lot of sounds like that and I guess they get used to it so they think it's like eggs frying or traffic moving, something like that. But the first time it's loud as hell, practically like thunder, and it can get you depressed.

There was a next time, another next time and still another next time. These kept coming at me like a lot of trains. I can't remember what all went on. It would start with Hilary the mentor and turn into Hilary the pleader before you could say Bill Shakespeare. Hilary the lofty and poetic mentor to Hilary the wishy-washy beggar. Even his words would change. From fresh, pungent, fascinating words to dumb old words like *just once* and sounds piped out of a broken organ. Then he would change back again to the dignified academician, eager to help the young, and I would see again the lovely shadow by night with the fierce mustaches, flowing robes and power absolute.

One afternoon I had to deliver my essay on Burke to Miss Kellogg's. I hadn't finished it by turn-in time and she gave me permission to bring it to her home.

It was snowing that day, a late spring snowstorm. The block of houses where Miss Kellogg lived was as beautiful as a Currier and Ives print, the red bricks bright as fresh paint and the snow white and pure. The steps of her house felt soft as velvet. I had been reading *Sister Carrie,* by Theodore Dreiser, thinking of Hilary as Hurstwood, the unfortunate restaurant manager, and myself as Carrie, the actress. I could see myself as Carrie being visited in the theater by Hurstwood. I felt the stage scene going on so keenly I was surprised when Miss Kellogg opened the door, and I heard the wispy voice saying, "Come in, please, Mercy, it's cold out there."

Poor Miss Kellogg, so kind and sweet and literary. She had been to the mountains for T.B. She was supposed to be cured but she still had pale, yellowish cheeks with red spots on each side. She would go out of the room occasionally when she had to cough. I closed the door quickly.

"Take off your things and hang them on the hatrack." Miss Kellogg was fully dressed and wearing an extra sweater and boots, even in the house. Her big, gray, dog-like eyes lightened when she saw me. We went together into her dining room, she had the entire first floor of her brother's house, and I saw she had a visitor, a big woman, over six feet and stout, who looked overwhelming in the delicately furnished dining room, with all the cut-glass in the china closet and the small, high-backed chairs and the fancy overhanging light above the table. The big woman putting on her coat seemed to threaten every object in the room.

"Gweneth, this is Mercy Bassford, one of my best English students. Mercy, have you met Mrs. Gardiner?"

I said, "How do you do, Mrs. Gardiner?"

"Hello, Mercy," said the woman. The hand that grasped mine felt big and powerful, with strong muscles you didn't expect in a woman, in fact the pressure was actually painful. She spoke in a big, gruff, masculine voice. It came booming at you like a football coach commanding a team.

I stood there staring foolishly at her. I hadn't had time to get used to the fact that there stood Mrs. Hilary Gardiner, Hilary's wife, Hilary, defender, mentor, pleader and would-be lover, Hilary of the thin lips and praying eyes, had a wife with bucketsful of money and there she was. She boomed at me again, "How's the storm doing out there, Mercy?"

"It's snowing very hard, Mrs. Gardiner."

"Oh, I guessed that!" she roared, laughing. It sounded more like a foghorn than a woman, and it went on much longer than the joke warranted. Miss Kellogg and I both smiled politely and waited for her to finish the boom.

"How deep is the snow, is more what I meant. How deep would you say, Mercy?"

"About four or five inches, ma'am."

"Four or five inches. Well, which is it, child? Four or five?"

"Five."

"Good. Well, now we know that," she roared laughing again. I wondered if she always went wild like that over her own jokes, showing the extra long, slightly yellow teeth she had. Did she think up a joke in bed nights and start roaring like that at Hilary? Maybe even when he was sleepy or enjoying a pleasant dream? Jesus, it would be awful to have to lay there wondering was she going to think up some joke and peal forth, and, if so, when? Like waiting for the second shoe to drop.

How much money did she really have, I wondered. And if she had all those barrelsful, in cotton and oil and land; how much did she give him and how was that arranged? Maybe she banged it down beside his dinner and made him count it. I'd bet whatever she did it was noisy as all get-out. She was wearing an expensive-looking brown wool suit, a simple wedding band on her finger and a plain gold wristwatch.

Miss Kellogg said for me to sit down, and I practically fell into the chair beside Mrs. Gardiner. She was pulling rubber boots up over ground-grippers. I wondered if the boots would go on over those shoes, but next thing she had pulled them up and was staring at me through gold-framed glasses. Her eyes were brown and bright as a bird's. "I said I thought it would lay when

135

I saw the flakes this morning," she boomed. "Cold out there, huh?"

The voice said, or implied, answer at once! No slumping there, girl, and I did. "Quite cold, Mrs. Gardiner."

"Wet, too? Or is it a dry snow?"

"It's a nice, dry, powdery snow, ma'am."

That must have satisfied her. She turned the bellowing on Miss Kellogg who was watching over a teakettle on a small gas stove. "Take care of yourself, now, Nancy. You hear?"

"Indeed I will, and thanks so much for coming by, Gweneth, in this awful storm, too."

"I was glad to come," boomed old Gweneth. I had the feeling she meant it, too. She liked poor, little beat-up women like Miss Kellogg. "Good-bye, Mercy." She threw me a boom, too. "Now, Nancy Kellogg, if you want anything, you give me a call, you hear? I can always send Hillie if I can't get over myself."

Hillie! She called Dr. Gardiner Hillie!

"Watch out for the icicles going home, Mercy. They don't announce it when they fall off the trees." She swung through the door like a big, husky man roaring that awful, loud laugh all the way through the hall, but closed the door gently behind her.

Miss Kellogg accepted my essay, which I promptly handed to her, then went back to the stove and started fussing with the coffee. "Well, Mercy, now you've met the principal's wife. I think you should have coffee and maybe even a slice of cake."

I accepted her offer and stayed on another fifteen minutes. But, my, it seemed quiet in the room after Gweneth left.

That night I continued thinking of Hilary as Hurstwood in *Sister Carrie* and of myself as Carrie; and then I started seeing us, and what I saw was clear as day. Hurstwood had left his restaurant and deserted his family for Carrie, or me, with this beautiful lightness I had, this fascination for men, especially for him. He had

136

taken the money and absconded like a common criminal
—for love.

We were in this very expensive hotel suite with these
heavy draperies and lamps with long fringe on the
shades, and a table set with expensive china, pale blue
with a thin gold line, and flowers, lots of flowers in
vases, long stemmed roses costing six dollars a dozen,
some from Carrie's stage door admirers, some from
Hurstwood. A fire was burning in the grate, and there
he stood, leaning on the mantle waiting for Carrie to
come down the steps leading from the bedroom to the
living room.

He wasn't exactly Al-Balkhi. Not now. Gone the
mustaches, the white horse, fierce teeth and flowing
robes. There was practically no sword, sheathed or un-
sheathed, and no *swive* of any kind. A gloomy, beaten
man devoured by love of me, like a piece of cheese
half-eaten by a mouse. He had holes where Al-Balkhi
was full and complete. He begged where Al-Balkhi commanded. This wasn't exactly what I'd planned on, if so
delicate a matter as the growing situation between Dr.
Gardiner and me could be called a plan.

Thel caught up with me one morning as I was walking to school.

"You've been avoiding me, huh, Merce?"

"No, I don't *think* so. Why?"

"Come on."

I had been avoiding both Thelma and Marian Swoboda and I knew exactly why, too. When you're involved
with someone, you're not the same as before. The old
rules of friendship no longer obtain.

"Admit it, you've been avoiding your old friends, and
we know why. At least, *I* do."

"You do, huh? Well, why?"

After a minute she answered with a question, "Are
you thinking of having an *affaieh* with Dr. Gardiner?"

We had all recently come on the word which we
thought meant flirtation, sometimes even a kiss, the sort
of thing Greta Garbo and Joan Crawford were doing

under soft lights in heavily carpeted rooms, and we were working it to the bone. Every girl seen talking to a boy or going to a movie or dancing class was said to be "having an affaieh."

"Maybe," I replied with proper hauteur. "Why?"

"Oh, nothing."

"What were you going to say?" She didn't answer, so I commanded, "Say it, and maybe I'll tell you."

"I don't think it's going to get anywhere."

"Oh, you read minds, huh?"

"Sometimes."

"And you know the future?"

"Sometimes I do, yes."

"Why didn't you tell your daddy when those stocks of his were going to fall?" I asked.

"I don't bother with commerce." She was smiling, that sly smile she gets that's so irritating. "Right now I'm interested in you and him."

I reached for my bag of tricks. I looked absent-minded, aloof and startled, all at the same time. "I hardly know the man," I said.

"Har-har," she giggled. "It's so obvious, Mercy. When you get that look on your face, you're a gone goose."

"What about *him?* Two people have to be involved in an *affaieh.*"

"He looks at you, too. Stands around stealing looks. Watches you from the windows." She sighed. "Lots of girls have had bad crushes on Dr. Gardiner. He's good-looking and he's interesting."

"What do you think will happen, since you're such a fortune-teller?"

"I think you'll keep on dreaming and so will Long Drawers."

"Stop calling him that!" I was screaming.

"See what I mean? I was just testing you!"

"You can't tell my future or anybody else's. You're too vague."

"Maybe you'll make the paper like that girl in New

Jersey. I can see the headlines. PRETTY HIGH SCHOOL GIRL WRECKS PRINCIPAL. MAN FOUND DEAD."

I didn't like this conversation. People like Hilary and Al-Balkhi didn't come down the pike every day. I had entered a special place and I didn't like Thelma Hodges coming in and moving things around. Yet I was curious as to how much she knew.

"I don't think you and L.D. are soul mates, if you want to know the truth," she continued. "And, if you were, Ground Grippers would kill you both—before you could get out of town. I bet she shoots from the hip. Hey, you'd be another Halls-Mills case. Jesus! SCHOOL GIRL'S HEAD FOUND UNDER TREE NEAR PRINCIPAL'S LEG." I ran ahead of her as we went up the school steps. Anything to get away from that conversation.

There was a next time after the lovely interval of playing mentor, with Hilary helping me with my lessons, giving my poems his special attention, giving me gifts of two books I wanted but didn't own. There was indeed a special, unforgettable time when he played mentor to the hilt. We had gone through *Measure for Measure*. I was getting tired of cloisters and dukes and holy fathers, and almost welcomed our return to old Richard the Second, with all the murdering and bleeding, which we handled pretty good by now. This time, we finished late. Hilary caught me by surprise as I was leaving by the back way.

"I forgot to give you this, Mercy," he said, touching my elbow to turn me back to the stage. I saw it was a book, a beautiful new book of Chaucer with a green satin bookmark. I went back in with him to the empty assembly hall. The janitor had already closed the windows and locked the doors. "You'll be reading it next year, or any time you choose, so I thought you might like to have it now. It's deep and amusing, both at once."

"It's beautiful." I sat down on the bench left on the empty stage and turned the pages, with him sitting beside me. He had stopped talking, I noticed immediately, and, stealing a glance, I saw he was biting his lower lip and looking at his feet. He wouldn't start the pleading thing now, I decided. He'd done mentor so long by now it was practically a habit. This thought just hit me when I saw an amazing thing happen. He stretched back over the bench, letting his long legs and feet go forward, while his whole torso including his head leaned backwards, as if he was getting ready for a doctor's examination.

"Kiss me, Mercy," he said, still with his head back. "Kiss me, kiss Hilary, now, please, now!"

I put my new book to my side, got to my feet and took his head in my arms, and there, leaning over him, as I'd dreamed of Al-Balkhi leaning over me, I kissed him on the mouth, thinking, "Holy God, what have I done now?" His lips were compressed and he started up the old animal moan. In fact, when I finally pulled away he had hold of me like an animal, not a real big animal, more like a baby puppy or piglet rutting into its mother. I had to pull hard to get loose, and I had the impression of settling him back where he was on the bench, as you might settle a baby back in his crib, I swear to God. He was making those awful sounds as I cracked out across the stage. Only this time there were different, more sucking or drinking sounds, greedy, too, like some thirsty animal trying to gulp down the ocean.

"Keep going!" I told myself. "Don't give the thing back there another thought."

Hilary was back to Hurstwood, whenever he came along in my head, but without the fine clothes, clean linen, jewels and sense of importance, and I was back to Carrie, but without all that changing color Carrie went in for when she heard Hurstwood was married and kept going on about the perfidy of men.

Al-Balkhi was nowhere to be seen these nights. He preferred young girls like Kute to Mercy, girls who lay around softly, having barely enough strength to imbibe the Arabian giggle-water before the rosy clouds came on and the old *swive* started up.

140

As for the "real" stage in the assembly hall at Wesleyan, Dr. Gardiner changed from Hurstwood-Hilary-mentor-absconder in Chicago to Hilary-Hurstwood-pleader-pauper-beggar and back again during the months of readings until the pleader began to take on a permanent cast, so to speak, peeping behind the shoulders of mentor, book-giver, Latin-reciter, sociological philosopher.

One late afternoon in spring found me on the bench, and Dr. Gardiner on the chair opposite, still appearing to read first from *Pericles,* then from Shakespeare's sonnets picked at random. I remember two lines:

This is his cheek, the map of days outworn,
When beauty lived and died as flowers do now.

It was almost dark in the auditorium. The rows of seats were grayish pink from the light filtering through the trees outside. I listened politely as Hilary read the sonnet lines, and was getting ready to go when he bolted upright and sat beside me, then suddenly let his legs go forward and his head spring back as if he had been stricken. I stared. An awful fascination held me as I watched. He wasn't stricken, I soon discovered, even though his eyes were closed. In the next few seconds he began speaking as he had the last time, I mean the last time it *happened.*

"Do it to me, Mercy!" was what he said. "Do it to me, please."

"Do what?" I gasped the words as if I had no idea what he meant.

"Kiss me," he replied. "The way you did it before, Mercy. Just the way you did it before. Only more."

Silence. Then I heard a voice say, "I can't." And then the same voice, "I mustn't."

"You can, dear. Mercy, *you can.* You know you can!"

He was laying there, I swear to God, with his eyes closed. Waiting. It was the Goddamnedest thing I ever saw, a man as tall as that stretched out there with his

141

eyes closed doing that waiting. A fairly famous academician, well-read, a man of parts, laying stretched out like that on this straight-backed wooden bench. Something was going wrong, had gone wrong. But I watched him spellbound. There was an eerie aspect to the whole business. What in hell was he going to do next? And what was I going to do?

I wasn't sure of anything at that moment. I had imagined Hilary Gardiner to be one of those people who knew the answers, who could take care of me in any situation, instead of which, holy God, he was looking to me to take care of him! Me, a girl of fifteen, brought up on Jesus and Thing. This big animal laying out there was looking *to me* to give him the answers! To do everything, even the kissing! Laying out there waiting for it, "Just the way you did it before!" Like I had some fix-it medicine. Like I was some kind of a nurse or something.

Where is he? Where is the big man I'd seen in Dr. Gardiner? Now you see it, now you don't. I knew by this time my parents not only didn't know much but went into a kind of litany whenever a crisis arose. They had this dead god they dragged out all the time and forced down your throat. Hilary was different, or so I thought. Now I knew to the contrary.

He and Al-Balkhi were part of each other no more. Al-Balkhi didn't ask for help. Not him.

Oh, well, the horse had gone, sunk deep into the floor. The sword had fallen back upon itself. Gone the flowing robe, the mustaches and flashing teeth, leaving in their place a creature breathing strenuously. Can you imagine such a change? And a creature who, or which, at that moment, in the glance I stole, resembled nothing so much as a large, bloated fish suddenly washed up on shore, still alive, but out of the water it needed to live.

His breath came in little gasps, his eyes were closed, his face was bright pink. Was he, maybe, going to have a stroke and get paralyzed? Men of fifty or so got strokes. Uncle Tom, Honey's father, had had a stroke.

142

But somehow I suspected that wasn't what was happening to Hilary, especially when I heard him speaking again.

"Help me, Little Mother, help me!" I listened, but I could hardly believe what I was hearing. He went on, still with his eyes closed and stretched out as if ready for the doctor. "I've never had it, Mercy. Never had any help. Fix me, fix me, please!"

Holy God! What to do now? There must be something. I thought of bolting, just getting up and running off, but that seemed so mean. Was it all really happening? Was that peculiar, bloated, fish-like creature the same who read Anatole France and Henri deGourmont and Goethe in the original, who knew Medieval History and Art. "Mercy, help me, just this once!"

Yes, it was the same. The inner man had crawled out and kind of smelled. I knew now what he wanted, too. He wanted me to take him in my arms like a baby and I didn't know what else. My mind and all knowledge stopped with a kiss, but I couldn't even do this. I couldn't deliver the kiss. I could not.

"I can't," I said. Then came the voice I hardly recognized as my own. "It would be wrong."

I was acting when I used the word "wrong" but I was telling the truth when I said I couldn't. There was something terrible and scary in him laying out there calling me "Little Mother" and asking me to fix him. And repulsive. He must have felt disappointed when I said it would be wrong. I know because he jumped or jerked slightly. Truth to tell, I didn't know what in hell he wanted.

I felt kind of desperate myself and, glancing across the stage, wondering when I could decently get up and go, I remembered I had to stop by Miss Kellogg's before long and then I remembered the honey cake Rose had baked for her last night and I was to deliver. There it was, right over there on the chair near the podium where I'd put it down, a big beautiful cake all wrapped in wax paper and stuck in a cardboard box. A honey cake, damp and rich and delicious. On a plate, too, a genuine

Haviland china plate. I had a penknife in my pocket and . . .

Inside of a minute I had opened the box and cut a big slice of cake which I carried back to the bench. He was still breathing heavily, murmuring, when I came back and then, seeing me in my place beside him, speaking. In fact speaking very distinctly, not at all to my taste. What he was saying was, "You're going to take care of me, Mercy." Only this time I was ready.

"Here, Dr. Gardiner," I said. "Have this and you'll feel better, I know you will."

He bolted up to a sitting position and stared down at the cake. His mouth fell open; he looked as if he wasn't quite sure what it was, but he had stopped that awful heavy breathing, I guess because all his energy was being consumed in staring at the cake. He looked nonplussed, if that's the word, I swear to God!

It was getting dark. I was glad about that because it is easier to say nothing and do nothing in the dark, and I was prepared to do nothing but hold the cake. I had come to the limit of my repertory, the end of the line. He would just have to eat cake and keep breathing till he got back into the water somehow or be overtaken by a big new wave like every other fish.

Where was I now after my discovery of the secret person inside Dr. Gardiner, ye prince on ye white horse, after my recognition that, while he had the steed, he not only couldn't ride it, but he was in fact looking to me to ride it for him and carry him along?

With Jesus, my first prince and bridegroom, by now practically a dead relative, and Dr. Gardiner unseated from his horse, what was left for all the beautiful, loose half-hours when, having finished the absurd problems of algebra and written my essay contrasting the sonnets of Shakespeare and Elizabeth Barrett Browning with those of Lizette Woodworth Reese and Edna St. Vincent Millay, my hungry psyche went searching for its counterpart?

Not Daddy, who was too busy eating, resting-in-leather-chair-at-club and pushing opinions on Mamma, sucking money from his own mother, drawing up "accounts," ordering plumbers and painters around and holding forth on current events as if his words gripped the attention of a huge crowd representing a cross section of logical God-fearing people anxiously awaiting his verdict. No, nothing here, and nothing there. Not President Coolidge. He was too much a wax figure of a man to fade in and out with Al-Balkhi, who was still waiting in the wings for his cue from me.

I hadn't too far to seek, for all along, since my days as a child of two alone in the street, I had fallen and he had picked me up in his arms and carried me home, I had Stephen Farrar III at the topmost peak inside me, casting a dark and thrilling shadow straight over my secret but busy sexual dreams.

And he was near, oh, was he near, right across the street in the great, gray stone castle on the corner, set apart from the red brick houses with porches and curlicue roofs by a beautiful and spacious lawn on all sides, planted with trees and white iron pots of flowers and further enhanced by a hedge six feet high and too thick to see through, there lived this god, this absolute god!

The architectural tone of the house, built well before the turn of the cenutry, was cool and distant, almost forbidding. It was set so well apart from the block of brick houses as to seem not to belong to the neighborhood, but, then, these unusual "countrified" properties appeared in quite a few Baltimore streets in those days and were greatly sought after on those rare occasions when one of them came up for sale. Almost as if the family had sensed the house's disdainful aspect, the lawns were of a different and more inviting ambience, bursting with the friendly faces of roses and geraniums, hydrangeas and bougainvillea in season.

Our house was almost directly across the street. In fact, through the shutters of our parlor windows, I would see Stephen entering the house, usually about six. Later at night, say ten or ten-thirty, I would sometimes see his

145

shadow against the drawn blinds as he moved about in his second floor bedroom.

Once in the late afternoon, I had seen his head quite near the open window. He was sitting in a chair, reading. A standing lamp threw soft light on his hair which was light brown and straight, but heavy in the front and back and unruly. Then I found I could see him better from my parents' bedroom. Their bedroom faced almost directly on his. This was a thrilling discovery. God in his own bedroom and me watching him.

I would look through the slats in the shutters and if I saw him, settle near the window. I stared transfixed as his face, especially when he sat down to read, grew clearer and seemingly closer by the minute. I would resent it bitterly if he disappeared from my sight and would wait impatiently for him to come back, which, often as not, he neglected to do. If he stood up and looked out the window I would stand there, my head almost level with his, and, when he sat down I would keep my stance till my legs ached or somebody came upstairs and I had to move on.

He was by now quite familiar to me. Stephen Farrar III was the only son of Mrs. Stephen Farrar, a widow whose husband had been shot in some mysterious circumstance. Stephen lived in the big house with his mother and those extra-smooth, shiny black servants, Beatrice and Oliver, neither of whom were ever seen outside scrubbing the front steps or hosing down the yard, chores that in our place were performed daily by Aunt Rose.

I knew facts about Stephen, as I had known facts about Dr. Gardiner. He was an "older man," thirty or more by now. He had studied at Oxford, no less, and now he was teaching boys at Oldtown Prep School just out of town, to which place he drove of a morning and returned by night on alternate weeks, substituting the three- for the five-day schedule every other week.

Sometimes I would pass him in the street, usually on my way home from school. He would always greet me and stop to talk. "How are you, Mercy?" he would say in a certain friendly but concentrated way, as if he had been waiting for me and really wanted to know how I was.

I would tell him, "Oh, I'm fine. How are you, Mr. Farrar?" And he would always correct me. "Stephen," he'd say. "Remember, we've known each other for fourteen years."

"Twelve," I corrected, but it was exciting to think he had counted the years since my fall in the street, even if he had it wrong.

He always wanted to know what I was studying, what my grades were, and if he reached for a book I happened to be carrying, "May I?" he would say, I would feel a thrilling sense of surrender and the closeness as he held it to his chest and opened it with his long hands.

It was as if we were the only people in the street, in the world, for that matter, and those others who came and went, in automobiles and on foot, some so close to our sides as to brush against us, were far off and dead to us.

They weren't ever long, these meetings, conversations of ten minutes or less, but when I left to go into my house I would feel as if I'd been near a great light and it was still shining on me; then the light seemed to be coming from inside me. As I passed the parlor and saw old Martha Washington staring disapprovingly down her long nose, her smug mouth muttering, "What have *you* done now that you think is so great?" I'd stare her down with half-conscious contempt, for she was dead, dead along with thousands of others, a good many of whom could still move and eat and speak. But I was alive.

Stephen's voice would stay with me sometimes well after he had gone, until something happened to catch my attention, such as ice-skating or going to theater or movies or reading a great new book, *The Death of Ivan Ilyich* or *War and Peace,* or *Crime and Punishment* or *Anna Karenina,* and then I would be in Moscow or Petrograd, in love or dying or both.

I liked to hear Stephen's voice. It was crisp but friendly, with a faintly British, or certainly foreign, accent, garnered no doubt from his years of living abroad.

Times would come when I wouldn't even think about him, much less stare through the shutters, but always, after these absent spells, passing the gray stone house or happening to glance in its direction, I'd remember he was in there, and then he would come floating back to my mind as a god I couldn't really know and might never know, and a combination of earthly men, too, say Edgar Allan Poe combined with Rudolph Valentino, someone like that.

Oh, well, it was nice to know there were men like these in the world, even if you didn't know them very well or how to reach them. But there was nothing, absolutely nothing whatsoever keeping me from calling them to mind whenever I chose, particularly this god across the street, and I did this in those periods when Al-Balkhi came to call.

Did I imagine it, or was there a slight, very slight, mind you, increase in the number of those accidental meetings I had with Stephen? I don't know for sure. I can only tell you that this particular period had a special kind of emptiness in which, for want of better companions, I often found myself in the company of Johnsy Dowse next door. We would walk through the park together, he on his way home from delivering flowers, and I from my dancing lesson.

"Why must you spend your time with him?" Mamma would ask. "He looks so unkempt—and he is so backward."

Those days I seldom gave her or my father what was called a "straight answer." I would say, "I thought we were supposed to be good neighbors."

She would put some pressure on her facial muscles, causing her lips to go out on the sides. "I didn't say you should be rude to him. Just don't let him keep coming here and don't be seen with him so much. You can't expect to have really nice boys for your friends with people like that around."

To do her justice, she thought she was giving me good

148

advice when she told me to keep away from "people like that." What she didn't know was that I resented Johnsy Dowse more than she did but I loved him, too, and needed him. I sought him out as much, if not more, as he sought me, because of the emptiness.

After childhood business, Sunday school and church and long family visits where meals last for hours on end, came high school and adolescence, when the old rug of religion was pulled out from under me, the entire red carpet gone in one piece. Every kid knows the sense of betrayal. They just didn't tell you the truth, is all. Well, anyway, some of the hurt of those nasty unfulfilled promises was soothed and comforted by the very people my mother called "people like that," Johnsy Dowse, Aunt Rose and Marian Swoboda.

Whatever Mamma thought of Johnsy Dowse, Stephen Farrar apparently did not share her opinion, or if he did, he kept it well to himself for, lately, though only occasionally, I had met him while walking with Johnsy, and he was as easygoing and courteous and interested in Johnsy as he was in me.

Did I imagine it, I asked myself, or were those meetings actually happening more often of late? I imagined it, I decided, and cursed my fate that Johnsy was so often along when they happened and hoped that Johnsy's dirty clothes, black fingernails and ungrammatical conversation wouldn't push Stephen further away.

I can tell you it's pretty easy to imagine almost anything in a state when religion and all the other bum rituals turn into things of the past. When passing my old church I'd look at the fancy windows, only it was like looking at faded photographs of rich relatives who didn't send Christmas presents any more. It was all gone, the great tuneful paeans to invisible beings—or dropped down into anxious questions—and nothing had yet arrived to take its place.

In our street, the Catholics had the Holy Mary and all the saints to do them favors, the Jews had Jehovah, the holidays and all kinds of shops and businesses, large and small.

The few Arabians and Indians, mostly tailors and small importers of odd foods, they had Buddha or Mohammed, something or other that kept them laughing among themselves.

But the Methodists had been taught to keep in with old Jesus or be in danger of hellfire and, when He began to fade, they themselves lost a great vision. They must have been sore about it, and, well, the anger and emptiness they felt got passed on loudly.

It's stupid as hell passing this stuff on to kids, especially real little kids, when they're ready to believe anything.

That's how it was, and I guess you can see it took little more than a spurt in the number of "chance" meetings with the fascinating Stephen Farrar to give a new impetus to my awakening emotions.

One sunny day I ran smack into Thelma at Tobin's Ice Cream Parlor. Marian Swoboda was having a soda all by herself at the fountain, so the three of us joined forces, claiming our favorite booth beside the window in the back of the room. I don't remember how we got started talking about a "soul kiss." Most of us knew what it was.

"Mamma told me that it can make a girl very sick," said Thelma, with such seriousness that Marian burst out laughing. Then Marian accused Thelma of not even knowing what it was.

"Maybe the whole Hodges clan just don't know nothing about it!" said Marian.

"I do *so* know what a soul kiss is!" Poor Thel was furious at the suggestion.

"Yeah?" Marian waited, then asked, "Well, what is it?"

"It's when a man's tongue goes in," Thelma replied.

"In where . . . ?"

"In your mouth, stupid. Where else could it go?"

Then Marian made a most peculiar comment, "I

could think of a helluva lot of other places," before bursting into guffaws. "You kids don't know nothing."

"Go on and tell her, Thel," I said. I felt I had to help Thel in face of these strange remarks of Marian's. We all knew from what we had been told by adults from our earliest days what terrible effects a soul kiss could have, and I longed to hear Thelma shout Marian down.

"Well, as I said," Thel began, "if a man's tongue tangles with your tongue it can be very dangerous!"

"Yeah?" For some reason Marian burst out with fresh laughter. "Tell me m-m-m-more."

"It's just *scientific evidence!*" I came to help Thel out.

"Just ask your parents," Thel commanded.

"I don't ask them nothing," Marian said.

"Why not?"

"I don't have to, that's why not." She giggled but stopped a minute. "Go on with what you was telling me," she said.

"Well," began Thel, "the pleasure, such as it is, just isn't worth the danger."

"What danger?"

"Because if the juice goes down your throat it can easily make a lump inside your stomach and then you're *gone.*"

Marian guffawed. "G-g-gone? Where?"

"Caught," said I.

"Pregnant," said Thel.

"Yeah? Well, you kids just better not swallow no juice," said Marian. "But I'll tell you something," she whispered, beckoning us to lean forward. "If you do swallow a hunk of that old spit juice, you just take a glass of hot water with a pinch of salt and gargle, just like you do for a sore throat."

"What'll that do?"

I listened eagerly. I hadn't had a real good soul kiss from anyone but Al-Balkhi. That practiced Arabian delivered his in the rosy darkness with safety, God bless his fierce mustaches, but I sensed it would be fun to get it from somebody else, and looked forward to getting my share with greedy excitement, meanwhile, giving them to myself via Al-Balkhi at regular intervals.

"That'll dissolve the j-j-j-juice, girls, and k-k-keep the lump from forming. You won't get no kid if you remember Dr. Swoboda's salt water suck."

She was still red from laughing as she paid for her soda. I was dying to have her talk more—Marian knew everything, I swear to God, but she had to go home.

I'd been told to keep away from Marian and girls from the same neighborhoods, waiting at corners, often accompanied by their mammas or the black girl of the house, were given the same word. She used bad language, was all. Despite the groups, the girls had a tendency to couple, unlike the boys who tramped by themselves through rain and snowstorms, joining up with other boys in the school yard for basketball, roller skating or general roughhouse. By the seventh grade, age twelve or thirteen, "best friends" had become more distinct and groups more recognizable as regular pairs of faces went together for swimming and dancing lessons or tennis in the park. Thelma Hodges was my "best friend."

Marian Swoboda didn't belong to any group. She was never included. She was Polish, lived in a poor, neglected neighborhood. Malcolm Street had big, ugly old stone houses, bursting with people and animals. You could hardly walk there of a summer's evening. Faces and bodies protruded from the windows of the houses, while people and automobiles fought each other for a place on the hot asphalt of the street. And sounds! The medley was so abrasive to the ears a person could go deaf just walking through those blocks. Kids played games and fought each other while adults played pianos and screamed songs from the parlors. Old people hung out the windows like tired old washrags, and boys played ball on the roofs, often hitting people down in the streets.

Marian was absent more often than any other kid in school except Johnsy Dowse, who had to work to help his mother. Marian was a plain truant. She played hooky by choice anyway, and, when fetched back by a truant officer, she would show up smiling as if only pleasant things had happened to her out there in the streets. She had long, curly black hair, not very clean, and bright, laughing brown eyes set in a round face. She was always grinning, as if about to burst with some kind of joyous force, showing dimples and teeth with spaces between them. Most of the girls who had been told to keep away from Marian, a "bad influence," obeyed instructions. Marian didn't mind. The whole business of school, education and status seemed to amuse her, and if no one but Thel and I would walk home with her, this, too, was funny.

One warm evening, when walking away from school with Marian, a group of girls passed us without speaking.

"Did you ever see a turd walking?" Marian asked the question out loud, with the girls just a few feet away. "They think they're people but they're *turds,* m'dear. Ask me why?" she went on, hands on hips. "Quick, Mercy, ask me why!"

"Why?" I gasped.

"Because, come on!, because we've just *passed them!*"

She grabbed my arm and howled with laughter as we ran hurriedly by them, leaving five enemies behind. Had I imagined it, or had I heard Edythe Burton say, "I'll tell mother and she'll tell *your* mother." No, I hadn't imagined it, because next minute Marian turned back and snickered, "You'd tell, only turds cawn't talk!"

The minute they were out of earshot, Marian said, "C'mon home with me 'n have some apple mazurek my aunts made."

I loved it at the Swoboda's. Marian's mother and her two aunts let her do as she pleased. The backyard and the kitchen were hers. Nobody sitting on porches overhead listening, nobody watching; a wonderful, easy freedom surrounded us at Marian's house. I felt disconnected from the whole world, loose in a wild, free atmosphere of pure joy.

It was dark and cool in the dining room. Marian's

two aunts, both widowed, wearing the Catholic widow's uniform, black dresses with white collars and cuffs, sat playing cards at the dining room table. They both had round, pleasant, ageless faces, no wrinkles, but no color either, a beige softness surrounded by light brown hair. Aunt Bert and Aunt Fossie. Aunt Fossie had the most gray in her hair and talked the most. "G'wan in and give your friend Mercy fresh cake, Marian," she said. "There's whip cream in the icebox."

"Charley come back?" inquired Marian.

"No, dear." Aunt Bert spoke in a soft voice almost a whisper, "That cat's gone."

"Cats are nevah gone, Aunt Bert," said Marian. "Charley'll be back, even if he's dead."

The yard smelled of earth as we sat in Marian's broken swing eating delicious cake and drinking coffee with milk. The lovely, illicit feeling of being with a bad, dirty girl crept over me, increasing my enjoyment of her.

"Didn't ya ever have no screwn, Skeets?"

"What?"

"No screwn?"

"What's that?"

"I guess you haven't been around so much. It's what you girls used to call sedshual indrakorz. Didn't you never have any, huh?"

The question terrified and delighted me. I took a minute to answer, "No."

"No kind at all?"

"No."

"You mean *nevah?* Not even you didn't try?"

"No."

She went on eating. I had never seen her doing anything wrong, especially anything of a sexual nature, but from the way she asked the question, I could tell she knew what she was talking about and most likely had had it. She got it for herself from somewhere much as other young people got pencils and paper. I was uncomfortable in the face of such sophistication. It went way beyond me, yet I heard myself ask, "You . . . have?" A person couldn't miss an opportunity like this to find out.

"Oh, sure, Skeets."

"You aren't afraid?"

"Aw, no, Skeets."

"But isn't it wrong?"

"Not the way I do it," she screamed, laughing.

I was quiet as I wondered all over again about Thing. She made it sound as if he wasn't in the picture. As if whatever it was she did, Thing did not get loose and try to kill her, as if he kept his distance. Gentleman Thing. Gee whiz! This was the first time I had ever seen or heard a real live person talk about *sedshual indrakorz* in this manner.

Up till now all I'd heard were those hobgoblin stories coming on apace, the aftermath of all human contact with Thing: the Black Death, the Black Hand, the White Slaves, Hell and Damnation, yet here was a girl, my own age, on the verge of womanhood, just beginning to break into bud, talking about Thing Himself as if she were talking about some friend! And right within her two aunts' hearing!

"C'mon, Skeets, y'ain't told me. Didn'sha' ever have any?"

"No."

"Well, Jesus, don't look so scared. I only astya a question, didya? There ain't nobody here in this here yard gonna give you none." She burst out laughing.

She had a new way of doing her hair. She said if you did it just once a week with this stuff she'd bought and then put it up in curls, it would stay in a whole week, from Saturday to Saturday. I noticed her hair had been looking better and when she offered to show me how to do it up, I accepted, and we went upstairs to the room she shared with her aunt, overlooking a yard and alley with low-hung shanties. Now as she worked first on her hair, then on mine, from time to time as I caught her impish face reflected in the mirror, I would become shocked thinking about her.

This girl must have done it, one way or another, maybe a dozen times, *maybe a hundred*. I couldn't even imagine how—the method was at this point still unknown to me; all I knew was a kiss and then the fog of roses—or where, and I didn't want to. I never saw it happen, but from the way she talked she got something for herself that pleased her.

This low-down kid, this Polack, this Polecat, this Hunky I was told not to see or associate with in any way, was already at the jug of life, and whatever she was sucking must have delighted her, because she was always laughing. It. Did It provide that constant grin coming from deep within her?

This "lousy Hunky," who smelled of garlic and onions, carp and red cabbage and peppers, and was glossed over with her aunts' cheap toilet water, she, Marian Swoboda, had some secret we didn't have and might never get!

It saddened and frightened me as I began to think. She was my superior. Hell, yes! She had something I needed, too, and in a deep, almost unknown but very earthy manner, she was kind. She would share the secret with me when the time came. Come hell or high water, I had no intention of giving Marian up.

Saturday was a special day, shopping on our own with money saved from work and allowances, a theater matinee or movies in the afternoon. One Saturday morning, as Thelma and I were walking through the park on our way downtown, I saw Marian slumping along in a nearby lane all by herself, yet looking as pleased with life as ever, and I called to her to join us.

Thel was furious. "What did you do that for?"

"Why not?"

"Because we just might meet *my mother,* that's why *not.*"

"Don't worry. Marian won't stay long."

Marian waved, but she took her time about joining us; in fact, as we came to the end of the path, we had to go over to see her.

All three of us slumped down on the nearest bench and began discussing the latest scandal at Eastern High School for Boys, a theft, but this time by a prominent doctor's son, which made it somehow more interesting.

Girls from Wesleyan High all knew boys from Eastern High. We had all seen the principal, Dr. Forbes, and Miss Leyten, the assistant principal, and many of the teachers. Earl Thiede had been accused by Miss Leyten, the large and competent assistant principal, of stealing ten dollars left stuck in a clip on her desk while he was waiting to be interviewed about truancy. Thelma, who had a crush on Earl Thiede, had all the details and told the story with passionate excitement.

"Ten dollars!" The sum seemed enormous. "And from Miss Leyten! The assistant principal! And while she was out of the room for a very short time! About ten minutes!"

"A dollar a minute!"

"What was Earl there for?" asked Marian.

"For an interview; a lecture. Maybe worse. About being absent from school!"

"Well, what happened? What's going to happen?"

"The nerve! The sheer gall that boy's got!"

"Sure," said Marian. "What about it?"

"Oh, boy! Wait till you hear! Leyten missed the money on Friday. She sent for him on Monday and asked him if he'd taken it, and he said yes. Then she asked him where it was, and he said he'd spent it. Then she sent for his daddy, Dr. Thiede."

"I bet the old man gave it to him."

"That's what's *funny*. Dr. Thiede asked him first why he'd stolen the money, and Earl said because he needed it. Guess what for!"

We said we didn't know and couldn't guess.

"To take out a girl, that's what for! To the theater and supper afterwards!"

"Jesus!" said Marian.

"All in the same night," said I.

"Now guess what Dr. Thiede did! Go ahead and guess."

We guessed the doctor whipped Earl or put him to bed or locked him in his room, but Thelma said no to everything. Eventually she filled us in. "Dr. Thiede gave Earl ten dollars, told him to take it to Miss Leyten and apologize to her and told his mother to increase his allowance."

"How do you know all this?" I asked.

"Earl told me." Thel waited, smiling, smug. Then she sprang it on us. "I was the girl he took to the theater!"

I was greatly impressed with this story. Thelma had won some sort of victory or prize, I wasn't quite sure how it went, but Marian Swoboda was not impressed.

"Why'n he work for the money?" was her comment, addressed more to the path and the trees than Thel. "Old Leyten worked for it. All those long days in that nasty, stinking hot school."

Thelma drew herself up as best you can on a park bench. "Earl doesn't have to work," she said, adding proudly, "I don't even think he *knows* how to work."

"You mean he's stupid? I'll say. Anybody's so dumb they steal from an assistant principal's office, they gotta be real dumb."

Thel was wild. "It's as good a place as any to steal!" she hollered. "Only it takes somebody daring. Nerve!"

"Oh, sure. He gotta bang outa hitting the old girl for a sawbuck, then getting it back from his pop. Oh, sure."

I listened, fascinated, as Thel went on. "Well, where would *you* steal it from?"

"Gee, I don't know." Marian frowned, as if she was actually thinking.

"You, Mercy?"

"What?"

"Where would you steal from?"

"I'd get it from my aunts or uncles. Some more friendly place than an assistant principal's office. How about you?"

Thelma admitted she had stolen from her mother. The idea was to steal just enough so it wouldn't be noticed at first and so you wouldn't be caught. Some kids stole regularly from department stores and candy stores, small stuff, beneath notice, and others stole money from various places.

Marian didn't seem particularly interested in the conversation. Not even the confessions drew her attention away from the paper bag of white vanilla candies she kept offering us, which annoyed Thelma no end. When she couldn't stand it another minute she turned on Marian.

"How about *you?*" She didn't even call her by name. "You haven't answered. You *know* you've stolen!"

"Uh-uh," said Marian.

"Aw, come on. We've told you. Now why don't *you* tell?"

"I ain't got nothing to tell."

"Maybe you'd tell Mercy, but you won't tell me."

"I'd tell you."

"Well, where'd you get your money from?"

"From home."

"All that extra money for movies and going to the fairgrounds and all?"

"If I want extra money I clean the kitchen and the backyard and run errands all over the place for everybody in my whole family."

"Are you trying to tell us you don't steal?"

"Uh-huh. I told you, I work. I cook pies and cakes and make thousands of painted eggs, Easter, Christmas and all them holidays, and I plant things and sew and all for everybody, and iron. God, how I iron. A dime an hour."

"And you *like* that stuff?"

"Sure. S'better than long division."

Thelma was angry and confused. "I don't believe you don't steal. Why not?"

"I guess I never thought much about it."

"It's not something kids sit thinking about. It's something they just do."

"Sure. Why not, if they want to? I got most everything I want."

Thelma got up. "Let's go, Mercy." I asked Marian if she'd like to go shopping with us, but she said she was on her way to Barston's to buy that fresh bread dough they have of a Saturday, so we went our separate ways.

"That damned dirty kid! Playing hooky all the time and then lying, acting so superior."

159

I said I didn't think she was lying. She might be dirty in Thelma's sense, but there was something more there, oh, much more.

One day in the autumn of my junior year I heard my Cousin Ruth was "back to normal." Maybe you'll understand better than I what was going on. I mean, there were some sinister underpinnings to those good old days, I can tell you for a fact. I wasn't too good at figuring these things out, I know. Most of the time I was just plain falling through space, but even the most foolish and the youngest people have reserves they hardly know anything about. They have wild courage and energy when they're cornered, when they're hit with a crisis.

Well, I was passing through the hall on my way out the front door on my way to Wesleyan where, as I told you, I was now a fairly prominent and popular junior, or so it seemed. My mother was practicing at the piano, as she did for two hours every morning before first getting on the telephone for interminable conversations and then to the Peabody Conservatory of Music for her daily lesson from Professor Francesca Maliardni.

She was practicing something that must have been difficult. I had heard her come at it twice as I sat listening at breakfast and now here she was starting up again. She stopped as I passed the parlor door and called to me. "Mercy, is that you?" She knew, of course, it was I. Who else would it be? In fact, by this time she could have seen me. Those ugly old folding doors were half-open, but Mamma, once at the piano, did not deign to turn away from the beloved instrument to look at a mere human being. I said, "Yes," and she said, "Come here, I want to speak to you."

I came obediently in and stood beside her at the piano, and she began speaking, only half-turning in my direction. "Your Cousin Ruth is coming for dinner tonight, with her things. I told Rose to make up the big couch in your room and she can have my old white wardrobe."

I waited until I saw her speech was finished; she must

have planned it well in advance, then I spoke in a strange, soft voice I hardly recognized when I heard it. "If you put her in my room I will leave this house and never come back."

My mother was silent for a minute. I noticed her hands laying still but tense on the keys, the tension showing in the tips of her long, delicate fingers.

"Oh, Mercy, why must you feel this way? A blood relative, your own first cousin!"

I stood there staring at her hands but not saying anything, and she was waiting, looking sad and wispy, the way she did.

Now my mother is a nice lady, pretty and with nice manners, religious and a fine musician. And she did get Ruth out of the house kind of fast after the steel bullet business. I could hardly believe she was inviting her back into the house, maybe to have the same performance repeated, or worse, and asking *me*, asking me softly and sanctimoniously, to forgive and forget, to go along with her and collaborate in my own undoing . . .

"Ruth is a fine girl, a fine young woman!"

"Is she?"

"A changed person. She'll soon be married."

"Ummhmm."

We continued not looking at each other as the conversation went on.

"We must all forgive and forget. We're all God's children. Jesus loves us one and all, Mercy. Jesus waits for us to receive Him."

"Jesus notwithstanding, if Ruth comes into my bedroom, I will leave home at once."

"There's so much she can teach you. She and Dale understand music. I see such a happy group."

"That is a chimera," I said. "Chimera" was the name of a poem I had sold to a little magazine for three dollars. I knew Mamma didn't know what it meant.

"Oh, Mercy, you used to be such a sweet, forgiving child. What is happening?"

"I'm trying to get to school, that's what's happening."

She dropped her hands from the piano.

"I'll have to put her upstairs," she said. "Virginia Ann will be furious, if she ever finds out, but that's what I'll have to do since you're so stubborn."

So it was decided Cousin Ruth was back to normal and was coming to share her normalcy with us, but not in my room.

"You'll have a friend in her *now*," Mamma told me, enthusiasm stirring in her voice. "She's changed so much you'll hardly know her."

"I'd know her," I said, but without expression. What was the sense of getting angry. It had already been decided, and there was nothing I could do to stop it.

"She's in love, you know. And she has a job teaching. And she's engaged."

I said, "Good-bye," and went on out.

I hurried through the streets, depressed but looking forward to my first class where I would see dear, fat Miss Pims in biology lab and escape into the microscope and the thrill of watching those silly spermatozoa jump around all over the place.

I was to go down to Grandma's that very evening where I'd have a chance to see Ruth all dressed up in her great new personality. Every opportunity was being given me to "make friends" with the "new Ruth," as Mamma put it, a prospect of which I took the dimmest possible view. Already fifteen, at a time when most American youngsters of that age were young in experience indeed, I sensed there are no "new people," although, of course, they might wear disguises of all kinds. People are pretty wonderful altogether. I'm kind of addicted to them, you might say, but you never know which of them is harboring a *spook*. Actually it's like you can't find out until you *see* the spook. It's really funny.

Another dark fact was I was poor in mathematics and would need tutoring. You had to give answers in math papers, for instance, not just show off your brilliant mind in the way you could in English Lit. But this, while bothersome, didn't seem nearly as important as the arrival of Ruth in the house. I tried not to think about seeing her face at mealtimes, but when I learned I had to "make friends" with her before she moved in I decided to rush into it and get it over with fast.

It was an arbitrary decision on my parents' part, this bringing Smile back into our house. What had happened in the past was as forgotten as last Christmas. It would be good for me to have an older girl companion, and they would be helping my uncle in marrying off Cousin Ruth and, I hate to mention it, but my uncle, well, *he had money*.

It's awful the way people act toward those who are rich, even if these richies wouldn't give them an old doughnut, and even if they're nasty and mean, people fawn over them. It's awful, actually.

I counted my friends at night: Aunt Rose, Marian Swoboda, Johnsy Dowse, Thelma, Honey and now Stephen, oh yes, Stephen Farrar, who had offered to tutor me free of charge.

What more could a young girl want? I thought, as I arranged my friends in a row in my mind in a place of Jesus and God, the unreachable. I had quite a row of people: four women and two men! Then, of course, there was Al-Balkhi who appeared only at night. He was the best of all, the strongest, too, but you couldn't actually call him a friend. But where would they all be if Ruth, let's say, should appear before me one night and instead of the new woman there would be old Smile herself? Who would rescue me? For some reason I thought of Dr. Gardiner. He looked at me kind of wistfully these days, as if I had something I wasn't giving him, and now there was no chance, just no chance ever of his getting it at all.

I wished that whatever it was that poor Dr. Gardiner wanted so bad could be slipped into an envelope, say, and left on his desk or somewhere, so he'd have it, and nobody'd be any wiser. But I wasn't very sure what it was, and, much less how in hell I'd get it into an envelope. Dr Gardiner wouldn't rescue me. Hell's bells, he needed rescuing himself.

And how would I do in a crisis more sinister than the

last one? Maybe Smile had other tricks to make the steel bullet "examination" look like kid stuff. I was older and wiser now—older, anyway—but so was Smile. Anyway, I was pretty uncomfortable thinking about her. I guess I was kind of a coward.

As I went off to have dinner at my grandmother's and meet the "new Ruth," passing the parlor and seeing Martha Washington staring down, I could almost hear her this time, "You'll never make it, not you. Never!"

Had I known how this visit would turn out I mightn't have rushed so, but then there's no such thing as seeing the future. If people could foresee, maybe they'd commit suicide in droves, driven like lemmings. Or they'd run to bed and not get up. I don't know what they'd do, but thinking about the future is pretty terrible.

I imagined Ruth was going to do something, show something of her old spiteful spirit, but she didn't. The dinner went off easy as pie. She was, in fact, everything my mother had suggested, and more; she was taller, prettier and somehow more interesting. She had been to Tilliton Girls' School, an expensive school for "correction of deportment." I heard one of my aunts say, "That was the only one where they let her stay." From the other schools—there were five, all costing more than my uncle wanted to pay—she had either been expelled or run away; but the last one "had taken."

She studied music, received a diploma, and was now a music teacher herself, besides being engaged to one Dale Stump who was coming to take her for a drive that very night.

I didn't know quite what to say to her; she sat opposite me at the table, smiling and staring to beat the band. I told her I liked her hair straight back with the bun.

"Oh, do you, Mercy? Well, I'll do yours that way," she replied. She said that she had been on a long trip since she had last seen me. She had been twice to New York City and once to the Grand Canyon, Texas, California and Mexico!

"I'll have lots to tell you, soon as I move on in." That

was when I saw Smile flashing like a steel trap. Some kind of animal force began down in the pit of my stomach, and I stopped midway on the roast beef.

I forgot what I had been sensing lately, a crazy idea that gave me a kind of awful comfort; I think maybe there's this great force somewhere, this enormous powerful force, and we are all pumping, trying to get it to come through. But most of the time only the least little trickle comes through, and that's all anybody gets. Meanwhile, we keep trying and trying to get turned on.

My parents had a religious idea, but it gave them only the tiniest little old trickle. That was why they kept on doing the same things over and over again, and that was why *nobody* cared much about anybody else, including parents. All they had to give was this mean little trickle because the spigot just wouldn't turn on. They kept asking Jesus to do it, but that didn't get much water up through the old pump, I swear to God.

There had to be another way. I hadn't found it yet but I would. Meanwhile, every time I ran into somebody who didn't have much to give, which is most teachers, relatives, etc., all these little trickle folks, I'd think about people trying to get help from a fellow dead two thousand years, and I'd think, there's got to be something more recent, more now.

"You prob'ly don't even *know* who the great composers are," Smile was saying to me. I ate some mashed potatoes and nodded agreement. She isn't even getting the regular trickle, I figured. *Hers is coming from somewhere funny and it's black.* "But I'll teach you, Mercy, and then you'll know."

I said, "I'm learning to play the violin," neglecting to mention I was pretty good, too. She would take me to concerts, she said smugly, as if I had nothing else to do and should jump at the opportunity. Meanwhile, my aunts and uncles went on talking at the other end of the table, having decided Ruth and I had patched up our differences and were now the best of friends, with me just waiting to welcome her back into the house.

She *had* changed in appearance. Her cheeks were

rosier, her wide mouth had tiny laugh lines at the corners, and her conversation was different, in a way. She wasn't sitting there *waiting,* the way she had before.

Pretty soon Beatrice, Grandma's pretty mulatto maid, was serving coffee in the parlor. The group had narrowed down to four women, Grandma, Aunt Jenny, Ruth and me. Ruth was waiting for her fiancé, and I was waiting for Johnsy Dowse, who was coming by to walk with me through the park to the Lafayette movie theater where we would meet Thelma and all three go in and see *Les Misérables.*

It was still light in the street. The lamppost just outside the house was already lit, casting its yellow glow across the pavement and part way across the parlor carpet. We were waiting for Dale Stump, the hero of the hour: four women talking, waiting. Grandma sat cosily on the rear sofa near the hall to the dining room. This sofa was part of an awful Victorian parlor set; it had big ovals of shining rosewood at the back, carved circular arms, garish feet, and it really was uncomfortable.

Grandma, a tall patrician lady with beautiful white hair piled high on her head, leaned against the plump beige-tapestried back and spoke small sentences as easily as if the sofa was as soft as her mother's arms. "It's barely eight," or "The streets are so crowded." Don't-worry talk.

Aunt Jenny was reading one of those "bad books" she kept borrowing from her friend, Josie Callendar. From time to time she would comment "Ummm . . . ummm . . . " or occasionally, "Oh, my!"

"What's happening, Jenny?" Ruth would ask in her over-eager voice, the one that said, "Look how nice and interested I am!"

Jenny would put her off. "Never mind now," and go on with her reading. The general idea was that Ruth and I would go on talking our way into this newly discovered friendship in which young girl cousin and older girl cousin would discover common interests. We had both worked at it during dinner, but at this point in the evening, after a long two hours, we began giving out.

166

Silence was settling heavily upon the parlor, interrupted only by Aunt Jenny's occasional literary criticism. I could see Ruth growing restless under the strain of the phony conversation and the apparent lateness of Dale and I was not surprised when she began on a new gambit.

"I got your cocoa butter at the Sprague Drug Store, Jenny."

"Oh, good. Thanks, Ruth." Jenny didn't glance up from the pages she was reading.

"That Mr. Sprague's son waited on me. He's a *fairy* nice boy."

"Oh, good," said Jenny, still without glancing up.

"I said he's a *fairy* nice boy. Not *very* nice, *fairy* nice, Jenny."

Aunt Jenny glanced up now, puzzled. Grandma muttered something indistinguishable from her remarks on the weather and the time. Then she said, "Sprague has a nice drug store."

"Oh, yes," Ruth was suddenly animated, "and old Mr. Sprague has this *fairy* nice son. Such pretty blue eyes and rosy cheeks. I bet you don't know what a fairy is, do you, Jenny?"

Poor Jenny had to stop her reading now, Ruth was so loud in her questioning. In a few seconds we were all three seeing Ruth. I wasn't quite sure why, except that Smile had appeared. "You're so darned innocent you don't even know what a fairy is."

Jenny didn't answer. She stared at Ruth, her small, friendly mouth moving lightly but emitting no words.

"This is Wednesday night prayer meeting," muttered Grandma, listening to the singing coming from the church next door. "It must be about over by now." In the silence, the voices from the church choir rose loud and clear. "We shall come re-joi-cing . . . Bring-ing in the sheaves."

"I don't know why you say I'm innocent," said Jenny. She and Ruth were staring at each other. Ruth was smiling her wide, terrible, mirthless smile. Jenny looked small and scared but she was not about to back down.

"I guess I know most everything I want to know. I not only know what a fairy is, I've been a fairy. I have a picture of myself in my class book, I was showing it to Mr. Hardy night before last. I had a dress with wings and stars in my hair."

"Oh, my God!" Ruth felt better now that she'd begun to laugh. "Listen to her. She's *been* a fairy!" Between bursts of laughter, she managed to say, "Just you keep on being dumb like that and you're going to get *raped*."

Jenny's big face flushed a bright pink. She must have had a problem getting up words to express her indignation but manage it she did. "You stop talking to me like that, you hear?" Then, "What was it you said?"

Thus inspired, Ruth continued but in a softer voice, way down, in fact, giving the words a new importance as we had to strain to catch them. "Raped! That's what I said. A woman of your age, soon be having the change, and you're dumb, just a plain damned dummy!"

Jenny held her book which was still open on her lap. "Why you, you just stop talking to me like that, you hear me? That's no way to speak."

"No way to speak to your aunt," muttered Grandma from her corner. "Young ladies don't use curse words."

"But she said she's *b-b-een* a fairy!" Ruth howled with laughter.

I watched, fascinated. I felt sorry for my dear aunt. She seemed caught in a maze because she didn't know what Ruth meant, and I was imprisoned with her.

I knew something funny was going on and it had to do with old sedshual, but just what it was I couldn't have answered if you'd put a pistol to my head. Now, Thing was a wild animal that got loose from men and went for women, that much I knew, but what on earth was a fairy. I could hardly wait to ask Marian. She would know.

I thought about "young Mr. Sprague" as he was called to distinguish him from his father. A blue-eyed, blond man with rosy cheeks, a pleasing voice and beautiful hands, who spent his evenings going to dinner at the homes of wealthy women, driving thither in a long, yellow automobile that seemed to become him. He did look beautiful and, well, something like a genuine fairy might be supposed to look, if he just happened to be a man.

Ruth was still laughing, and Aunt Jenny grabbed her bad book and walked out of the room, followed by Grandma.

"She's been a fairy," Ruth repeated, looking toward me. "You heard what she said. She's been a fairy."

In her joy, she seemed to have forgotten all about Dale, her soon-to-be bridegroom. She stood up and was about to go after Jenny, follow her into the dining room and tease her some more.

I don't know what would have happened, but through the two windows a new figure could be seen appearing out of nowhere. Walking straight as an arrow, head held high, face flushed bright red, hat crooked and tie askew, came my Uncle George, drunk as Bacchus and singing at the top of his lungs! "Stand up and cheer! Stand up and cheer for old Col-um-bia!"

He reached the steps of my grandmother's house and collapsed, lying in his now familiar position, the one favored whenever he returned home drunk, on the first step, elbows on the second step, back supported by the marble steps behind him and legs sprawled out across the pavement, causing passersby to either circle him or gingerly step over him.

> For today we meet—
> The Blue and White against the Red—
> Our boys are fighting
> And we are bound to win the fray.
> We got the team,
> We got the steam!
> And this is old Columbia's day!

The college song completed in his great, bawling voice, he clapped his hands, settled back on the steps as for a long sit and called out, "Fuck everybody in this block!" and sat chuckling to himself. Ruth and I both jumped up and ran to the window to watch. We saw him moving his hands around, searching for some lost object. He finally found it, a pint bottle of whiskey newly bought from a bootlegger and nearly full, and took a good swig before putting the cork back in and placing it beside him on the step. "Dirty dogs in these houses," he commented. "Nothing but dirty dogs, whole bunch of 'em."

A well-dressed couple walked past Uncle George's feet, which were now stretched out full across the pavement.

"Glad to see you," he muttered, reaching to tip his hat which he couldn't seem to locate. "You wouldn't care to stop by and have a little drink?" The man stared back, but the woman ignored him completely

From inside the church, the choir singers' voices began echoing out into the street, the resonance strengthened by the acoustics of the alley between the stone church and my grandma's big, old brick house. Uncle George joined in the chorus. "Rock of ages . . . cleft for me . . . Let me hi-i-ide myself in thee." Then he began again. "One important thing we got to do is have a little drink!"

Meanwhile, Aunt Jenny had crept into the parlor and was standing at the window. She lifted the window up from the bottom, stuck her head through the opening and hissed angry instructions at her brother.

"You come in here this minute, George Honeycutt, you hear? Don't, I'll pour water on you from upstairs!"

Uncle George turned his head and stared in our direction, squinting as if he were having trouble seeing. "Seems like I heard a voice from somewhere," he muttered. "Some old biddies in there, afraid of what I'm going to tell." He leaned back and laughed. "I could tell a whole lot about what goes on in there. Anybody throws water on me, I'll let loose. Ain't a good piece of tail in the house. Another thing, there's people in there been in the booby hatch."

"Get him in!" Ruth was suddenly frantic. "Dale'll be coming any minute."

Jenny put her head out the window again, this time hissing louder than before. "You get in here, you drunken bum. Don't, and I'll call the police!"

Uncle George chuckled. This time he gave no sign of having heard her, but I was sure he had. "I'm a first-class newspaperman," he announced. "I know things about most people in this town. The people in that house back there, they're terrible, I can tell you that much. They get put away and they run out. Crazy as loons."

"Get him in!" Ruth was screaming. "Get him off those steps!"

"How?" Jenny stood up and stared at her. "I can't move him."

"You can if I help you. Mercy can take his feet, and I'll take his head."

Grandma appeared in the dining room doorway. "You better send over for Randall, Jenny." She spoke softly, as if nothing unusual was happening. "Send Mercy over to Riggs Alley for Elvin Randall."

"All right, Ma. But suppose he's not home?"

"One of the boys'll be home."

I got ready to run out through the backyard. This was common procedure whenever Uncle George collapsed out front. Somebody ran to the alley to get the big Negro, the only one able to manage Uncle George.

"I'll run right over," I said. I had just started through the dining room when I heard Ruth coming behind me. We ran all the way over to Riggs Alley, three blocks down, turned left through two blocks of nasty-smelling shanties until we reached the Randall place, third from the corner. Elvin was sitting in the tiny living room, playing with his dog, and when Ruth and I appeared at the door he got right up as if he knew what we wanted.

"Evening, Miss, evening."

"Elvin, could you come over and help us with my uncle?" I began. Ruth moved right in. "He's pretty bad," she said.

"Stretched out, is he?" Elvin chuckled.

"Yes, *hurry!*"

Elvin muttered something to somebody inside and came right along with us. He was six foot four and, with his long legs swinging on ahead of us, we were hard put to keep up with him, even with both of us running. I caught half glimpses of Ruth's face as I ran beside her; her teeth were pressed together, her mouth stretched wide and her long neck showed strained muscles. Altogether, she looked hardly human, more like an animal trying to get out of its cage.

Uncle George seemed asleep as we turned in from the alley. He was now fully sprawled out on the pavement, as if for the night, his head resting on the bottom step with the bottle standing upright beside him. One of his shoes had found its way miraculously to the curb, his hat was halfway to the house next door, his eyes were bloodshot, but he went on singing, this time in a softer key. "Gladly the cross-eyed bear, Gladly I'd die."

Dale Stump apparently hadn't arrived, as there was no sign of his car parked in the street. Ruth and I rushed up the steps and into the parlor where Aunt Jenny and Grandma sat waiting. The three of us stationed ourselves near the window, Ruth first, on the sofa, Aunty Jenny and I huddled together in one chair.

Even Grandma pulled her rocker up front, rocking and talking softly in that special way she had, not sadly, more philosophically, tying up loose threads and pouring oil over wounds. "It's too bad Grace had to die so early. He was happier when she was there with him. Oh, well, he'll be better tomorrow."

"He'll never be better. He's a dirty drunk." Ruth didn't even look at Grandma. "I wish he was dead!"

Meantime, the scene was going on out front. Elvin was settled down beside Uncle George, the two of them talking together like old friends. They sang "Jesus Loves Me" together, then Uncle George took a great, long swig from the bottle and handed it over to Elvin who pretended to drink from it. It went back and forth until it was empty. Uncle George's head fell further down until it was entirely on the pavement. Elvin stood up quickly, making a circle with his hands. Aunt Jenny and Ruth opened the front door while I placed the iron dog to hold it open. Before we knew it, Elvin came through carrying my uncle like a baby in his huge arms. He swept through the back hall and then through the dining room, depositing the sleeping man on an old leather couch in the kitchen.

We heard Uncle George call out once for his whiskey bottle which Elvin quickly gave him, but he was too far gone to imbibe and the only sound he was capable of emitting was the long, even snores of drunken sleep.

I'll tell you about Dale Stump as he is a key figure in the eerie events that were to happen. But it's still difficult to think of Dale as a key figure. It's difficult to think of him as a key to *any*thing in *any*body, much less the key to my complicated Cousin Ruth. He was typical of the white-collar worker of the twenties, this admirable, church-minded young man who played rather ordinary music by night while by day he worked in the personnel department of Lane & Co., the big plumbing manufacturers, looking over applicants for positions as typists, salesmen, truckers, porters, clerks, that sort of thing, examining their references and religious affiliations, length of stay in their last position, where they went to school, lived, and moved.

He arrived five, ten minutes after the coast was clear of all drunks, and hat and shoe were recovered from the street. A long-engined, slightly aging Hupmobile drove up, the door banged to and a young man walked up the steps and rang the bell.

I thought when he first entered the parlor that he was handsome. Indeed as Ruth said, "This is my Cousin Mercy, Dale," and he moved forward smiling and saying, "How do you do, Mercy?", I was rather impressed, I can tell you. I saw a tall man with an open grin, wearing a light-reddish tan suit, a white shirt with a red tie and tan shoes. And I liked his sideburns, but I have to add that this impression of a matinee idol was marred by the fact his hand was soft, cold, and damp, and that

173

he shook mine as if he were touching a dirty rag. Something or other was said. Then Ruth said, "Let's go!" And the sideburns I at first imagined were interesting growths of hair, were not sideburns at all but oblongs of pimples, half scabbed over and half still erupting; he had cleverly tried to conceal them with some repulsive brownish cream.

I remember watching this couple on the way to their car and thinking about them. There was something strange about them, as a couple, I mean. They didn't belong together, I'm not sure why. What did they have in common, besides the fact that they were both alive? Then for some reason I suddenly saw again that bathroom scene, Ruth holding that thing, and I felt scared the way I had when I was just a little kid. I also recalled my recent glimpse of those splotches Dale had covered up with that cream and I thought, Jesus, suppose they have a baby! Brother, that'd be hairy, all right. I guess I'm not too nice about this kind of thing.

I just watched the engaged couple as they sat talking. Dale said something. Then I noticed he looked at her eagerly, only she was staring straight ahead. I could almost hear what he said, some question requiring an answer, "Where'd you like to go?" something like that, and Ruth kept staring at the street. Then he must have asked her something else, possibly some question she didn't like, because I heard her answer. It sounded like "Shut up!" Dale turned quickly back to his wheel, and the noise of the car starting up filled the street.

As I sat in the parlor I heard a soft clump-clump somewhere. I quickly recognized that sound as the same damned nerve-racking clump-clump I seemed to have heard all my life, beginning at the very moment of my birth, or maybe even before, yes, definitely before. That same sound had pressed against the tiny auditory nerves in the fetus forming in my mother's womb. Tonight it was comforting, the sound of the ball against the wall in my grandmother's yard, hard, then soft, clump-clump, clump-clump.

I remembered I had a date with Johnsy, if any arrangement a person ever made with Johnsy Dowse could be dignified by such a phrase. You saw Johnsy, heard Johnsy, walked and talked with Johnsy. He was just there and sometimes he came in handy, oh yes, that much he did. Now standing up in the parlor, I could see straight through the dining room to the box of green ivy and pink geraniums on the porch and on through to the backyard, and there he was in ill-fitting long trousers throwing a ball against the back fence and catching it in his hands.

I often sort of didn't *see* him; I was aware of him, though. Practically all this time I was deep-down aware he was in the world; alive, next door, mine. People said Johnsy wasn't "bright" or they said he was "slow."

I guess maybe he was slow at school because he had a hard time passing his grades, no matter how his teachers kept pushing him, but he was always in good humor. He didn't seem to care what people said or how he looked, he didn't care. Johnsy was always a mess in his clothes, his table manners weren't any too good and his grammar was sometimes worse than Rose's.

I might as well tell you, I was aware of Johnsy as of some almost unknown, maybe even half-deformed part of myself. Say you had a hand with a finger missing. You'd hate it sometimes, you'd be sorry your hand wasn't normal or pretty like other peoples', but you'd always need it desperately and it would always be there.

Johnsy saw me through the dining room window and yelled, "Hey, Merce, you ready for the movies?"

I said "Yes, sure," as I came into the yard. He opened the back gate, and we were out like lightning.

I had a hazy feeling of guilt toward Marian Swoboda. These guilt feelings had nothing whatever to do with my parents' edict, in fact quite the contrary; and whenever I would hear the admonitions—Marian was supposed to be "dirty," to have "a bad reputation," that kind of thing—I would nod my head mechanically and promptly forget what had been said.

175

The embarrassment came over me whenever I considered the good times Thelma and I shared, in which she was not included. Thel's mamma and daddy wouldn't have dared take Thel to New York without including me, for fear of her plain refusing to go. They had tried it once and, finding Thelma adamant, they had promptly done a turnabout and invited me. Our sophomore and junior years were happily broken up with these lovely trips to New York where we would lap up the big city atmosphere together, escaping from the Hodges whenever possible, going off on buying sprees and into restaurants and theaters and talking animatedly to any number of strangers.

We bought pearl-colored skirts on Broadway, went ice skating in Central Park, saw John Barrymore on the stage, stuff like that. We sat on velvet settees in a restaurant on Madison Avenue where they served these huge cups of hot chocolate topped with inches of whipped cream, while waiting for Thel's daddy to pick us up, playing the game of thought-guessing. Thel, who was first, said, "Him."

I asked, "John?" And she nodded. I was one up.

"You?"

I said, "Same."

Thel asked, "What for?" and I admitted, "Anything!"

We discussed going backstage to see him, but Thel's parents frowned on the idea and, since we couldn't get away from them before leaving, we decided to wait till John and we were all older.

I always brought back a present for Marian and told her what had happened, as by now I prized her friendship. "I wish you could have been with us," I would say.

"Gee, so do I, Skeets. Maybe sometime we'll go ourselves."

All too soon we were all back in school from the Easter holidays, Thel and I both receiving the marks on those mid-term exams and finding out we had both failed algebra. "No real grasp of figures," Miss Talbacher wrote in her big, nasty scrawl, giving me a D. I passed English Lit with E double plus, but that ridiculous group of algebraic symbols and equations, especially that grisly "X," had thrown me. Hadn't Dr. Gardiner suggested to my parents the need for a tutor before I could ever hope to pass the finals? Nobody understood algebra that much, I knew. The knack of solving equations seemed to come most easily to those I considered the dumbest kids in the class. How do you figure that? Thinking it over, I caught my first genuine glimpse of the cruel fraud, I mean the absolute waste of all these hours of "education."

I felt sorry for Marian when I heard she received D's in all subjects except gymnasium and homemaking, in both of which she received E double plus. "You can make it all up during the summer, Marian," I said when I met her in the park.

"Gee, Skeets, don't look so sad," she giggled, putting her arm around me as we walked on. "I don't care what grades I get. All except what I'm using. Exercise and cooking and sewing."

I stared at her in amazement as I saw she honestly didn't care. At fifteen she was actually *living,* doing what she wanted without having to think about it. It was often like this with Marian and me. I mean, I would start out feeling pity for her, feeling I should uplift her; help her out. Then I'd take a good look and see that she was already uplifted. What I saw was raw, dirty, bleeding, laughing life, and beside all this I felt inferior but, well, strangely invigorated.

"What do you want to do, Marian? What is it you want?" I'd ask stupidly.

"I wanna be somebody's girl, a' course. I can make good money in a factory or being a maid or a cook like Aunt Alicia."

"A *factory?*"

"Sure. Whatsa matter with a nice clean factory? I won't stay long nowheres 'cause I'll be married. Come on home and see the dress I made. I'm going to a dance tonight with Boonie. Tried it on with him last night and he went nuts. If you like it I can run up one for you."

She was in the house again. Ruth! Smile! I spoke of her as She or Her. She was waiting in the parlor for her fiancé. *Her* footsteps were banging overhead. *She* had the room above mine so I could hear her come in and go out because, with Virginia Anne away at college, Smile had been given her room, against Virginia Anne's will, of course, as Virginia Anne's room was supposed to be kept untouched for her Christmas and Easter vacations when Ruth would go back to Grandma's.

Now that she was overhead she wasn't so soft and sneaky as she'd been before. She came in and went out, banging doors and dropping shoes as if to say, "You, underneath there, you refused to let me share your room, so take this and that and now this," as first one heavy object then another would bang down on the bare hard wood, the part of the floor where the rug stopped, often waking me out of a sound sleep.

I was just beginning to get on to this thing about people, about how wild and furious some of them are. Now, this knowledge was pretty new to me. You could say it was just beginning to bud. Girls get on to this stuff real early in their adolescence, sometimes even in their childhood, and mostly it bothers them. Boys don't seem to care. They just accept it or they hit back and laugh. Women creep around and get you from under. But don't get me wrong. I wouldn't want to be a boy. Hell, no! I'd have to be too damned strong, for one thing. And for another, I'd have to marry a woman!

I knew, for instance, something was driving Smile. Something had hold of her, I knew that for sure, and what's more I knew this force, or whatever the hell it was, was *directed at me*.

It's hard to figure out, but now take any private circle of nice, average people, well, one out of every five is likely to be a spook. In my own group of relatives, first there was Smile, a genuine, bonafide Halloween spook, nobody'd deny that. Then there was Honey's father, my

178

paternal Great Uncle Tom, a Biblical spook, all right, but a spook just the same. I was beginning to wonder about some others, especially Dale Stump. Was he or wasn't he? You can wonder like this about most spooks, are they or aren't they, because how do you know till you see them in action?

Mamma was at the piano either at home with the parlor doors closed tight or at her music teacher's studio getting ready for a concert, or else she was on the telephone planning her social life. Daddy was busy "seeing people on business."

They did not know me at all; this shadow growing up in the house, wrapped up in strange worlds they neither recognized nor admired. They didn't like my sister too much, either, come to think of it, but she was a more "normal" child, in their sense. She was more obviously manipulated, whereas I had secret documents, diaries and such, kept hidden in strange places, not readily available upon sight on those occasions when Mamma rummaged through bureau drawers.

What would Mamma have done had she found one of my most secret notebooks, containing most interesting and complete sketches about her and Daddy? I would listen for them to come upstairs to their front bedroom of a night, that beautiful forbidden land of canopied bed and soft, faded green satin chaise longue, of marble bureau tops with Mamma's engraved silver brush and comb set, her bottles of perfume on a tray, her jewelry case with the ruby red ring and the sparkling earrings and necklaces, cameos and brooches, and their clothes, his and hers, in separate wardrobes, in chests of drawers with fancy brass knobs and marble tops.

Mamma would come up first and Daddy would follow ten or twenty minutes later. Often as not the door would be left open, and if awake, I would creep down the hall and listen to them. Listen is actually too mild a word to describe this most purposeful act.

My actual spying expeditions were quite different from ordinary everyday eavesdroppings. I began them at the age of seven or eight, when I would be awakened between the hours of midnight and one o'clock by the sound of my mother and father, quarreling about something or other. I'd know that immediately as I'd had learned to recognize the pattern.

Daddy had a dexterous, adroit way of pushing whatever he wanted toward Mamma. He pushed hard and firm in short, terse sentences. Mamma retreated, answering at a slower rate, but sometimes reemerging with more verbal self-possession, though her platform was never quite solid. He'd come at her again even more terse and slightly louder than before, and, at length, sometimes after a long pause in which he'd bark his demand for a reply, once again she'd retreat as she went off into the old conciliatory refrain. I knew when they were wrangling about money, I could tell that from the very rhythm of the voices. I knew this quarrel by heart. My father wanted to save all the money he possibly could for his business at the expense of his home. His sole exception to the rule of frugality was in restaurants and show-off parties, saving face with other people who often had more; my mother, however, liked to spend.

He had a righteous seriousness about his dollars, whereas she had an almost sportive, frolicsome way with them that I found adorable. You could, at least, touch and feel Mary Jane patent leather pumps, lovely white silk socks, gold heart-shaped lockets and chains, organdy dresses with blue satin sashes, and you could smell and taste chocolate ice cream sodas and that expensive pound cake she loved to buy.

She ought to say something hard and snappy to him, I decided, but I knew she wouldn't and decided it wasn't interesting enough to chance a walk down the hall in which a loose board had to be straddled in order to reach the stairway and lean over the banister. Once your foot happened on this particular loose plank, it creaked and groaned like a struck animal, making a long, harsh, grating sound before it settled back into place. Often as not, venturing out on a spy hunt, walking barefooted and close up to the wall, I would hit it by mistake, and Mamma would call from downstairs, "That you, Mercy?"

I had the answer ready, delivered in a voice loud but bored, "I'm going to the bathroom." Sometimes I wondered how they always knew it was I and not Virginia Anne who walked the halls by night, and then I would remember how often I had heard them say my sister was a more normal child, "so different from that one."

The pattern was that they'd start downstairs going on about their families. Daddy would say, "My great-great grandfather's grandfather came over heah in sixteen hundred and twelve. They settled in Gawgia . . ."

Mamma would listen politely, then take up for her side of the family tree which was not too interesting. She dwelled on who married who. "Helen Louisa Haymarket married a Merriman . . ."

Daddy would wait his turn and go into how his ancestors "came ovah heah on a grant from King Charles." We believed that, all right; he liked grants or anything free, but the sound of the name King Charles was a signal for all doors to close, as we knew it was going to be boring from then on.

Sometimes there were special frantic quarrels, and most of them ended badly, which is to say there was no end. Usually Daddy ran out of the house, slamming all doors behind him and, often as not, staying out until supper the following night, sometimes longer. Once he had gone off on a hunting trip for ten whole days without letting Mamma know where he was. I must say he returned home jovial and exuberant, with a carful of dead birds and animals in bags. It's funny how hunting trips kept menfolk cheerful.

But after these special quarrels, the house was tense, life lived in it uneasy, Mamma moody and remote. I remember hearing one where I decided the floodgates must have burst. No use to try and sleep. Besides, who wanted to?

It got started downstairs.

After some ten minutes walking faster and faster,

Daddy ran up the stairs and burst into the bedroom. Actually what he did was to run up the stairs loud and fast, two at a time, open the door and bang it so hard it fell open again. Loud voices could now be heard and the words understood, at least in part.

I heard Mamma say, "Don't you dare!"

"Don't tell me what to do," Daddy replied loudly. What was it he wanted to do? I got out of bed and, in fact, was just opening my own door, the better to make out what they were saying, when they shut theirs. I could still hear the voices, but now the words were muffled. A real humdinger, it went on and on, with intermittent silences. You'd conclude they were just about giving out when, bang, it'd start all over again. Toward the end, I mean toward the climax, the door opened, and this time I heard them very clearly. They were trying to keep their voices down, but the tense words banged out into the hall like gunshots, ricocheting into my eager ears.

"If you touch me that way again, I'll go right home and tell Pa!" Mamma cried. She was cornered, or that was how she sounded, and desperate.

"You'll do no such thing."

There were other frantic phrases, coming out stunted and staccato, in the desperate efforts to keep from being heard.

I wish I could, but I can't remember them. This was a long one, with no smooth spots, no openings for reconciliation. They must have reached vast inner resources, hit old wounds which once opened, bled on. Questions filled my mind.

What would I do if they separated and I lost my home? Suppose I lost Rose, the kitchen, my precious bedroom? Suppose they both ran away, he to hunt, she to do whatever it was she wanted to, become a concert pianist, go to New York, that kind of thing? I was just deciding if some new terrible crisis was afoot I'd better know it and confide it to Virginia Anne, when the entire matter was taken from my hands as their door banged open. Daddy dashed down the stairs, through the hall and out into the street. I stuck my head out now with ease, listened, and in the silence I could hear his footsteps clattering on the pavement outside.

I opened the door to my sister's bedroom, thinking that if she were awake by any chance I would tell her what I had just heard. She wasn't awake, of course. Noise, even troubled, personal noise, screaming right under her window, increased the depth of her sleep, so the portentous quarrel I'd just heard, going on first beneath her and then a few yards down the hall, was probably like some lullaby.

I kept wondering what on earth Daddy wanted that roused Mamma to such heights that she threatened to leave. She meant it, too, and occasionally did it, went "down home" to "tell Pa," when my grandfather was alive. The particular fight above occurred when Grandpa was still alive and available for serious matters. Mamma, often remote and chill-of-hand; she was pretty, well-behaved. What caused her to change into a fierce and angry woman? And he, my Daddy, in those long nights out, where did he go? Once his footsteps stopped sounding in our block, down what street did he turn, what house did he enter?

Years later, in high school and after the death of my grandfather, who was my mother's eternal defender, I broached the subject to Marian Swoboda. We were sitting in the soft darkness of the Swoboda kitchen, with only an oil lamp to light the great, thirty-foot square room, to which the roof of the porch closed off even the pale gray light from the rainy day outside. Marian was safe to talk to. Even if she wanted to betray me—which she didn't—she was as ostracized from school society as a leper. My mind was now a confused mass of questions supported by small facts, softened by the dark, and my appetite appeased by something Marian called *peerogeet,* actually noodles stuffed with cheese and raisins. I spoke up.

"They fight so long," I began, carefully suppressing the fact that I listened, fascinated.

"Yeah, sure, alla married couples fight like cats and

dogs," said Marian. "My pop can't fight no more 'cause he's dead. Dropped off the side of a building and cracked his skull. Stopped him cold."

I finally got to the big question after describing the nature of the most recent quarrels. "What do you think he wants?" "Gee, I don't know, hon. Maybe he wants th' old girl to take off her clothes."

"What!"

"Lotsa people don't want to take off their clothes. Women don't. Even if they do take off their regular clothes, they won't take off their nightgown. Or let nobody pull it up or nothing. Expect a man to crawl in from under the bed."

"That doesn't seem like what he wants."

She thought that over. "Maybe he wants to stick it in, is all." This made more sense. "Women are funny, Skeets. There's times they'll let 'em do it, and times they won't. They just won't."

"Well, where do you think Daddy goes, when he takes off?"

"To a hoor house, a' course. Your old man's got the money. They get two, three dollars, them hoors." She ate some more. "They're dirty dogs, but they give it to the men, all right."

"Well, what do you think'll happen?"

"Nothing. He'll just get a hoor an' come home."

I had been told that men who went with whores got something like the bubonic plague, at least they turned black and were never the same again, and now I voiced my fears.

"Naw, not if they wash first with soap," said Marian, the wise. "Ya just take ya hoor and wash her down good with yellow soap. Plenty times my mom wouldn't do nothing with my pop an' he went to a hoor. Always took along a bar of kitchen soap t'wash her off."

I am in my senior year at high school. Virginia Anne, two years older, is home from her first year at college, majoring in art history. We are both sitting in the dining room. It is after midnight. We are well-dressed in our

184

"good" dresses, hers is black crepe de Chine, mine is blue velvet with puffed sleeves. We have been driven home by my Uncle George from a party given by the estimable and socially prominent Mrs. Harriman Teague, a huge pigeon-breasted woman with a wide, fixed smile who had helped to endow the Partridge Conservatory of Music.

The party was to celebrate the doings of the conservatory president, Howard Farraday. He was a bachelor of indeterminate years, a tall, thin, loosely-constructed man; his long arms and legs and narrowed head had to have wires at their sockets, just perfect for bowing and strutting. I remember him saying, "Ah, yes, Helen dear," and, "You're right there, dear," to Mrs. Harriman Teague.

They were intimate, Farraday and Teague, in some totally asexual way, even I could see that. In fact, when they ate from the plentiful buffet, caviar and orange-colored mousses, fowl and meat, vegetables so fluted and dressed up you could hardly recognize them, they ate together. What I mean is, he waited for her to taste something and comment on it, and then she did the same for him. There was something funny about it. It was sort of like two people feeling each other, looking for the right spots.

"Those are her girls," I heard old Farraday say, about Sister and me. This Mrs. Harriman Teague stared at us, gave the required smile and went right back to her asparagus. We were there on sufferance, I knew that much. My mother was invited, of course, with several of the other pianists and singers. She hadn't planned to bring us along, but Uncle George had failed to show up in time to collect us so we tagged along with the crowd.

"Go along with him, Mercy," Mamma said to Virginia Anne the moment she saw my uncle. Sister stared at her and so did Uncle George, whom she barely greeted. "You, too, go on now, Virginia Anne." She pushed me, not hard, but in a quick, dismissing manner.

"Congratulations, Susie May," poor Uncle George

whispered. He had whiskey on his breath, but he was not drunk.

"Tomorrow," my mother said and disappeared in the crowd.

Now back to the dining room where Virginia Anne and I are smoking Melachrino Number 9 cigarettes and drinking coffee. "She looked pretty when she was playing that Bach thing," I say.

"What . . . ?"

"Mamma looks great with her hair up."

"Uh-huh."

"They really did applaud her. She came back three times."

"Uh-huh. That was because she had a claque."

"What. . .?"

"A claque. She has Bertie Hildebrandt and her sisters and that group of women back there clapping for her like their hands couldn't stop." Sister thought further. "She had too much rouge on her lips. She's drinking champagne, did you notice that? By now she must have put away a lot."

"You're pretty mad at her, aren't you?"

"Certainly not."

"It's because she forgot your name and called you Mercy."

"She does that all the time. She called you Virginia Anne."

"She doesn't really see us." I found myself defending her. "She didn't really know what she was doing. She's having a career." It seems funny telling about it the way it was. Writing it down. Of her two girls, Mamma generally preferred my sister. Virginia Anne was on to her, whereas I loved her madly. I had just learned to smoke, I detested it but kept at it continually. I said, "I think she's pretty plucky, going right ahead with her career, and Daddy off on one of his sulks!"

Virginia Anne started unbuttoning her dress, it must have had fifty buttons and buttonholes. "She made us leave before we got anything to eat," she announced.

186

"Remember what Aunt Margaret told us she said when they came back from Paris after their wedding trip?"

I knew but I wanted to hear it again, just to make sure I'd heard it right the first twenty times. "What was it? I've forgotten."

"She said, 'I've made a *fatal* mistake.' Not just a mistake, something that might get corrected, but a fatal mistake. Do you know what that means, fatal?"

"Sure, lethal. Deadly. Like taking poison."

"Right. Well, she made this fatal mistake, as she said, and then she went right on having children."

"But she couldn't help that."

"She could, too. She could have made him wear a rubber."

The front door was just opening, and Ruth came in. She had been to the concert with her fiancé and wanted to talk about it, but my sister closed up like a clam.

It was a mean, bleak day. One of those long white days when the sky stays folded over dirty white snow and the whole mess of street and sky is about as inviting as a dish of cold oatmeal. The house was empty and silent when I came down for breakfast.

By this time Ruth had been removed by fate; yes, that was how I thought of her marriage to Dale Stump. After standing in the church, then attending the reception, then having to wait till the newlyweds went off, all I could think of was, she's going, she'll soon be gone, she's gone! I can go home, and she won't be in the house!

Rose was standing in the dining room, wearing a freshly-ironed pink silk dress, one of Mamma's from year before last, and wiping the cut glass on the buffet with a soft rag.

"Anybody call?" I asked, but I knew the answer.

"Nobody."

"I thought I heard the phone."

"Didn't nobody ring here. What you wanna eat?"

There had been no invitation to the big Burton party so far in the mail, and all week long, as invitations flooded the school, sticking out of algebra and history books, desks and book bags, and it seemed the entire school had been invited, I began to feel left out and depressed.

I didn't care really, I kept telling myself. It wasn't warm enough for the garden party they had planned for the celebration of Edythe's sixteenth birthday. The party would be a flop if they used the garden. Why, there could even be a snowstorm. It was April, after all. A nice big hailstorm with great pellets of ice banging against the guests' umbrellas, that'd be great! They had that big two-acred country house in the city up on Calhoun. I hated that place now, especially the gardens and lawns, as they floated into my mind, and if, say, hailstones big as lemons would hit the arriving guests, bang, smack on their heads and break the whole damned canopy to pieces, that would be fine. I was so sick of hearing about that pink and white canopy.

The beautiful flannel cakes Rose had put before me felt heavy and thick against my tongue. Then hope fluttered suddenly and I ran out into the hall. Invitations slipped under the door at the last minute sometimes found their way into the hall tray. In a second I knew there was none. The tray contained nothing but a bill from Eisenberg's Coal and Feed store. Along with this unpleasant sight I saw the vestibule filling up with the figure of my Cousin Ruth, now Mrs. Dale Stump.

She followed close behind me as I went on back to breakfast.

"Did Aunt Susie leave a package for me?" she demanded of Rose.

"Yes, she did." Rose handed her a small box from Hultzer Brothers, wrapped in white paper and tied with a red cord. I'd barely spoken to her; she seemed in a hurry, which was fine with me, but I noticed she was stopping by the dining room table to show off her new black silk suit, I supposed, and to open the present right in front of my eyes.

"Rouge," she said. She held up a small gold box from which she extracted a puff and applied it to first one

188

cheek and then the other, as she looked at herself in the mirror of the box. "Like it, Mercy?"

"Ummhmm. Very nice."

Then she said something else. "It's a present. Aunt Susie gave it to me for the party tonight."

I wanted to ask her, no, it couldn't be, *it couldn't be!* She didn't even know the Burtons, or did she? Oh, yes, I wanted to ask her but I couldn't set up the words. There she was wrapping the present my mother had given her, and then she stood staring at me. I could never tell about Ruth's eyes, because her mouth stared. I swear she *saw* with her teeth.

"Doctor and Mrs. Burton understand Dale's talent. They always have us at their musicales."

Was it true? Had she even said it? Remembering how she used to go up to strangers in the street and end up friends with them, I began to think, with whatever was left of my mind, she just might have gone up to Edythe's mother, or telephoned her, or in some way got herself invited, most likely by offering Dale.

"The dancing won't start until late, I guess; nine or ten, after supper. Dale's Charleston is pretty bad, but there'll be plenty of other good dancers, don't you think?"

She was telling the truth. I winced at those words about Dale. The poor man just didn't have rhythm, he moved heavily on his feet. So she *was* going, Ruth, Smile, the married woman. It didn't matter, I told myself quickly. *A hundred other people are going, maybe two hundred, three hundred. Countless people, dressed and smiling and happy.*

"I guess I won't see *you*—after that trouble at school."

She was playing with the string around her present when I heard a voice say, "Oh, I don't know. Maybe you'll see me!"

In a flash she was gone. There was Rose wiping off the telephone table. I remembered Thelma persuading me to buy the pale gray chiffon dress with the white collar, using up half my savings, now hanging upstairs

189

in my wardrobe. How she had said, "But of course you're invited, Mercy." When I confessed I hadn't received an invitation, she added, "They can't send invitations to everybody. Those things cost *money*—printing and mailing and all."

"You got one, didn't you?"

"Well, yes, I got one, but lots of girls didn't. Edythe just told them and they're going. You're invited, I tell you. Everybody's invited!"

The day was crowding in on me, as they say in those books people used to write, the kind I was reading. Actually, it's not the day, the interval between sunrise and sunset, that crowds a person. I was being crowded, pushed into a corner by people, important people, over whom I had no control. My mother, off somewhere for the day, had given Ruth a present to help her look pretty at Edythe Burton's party.

"She—she likes Ruth."

I must have said it out loud without thinking. Rose chuckled to herself. She wasn't going to talk to me, I could tell from the way she went on with her work, but I had to have somebody to talk to, even if she didn't talk back.

"She—she brought her here to be a companion to us. That's really a joke, Ruth a companion! But she wanted her companionship. Sometimes she can't remember our names but she remembers old Mrs. Smile!"

These bitter words hit only flab in my big, soft Aunt Rose. She gave no sign of hearing, not even the familiar Southern throat sound, *Ummhmm*. What I was trying to tell her, and anybody else in the world who'd listen, was that my mother, my very own mother, the soft-spoken one whom everybody else thought was so sweet, so "artistic," so interesting, was collaborating with Ruth and with any other enemy who happened to come along in my undoing. All this framed itself into a question demanding an answer. "What kind of woman is she really? I'd like to know. How could she?"

Rose stopped dusting. She wasn't turning around even, but she was getting ready to speak.

"Well?" I demanded.

"They's people that're assent-minded."

Absent-minded, oh sure, attracted here and there, to Ruth, to her piano teacher, to those sheets of music. But where was she going? I often wondered. What was she looking at? Waiting for? Waiting, that was it. Oh, that's what Mamma and Smile had in common. They were both waiting.

Rose has gone out of the room, back into the kitchen. I'm alone again, all I have for comfort is sounds, old sounds from Riggs' Alley back there. Blind Albert, that gray-haired minister, is leading the hymn singing, "Rescue th' per-ish-ing, Care for the dy-i-ing. Jes-us is merci-ful, Jes-us will sa-a-ve!" It stopped suddenly and then the prayer began. Jesus again, no doubt. I couldn't hear the words any more. What I heard instead was the heavy familiar *clump-thud* of that damned ball. Johnsy out there in the yard next door, hitting that damned ball against the wall under the shed. *Clump-thud . . . clump-thud.* These sounds began slowly, almost imperceptibly, to change until you sensed how the hard ball hit the damp brick house with increased speed and impact, harder and harder, faster and faster.

Rose was moving about in her bedroom off the kitchen, opening drawers, all those going-for-the-day-off sounds, and I was sitting there waiting for the telephone to ring. I must have hollered something. I don't remember. Next thing I know Rose was standing there buttoning up her black cotton dress with the white piqué collar.

"Whyn't you let that poor boy play, Mercy? He works hard enough for ten boys."

"I don't care what he does."

She sighed, a critical sigh. "They's heaps of ways going to parties without them invite notes."

"Well, mention one."

"You just comes along in with other peoples is one way."

"What other people?"

"Peoples been invited."

191

"Just how do you do that?"

"You gets es-corted is how."

"How?"

"Anybody knows about es-corted. I been es-corted to lots o' gatherings of that kind."

"Well, who'll escort me to this one?"

"They's plenty peoples going."

"Oh, sure. That doesn't include me. I'm not invited."

"Your escort is invited and he es-corts you. You cheer on up now, you hear?"

I must have stayed there doing nothing all the time Rose dressed, I must have been half-alive, because I was surprised when I saw Johnsy there in the dining room. I've told you how something inside me went up and down both at the same time whenever I saw him. He was always dirty and disappointing, and I always needed him. You have all known such people, usually intimately and ultimately much more than you want to admit.

The blacks were the intimates and the ultimates of the whites then, intimate because you could do anything in front of them, and they couldn't fight back, ultimate because there ended the whole process of deception, there fell out all your grimy insides, the end of all withholding. *Ultima thule.*

Johnsy was standing on the other side of the table in the tight, dirty trousers which always made his behind stick out too far, and the checkered coat his mother gave him the year before. He had thick, reddish hair, too heavy for even *his* big head. It fell in waves and ringlets over his forehead and ears and down the back of his neck like an overgrown vine. He had thick lips, reminiscent more of a black than a white boy, and they were always smiling a foolish smile, breaking over protruding but quite perfect white teeth. He had big, hazel eyes, with brown flecks; sometimes they looked blue, draped with long, black, silky lashes. He was rather short and skinny, but his backside was fat, slightly out of proportion.

"He musta had a father," Thelma allowed. "Most people do."

But no one had ever heard of his father. His small friendly, Scotch-Irish mother had never been heard to mention him, she didn't even bother to make up a story, but someone, at some time, must have left her the house which she and Johnsy, together with a parcel of roomers, two telephone operators, an aging traveling salesman and his wife, managed to keep up, Mrs. Dowse by hiring out as a housekeeper, and Johnsy by doing anything he was asked to do for whatever he could get.

"The thing about that poor boy is," this from Roberta Thomas, Judge Thomas's daughter and a nasty snob, "he doesn't seem to *know* he's poor or dumb." She cleared her throat whenever she made these pronouncements. "Whenever you see him scrubbing people's marble bases, looking filthy and wet, he smiles and speaks to you as if he was your equal. That's because he's too dumb to know what he's doing. He just doesn't see."

I heard myself say, "But he's so much prettier than you are." The words came rising out of me, and Roberta's face turned pink. She hated me, anyway, so it didn't much matter.

"What! What did you say?"

"I said he's so much prettier than you are. What I meant to say was he's so much more beautiful than you are."

"What do you mean by that?"

"I mean he has beauty, and you haven't. He doesn't know or care what you think. He's beyond you." I could say these things when some button was pressed and not be able to stop.

"Don't you dare compare me to that backward child!" Roberta spoke in a low, angry voice.

I shrugged. All this was true about Johnsy. He had some animal secret. I swear to God he did, some deep-down contact, maybe with the earth, I don't know, that made him contented. Maybe, I sometimes wondered, maybe it was from doing the very work Roberta so despised.

Anyway, the day of the Burton party, seeing him standing there in the dining room, dirty and damp, with his face sweating, dragging muddy feet across the floor, I, well, I didn't feel quite the way I did that day with Roberta. Whenever I saw Johnsy or heard him about, like I said, something came up and went down in me, always both at the same time. Love, or need, and sorrow, disappointment, hope and need again, something like that.

"Whatsa matter, Merce?"

I didn't answer.

"Guess you're mad about something, huh?"

Rose appeared, dressed and carrying her old black pocketbook. "I'm going out now. You quit worrying about that ole party and do like I said." I didn't answer but smiled my good-bye. "Johnsy, you take care of her now, you hear?"

"Yes'm."

Johnsy never knew what to say. You didn't dare tell him anything or he'd blurt it out to precisely the wrong person. He trusted everybody. He came at things head on and, often as not, he scratched himself.

"You're mad 'cause you ain't been invited to the party, huh?"

"Haven't been invited."

"Yeah. Haven't. That's why you're mad, huh? Aw, gee, Merce."

Silence.

"If you hadna tole that story they'da invited you."

Silence. At least he called it a "story."

"That was ages ago. It's ancient history."

"Yeah, sure. Anyway, it didn't mean nothing."

"Anything."

"Yeah. Anything."

Silence.

"I gotta deliver flowers up there to the Burtons. Listen, they'll ask me to stay and dance."

"Maybe they won't."

"Sure they will. I can dance like a bassard."

"Bastard."

"Yeah, bassard. I'll take you, and you can stay, too."
Silence.

I didn't want to go anywhere with Johnsy Dowse except to walk somewhere or sit in a swing in my own backyard. Yet three hours later there I was sitting opposite him in the park, big as life, playing a sad, heavy game of five hundred. Not talking. There was nothing to say. I was playing in a desperate mood as if my very life depended on it. Johnsy followed suit trying to placate me. People came walking by in the lane near where we were sitting, our cards spread out on the concrete bench, a fancy affair with lions' heads for legs and a flat surface, but without a back. We heard voices, footsteps, children running and screaming, then silence and more voices and people coming closer and going away. At some point in the game I became aware of footsteps that seemed to stop suddenly. I kept on playing, waiting for them to move on, but they didn't move. They had stopped. I was just getting ready to play a king and was staring down at it. The cardboard eyes looked out, remote and impersonal. I stared back at them with what might have passed for intense interest, but, actually, I hardly saw the king. I was on the qui vive, sensing something was about to happen.

Johnsy was busy studying his cards, too, when suddenly I felt it, someone standing there observing us. A man's legs. Johnsy played his jack. I looked down at my cards and quickly played my ten of clubs—I'd been ready to play it for some time—and as I did, I turned my head backwards, showing off my long hair, and incidentally, looking sidewise. I knew it for sure in the first glance.

It was he, Stephen, standing there watching us and smiling happily. Damn Johnsy, I thought, damn him to hell. Why'd he have to be hanging around at a time like this?

While I was waiting for Johnsy to play his card—he was always slow beyond belief—I couldn't resist looking up. This time my look came on up straight to his face, to his eyes. I remember I had a funny feeling of falling—

as if I were going to go right through his eyes. I don't know how long this continued. It was kind of the style, this looking business. A lot of that stuff went on in the movies, and all of us school kids knew about it from the experts of the screen, people who looked and kissed those long "soul kisses," enough to give them thousands of children. And now here I was doing it, too, and this Stephen Farrar, this god from the stone house on the corner; *he was doing it back*. Only, he was smiling, which isn't exactly in the game. Anyway, we were just getting into it good when bang, right in the very midst of it Johnsy spoke up. "Hey, what you looking at, Mercy?"

Thus interrupted, Stephen came quickly across the grass. I could have choked Johnsy, particularly as, having spied Stephen, he went on, "You better watch out. You're taking all the looks off him."

"More likely I'm taking all the looks off her," said Stephen. We all said hello. "Go on with the game now, you two, I'll just sit here and watch, if you don't mind." I was glad I had on my good camel's hair skirt and the new silk stockings that cost one ninety-five.

He settled on the grass, sitting on his haunches, his arms around his knees, his face up near the bench where he could watch the cards we played. Oh God, what will Johnsy do next to spoil things?, I kept thinking. Johnsy knew everything about me from the day I was born, not only the bad things I had done as a child and older, but all the mean dirty thoughts I had, the lies I told and the people I hated. I spoke out loud to him as if I was talking to myself.

What terrible recent encounter would he seize on to blab? How I followed my father on one of those night walks of his, trying to find out whether he went in the direction of the red-light district? I'd told him all about that damned walk, including how hard it was to follow Daddy because he kept turning around at the corners, searching the blocks behind him to see if anyone was watching, and how I had solved this problem by running faster than he could walk and hiding behind trees and steps.

Stephen was watching us, not saying anything much till we finished our game, but all the time I could tell he saw everything, how slow Johnsy was, for instance. We would talk while waiting for Johnsy to decide which card to play. "I had a date for *thé dansant* at Rennert's Hotel," he said, "but the girl can't make it. Why don't you two come along instead?" I couldn't help seeing something else. We both pleased him, he liked us, me first, of course, and Johnsy second. He seemed so happy, as if he had discovered something by running into us. "Come on, Johnsy," he almost pleaded, as we finished the game. "We'll eat, drink and be merry!"

"Aw, I can't do nothing like that. I gotta work at Ziegler's candy store Sundays."

"You come along. I'll explain to old Mamma Ziegler I need you for something.

I said, "Let's go, Johnsy," but Johnsy never could pick up a new vibration, get on to any idea. Besides, he seemed to have no special interest in Stephen Farrar, who was by all odds the most exciting man in our street. He just didn't know obvious things like that.

"Aw, she won't believe you," he said.

"She will if I give her an order."

"What'd you give her an order for?" he asked stupidly.

"I'll buy a ten pound box of chocolates."

"That'd cost twelve dollars, if you get it wrapped up." Oh, my God! He was being so dumb, holding up the party. "What would you do with all that candy?"

"What? Oh, I'll take it to the Burton's, that's what I'll do with it. Come along now. Mrs. Ziegler doesn't get those nice greenbacks every Sunday, and you know she eats them with cream and sugar."

For reasons unknown to me, Johnsy, always a diehard about his work, afraid of being fired, actually laughed at Stephen's joke. I knew he had finally succumbed to the idea of going along.

I could tell Stephen Farrar knew what he was doing.

197

He had great spontaneity and humor and imagination; it showed in the first ten minutes. He picked us up out of our humdrum lives, my humdrum life, I mean—Johnsy didn't know about things like that—and carried us along in his own special chariot. Suddenly, fast. I was the attraction, the magnet, I knew that, and Johnsy, awkward and bungling, dirty and illiterate, was generously included, I thought, for the sake of propriety.

It was all done so casually, yet fondly, even affectionately, the older man with superior advantages, drawn to the younger twosome, raw material of the future, that kind of thing. Like I say, he knew what he was doing, he wasn't falling through space. And there began the early grace notes of the first great symphony, foreshadowing the exuberant fun and the whisperings of some darker, more *fateful* side. We'll get to that.

On our way to the *thé dansant* at the hotel we had to pass the promenade near Grace Church where everybody walks on Sunday. Groups of people filled the sidewalks, coming from the church or the park or the museum down the street. I saw faces I knew. Roberta Thomas with her father, the judge, and there was Edythe Burton hurrying toward us with her mother. We were almost abreast of them when my beaver hat blew off and stuck in the wheel of a car parked near the curb. Stephen ran for it and was just putting it back on my head as the Burtons stopped to speak to him and were forced to acknowledge Johnsy and me. "So nice to see you, Stephen. And you, Mercy, and that's Johnsy, isn't it?"

"Yes, ma'am. I'll be bringing you your flowers."

"Of course. You must come and stay awhile."

The Thomases stopped, too, when they saw Stephen. Then they all walked on, and we went in the opposite direction. I knew they would all be going to the Burton party, but for some reason it didn't matter. I didn't even wish that a storm would come with the canopy blowing down and the hailstones banging the guests on the head. It just didn't matter anymore.

It was real nice and hushed, walking into the dining

198

room at the Rennert Hotel, like walking into a velvet tunnel. A small sign supported on a stand informed in gold letters the *thé dansant* was on. We arrived just as the band finished the last rhythms of "Yes Sir, That's My Baby." The players were wiping their foreheads, the dancers were just leaving the small rotunda set apart from the tables, looking back at the players to see if there was going to be another sound, just as the headwaiter showed us to our table. I like this luxurious type of hotel dining room, especially when it's all set up for a *thé dansant*.

After the wild jazz stopped and it was quiet as a church, well, then came the soothing personality of the place, so comfortable and pleasant, with deep, purple carpets your feet could sink into, satin draperies so long you couldn't tell where they began or ended; the chandeliers with tiny lights like candles. I liked the little pink-shaded lamps at the tables, too, because they had real candles burning in them. I always like it when you come in—the sounds, the tinkle of china and crystal, and I like to hear those covers the waiters put on trays being lifted, and the ice tinkling in the glasses and the hum of voices. You feel that in a place like this, something could happen.

Stephen sat in the center chair facing the door, with Johnsy and me on either side of him. He looked taller sitting down. Maybe it was the way we were sitting. Johnsy was slumped down, but I straightened up to be nearer Stephen's height, I guess. A waiter appeared at our table and gave us three menus.

"I want a tall glass, ice and soda," said Stephen, "right away."

The waiter, who seemed to know him, gave the prohibition nod and said, "Yes, Mr. Farrar. Now how about the tea menu?"

"Oh, yes. Have the full tea, Mercy, it has marvellous things with it. And you, Johnsy? What looks good to you?"

Johnsy kept staring down at the menu as if he'd never

seen one before. The waiter came to his rescue, but he kept staring with that glazed look of his.

"Maybe you'd like something more substantial, young man," said the waiter. "Here, on this side."

Johnsy followed the waiter's finger, and slowly his expression changed. "There, I'll have them." He pointed to something.

"You want the fried potatoes?"

"Ummhmm."

"A whole order of French fried potatoes? Nothing else with it?"

"Uh-uh."

The pink lips smiled as the waiter wrote out the order, and Stephen told him, "Bring him the tea, too, Peters." Johnsy's stained jacket and soiled yellow sweater stood out in its muted elegance; even in the candlelight you could see there was something funny about the boy in the seat over there. But he didn't seem to know or care. In fact he began taking over, talking a blue streak.

He began on Stephen. "You gonna drink hard liquor?"

"Yessir. You don't mind, do you?"

"Naw, I don't mind. What kind, whiskey?"

"Bourbon. Ever taste it?"

"Sure. Often. I often tasted bourbon."

"When, for instance?"

"Aw, holidays. Everybody has mince pies and sweet potatoes pies. And when you're sick sometimes. With a cold or something. And in punches."

"You, Mercy. You're a toper, too?"

"I've had highballs and champagne. I love champagne. And sherry and port and cordials."

"Me, too. I had cordials an' highballs."

"Well! I see I'm in good hands. Out with a couple of hard drinkers."

It was nice being there and all of us talking like that. The waiter, this Peters, came in with Stephen's "mix." Stephen reached into his hip pocket and came up with a silver flask, slightly curved, the kind my Daddy carried around, poured a good shot into his glass and stirred it. He asked us would we like a highball, but we said no, and he began to lift his glass in a toast to us both.

I was getting a bang out of all this; then I noticed a handsome young man come in and stand near the door right in front of Stephen. I saw him first in the big mirror and caught him watching us. There was something in that mirror image that caught my eye, right away. He had on a tie, a bow tie, with these bright colors, red, white and green, and he wore a white carnation in his jacket's lapel. He looked like a young movie actor and he seemed worried and restless. Stephen was just completing his toast, glass lifted, "Here's to us, we three and nobody else." He took a big swig and was just putting down his glass when this young man made a beeline across the floor and there he was standing beside our table.

He looked at Stephen. In fact he stared at Stephen. Stephen said, "Well! Hello, Holmes, come sit down with us." Holmes didn't answer at first, he looked kind of mad. I didn't know what to make of it.

"Come on, Holmes, sit down, please, Holmes." Johnsy piped up like a damned parrot. It sounded so funny you couldn't help laughing. I mean, I laughed and Stephen laughed and Johnsy laughed. Everybody laughed but poor Holmes.

"Thanks, never mind," he said. He spoke kind of pointedly to Stephen. "You seem to have ample company. I get it. Well, so long, *Mister* Farrar," he added and then rushed across the room toward the door. Stephen excused himself and went after him, but Holmes was gone before he could reach him. Stephen didn't seem to mind. He came back and went right on with another toast, or maybe it was the same toast with just another gulp. "Here's to us, and all the good times we're going to have. I can see them coming."

He made it sound like we were already close friends. He talked a lot. I can't remember what all. The war, I remember that, and why it had to happen. I remembered the time he was in the demonstration against the war, and his face lighted up. "Say, we go back a long way, Mercy, we damned well do. I remember you two babies waving at me."

Johnsy remembered the parade and the police officers but he couldn't remember Stephen and his friends. That was one of Johnsy's problems, not being able to remember. Stephen talked books to us, as if we both knew them all. Hemingway and Westcott, e. e. cummings, Edward Bellamy and Mark Twain and Gertrude Stein; Big People.

I was thrilled when he mentioned Remy de Gourmont, as just by chance I'd picked up the book in the Hodges' library when Thelma and I weren't reading *The Arabian Nights* or playing five hundred or talking about the Deacon murder; that was a real hot story running on the front pages. Then, of course, we got to the Russians. I heard my voice say, "There aren't any other writers like them in the world, not in the whole world." It sounded as if I *knew,* as if I absolutely knew. "There can't be," I went on, "because they see from some mountain top." I meant it, but that was pretty good, actually.

Stephen put down his drink and looked at me. He had a nice mouth; when he smiled his whole face was in it. I felt myself come up to him. It was like something came rushing all the way up from the bottoms of my feet; the damned thing went through my body and on up to my face. We locked eyes for a moment, and I thought, Jesus, a person can't figure what's happening to them sometimes. I felt a strange kind of silence around us, wild and sweet. "Well, I'll be damned," he said after a moment. "You know about the Russians. You really know that. Tell me what you think, please. Right now."

"They're not just talking. Not making something up."

"Right, oh, so right." He seemed to actually think about what I was saying. "Not just rhetorical indignation. Not making things up, and you know that! Well, I'll be damned. I am in good company."

Peters finally came with the tea, and I must say it was all Stephen had promised. There were these tiny sandwiches, Virginia ham and cucumbers and some kind of delicious white cheese, with watercress, then pound cake cut thin and tea in fine china cups, white with bands of emerald green and threads of gold. And ice cream, three different kinds on each plate. Even Johnsy's platter of French fried potatoes was trimmed up with greenery.

People came up to our table from time to time to speak to Stephen. A Mr. and Mrs. Vincent, Tom and Marjorie, a good-looking young couple. Stephen introduced us, and they seemed glad to make our acquaintance. Then a stout older woman with her tall husband. They looked like people out of those old melodrama posters; I discovered that the woman was the Mrs. Teague who'd been so snobbish to us the night of Mamma's recital.

I remembered her, all right. Mamma liked to read about her in the society pages. "That's Anne," she'd say. Mr. Teague had great black mustaches, dyed no doubt, and white hair with black streaks in it. Mrs. Harriman Teague had the exact same smile she'd worn the night of the concert. Big but permanent, this smile, while her over-plump cheeks trembled like pink jelly.

We all stood up as long as these people were at the table, a long time it seemed, as this Mrs. Teague and Stephen went on about some play of Eugene O'Neill's they were going to do at the Little Theater I heard she'd financed.

"Look here, Anne, what about Mercy for the part of Marjorie? I'd like to have her read for it."

Mrs. Teague looked suddenly kind of old, her smile shrunk; I mean you could see it going small at the corners, but what she said was nice and ladylike. "That's a good idea, Stephen. Can you come in and read for us, Miss Bassford, or may I call you Mercy?" I said I could and I'd like to, and Mr. Teague said, "Jolly good idea that, Stephen."

The band was starting up "Happy Days Are Here Again," and before I quite knew what was happening, I was dancing with Stephen. He could dance like a bastard, but then, so could I.

The floor was an oval of shiny, polished wood, nowhere near large enough for the couples who crowded up and started whirling and twirling in two-steps and fox-trots, Charlestons and lindy hops and Black Bottoms. We danced wherever there was a spot and nobody collided. In fact, I wasn't even aware of being crowded. I was glad of those practice sessions I'd had with Thel and her brothers. I could do all the steps, changing as the band switched tunes.

I was dancing with an older man, I knew, and most of these people flinging themselves wildly around the floor were older people, anywhere from twenty-nine to sixty. Tell the truth, some of them looked half dead. One real old man with a mane of white hair kept flying past us, smiling a wild, scary smile as if he was about to do something crazy, maybe fly away.

This was the right place to be. *I'm here, and these are the right people. This is real life.*

Johnsy sat watching us and eating his way through the rest of the food. The band switched to "Ain't She Sweet?" and we all went so wild with that one, I wondered how the mane-flying old man would manage the corner. He was throwing his feet right off the edge as if he had more where they came from. As we passed our table I saw the French fries and sandwiches were gone, the ice cream had disappeared and the cake dish cleaned down to the crumbs.

Johnsy hollered, "Hey, Mercy, you're doing it great!" Everybody laughed, people from nearby tables turned to stare. What they saw was a shabby, happy boy getting to his feet. Before I knew it, he had cut in on Stephen and was dancing away with me. Johnsy could really dance—he was so light on his feet, he had such rhythm. He wasn't dressed right or anything, but I didn't care. Great things were about to happen, they were already happening, there was no telling where it would end.

Between dances we all three sat around the table talking our heads off. I don't know if I imagined it, but

204

Stephen's face kept changing. The average face is pretty much the same all the time. It changes *somewhat,* of course, when the owner gets angry or laughs, things like that. But this Stephen Farrar actually looked different at different times. I couldn't quite figure it out. He spoke and acted like a very handsome man, maybe that was it. Of course, half the time during that *thé dansant* business I saw Stephen in a kind of haze, I'm not sure why, except that the whole thing happened too quickly to catch it fully.

But there was one time when I caught him, you might say, like a camera, when he wasn't looking. He was standing at a nearby table talking to some people, and the light, what there was of it, coming from the chandelier lit his head and face. I saw then he wasn't actually so very good-looking, he wasn't nearly as handsome as Johnsy, for instance. His skin was darker than most, maybe from the sun in all those trips abroad, his hair was too long and he had a scar under his eye. His head and face would be just right in one of those paintings you see in museums, say of a Scottish knight or a prince or something like that. He had nice brown eyes and a look, an expression, as if he were genuinely curious and eager, sort of searching, which is pretty interesting if a person wants to be searched. Anyway, he wasn't all that handsome; he looked almost ugly. Good, I thought to myself. Very good.

The minute he came back to the table he was his old self, easy and jovial, ready to do anything we wanted, so I forgot the secret picture I had taken.

"I gotta go now," Johnsy announced. "Old lady Ziegler'll be sore as a boil." His voice sounded childish and unreal in this world of real people talking about real *things.* I hated to go. I wanted to hear more of what these real people were talking about—Wall Street, and stocks and bonds, real estate; *The American Mercury,* I knew that one. I heard talk of Marxism and Greenwich Village and someone named John Reed and this writer Scott Fitzgerald.

These real people were all living some remarkable,

interesting lives but they seemed to like Johnsy and me, maybe because we were young. As we walked between the tables with Stephen on our way out they looked at us with actual interest and those I met called me Mercy. I felt tall and willowy, tell you the truth, and kind of unusual myself. And there were mirrors along the walls. With this looking-glass support, I had some magic that was drawing people toward me, I decided. I'd seen it in Stephen when he talked to me and when he was dancing with me; I had something he needed.

Stephen did stop by Ziegler's candy store. I know because I remember seeing Mrs. Ziegler surrounded by teddy bears with soft pink feet and dolls with cottony yellow hair, scolding Johnsy for not showing up, and Stephen saying, "It's my fault." I remember Stephen paying twenty-four dollars for three ten pound boxes of chocolates, telling Johnsy he was taking them to the Burton party. But I remember it much, much more clearly because of the important conversation in the street outside that store, with Stephen asking us, "What time are you going to that party?"

"She ain't invited," Johnsy piped up.

Stephen spoke quickly. "She is! Let me take you, please, Mercy?"

I guess I said, "Thanks."

"Hey, I gotta deliver flowers." Johnsy started off when Stephen halted him. "You'll have to change, won't you?"

"Yeah, sure. I'm gonna dress up good."

Stephen said he'd pick us up at seven, and Johnsy rushed away. Once inside my house, I went into the parlor and watched Stephen cross the street with the candy boxes and climb the steps into his house.

Six o'clock. A whole hour to get dressed. I turned on all the lamps in my bedroom. Every move I made was careful; every object carefully selected, from soap to powder to brush and comb to dress and lipstick. I was glad Thel had made me buy the gray crêpe with the pleated skirt and the red leather trim, thirty dollars of my college money up in smoke. But who cared? I must keep cool, above the situation, act quickly but efficiently. Everything must be done just right. *Give yourself a hard look. Arrive downstairs finished.*

And at the Burton party, nothing but good will and good manners. Everything floating. No showing resentment or even victory. Nothing must show!

I did wonder about Johnsy, would he be ready when Stephen called for us? And if he was, what mightn't he blurt out, maybe right at the Burton shindig? *Cool. Float.*

As I dressed I was aware of some new sense of myself. Hair, legs, face, eyes, mouth, even my feet, all of these familiar pieces had become like precious possessions, gifts, you might say, to be watched over and enjoyed. I used to imagine there was this great darkness coming from behind the piano; it was so powerful, it blew hard, it made Mamma forget my name, making me a nameless creature, not a child, not even a female. Well, that was going now, pushed so far back it might never get up again. I had been recognized. Why, everybody at *thé dansant* recognized me—or practically everybody. *Mercy Bassford, that's Mercy Bassford.*

Downstairs, I turned on all the lights in the parlor, the chandelier and the soft lamps on the mantel and beside the sofa and the piano. It's funny how you really enter a place when you get this feeling. Identity!

I think everybody has this problem, one time or another. Or is it just every American person? Identities come and go. Now you see it, now you don't. Clever people set up identities. They dress a certain way, talk a certain way, and people say, that's So-and-So. And So-and-So says, that's right. That's me! But suppose people say that isn't So-and-So, then who is it? What does So-and-So answer? This thing comes and goes. Well, here I am in the parlor and I have it.

I could see and feel everything so clearly. The horsehair sofa pressed against my legs, the carpet soft underfoot. The picture I had in my head, myself, me, the way I looked. I got up and stood before the mantel.

Martha Washington stared down. "Where do you think you're going, you?" But I had her. "You're a dead old woman," I said, not out loud, but she heard me. I was just getting ready to say more when the doorbell rang.

Stephen came promptly at seven with Johnsy in tow. From Stephen's head and face some marvelous lemon and cinnamon scent floated down. But at one glance I knew Johnsy hadn't changed his clothes; only his hair had been slicked down with some shiny black stuff from which his curls were jumping up like snakes caught in the ointment as he jogged along whistling "Margie." I walked in the middle. We were fairly quiet, but there was this communion we had between us, as if we'd known each other for years and gone to maybe a hundred parties together.

We walked through streets of big old stone houses, where blacks were just beginning to move in, say three or four houses to a street, the rest white. The Burton place looked kind of shabby when you first saw it, something like a house in a spook movie. It was way up on a hill, with a big lawn sloping down to the street. It was too large for any normal-sized family, especially a family of three, had a chipped roof with windows of all shapes and sizes, big old shade trees and a porch going around the entire house. It was covered with wooden shingles, so it had a kind of permanent shabbiness, dark and old, graceless and ugly. Dr. Burton's father had it built in the 1880's. I heard it cost a lot of money, maybe five thousand dollars, maybe more. Anyway, it was one of those country houses in town and it took up over half a city block, so it looked like a small plantation complete with out-buildings added later, a tennis court, a pond for swimming, a stable for Edythe's horses and, combined with the garage and these acres of gardens with lanes and benches, was pretty impressive, especially when all lit up for a party.

We came up on the porch where we could see the party going on inside. It looked like a big happy crowd. Parties always look that way, even if the people are dying. Sounds came buzzing through the windows, cars were still stopping in the driveway; a butler opened the door, Stephen stood back to let me walk in first.

I'll tell you about that shindig. I know how people love to be invited, how hurt they feel when they're left out. I even know how elaborate the system is, the crazy way grown-up, sophisticated people think a party may change their lives.

Well, this one was a whole lot of something, I'm not sure what. The interior of the house looked dark and gloomy, even through the festive crowds and the many lights, you could see the damned house *frowning*. The wide stairs going up to the balcony had carved woodwork banisters with ornamental wooden curlicues and they were floored with heavy dark carpet. The downstairs floor was covered with Oriental rugs, and there were more books in ornate bookcases, plants on marble stands and statues standing about than I'd ever seen outside of the movies.

Dr. and Mrs. Burton received us with outstretched hands as if we were relatives. "How are you, Mercy, my dear?" and then that "So glad you could come." And to Johnsy, delivery boy converted to guest, "Johnsy, how good of you to come back." Now, it's pretty nice, that kind of thing, even if people hate your guts, it's nice, it make things easy. But our greeting, Johnsy's and mine, was glassy in comparison to Stephen's. Especially from La Belle Burton; you could say she fawned on him, while old Dr. Burton moved in fast and started fawning on me; at least he held my hand in both of his. They were hot and sweaty, but I left it there as if it felt great. "You're Mercy Bassford, Edythe's good friend. Well, it's really good to see you, Mercy. How are you?" That kind of talk; these Burtons sounded like they'd been doing it for thousands of years. He was going real good when I caught Edythe's eyes. She was standing in a group of girls, and I was wondering how to get away from Hot Hands and say something, Happy Birthday, anything to Edythe, when Thelma appeared out of nowhere, and we greeted each other like long-lost sisters. "Told you, didn't I?" she screamed with joy.

"Food!" whispered Stephen. "We're going to starve. Punch first. How about it?" We all four careened wildly toward the larger buffet, making our way through people and tables and carts, past maids offering us drinks from trays. And we ate something; I was too excited to notice what it was.

We got caught up in a group of women standing near the mantel who were listening to Myrtle, the Burtons' cook, a large queenly lady, explain how she made the Lady Baltimore cake, which was just being placed on a separate table. "I whips up ten dozen egg whites, good and stiff, then I folds them into my batter and bakes 'em. Then I chops up my figs and my seeded raisins . . ."

"Let's dance now," said Stephen. He took my hand and we pushed our way into the big dining room, which had been emptied out, the floor waxed and a platform set up for the band. The room stretched completely across the house, straight to the kitchen, sixty feet or more, but I guess it wasn't quite big enough for the eager crowd. As soon as the band got going good it was so crowded only good dancers could hold their own. Just once Stephen and I got stuck in a corner where, during a letup, we heard two older men talking as they watched us. "Works with boys," one man was saying. "Fine chap. Grandad owns that big old house out on Calhoun Place."

"That's me they're talking about. I'm a fine chap. Remember that."

"Why won't they sell that house?" the other man asked.

"Old man's peculiar, I reckon," the first one replied. "Been kind of funny since his son was killed. After that his wife passed away and, well, he's been kind of strange ever since. He keeps it up nice though, the house. They says it's just like it was when the family lived in it."

Right after this, which was news to me but must have bored Stephen, they started on families. "She was a Roundtree. The Roundtrees came from Georgia. Her father was William Langford Roundtree." We danced away, but when we circled back to avoid another wild

210

couple, they were saying the same things over again. "The Roundtrees came from Georgia . . ." Stephen started chanting a song he made up, "The Roundtrees came from Georgia, the squares from Tennessee."

"This is what people talk about at these things," he whispered. "And these are the lively ones."

I saw what he meant. Half of them just weren't saying anything. "Imagine what it'd be like without the dancing."

"You imagine it, Mercy." We laughed at that.

Once, during a hot Charleston, I saw Dale Stump knocking around on the floor hitting into people. The bumps had come out on his face something awful in a peculiar design almost like a stigmata. Stephen made a wild turn and we barely missed him, but Ruth caught my eye as we danced by. Her mouth fell open, she forgot to steer Dale, as she stared from Stephen to me. Then slowly the old smile came back. "Why, Stephen, hel-loa! Imagine, dancing with little Mercy."

"She's not so little," Stephen was saying, as the Stumps tried again. Dale couldn't even do the two-step and his Charleston was comical, especially with Ruth leading him. He almost fell over Thelma, coming down hard on her instep. Thelma cried out in pain, the "ouch" echoed over the saxophones, but Dale apologized and kept right on bumping into people until Ruth pulled him off the floor.

The next time I passed her, an elderly man had her in tow. He was determinedly doing a waltz to fox-trot music. I saw her watching us as Johnsy cut in on Stephen and we went off in those crazy steps we do. The old Smile was opening up like the Grand Canyon as she and Elderly went waltzing by.

People were eating and drinking their heads off. I know it sounds silly but I had this idea I was going aboard a big ocean liner. Soon, any minute now, the ship would leave port with me on it. Now, when this ship business got started, why, then the Black Thing that was after me, you remember, behind the piano, well, it would be outwitted.

Next thing I knew we were leaving. Mr. and Mrs. Burton were seeing us out and saying exactly what they said when we arrived. "How good of you to come," the same damned thing, I swear to God.

We got home pretty late, but the house was empty, so it didn't matter. I sat down in the parlor long enough to watch Stephen cross the street and go into his house. He is going to bed and so am I, I thought, childishly comforted by the idea.

I slept late the next morning. It was a Monday, but every now and then I did skip a Monday at school. The doorbell rang early. I remember peeping out to see what time it was. It was five to eight. So I stretched and stayed abed, the joyous awareness of the Burton party still spinning in my head. And in my mind's eye, I saw something. Just over me, where Al-Balkhi used to arrive on horseback, the person of Stephen Farrar was waiting, his face there in the room. It was too early to savor the secret knowledge to the full. I went back to sleep. But it seemed I was barely off again in my dreams when I heard voices downstairs. I listened, half awake. Wasn't that the pushing voice of my Cousin Ruth and the retreating voice of Aunt Rose? I tried to wake up for a few minutes, as Ruth pushed harder against Rose's staunch, ameliorative answers, whatever they were. But I couldn't catch the words. The question and answer period went on for quite a while. I must have fallen back to sleep still trying to catch what was being said. When I woke up I saw it was after ten and hurried down to breakfast.

"There's a present here on the buffet," Rose informed me as she brought my breakfast. I opened a neatly wrapped package to which a handwritten note was attached written on Stephen Farrar's personal stationery. The flap of the envelope was loose, as if it had been opened by someone. When I took the note out to read it, the paper was wrinkled as if it had been crumpled in someone's hand. "Mercy, dear. Here's the book I mentioned. We'll talk about it tomorrow night. Until then, Stephen."

Last night, seeing how popular he was, I wondered if he mightn't just forget me. All those people he knew, all those invitations, he must have collected a dozen right there. I kept hearing people invite him as if he were the only man left alive in the world. He hadn't forgotten me! I read the words again, *"Tomorrow night. Until then Stephen."* At that moment I knew something else, too. I don't know how I knew it but I did. He needed me. Now why in hell would a man of his prestige, rich and important, need me? Answer to come.

I ran my fingers over the name engraved on top of the page. Stephen Farrar III, 1428 Hollins Street. I liked feeling the letters against my fingertips. I'd always have engraved stationery, I decided, so people could feel my name; none of that cheap printed stuff. The package contained a small, leather-covered volume, *The Oxford Book of French and English Verse*. As I fingered the soft leather, the thought that Stephen might have come to my house to deliver it in person was just getting to me.

"How did it come?" I asked Rose. I wanted to hear her say it.

"Way most presents gits delivered. Deliverers brings them to the doors."

"You mean Stephen was here this morning?"

"Five past eight."

"That must have been the bell that woke me up."

"Maybe so. More likely it was that Ruth's ringing woke you up. She rings so hard."

"Ruth was here? I thought I heard her."

"They come almost the same time, that Ruth and Mr. Farrar. I bare took the package from him in my hand when the bell starts ringing again, and there she is, waitin' to get in. They coulda butt right into each other, the way she come in right soon as he went down the steps."

"What did she want, coming by so early?"

"She come by with the chair covers she borrowed

213

last week. Says she's copied them already, but I didn't believe it."

"Oh, Rose, what did she really want?"

"Now don't you worry none about her. You go on eat your breakfast and I'll tell you after you're done."

But I couldn't eat until I found out. I had the idea I was another person sitting there at the table with my new book and the note from Stephen Farrar. I was no longer miserable energy moving around in a large circle, trying to enter somewhere. I saw now a beautiful and interesting person with untold possibilities and capacities, entering life. Could it be possible Ruth knew, too, and had something in mind to stop me? No, that wasn't possible. Ruth was married, thank God!

Rose was standing with her back turned to me, wiping the china closet with an oiled rag. "I hear tell you was the big thing at the Burtons' shindig."

"I went with Stephen Farrar."

"So I heard."

"How'd you know?" She didn't answer right away, a way she had of going absolutely silent when she wanted to keep things back. "What was all that conversation you were having with Ruth?"

"What conversations I had with Ruth?"

"I heard you talking your heads off. Come on now. She told you about last night, didn't she?" I kept on and finally I wormed it out of her.

"She's goin' wild about your goin' out with that Mista Farrar. Come on over here to trying to get your mother to stop it. Only she ain't found nobody here but me so it didn't do her no good."

"What did you tell her?"

"I told her plenty, don't you worry none, you hear? You got a right to be escorted to a party. You got full age now, you goin' to be sixteen. You can go anywheres you likes and she can't do nothing about it."

"But what did she want to do? What business is it of hers?"

"Wants your Mamma to stop you going out with a man that old. But I tole her that won't do her no good.

They's already hired him to tutor you, to push up your schoolin'. That did her in!"

"Did she touch my present?"

"I dunno. I been busy kneading ma bread. I just talks to her and then I gotta go back to ma work. Told her nobody wasn't home but you and me and there wasn't no more to say. She set down to use the phone, and I went on about ma business."

"You left her alone here in the room with my present?" I know it sounded silly—*alone with my present*. As if she could hurt an object, perhaps even murder it, but that was how I felt.

"She just set down and called up somebody that wasn't home."

"What'd she do then?"

"Stood around is all she done. Took a muffin off the table and et it up and went out."

Ruth had opened my note. She had read it and shoved it back into the envelope, and I was furious and uneasy, both at the same time. "Someday I'll kill her!" I cried the words, meaning them, too. I had so few friends, I was always counting them, Rose and Johnsy, Marian Swoboda and Thel and now Stephen. I stood them up in line in my mind as I ran my fingers over the note again, trying to press out the wrinkles.

Thelma and I were as thick as thieves. Together we snatched secret sweets, satisfying our longings. Experiences, such as Gardiner, Al-Balkhi and now Stephen were all divided and shared, sometimes unwillingly. The long afternoons would find me side by side with Thel in dark movie palaces, watching our favorite movie actresses suffer like madwomen. They were large, overfancy, over-heated and ugly, those old houses where people laughed and cried unashamedly, laughing at Charlie Chaplin, Harold Lloyd and Laurel and Hardy, crying over Lillian Gish, Joan and Greta.

These theaters smelled of cheap perfume, disinfectants, people's armpits and hot backsides, but we loved every minute of it! I claimed Joan looked like

215

she'd just killed her mother. Thel said Garbo looked like a boy. But we were in love wtih them both, we shared in what they did and said. We were right up there in those over-furnished drawing rooms with the beaded lamps and draped pianos. We were actually wearing the long black dresses and we flirted with the tall, interesting men.

We knew we were going to get it. Thing, but hidden in a velvet dream. All disbelief was suspended. In fact by the time the handsome men finally got to kissing the girls, those long soul kisses where the girls gave their all and the tall men would dip into them—and us —bending over them with grace and agility, we, breathing heavily, were willing at least to have our clothes torn off! Nothing came of it. The scenes would change after a good soul kiss, but when we saw the girls again we knew they'd had it because we'd had it, in our minds, anyhow.

Now, after we'd all had it, Joan and Greta, Thel and I, we'd be abandoned, of course. But, oh, those sunken living rooms with those Oriental rugs, they were great places in which to be abandoned. We would stand at heavily draped windows wearing long strands of genuine pearls or ride around in long, black chauffeured limousines saying good-bye forever to eight-foot men in tuxedos who were about to abandon us, having slaked their lust, and ours, to boot! Not to mention having stolen the best ten minutes of our lives.

Late afternoons we'd leave, with damp seats and damp eyes, for the chill twilight of the street and as often as not we were sad and quiet. Because what could you say? The women back there, Joan and Greta, and Thel and me, we had been sweet and weak, and the men had been cruel in the end, to a man they had, but, oh, did they ever know what to do? The way they kept kidnapping people and having their way and then abandoning them, wasn't it awful? And wasn't it wonderful?

There was something terrible about it, too, because these men in the movies had something the men we knew didn't have and it wasn't just the long limousines or the dropped living rooms. What they had to drop went deeper than mere material trappings. Not that we disparaged these. In fact, those paintings in the drawing rooms, lighted from above, made the steel engravings of dead squirrels and George Washington in our homes look squalid indeed.

But it was the men themselves and what they knew that had us going. Take a man like Clive Brook. He was fascinating, smart and poised. Take even old Rudolph. He stared at his girls, he stared into them, he ravished them one and all.

Bereft of all this sophisticated loveliness, Thel and I would traipse through the slushy streets, beating our way to Tobin's Ice Cream Parlor where we would fall into the first empty booth, light up our Melachrinos and puff pretentiously, impatiently awaiting, to quell our sorrows, long ice cream sodas to be followed by coffee and chocolate éclairs. We ate like crazy and never gained an ounce.

"Clive was wonderful, wasn't he?" Thel would say to the twilight outside the window of our booth.

"Yes, different from the people we know."

This exchange would often quiet us through a whole cigarette. Those men in the movies were neither awkward nor repulsive, they were never boring, their teeth were never dirty or crooked.

"I wonder why so few boys are interesting," Thel would sigh.

"Hard to find one, just one, who can really talk."

The men in the movies did not make remarks at Joan or Greta, they spoke to them. They did not grab at their girls, like the boys we knew did, who, by the way, wouldn't know what to do if they did manage to catch hold.

"You at least had old Bright Eyes. Hilary knows how to talk."

"Oh, yes. Academic conversation. Quite literary."

"I'm sure." She was waiting, but then so was I. Meantime Tobin's was emptying out. It was growing darker outside, getting nearer to dinner time. "Can you do *any-thing*, Merce?"

The question was startling, but I was ready. "Of course I can."

"Like what?"

"What do you *mean?*"

"Could you, you yourself, a girl, do anything like the men did? Like Clive, fr' instance?"

"I can kiss," I announced, smug but reticent.

"How much do you know about it?"

"Everything."

"Jesus! Do you really?"

"Of course." I stared out the window. "Don't you?"

"Well, not the way they do. I'd need practice. Besides, who would I want to seize and kiss?"

"Nobody."

"Exactly. And anybody'd want it wouldn't be the one you'd want t'do it to."

"Right. Exactly right." There was something Thelma knew. A boy named Melvin, not very attractive. "You were going to tell me about Melvin?"

"You never finished telling me about Long Drawers."

"I did. Ages ago. There's nothing more to tell."

"That ain't all now, Merce."

"Well, let's see. He, he was more like, let's see now. He wanted me to do it all to him."

"Jesus! With all he knows?"

"Ummhmm."

"But isn't that peculiar?"

"Ummhmm. I thought so. Now about Melvin?"

"Oh, Melvin."

"He's got nice eyes," I said, hoping to find out at last. "His conversation's terrible, but I like his parents."

"He drives a car, too."

"Did you do it with Melvin?"

"Uh-huh." She looked through the window where tiny stars were starting in the darkening sky. "We better go home."

"Did you do anything with him or not?"

218

"I don't know, Mercy." She whined so she sounded confused and saddened by the question. "I guess so."

"What do you mean you guess so? Did you or didn't you? Yes or no?"

"I said I did, didn't I?"

"You said you guessed you did."

"Well, what are you so interested for?"

I stared back at her without answering. At this point in our lives, the idea of love moved in the arc towards *sedshual indrakorz,* the dark monkey on top of the budding bush. But here the great transformation began. If, somehow, you climbed up and *hit* the monkey, this situation no longer meant death and destruction, as our parents had said. The monkey was more vague and less malignant by now, he had even been seen to smile, confer favors, lift the heady climbers in his hands and hold them aloft. Besides, even if he threw you into a black pit, the hunger was there, the crying need for the kissing and touching, the words. What to do about that?

A great natural force was erupting and, whether you used Al-Balkhi with his sword or Dr. Gardiner or whoever turned up, it had to be. Now, right opposite me sat Thelma, my closest friend, saying she had been in the monkey's claws. "Tell me this minute, Thelma Hodges."

"Well, I did, but not completely." She put down her fork beside her half-eaten éclair."

"What do you mean by that?"

"I mean, well, *he* did, but *I* didn't." She looked scared. "Now listen, Merce, remember I only did it with Melvin."

"Were you in love with him?"

"No, I, I did it to save *him*."

"Save him from what?"

"From being a cripple. For life."

"What?"

"He said if I didn't let him do it, he couldn't go home, because of his thing. He said it hurt him something terrible, so he could hardly move. If he didn't get relief he'd be crippled for life like his Uncle Harry was."

"Crippled? Why? What were you doing, kicking him?"

"Of course not. Oh, Mercy, don't you know anything? A boy can get crippled easy as pie if he gets excited like that and can't go on with it."

"He can?"

"Sure. Melvin said it's nature's punishment and nature is very cruel. He said a doctor told him if he got like I said and then he didn't do it, why, his thing would get crippled and never straighten out. And he'd go through life bent over double!"

"You didn't believe that?"

"Not exactly. Only he said he knew a way to do it so I wouldn't get caught. And I, I thought I'd like to try it."

"Sure."

"So I let him."

"How was it?"

"Awful."

"I mean, how did he do it?"

Her face turned bright pink. "Through my petticoat," she whispered.

"Through your petticoat?" The image was as unpleasant and anonymous as a poison pen letter. "It sounds horrible."

"He seemed to like it."

"How did you feel afterwards?"

"Wet."

"I'll bet. It sounds depressing." I thought it over. "Clive would never stoop to such carrying-on."

"I guess not. Let's not talk about him."

"All right. What about Melvin?"

"Oh, he was fine. Wanted to do it again next day."

"You didn't?"

"Oh, he kept at me so hard I said if he wanted it so bad, he could have it."

"Have what?"

"My petticoat."

The picture was so funny I burst out laughing. "Oh, no, Thel, you didn't?"

"Yes, I did. He took it, too."

"I guess a person like Melvin would take anything. Imagine Clive or Rudolph taking somebody's underskirt."

Thelma laughed, then we both burst out screaming. She was feeling better. "I got it back," she admitted.

"Have you told anybody?" I felt more kindly and protective toward Thelma now that I knew what she'd been through.

"Not a soul. And if you do, I'll kill you."

"I certainly won't. It's not the kind of thing a person talks about. Thel?"

"What?"

"Did you lose your maidenhead?"

"I guess so. I don't know. Oh, how do *I* know what I lost?"

"Well, I think you ought to know."

"I figure maybe it went in my petticoat."

"Did you look?"

"No, of course not." She thought it over. "Melba was washing clothes when I came home, so I just stuck the damned thing in the tub. I never wanted to see it again."

Imagine! A precious thing like a maidenhead jumping around in a laundry bucket! I was beginning to feel so sorry for poor Thelma. I wanted to help her, but I was confused and somewhat depressed myself. "Oh, well," I began, "most people don't know too much about their maidenheads anyway, not till after they're examined by a doctor."

"Oh-h-h-h-h!" wailed Thelma, so loud the waitress must have heard us all the way behind the counter because she turned to look. I glanced back at her defiantly, lucky fat woman of thirty, far removed from the horrors of the young. "Why didn't you go to a doctor right away?" I whispered.

"Why, Mercy?"

"Well, because maybe it's still there. Maybe it's stuck, half in and half out, and in that case, a clever doctor might push it back in."

"It wouldn't stay. It'd only fall out again."

"Not if he pushed hard enough."

"I thought about going, but Mamma always comes with me. I'd be scared the doctor might say something in front of her."

"Wait!" This was when one of those sudden flashes I get came over me and I said almost without thinking, "Thelma, don't be afraid. You don't have to go to any doctor. You still have it!"

"Oh, God! How do you know?"

"I don't know how I know but I know. Like you say, *he* did it, but you didn't." I felt absolutely sure of myself as I delivered my edict. "He did it to your underskirt but not to you."

"You think it didn't happen?"

"Exactly."

Thelma let out a sigh I could feel all the way across the table. "I'll bet there's a whole lot of that kind of thing going on all over the world."

Stephen was to tutor me. It was Dr. Gardiner's suggestion. With all my talents, I was going to flunk math, and to our surprise, Stephen had not only agreed but had offered, in person to Mrs. Dowse, to include Johnsy. As he told me about it, his eyes actually sparkled, he kept grinning as he talked. "We can use my grandpère's place," he said. "Say, that'll be just the ticket. It's a beaut! Come to think of it, the damned place is made for tutoring." We were to meet that very Thursday, Stephen, Johnsy and I, in the famous old Farrar mansion.

From the moment we entered the house, Stephen acted as if he owned it. In the dining room he picked up a Chinese porcelain dish from one of the open closets. "Look at these pale pinks and blues combined with the bright reds and greens," he said. "Pretty! This has to be from the Ming dynasty. The old girl knew what she was doing. Any idea what it's worth, Mercy?"

I said I didn't know. But Johnsy was on a more secure footing. "It won't be worth nothing if you drop it."

"Oh, yes, it would," Stephen corrected. "Even dropped and broken into pieces this dish would still be

222

worth a mint. You know I'm the only grandson. It's just a question of time before this place comes to me."

I was impressed, but Johnsy didn't seem to hear him. "You're going to inherit this house?"

"Who else, Sunshine?" He started calling me by this nickname about this time. "Well, suppose you were a very old man, barely able to sit on the lawn of an expensive hospital and you had this house as part of your estate. And one grandson named Stephen Farrar III, who visited you every week and read you to sleep, to whom would you leave your old empty house?"

"Oh, I see."

"Some of my friends call me a professional grandson!" Stephen laughed. "And in a way it's true. I do try to make life easier for the old boy. Last time I visited, guess what I did for him?"

"I betcha asked him for the money," Johnsy allowed.

"No, I don't have to do anything of the kind. The will's been made long ago. I wrote his obituary for him, to his dictation, of course."

There was something about the interior of the house that chilled and excited me, both at once. I don't know how to describe it. The narrow blinds were pulled down just below the center of the long French windows opening out on a balcony with iron grille work overlooking the garden. As we walked down the wide stairs leading to the floor below, our footsteps echoing loudly, I began to feel maybe we were doing something wrong coming in here like this, that the rightful owners might come in at any minute and discover us. I had to remind myself that Stephen had the keys.

The lower floor, or basement, was unlike any basement I'd ever seen, a long, wide room running the entire length of the house. "Nearly a hundred feet, and look at the fireplaces at either end! Let's examine all this. Say, you two can help me decide what to sell and what to keep."

He was laughing, a certain mocking laugh he had. I noticed it especially whenever he spoke about anything connected with his family. There was something mysterious about it. Part of his joy went under whenever they came up; he laughed as if that was the only way he could come at it.

"Look like folks is still living in it," Johnsy commented, as we walked about, poking into things, touching andirons, chairs, tables, books. There were hundreds of books in long shelves going up to the ceiling, reached by a stepladder made like a small stairwell, quite graceful and handsome in itself. "What'd your grandpa do in this big old house?" Johnsy couldn't seem to understand the place.

"He lived and had his family, his wife and their servants."

"And just one kid, eh?"

"Yes, he had one son, who is dead."

We stood still, staring at faces looking down from photographs, with Stephen introducing us to all these silent dead people who seemed to be watching us. "That's my grandmother, a beauty, wasn't she? There's the old man, that's my great uncle. And there's my father." Everybody in the street knew his father had been killed shortly after Stephen's birth, but no one knew exactly how. Watching Stephen stare at the photograph, waiting eagerly for him to say something and noticing his silence, I wondered if anyone knew for sure how it happened.

"Hey, look at this thing! It turns around." Johnsy had discovered a globe of the earth set in a brass fixture and was eagerly turning it on its axis. "Hey, there's Italy. Don't look like no boot to me!" said Johnsy.

"Any boot," Stephen corrected him without even turning his gaze from his father's photograph. "Or, to be absolutely correct about it, it *doesn't* look like a boot to me."

"Yeah, it *doesn't* look like a boot to me. It looks like a leg to me." He noticed Stephen staring at the photograph and came over beside him. "That your father?"

"Yes."

"I'm sorry he's dead. I never had no father. Any father, I mean. Maybe I did. I never knew no father nohow." Neither of us answered Johnsy. Most of his comments didn't require any answer. "How'd your father come to die so early?" Johnsy blurted out.

"He was shot!" said Stephen, still without looking away from the eyes of the photograph.

"Shot! Gee whiz! That's awful!" He waited, then, "You mean he was murdered?"

"You could call it that. He was on a hunting trip, and one of the hunters in the group shot him, unintentionally, of course."

"Gee whiz! That's awful." Johnsy was so interested in the tragic news, he went on, asking, "Which one of the hunters got him?"

"My uncle," Stephen replied, as coolly as if he'd been asked the time.

"Your uncle?"

"Yes, my maternal uncle. My mother's brother."

"Gee whiz! That was a terrible thing!"

Meantime, I'd been taking in the house. I'd never seen anything like the so-called basement, complete with books and desks, soft chairs and couches, Oriental rugs and brass lamps and a solid mahogany bar with a rail. It must have been the old man's study or retreat. It reminded me of rooms in movies about the doings of big tycoons, or rooms set off behind heavy cords in museums, requiring only a knight in armor to complete the picture. There were some fine old paintings over the mantels at either end, one of Stephen's grandmother as a young girl out front, another of his grandfather, with mustaches and beard, but none of the son.

Stephen turned away from the photographs at last, and we all moved to the bar and stood there, half expecting a bartender to rise up and ask us what we wanted to drink. On our way across the floor, between the rugs, we stepped on marble tiles.

This place was so different from our basement at home, with its lifeless painted brick walls, its bins with shelves of glass jars filled with preserved foods for winter, peaches and tomatoes, plums and pears and apples, its old rocking horses and tricycles and its player piano and Victrola and child-size pianos with broken keyboards. Nevertheless, you felt life had been lived here, at concert pitch, too. In a sense, it still resounded with it. Something was still going on here, and more was going to happen.

A sense of unfinished business hit me as we settled in the big chairs. I pick up things like that, atmosphere, spooky stuff. Stephen put down his bundle of books on the library table. "Why don't we use this place down here to study?" I liked the idea and began to look for firewood.

It was the perfect place, and doubts about whether it was all right for us to be here were quickly dispersed. A private place, remote from our neighborhood, a house off by itself in a street where all the houses were made of gray stone with receding lawns and long, plate glass windows usually covered with draperies from top to bottom. A street of expensive houses from which no faces peered, houses whose front steps were covered with ivy instead of people. The very name, Calhoun Place, had a special cool sound.

We talked about algebra. Johnsy stared. I listened. Stephen expounded, but not too seriously, not at all like Miss Talbacher, and I began to learn a little. Before we knew it, it was getting dark. "Let's take a break," said my tutor. He pressed a button, and lamps turned on everywhere. Even over the portraits, small lights appeared. The room came toward us like a great lady from bygone days, smiling and extending her hand eagerly, as if she had been waiting a long time for the party to begin. "The old boy put everything he needed down here." We walked around, examining nooks and crannies. "Mercy, come look at the kitchen." I came over and found a marvelous room with an ice box and a stove, a complete kitchen with closets and dishes, pots and pans and food, jars and cans of beautiful fruits and vegetables.

Johnsy had never seen whole sets of books. "Are those books real?"

"Are the books genuine?" corrected Stephen.

"Yeah. Are the books genuine?"

"Certainly are. Come look, you two." Stephen ran over to examine the titles. The shelves were divided into special classifications—law, medicine, fiction, occultism. "Here, Mercy, occultism, witchcraft, no less. We've a pile of wild reading to do, once we've passed over algebra."

There were books about Albania and Russia, Rumania and China and Japan. I could hardly read the titles. I was becoming aware of a rush toward some powerful, well, crisis—danger to one of us, or all of us. Then I began to figure the calamity, whatever it was, had already happened to these other people, these young strangers on the wall, maybe even killed them or caused their downfall so that only the old man was left, a rich ogre sitting on a hospital lawn with this professional grandson, Stephen, showing up now and then. No matter. With each passing minute in the strange place, I knew a little more about my new mentor and favorite man. "We're going to be comfortable while we work away. We can keep groceries in the ice box. What you say, Sunshine? Have a spot of tea if we get hungry, maybe even dinner if we're running late."

"Yeah, let's have dinner!" said Johnsy. It was going to be fun and interesting.

Stephen was to tutor us two or three times a week, depending on the amount of work required of him at the Old Town Boys' School. I'd rather not have had Johnsy along, but that's how it was and, for some reason I couldn't figure, it was going to be all right. Stephen was determined to help Johnsy with his education, to get him out of his rut. That was how noble he was. Besides, there was a relationship growing between the three of us by leaps and bounds, and I even began to like having Johnsy there. There was something so honest and masculine in his big, frank eyes.

"Hey, Stephen, here's a room full of bottles," the object of my ruminations called out. "Was your old grandpa a drunk?"

"That's a wine closet." Stephen and I came over to

227

the room Johnsy had discovered, a small, stone-lined enclosure off the kitchen. What looked like hundreds of bottles were laid out flat with the corks or covered tips staring at us like eyes.

Stephen began taking out dusty bottles, reading the labels. "No, he wasn't a drunkard. Before this damned prohibition law, every gentleman was expected to lay down a cellar of good wine. Grandpa's got quite a small cellar, but because of the damn law, these wines are almost priceless now."

It was so chilly in the wine closet I was glad to get back to the fireplace. Through the windows you could see it was growing dark outside. We ran through a little more algebra, and Stephen concluded his lesson. "Day after tomorrow, Sunshine. Let's see, that'll be Saturday, four o'clock." He took a small notebook from his pocket and wrote down the appointment.

Just once, as we all three started fixing up the place, putting away the books, banking the fire, putting out lights and closing doors, I heard footsteps outside, very near the house. I stopped what I was doing and looked up at the windows facing the street. I saw the outlines of a face staring at us but I couldn't see who it was. "Did you see that?"

Stephen said, "Yes, somebody snooping. We'll close the draperies next time."

Once again I had the feeling of some catastrophe, as if in the cosy, inviting room a wild thing were alive, rushing like a river concealed beneath a city. But outside in the empty street, there was no one, no car, no children, not even an animal moving.

One Tuesday morning before school I had gone to the bathroom with my Cousin Honey, having promised to be with her the night before, as she had "a big day" coming up, a date with Clarence or Raymond or that new, quite handsome man named Richard something, and wanted to be up early and finished with her work so she could start dressing early in the afternoon. I was dutifully there sitting with her when she informed me

228

her date had been put off till tomorrow, Wednesday, and asked if I could come help her to dress, but I said, no, I couldn't.

"I have to meet Stephen right after school," I told her.

"You have to meet who?"

She looked at me, surprised when I mentioned him, and then rose immediately and completed her spell on the toilet in a great hurry. I assumed she was disappointed because I couldn't come to help her dress the following day. She often liked a second pot-sit in the afternoons and that, too, would be denied her.

"I guess I could make it later," I said. "Say, six o'clock, maybe."

She didn't answer. She had flopped into the little chair before her dressing table, so I took the big soft chair in the corner of her bedroom. From where I sat, I could see her face reflected three times in the three mirrors of her dressing table. She picked up the comb but put it down without combing her hair.

"Did you say you were meeting Stephen Farrar?"

"Yes. He's tutoring me. Algebra and French."

"You didn't tell me."

"I thought I had. Maybe you just forgot."

"You didn't tell me, Mercy. You never mentioned any such thing."

Her voice sounded funny, as if it had moved further back in her mouth. From where I sat I could see three of Honey's faces staring at me from the three mirrors. Three whole pink faces and three sets of round, green and white eyes, only she wasn't smiling and none of the faces looked right without the dimples showing.

"He's a fine tutor, you know," I began explaining. "He's very brilliant at math and he's a linguist, too, and Dr. Gardiner suggested him. He thought it'd help."

"Yes. I know he's brilliant."

I was sorry I'd mentioned anything to upset her. And, then, on top of this, here I was deserting her tomorrow. No wonder she was worried, considering how lonesome she gets when she has to do it alone.

229

"Look, Honey. I think I can come over lunchtime. We could come upstairs and afterwards I could help you start getting dressed."

"How long could you stay?"

"An hour. A whole hour, maybe longer. Maybe an hour and a half."

She nodded. But she wasn't making up her face, and this was a bad sign. "Mercy?"

"Yes, Honey."

"You're not . . . ?"

"What?"

"You're not doing anything with Stephen, are you?"

"Doing what?"

"Anything wrong?"

Well, I was dreaming plenty of "wrong" dreams at night as I lay wide awake. But these were highly personal matters I was not about to reveal, not even to Honey.

"What could be wrong about passing that damned algebra? Or speaking proper French? Reading Remy de Gourmont and Anatole France in the original?"

She thought that over, but she still wasn't showing her dimples. "I don't mean anything really wrong. What I mean is, well, where are you taking these tutoring lessons? At home?"

"Sometimes." It was only partly true. I had taken exactly one lesson at home.

"And sometimes other places?"

"Other places, yes. Sometimes in the back room of the library."

"And any other place?"

"Anyway, Johnsy Dowse is always there with us. Stephen is trying to help Johnsy pass so he can be a junior someday." I went on a bit about that, having actually ignored her question.

"Johnsy is *always* there?"

"Ummhmm." I said it quickly. There had been times when Johnsy came late or couldn't make it at all. Honey seemed relieved. It was the first time I had ever told her a lie. There's something luxurious in having a friend to whom you tell the truth, the whole truth, not holding out the nasty parts. You know, bits and pieces we all keep hidden. And now a thread in the luxurious tapestry of our friendship had been torn.

I could just as well have told her the truth about the basement study with the rugs and the fireplace and the floor-to-ceiling bookshelves, but this was a secret between Stephen, Johnsy and me. We'd all vowed not to mention it, I'm not sure why. I had another motive, too, of which I was becoming aware as the minutes wore on. I wanted it to be mine, all mine, my own secret. I felt saddened at the loss of this totality, this blissful ease I'd had up to now with Honey, whereas Honey was feeling happier. Her lips began opening wide again, showing her pretty teeth, and her dimples came flashing back.

"I guess it's all right then, Mercy darling." She had already started combing her hair and making curls to be tucked up later. "I just can't help worrying about you sometimes. We're first cousins, I know, but you're more like my baby sister. And you know everything about me, almost everything."

She got up from the dressing table and came over and hugged me, and I was happy, blissfully happy as I hugged her back, good and hard. I knew nothing had changed between us, at least not on Honey's part, because she went straight down the steps and sat on the toilet again and began talking away.

I probably wouldn't have thought much more about this conversation with Honey except for something that happened a few weeks later. It was on a Friday night. I was on my way down to meet Aunt Margaret for a séance at Aunty Berty Hildebrant's, looking forward to it no end, as Aunty Berty, a middle-aged, plump woman with soft brown eyes and, when not in a trance, had the most lively smile and friendly ways. Sitting in one of the straightbacked chairs Berty had set out in rows ten across in her forty-foot parlor, watching Cousin Berty go into a trance and receive messages from the dead—occasionally expressing accurate information, sometimes

231

juicy, sometimes terrifying—was a marvelous thing to do of an evening.

I was walking down Gilmore Street just before six o'clock, planning to take the streetcar any minute, but, as I got to the park block, the promenade looked so inviting, with trees hanging overhead and the fountain splashing in the distance, I decided to walk instead. Now the park at Gilmore stretches on for eight blocks and, strolling along at an easy pace, I must have walked through barely half of them when I saw Stephen's car parked under the big oak just a block ahead. There were other green Stutz Bearcats around town and maybe this was one of those. I slowed down. I often thought I saw Stephen's car coming toward me or moving away, when in point of fact it was some stranger's car.

Then I saw something else that consumed my attention. Honey, walking fast in those navy blue, high-heeled shoes, the curls on top of her head bouncing up and down, and wearing the very same dark blue serge suit she had tried on in my presence, asking of the skirt, "Does it hide my fat behind?" and me saying, "A person wouldn't know you had a fat behind!" And of the jacket, "Does it show my bosoms in profile?" And me responding, "Perfect curves. Shows them just right." She went on about that suit, asking me how she looked, front, back and sideways, always ending up with her sorrowful defect, the big plump bottom.

I was just getting ready to call out to her when to my amazement I saw Stephen step out of the car, on the park side, and come around to meet her. I stopped dead, waiting, and pretty soon Honey caught up with him. He watched her as she came toward him.

He wasn't smiling the way he smiled when he saw me. He was staring at her, though. I just stood there, slightly hidden by some low-hanging branches and a park bench, watching them. I began to feel kind of funny. I didn't feel dizzy or sick exactly, but my face felt hot and I almost forgot where I was. The familiar street and the park and the houses opposite became vague and misty, as if they were receding.

This was foolish, of course. I didn't see anything spectacular, nothing but Stephen, my friend and mentor, opening the door of his car for Honey, my beloved cousin, and her getting in, and then him going around to the other side and hopping into the driver's seat. That was all I saw. I couldn't hear what they were saying. It seemed to me they weren't saying anything. They moved like people in a silent movie. They didn't do anything, either. As far as I could tell they didn't even move their mouths to say hello. They simply looked at each other, and they didn't even smile. Come to think of it, they acted more like people meeting to do some task. Yes, that's it! Something inevitable.

The street was almost empty of traffic. The sights and sounds I'd seen and heard in the first few blocks of my walk, people talking in the park, children playing, the big red brick houses with pots of ivy and geraniums, their lighted lamps showing through the lace curtains, the faces here and there in the parlors or on the steps, now looked far away and unfamiliar. The whole scene stretching before me was more like a strange street in a foreign city to which I had suddenly been transported.

I heard Stephen's car start up and move on down the street; I discovered I had been standing still leaning against a park bench which was pressing into my stomach. I moved back.

I felt relieved that they'd gone; the last thing I wanted was to meet up with them. Then I remembered I was headed for Aunt Berty's séance, but I continued my walk more slowly. Everything was different now and I had the idea I might fall down.

Aunt Berty said I could bring Thelma and Johnsy to the séance. I would see Aunt Margaret and Thel, and Johnsy would catch up with us later, after he'd cleaned up the florist's shop, and remembering all of them, I began to feel slightly better. I started walking faster, figuring that might help me stop thinking about Honey and Stephen. But it didn't help. The question kept coming.

What was going on between them? Why weren't they

glad to see each other? I couldn't see Honey's face, just the profile as she stepped into the Stutz. What were they going to do, what act that they had to do and maybe didn't even actually want to do? Or both wanted and hated to do?

Was it the same act that went on between people that made them happy to see each other, or the dangerous act that ended up all those poor, soft women who weren't married, or the act that was entirely different from a kiss, the act you never saw in the movies or anywhere else, the thing that should only take place properly about a year or two after marriage and, even then, could cause the most awful trouble? Quarrels, jealousies, blue babies, death and transfiguration, that kind of thing.

And where were Honey and Stephen going to perform this act? For some reason I thought of the graveyard at Goose Hill, the one behind the park near the Lake, where lovers walked of a night. There was just about everything out there at Goose Hill, restaurants and hotels and old houses with haylofts, a lake with swans and rowboats and canoes, and lover's lanes, and beautiful cemetery with monuments! A likely place for two people who had to meet each other, a perfect place to commit a crime. That was where they were headed, I began to feel certain.

I couldn't do anything about it. I thought of following them but I knew that would be a wild goose chase. I couldn't do anything at all. I began again walking fast, very fast.

During the weeks that followed I said nothing of what I had seen. Honey sent for me, if anything, more often than before. For pot-sitting, dress-watching, bath-watching, makeup helping. Her need for general and specific conversation from me, and only from me, was growing. She laughed and cried in front of me, asking me all kinds of questions.

"If you passed me on the street and didn't know me, would you say I was good-looking?"

"Yes, Honey."

"Pretty?"

"Very pretty."

"Really beautiful?"

"Yes, I'd think you were beautiful." Those answers would quiet her down, but not for long.

"Well, Mercy darling, now if you were a man, would you say I was an interesting woman? I mean, an interesting companion?"

"Yes, I would, Honey. If I were a man I'd like you very much." This didn't seem to satisfy her. So I went on. "You're accomplished. You play the piano beautifully. You have a fine soprano voice. When you sing, people feel it, they really do."

"What else, Mercy? What else, darling?"

"Well, you can cook like a dream, when you want to, that is, and you throw a wonderful party, and you dance like a professional." She thought all this over, her dimples barely showing. "Raymond and Clarence are both madly in love with you. And that new man . . ."

"What new man?"

"That Richard—I keep forgetting his last name."

She said, "Oh, him. Well . . ."

"Can't you make up your mind between one of those three and get engaged?"

Her bright smile receded like a curtain falling. "I cain't, Mercy," she said. "I cain't make up my mind."

"But they'll catch you at it one day, Honey."

"Not the way I do it. Raymond Mondays, Wednesdays and Fridays. Clarence Tuesdays, Thursdays and Sundays. Dickie Saturdays."

"What about the other people you see?"

She stared at me, a sidewise glance uncommon to her. "What other people?"

"I don't know. You said they weren't the only ones."

Silence. "Well, when I see other people I call up and say I'm tired or Mamma's sick, something like that."

"Aren't you afraid they'll find out?"

"Sometimes I am. Sometimes not."

"Aren't you afraid they won't marry you—if they find out about each other?"

"No, Mercy, I'm not."

"Well, why not?"

"Because, oh, suppose I do get married. I'll be so lonesome, going to the bathroom by myself, and times like that. It'll be even worse maybe."

"No, it won't. Maybe you can take your husband to the bathroom with you," I said.

"They think I'm a goddess, darling. They don't think I even do anything like that."

"But in time they might find out you do, Honey."

"Oh, no. No. I'll just go on being lonesome. That's all."

Honey had become more generous with me than ever before. A trip down the street to the tailor to pick up a skirt brought half a dollar, a single pot-watch was up to a quarter, and rouge, tooth-white and a mended curling iron often as much as a dollar, or whatever she had on hand. Since she was now on a buying spree for new clothes, she gave me the most beautiful of her older clothes, a green satin cut princess-fashion in a dozen gores, a georgette crêpe with a pleated skirt, a coat with a fur hat and muff that she'd hardly worn.

"I'll take them all in around the back and let down the skirts; your Cousin Louise is heavy around back and short, whereas you're small down there and tall," commented Cousin Maria, the deaf relative who came to us to sew every Monday and Tuesday, and to other members of the family on the other days of the week.

But although Honey seemed to love and need me more than ever and to trust me implicitly, a new element had entered into my feeling for her. I found myself watching her curiously, listening on the alert for clues to what was actually going on between her and Stephen that neither of them saw fit to mention.

I remembered the way Aunt Gus would scold her daughter. "You keep on playing cat-and-mouse with men, one of them's going to get you good and hard someday. And you'll be sorry. There's no telling what

236

your pa will do to you, and to him. He keeps his shotgun polished up good."

It wasn't the gun that worried me. All the men had shotguns, some of them had half a dozen. It was that about the man getting her "good and hard." As I thought about Honey with Stephen, I remembered how, as a child, during the war, when I went into the parlor to look for my picture book, I had found Honey's feet sticking up from under the piano, together with the big feet of the soldier who was courting her, her voice saying, "Go away, Mercy. Go on home now, you hear?"

Those same legs and feet I had seen under the piano and under the soldier had been the exact same ones beside Stephen the night they had driven off together. The exact same legs, now more than a decade older! Twenty-seven-year-old legs. The legs of an older woman. Honey was no longer young and still she was not married and she was dissatisfied with her life. Once she had been engaged to three men at the same time and kept changing her rings as each giver appeared. I began to believe she lived another secret, terrible life, and to think that this very drive might be what made her so lonesome and scared, so scared she couldn't even go to the toilet by herself.

One day Rose came to the door as I came home from school. She gave me a cryptic message. "Your Cousin Louise wants to see you right away."

"What for? Another errand?"

"I don't think so. Not this time. You better go on over for five minutes."

Honey was waiting for me. She was already upstairs this time. "I'm going to a hop at the Naval Academy this Saturday, Mercy. Tell me which dress looks best on me, will you please, darling?" She had three dresses laid out on her bed, and I waited while she tried each one on, giving the try-ons my full attention.

"You look prettiest in the white," I said finally. "White silk is just wonderful on you. It floats even

237

when you're not dancing." She tried it on once again, and we both decided it was best.

"I have to go now, Honey."

"Not this minute. Stay just three more minutes."

"All right." I saw she was serious, there were no dimples, and she was sitting up very straight. "What's the matter? Do you have a new man?"

"Yes."

"Well, you'll look great. So don't worry."

"Mercy?"

"Yes, Honey."

"If I got married, would you come and live with me?"

"Certainly. You bet I would."

"You would, really? You could go to college and write and have your own room and everything you wanted." I thought how wonderful it would be, living with Honey. Virginia Anne had already left home, and Mamma and Daddy didn't seem to miss her at all. "I'd give you a heap of presents all the time, and we'd have parties and *fun!*"

"Oh, I'd love it, Honey, but have you made up your mind?"

"I have to," said Honey, very gravely. "I feel better now that I can count on you." We hugged and kissed and, for the time it took, I forgot all about Honey's deceit, also about the unlovely chores that might be required of me in the palace we seemed about to enter.

Those afternoons in the beautiful house with the delicious unsafe feeling, a revved-up motor underneath my heart! Discovering you could get loose from your mind. More or less, anyway. "Let's remember not to be repressed down here," Stephen would say. "Mercy, girl, d'you know what I mean by repression?"

I'd say, "Yes. I think so." But I wasn't sure.

"Johnsy?"

"Naw."

"It means putting down. Putting the lid on. Quelling."

"Yeah, quelling."

"Let's not keep things under control."

"Yeah, you're kidding us," Johnsy said.

"No, I'm not. That's my way of teaching." Algebra, he told us, is just one of the subjects one has to learn in school which has little or no relationship to what most people will be doing in their later lives. "I don't think either of you two are going to have any use for algebra, except in the sense people use all forms of mathematics as a training, an introduction to logical thinking, if they can make any sense out of it."

Stephen walked as he talked, explaining how in olden days mathematics was considered a part of magic, fit only for priests. Then it became part of the stock in trade of astrologers and alchemists, even took on a mystical slant which was probably why these brilliant mathematical people were called wizards. Some of these exceptional students might go on to study calculus, trigonometry and other higher branches of mathematics and become engineers, architects and industrialists.

He had boys in his class who were so serious about charts and slide rules they couldn't keep their minds on any phase of art or literature. "They can't *see* things. They actually don't read!" He made us both feel better about ourselves. Then he shifted his conversation, bang, into the actual kind of test problems in algebra I'd have to solve at the mid-term examination.

He made us both talk. Even Johnsy began to speak up. It was the freshness in him that made you feel relaxed and kind of eager. My world was being extended. A relationship was building up among the three of us, as I began to catch on to algebra, and Johnsy caught up in his school work. I began to feel Stephen's presence in a special way. He reminded me of somebody. He didn't remind me of Jesus, the old dropped lover, or Al-Balkhi, laughing rider with sword. He was not like anyone else. He was unique, complete to himself, and mine, all mine.

He brought with him a Christmas Eve feeling. Rewards in the offing? And the way he'd grin! A special light came with this grin, I swear to God. It made his

239

rather dark skin come bright against his white teeth and the white in his brown eyes, and I would feel a flash come up from within me like a train signal, *I'm coming through!* He took nothing away from you, the way a lot of boys and even adult men tried to do.

At school there were moments you could remember, first sight of the omega separating under the microscope, getting the basketball into the basket, hearing your own voice winning in a debate, but the afternoons in the old Farrar place *all* had something you couldn't forget.

Many afternoons when Johnsy failed to show up, Stephen and I would discuss him. Junior, we called him now. He could be seen at all hours of the day and often at night, trudging through snow and sleet, toting large, heavy packages, when he wasn't washing down steps or basements, shoveling or piling snow. Yet the hours he spent learning how to study had had a telling effect. He wanted to pass now, he said, so he could get a job, and to this end he tried to study in the little free time he had left.

It was getting dark outside one afternoon, and Stephen was just banking the fire, when he began talking about Johnsy, who hadn't been able to come. "It's not right," he said, "working a boy that hard."

"No, it's terrible," I agreed.

"You know, he's not retarded. He's actually bright. And he's such a beautiful child. Natural. Untouched."

"Yes, uncontaminated." I thought that was pretty good. I meant it, too. As Stephen was speaking I saw I had changed in my feelings toward Johnsy Dowse.

"Masculine," Stephen went on. "A masculine boy. Not above work. Loves it. I've seen him shoveling snow when he was just a kid. You wouldn't believe how he could shovel with his small arms. And always smiling and laughing as if he were having a good time. A man, Sunshine, a genuine man, male-child!"

This was Johnsy we were talking about! It's funny how you can change your feelings about something like that, looking at it through somebody else's eyes. Like I say, I'd begun looking at Johnsy through Stephen's eyes. All the facets of Johnsy's personality and his big eyes and big mouth, dimples and even dirty clothes, had changed magically into desirable attributes, so much so that Johnsy was fast becoming another person. In fact, for quite a while now when I heard his voice coming from the backyard next door I had felt a quickening inside, like any young girl made suddenly aware of a not unattractive male person nearby. Then I would quickly remember it was Johnsy, but the feeling did not immediately subside.

Stephen mentioned something about Johnsy being "pretty gone" on me. He slipped into it so easily I hardly thought about what he was saying, but then this was the rule in the Farrar basement, this easy, open sharing of innermost secrets. Before I knew it, I was telling him all about Johnsy and me, recalling Johnsy as I had known him before Stephen. "It was sort of like we'd come out of the same litter," I said. "Why, when I saw Johnsy it was like seeing my own arm or something." I told him about the fights we had had as kids, knock-down, drag-out quarrels ending in real fights. He'd tease me. I'd get mad and attack. I'd hurt him, too. He'd sometimes conquer me, pin me down, but he would never hurt me.

Before I knew it I was telling Stephen about the time Johnsy had "tried something." We were behind the piano and he had me pinned down.

"Behind the piano?" Stephen smiled languidly.

"Yes. We used to have this upright piano stuck slant-wise in the corner."

"A marvelous place for such a thing, with those long Spanish shawls hanging down."

Thus inspired, I continued, "A big carpeted space. It's always dark back there, even on the sunniest days."

"Of course. I see that. How clever of you two." His eyes were half closed as he talked. "A big space, plenty big enough for two full bodies, covered with that Brussels carpet you have, green with the red roses. Everything going on around you. You can hear and even see but you can't be heard or seen. Tremendous. Go on."

"Well, there we were," I said. "Me pinned down. Johnsy put his one free hand on my thigh. Then he started to press against me. I told him I'd holler if he didn't get up, but he just grinned and said he didn't care, and I knew he didn't. He just didn't care."

"He just didn't care," repeated Stephen. "This male-child just didn't give a hoot. Go on."

"He pressed harder and harder. In fact, the doors to the parlor rolled back, Mamma came in and sat down at the piano and began playing that damned concerto in D Minor. As the music grew louder, he kept pressing so hard I thought I'd go into the floor."

"Wonderful! Like making love in an opera box. Down on the floor of one of the carpeted tiers, with the opera going on."

I said, "Yes," as if I knew exactly what he meant, which in a sense I did. I'd begun to pick up on him, feel with him, if you know what I mean. Sometimes when we parted I felt like I was going back into my old self, almost like entering a familiar town where I'd once lived and where I had again to get used to the lonesome streets.

"Suppose your Cousin Ruth came in? Suppose Ruth decided to play the piano?" I stopped talking. "You're afraid of her, aren't you, Sunshine?"

"Ruth is terrible. You never know what she is going to do. Thank God she's married."

"If you can call that a marriage."

I knew exactly what he meant. Dale of the pink and purple pimples, and Ruth the Smile, were certainly a bizarre couple. "It was awful, having her live with us between schools." I was not about to tell him what had actually happened.

"But you haven't finished telling me about you and Junior. You're still behind the piano."

"He's pressing so hard I think we'll go right through the floor." I stopped there. I noticed the way Stephen was staring down at me, his mouth slightly ajar.

"Go on." His voice was so low I could barely make out the words. But something stopped me. I couldn't go on. I looked up at him. His eyes were lowered. I could see the lids with the heavy lashes come down partway. I thought I heard a sound, a door opening and clicking to, and when I finally looked away my cheeks felt warm. "You want me to kiss you, don't you, Mercy, dear?"

I didn't answer. I heard him get up from where he had been leaning against the table and come over to where I was standing. I knew I should stay cool and speak casually, but I couldn't make it, not this time. I couldn't even lift my eyes, though once I tried and stopped at his chin. He took my face in his hands. My lids felt heavy and dead. Maybe I've begun to die all over, I thought. Of course, this is dying. You rise up out of your body, and then you fall and you go down this bright pink cone, down, down, forever.

PART THREE

1929

GRADUATION arrived at last. A soft summer's night, blue skies hanging over the streets. Dresses of organdy, voile and silk fluttering down the blocks of red brick houses as girls run down white marble steps into waiting cars. Shiny black limousines and town cars dot the streets. Old streets look younger, old bricks and stone have a new brightness, old cornices on rooftops gleam in the fading silvery sun. The pavement glitters under my satin feet as I walk out in my white silk dress and head for the long black limousine waiting at the curb.

The car is empty. I'm its first occupant. I choose the best seat beside the window. The polished brown face of smiling James Caulfield, he had been driving girls to graduations and families to and from weddings and funerals as far back as I could remember, looks in the window as he closes the door. "Good evening, Miss Bassford. I hopes it's a mighty fine time ahead now. You just takes up your diploma and don't be afraid of nothing."

"Thank you, James." Funny how black folks are always telling the white folks not to worry. "Don't worry, you hear?" Aunt Rose forever admonishing me. "The spirit don't want you to worry. Everything's going to be all right." Rose, before she goes home to her alley on Sunday, says she's "not gonna to do no cooking.

Gonna to eat cream-muffs and milk," cautions me not to worry, and here James Caulfield is telling me, "Don't be afraid."

Thel is the next girl to be collected. She has on a satin dress, coffin white, more fashionable and expensive than mine, but not as soft and pretty. "Hey, Merce."

"Hey, Thel."

"Let's grab both windows before that fat Merle gets in."

"Uh-huh. Good neighbors is what we are." We're still laughing a mile or so later as the limousine stops on Mulberry Street to pick up Merle, who looks chic but boyish in white linen and no makeup.

"Hey, you kids hogged the windows. I'm stuck in the middle with my fat ass."

"You can have my seat."

"Aw, no, Merce. I can see the sights from here."

The sights are like ceremonial scenes in some movie as girl after girl in coffin white or cake pink or sky blue comes down marble steps into limousines where black men wait beside open doors to let them in. Thel says her daddy was forced to tip the headwaiter at the Southern five dollars to assure the Hodges' seat at the corner table. Merle, whose family relies on a rich uncle for extras, says Uncle Howie is taking them all to the country club. Merle doesn't like boys and is being escorted by her Cousin Robert, under protest.

We pass houses and parks until, as we near the crowded downtown section, there are no more groups of girls and we watch, instead, the backs of streetcars, automobiles and ugly office buildings on our way to the hall. A silence is forced upon us by honking horns, clanging streetcars, the harsh scream of city traffic. Then the traffic quiets, as we near the hall, and the questions and answers begin.

"Where *you* going, Merce?"

"To a private party."

"Where?" demands Merle. The car lurches forward. From where we sit we can already see groups of girls

247

getting out of cars, making their way to the stage entrance.

"There's Candice Vincent, she's wearing the dress she told us about, showing her bosoms." They both stare.

"You didn't tell us where you're going," Merle begins again with the questions. "What's the big secret? Who's the man?"

Thel looks over at me. "I bet I know. She's going to the Castle, m'dear. She goes with an older man, socially prominent."

"Who? What castle? What's Mr. High Class's real name?" She takes hold of my arm. There's something funny about Merle, the way she walks, steps so long you can't keep up with her, the way she fights with boys. "You better tell me or I won't let you out of the car." She pinches my arm so hard I forget Stephen for the first time that day. *This is all a dream and now comes the nightmare part. Wake up!*

"Let go of me, Merle. You're hurting my arm."

"Well, now, Miss Embroidered White Silk, I just bet I know who your fellow is. What d'you know about that? I know a whole lot about him, too, and for half a dime I'd tell you!"

"Let go of her, Merle." Thel pulls at Merle's hand. I'm glad when the car starts rolling. I'm ashamed in front of James Caulfield who looks so dignified but who can hear every word we say.

The ceremony is like a sequence, in one of those silents, where the actors move in jerks as if they have St. Vitus's dance. It is interrupted by great blobs of color and sound, and these keep getting interrupted by darker blobs of silence and terror. It comes back to me in waves. The girls all talking, some whispering, some screaming about where they're going for the summer, what they're going to do.

I settle in my small red velvet chair among the hundreds of others set up in tiers, my embroidered dress falling over my legs. I'm aware of myself with a dress that has dozens of tiny tucks, scallops and small white stars, as I prepare to endure the endless speeches about dedication and the future. I feel slightly queasy. Suppose when Dr. Gardiner calls my name, Miss Mercy Bassford, instead of getting up and walking downstage to receive my diploma, my legs become paralyzed and I can't move.

The soul kisses I'd had with Stephen come to mind, sweet, exciting but threatening. I hadn't swallowed any saliva, or had I? Could you swallow saliva and not know it? Of course not, no more than you could swallow coffee and not know it, but wait, maybe Stephen's saliva, nectar that it is, was different from coffee. It might go down by itself, slip through the tonsils in secret drops and have some odd effect. This was crazy, a childish idea floating back. Nobody can get anything from a soul kiss, except another soul kiss.

Miss Bonner is standing at the podium, tapping with her steel stick. We rise in a body. The corny singing starts up.

Silent o'er the waw-aw-ters gli-ding . . . In our bar-ruks we ride. Where would Stephen be sitting? I think I can see Mamma beside my Aunt Jenny but I can't seem to find Stephen. *Far a-bove the star-rars are gleam-ing, mir-rored in the dee-yup . . .*

That head near the column, that's Stephen, with Johnsy sitting beside him, grinning. The singing goes on and on. Then, in between, noisy talk in the auditorium and then silence and then the speeches, so full of words and those awful jokes and then the pseudo-serious part that always sounds as if the speaker is going to really say something, but never does.

It seems like hours before the diplomas are given out. First five girls—Able, Addair, Aranson, Arnauld, Atkinson, and then comes Miss Mercy Bassford. My legs work fine! So do my feet, hands and eyes, and I have my diploma and am back in my seat before I know what I'm doing. My face is hot, but I'm relieved. I see Mamma and Aunt Jenny again, then Stephen and Johnsy, all clapping for me. It is hot on the stage and the odor is terrible, all those roses, orchids, gardenias mixed with heavy perfume, I can smell Christmas Night, Mitsoukou and some cheap stuff, Jasmine or Gollywog, the smell of girls' sweat, powder, and rouge. I wonder how the same number of boys would smell in their graduation ceremony, a few blocks away.

Stephen's head is bent over toward Johnsy. Just think, Stephen, way up there in the cultivated world of men, he's chosen me. *And tonight, this very night, in a matter of hours, anything may happen!* We're going to have a party after this graduation. Stephen and Johnsy are giving a party for me, all by themselves in the big house. *Maybe this will be the night I'll get it!* I'll take it, too, no matter what happens, gracefully, as if I'd had it maybe a thousand times before. I feel dizzy with excitement. Suppose I get sick, about to faint or be sick at the stomach. Imagine having to run through the crowd and look for the bathroom, and having a doctor come. What would I say to him? Miss Bonner is tapping again. They've already started that damned singing, way over on the left side. *Merrily, merrily, merrily, merrily, life is but a dream* . . .

Outside at last, the corridor is bursting with families in smiling groups waiting for their overdressed darlings to show up. Mamma says, "Mercy dear," and kisses me. When I turn, she has disappeared, leaving me with my two aunts. Daddy hasn't been able to get back from his hunting trip but has sent me a telegram. I notice Aunt Jenny's bosom; it's the biggest in the entire corridor, in which quite a few mammas, aunts and grandmothers have plenty up front. Aunt Margaret has rouge on her face in the wrong places, but I love her.

My two aunts are standing beside honorary Aunt Berty Hildebrandt, the spiritualist, tall, nearly six feet, and quite plump, nodding her head, her face lighting up. You can practically see the spirits communicating with her. Stephen appears out of nowhere, and kisses me on the forehead, whispering, "Congratulations later." Johnsy bites my ear. "Hey, I heard your opry voice all the way to the back seats." Everybody laughs. He has on his good suit, his hair is plastered down with Vaseline, his curls are running out from under.

Thel, standing with her mother and father, leans over. "You're not supposed to insult her tonight. But she does sing awful."

It isn't much of a party back home; everybody knows I have a date, thank heaven. Rose has baked a lemon sponge cake with white icing. So we sit around the dining room table playing with the cake and sipping white wine, my two aunts and Berty Hildebrandt on one side, Stephen, Johnsy and I on the other. We three are getting ready to leave and Johnsy is already standing when Aunty Jenny makes shhhh sounds as Berty's head falls back, sure sign she's going into a trance. In a minute, her hands fall to her sides, her mouth opens, her eyes close.

It seems like about a year passes before Aunt Berty begins speaking in a husky, masculine voice, mostly muttering in a foreign tongue; these stop, and when she begins, "Yes, we are ready," she sounds more normal. Next thing she's whistling, practically warbling. Berty has this Indian guide who comes on whistling, and we have to wait till he finishes up. Then it comes. "Be careful where you go, Mercy and Johnsy," a man's voice cautions. "Watch out for an accident. Be careful!"

"You'd better rest now, hadn't you?" whispers Aunt Jenny, as Berty begins to wake up. We say good-bye, politely thanking everybody, and are out on the street before Berty can resume her performance.

"You think she seen anything?" Johnsy asks me.

I say, "I don't know. She looked like she was off somewhere. She's a famous medium," I tell them. "People come from all over to receive messages through her." Stephen simply says he didn't like what she said, even though he didn't believe it. He has his arms around us. "I'm happy and I don't give a damn one way or the other."

"Aw, anybody can say you're gonna do something or have something happen," says Johnsy. "I seen lots of people talking to spirits."

251

"You have?" I ask.

"I can do it myself if I want to."

"Do it for us tonight?"

"Sure I will. All you gotta do is get in the mood." Johnsy is already in some kind of special mood. He almost drops the large package he is carrying. "I'm an old witch-man. What do you want to know?"

"Plenty."

"Well, wait till I get a chance to sit down and I'll tell you." We begin doing a Highland fling together, taking giant steps as we hurry on.

For some reason, the Place looks especially inviting and luxurious. There's something different about it. Stephen closes both doors as we begin moving about, putting down packages, getting out records, adjusting windows, before I discover what it is. "Somebody's been in here."

Stephen grins that lovely grin he has when he's happy. "You're imagining things, Sunshine."

"Only us three's got keys! Musta been one of us." Johnsy is opening a huge brown grocery bag, removing package after package, a box of chocolate-covered cherries, three bags of potato chips, a cake wrapped so carefully in wax paper you can hardly see it, bottles of Coca-Cola, packages of pretzels, peanuts and cigarettes.

Stephen begins helping him. "We could hole up here for years."

"Yeah, that's right."

After the food comes packages from Johnsy's booty. My gifts.

As I look across the room I realize I must have been crazy not to notice the flowers, flowers everywhere! Roses and gladiolas and daisies fill all the vases. The place has been cleaned, too, the floor is waxed and shining, the Oriental rugs swept and wiped clean and there are fresh candles in the two candelabras beside the fire place and on the table.

"Who did all this? You?"

"Pixies, Sunshine. They come on call." Stephen is busy at the icebox. A new block of ice has been put inside, whole rows of bottles are chilling on the shelves, beside covered dishes and platters of beautiful food.

"Let's just stay here. Would you dare?"

"Yes. Mamma's away. I'd dare."

"You, Johnsy?"

"Sure. Let's hide out. 'At'd be fun."

Stephen must have been here working for hours. There's an extra thrill about that, a man fixing up a place for a girl, trying to make her comfortable. I felt relieved, seeing it all. This is kind of an emergency, I know. I have a general shakiness about everything of a sexual nature. But he knows what to do. I wonder what Johnsy will do besides depositing food and grinning and saying those funny things he says. What will he do? But Stephen is in charge. Stephen knows.

I move around fingering flowers, lighting candles, touching things, wondering what's coming next? *I'm the heroine here. I have two men, a man and a half, anyway, and they're both in love with me. But look at me, waiting around big-eyes, dumb as some corny movie heroine. Buck up, say something. Heroines aren't all that dumb. Not necessarily, anyway.*

I couldn't think of a word.

Stephen lifted a bottle of champagne out of a bucket he had carefully filled with bits of ice. He twisted the top, and the cork popped. Johnsy and I screamed delightedly.

"Here come the elephants," said Stephen pouring the lovely beige liquid into crystal goblets. I remember noticing how clean and sparkling the goblets were. He must have come there and washed them. Everything was so alive! "Here's to a national emergency," Stephen lifted his glass to touch ours. We all three said it at once, "Emergency." Johnsy drank as if he was drinking ginger ale, and Stephen refilled his glass. I sipped mine slowly. It came down to my chest with a sweet, prickly pang. A woman wearing a large flowered hat passed the window without even turning to glance in at us. Aside from the goblets and the expensive goodies, Stephen had provided paté from a thick crock, which he spread on crackers, and other more sophisticated food, caviar and the like, some of which I had never before tasted. Johnsy's pile looked like kid stuff.

In the summer's night, through the open windows on three sides of the big room, an odor of damp earth and trees seeped in, mingling with the scent of honeysuckle and lilies of the valley from a bed close to the house. I sniffed the liberating pine tree smell, clear as new stars. I glanced up at the familiar branches of our spruce, with its emerald-green buds. It had pushed its way so hard through the small opening we hadn't been able to move the slats.

After maybe the third glass of champagne Stephen looked more than ever like Clive Brook. Suave, tweedy, British, reserved, controlled. He knew what he was doing got to me. The way he set the table and arranged flowers and plates, knives and forks and glasses. A man of the world, I can tell you that for a fact. Johnsy was dancing around by himself.

I kept staring at the branch of this damned spruce tree, these new green buds turned brighter; they looked like fuzzy green lights. Stephen struck a match and lit more candles. When he finished with them he stared at me. "That white silk dress is a wonder, Sunshine. You must keep it all your life. Silk of that kind won't ever wear out." I could feel my skin come up against the silk as he spoke.

Johnsy drank the last of the wine in his glass. "Hey, that stuff's pretty good. Feel like I could dance all night. Got any more?"

"Just about a dozen bottles. Here, let me have your glass, but don't forget we're eating something now."

"Why?"

"It'll last longer . . ."

I wondered, as we sat down at the table, how much of this will I tell Thel? It's so much like a movie setting, only better. Stephen is better than Clive. For one thing, he talks. And all the things he can do. Teach, set tables, converse. Whereas Clive just mutters "shucks," or "I love you," or "Let's go somewhere." That's what it seems he's muttering.

The buds, the tiny, bright green buds on the tree branch had changed when I saw them again. They were moving, crawling on the branch, which was coming nearer.

"Damned thing's grown a foot since last week," Stephen was saying. This trait he had was often irritating, the way he kept his head as he read exactly what was going on in mine.

"If it's grown a foot, maybe it'll grow legs and a hand," Johnsy giggled like a child, but somehow, as I watched him, I could see he was a very male child and he fitted in with us. We were eating and drinking the champagne. I don't know what all we said. While it was going on, Stephen had been stroking my fingers gently, slowly up and down. I smiled at him and, as I did, I felt something else, Johnsy stroking the fingers of my other hand. Johnsy's fingers imitating Stephen's. It was funny, we all laughed, but it was something else, too. Johnsy's fingers felt different from Stephen's, they were bigger and rougher, but they affected Stephen's gentler touch, made it more thrilling, I don't know why.

"Did you know we're living in a tree house?" Stephen moved up closer beside me.

I wanted to say something, to prove that I, too, could keep my head but I couldn't think of anything. It seems just right having a tree growing in a room, with the buds crawling. I was thinking that, but found I said it aloud.

Stephen got up and opened another bottle. He managed it cleverly. When the cork popped, we all screamed, "Emergency!" just like kids. He filled our glasses and came back to sit besides me. "There's such a thing as a real tree house, but those are for children and I'm not talking about those. I'm merely wondering why more people don't build part of their houses around trees. A country house in town, with a tree going up through the porch. That would be marvelous. That's what we'll do as soon as we're settled somewhere. If we ever are, that is." The words hit me like gobs of hot caramel. As soon as we're settled, *as soon as we're settled!* I imagined being settled in a house with Stephen and having part of it built around a tree. I started seeing the house and him, and then I started feeling it and then I was actually there, *in the house with Stephen and Johnsy, and there is the tree right before my eyes.* Every single object I saw, touched or smelled then came nearer and was bigger and brighter than before.

Stephen began gently rubbing the inside of my palm. I was looking at the branch of that tree, and noticed the needles resembled great emerald-green darts. Then I saw each needle was a small tree in itself, a long oval tree pointed at the top, dark green and then lighter green with a fine line going down the center and, on both sides, a silvery shine. These needles were so alive they seemed about to speak. A silence had come over us, but the house wasn't quiet: it made a slow, beating, rhythmical sound, as if there were a drum concealed somewhere in the woodwork.

I thought if I once lifted my arms I'd float up off the floor and go dancing up toward the ceiling. I'd follow this strange new beat, even if it lifted me up, way up dangerously near the top of the room and then maybe dropped me down when it stopped. Dangerous, but I was looking forward to it.

Johnsy was sitting there in one of the big chairs, smoking and smiling. I was thinking, don't start talking. Then I saw Stephen at the Victrola, looking over the records, and I hoped he wouldn't put a record on; there's already this other music, this beat going on in the woodwork. There was something waiting, no doubt about it, and we were all three waiting with it.

After a while, we were sitting around the table when the Victrola started playing all by itself. We laughed. We didn't find this unusual. We acted as if records went on by themselves every day. It was Armstrong's, "I Can't Give You Anything but Love." You couldn't resist the commanding horn sounds. Stephen started dancing first, then Johnsy and I both started at the same time. I was dancing with both of them, and this seemed so right and we were doing it so perfectly, I wondered why more people didn't dance this way, a girl between two men, both of them twirling her this way and that; it made a marvelous whirling rhythm.

I had been afraid this waiting thing might disappear with the first loud sound and never come back, but now, as we all danced faster and faster, enjoying ourselves to the hilt, the same sights flickered in my eyes, and I knew it was still there, it was going to stay.

Now all this physical enjoyment, this flood-tide, end-to-end fun we were having, while entirely new to me, was not without some insights. I could feel my insides liquefying with a silvery heat. *I'm free now and I can do anything. I'm something special. I can see and feel and know everything. And I will, oh yes. I have these two men, these two remarkable people, and they're both mine, and I'm theirs, too, come to think of it. We're all three part of each other. I can feel us pouring into each other.*

This minute, this *now* feeling was so strong I could feel it running through me every which way. Through my skin, in my mouth, my nose, way up through my hair. Stephen actually was a god. Look! He had become extraordinarily tall, his eyes were larger, why, his whole head was twice life-size. Johnsy looked different, too, I saw how beautiful he was, the shining red curly hair caught up new lights, only his mouth was slightly threatening in its slowly awakening masculinity.

They're both mine, and I'm theirs. We're all three caught up in this great, quivering, waiting thing, this life thing, and this is forever. I'm going to get it soon. This love thing, and then I'll know. But what about Johnsy, this strange, tall boy with the red head and the eager eyes, smiling at me? What will we do with him, or was he a part of what was about to happen?

We were all quite close together after a dance. I don't know how it happened we were all three kissing each other, lightly, happily, foolishly, yes, that must be it, three happy fools. Stephen kissing me, then John-

257

sy kissing me, then Stephen kissing Johnsy, foolishly on Johnsy's foolish red curls, then Johnsy kissing me again. *Some part of me is dissolving.* I managed to notice that. *My old self, yes, that's it, my old self is becoming obsolete.*

I began to laugh because they were both laughing. *I don't know how or when or, come to think of it, even with whom, but I'm going to get it. And it's not a sin, it's not going down a bottomless pit, it's more like rising up, way up!*

"I hope this night never stops," I heard myself say. And Stephen said, "It won't." "How do you know?" "I'll see to it, Sunshine. I have ways. I promise."

Johnsy had started cutting the cake. The slices lay there, the creamy icing falling slightly to the side. "I'll see to it, too, Sunshine." Johnsy looked happy. "We'll see to it, huh, Stephen?"

It went on like this. It had this rhythm, pushing us onward toward its own climax. Whatever we did, drinking the champagne, listening to the records, or kissing each other, or dancing together, we moved in a queer kind of precision, as if we all heard the exact same sound. I have a memory of us stopping somewhere, I think at the end of one of those wild dances, and Stephen saying, "We love you, Mercy." He wasn't looking in my direction, a sure sign he was dead serious.

"Do you, really? Do you both love me?"

Then Stephen answered, "We do." And Johnsy, "We do." It sounded like some kind of a vow. Of course, I was at a wedding, my own, and I was the bride.

"I love you, too," I said. "I love you both." My voice came out loud and echoed in the vast space. It was a kind of ritual. *I am being chosen, I really am. This is my initiation. Stephen and Al-Balkhi have been with me many a night before, with Johnsy faintly outlined, but that was just dreaming. I was in control then, but this is different. It will hurt, maybe it will hurt real hard. Everybody says it hurts the first two years or so. But this is love hurt, different from other hurt!*

How it happened is that I was half sitting, half lying

stretched out on the wicker chaise longue. Two men seemed perfectly proper and natural to me. I know Stephen moved quickly and took me in his arms, pulling me up close to him. It wasn't our first kiss, not even our first *soul kiss,* but it was the deepest and longest.

Then he lifted me up off my feet and carried me across the room. My shoes fell off. I remember hearing them plop on the floor, first came one, then the other. Then he was laying me down, bending over me. I wasn't quite certain where I was lying. I thought I felt crumbs underneath me, under my silk dress. I even thought I smelled the cake. I forgot all other smells in the smell of Stephen, his face and his mouth and that Russian toilet water he used. Then, what's this? Why, Johnsy was taking me in his arms. Johnsy wasn't as gentle or as subtle as Stephen, his smell was entirely different—Kirkman's Borax soap covered over with some cheap toilet water, a smell of recently eaten olives and potato chips. Different, but very sweet and young.

Johnsy was lifting me up toward him. "I love you, Mercy," he kept saying, not realizing, of course, we were beyond words. They slowed the action. I must have forgotten our recent ritual. I was in a queer position. Stephen had hold of me, he was kissing my neck. At the same time Johnsy was kissing my lips. I remember wondering, two sets of hands, one was Johnsy's awkward, half-scared, the other was Stephen's, practical but gentle, always careful. Even Al-Balkhi couldn't do anything like this, I can tell you.

Quick images come flashing in like dreams and nightmares and I'm barely aware of us as different people; we seem to be the same person. I know Stephen is lifting me up in his arms but I wonder why he is putting me on that high table, the one we have to stand beside to reach for our books. But just feeling his arms and the sensation of being carried is too good for quibbling. He lays me down gently; is pushing up my dress together with the silk petticoat, and then his hands are unhooking all the tiny buttons down the back of my dress.

He does it quickly, gently. The dress makes a sound hitting the floor—I'm still half dressed now, but the petticoat is up, and my silk brassiere is showing. The scallops on my petticoat hit the sides of my bare thighs. What would Aunt Gus think if she could see me now? And Uncle Tom, the Bible quoter? What would old Al-Balkhi think? But Al-B knows me, he even knows Stephen and Johnsy, all of us, everything! Why, even his horse knows! Al-B knows better than I what's happening now.

Why, Stephen is behind me. He must be. I can feel his hands on my hips, then going down under me. And yet he, or is it Johnsy, is up front there. "Gently now, old chap, not too fast, not so rough." Is this really happening? They are both petting me, fixing me—angels, doctors, lovers. Anything is possible. Is that Johnsy up front, pulling my legs toward him, around his waist? I don't know for sure. I know Stephen's long, strong, silky hands. He has my bare waist in his hands. Then, oh, his hands are covering my breasts, cupping them, pressing gently on the nipples. I knew I had nipples, of course, but I didn't know they could stand up and feel like this.

His hands move under the silk bodice which is half open, touching me everywhere. "Empire cut," he whispers, recalling my description of my new dress, "over the most beautiful pink points in the empire." His head leans over me, kissing my forehead, my neck, my ears. Johnsy, standing down there somewhere, is awkward, he's pushing hard against me, he hurts, but just then Stephen's hands come down around my thighs over the cheeks of my bottom. I didn't think a bottom could burn like this. I didn't know.

Then I feel his big hands going under me, lifting me up. It's all done so deftly I'm not sure just what is happening. Then something starts entering. Gentle. But even so it hurts. Johnsy, it must be Johnsy, hurting me, pushing into me. It hurts, but there's another feeling, too, terrifying, thrilling, intense, of pleasure riding side by side with pain. I resist, but Stephen's touch on my stomach makes me pliable, my body opens up inside and stretches every time his hands move. I feel him kissing my ears, and everything inside me starts opening like a plant left burning too long in the sun at last feeling the rain.

Sounds from somewhere, sound of music, that victrola record must be stuck and keeps on playing. The sound of hands, breath coming faster, then a solitary, authoritative voice. Is it Jesus? Al-Balkhi? Stephen? Johnsy *and* Stephen? or maybe even God? Love is taking on new dimensions. "Move back, my darling. Oh, yes, that's it. Open your legs. Now come up, up." That couldn't be God. More likely Al-Balkhi-Stephen or Johnsy, or both together.

I am in a house of hands. A hundred little dams rising inside. They start to break into rivers going every which way. Did I imagine it, or was that Johnsy saying, "I am so a man!" The music rises loud over a sense of pain gone wild. I try to see what's over me. Is it skin? It looks like a blanket of skin, pink in places, dark in other places. Oh, a big star is rising inside me! Too big! It's going to burst, I know it is! It'll burst open like a rocket. It's beginning now, and pieces, pieces of myself, are breaking off.

A part of me senses what's happening. Stephen, directing this magic. *Him,* that's who's behind all those hands, those bodies, hot and hard, pressing into me everywhere. I see eyes. Are they Johnsy's eyes or Stephen's eyes, or the eyes of all men, staring into mine? I'm going to die, as this great, pain-filled star starts to fall. But maybe I'll live. Life or death, which will it be, or are they both the same? Then the hot pieces start falling down inside me, and I know I'm part of the star that's bursting into flames, falling, down to nowhere.

Do I hear Johnsy? "Aw, no, that'll hurt her." I'm not sure, because just then I see Stephen's face. He looks like that sculpture of Jehovah in the museum, and if at that moment someone had asked, "Is this the face of God?" I'd have answered, "Yes, of course!"

A short time later, it started to hurt a lot more. It hurt so hard, the whole place went dark with brilliant flashes of white light. *This is the love hurt.* I kept trying to hold on to that idea. *Different from all other hurts.* And I did think once, ignoring the ritual, *does it have to hurt this much?*

On a Saturday, a few weeks later, I awoke to the realization I had the whole day off from my summer job at Lane and Co. Ltd., the international plumbing cartel where Dale Stump was personnel manager and had recommended me. By dint of working on Friday till eleven, I was given the whole day off instead of just the afternoon. I'd collected my salary and promptly added the entire twenty-eight dollars to the hundred and forty in my cash box for my college clothes. Now, with another twenty-one due from Honey for uncollected pot-sits, dressing helps, general listening and counseling about her impending marriage to Clarence, I'd have quite a sum of money which I was planning to spend in a happy shopping spree with Thelma.

Hearing rain splashing against the window screens, I looked forward to my date that night with Stephen and Johnsy, yawning and stretching and luxuriating as I thought, we can stay home tonight, light all the candles, even make a fire. Rain like this might just add a new dimension to love, make it even sweeter with us three closer, listening to the rain.

Downstairs, I ate breakfast hastily, so Rose could go off to her shanty to take care of her sick mother and finish ironing clothes.

"What's happening to the plants?" I asked, as I heard her dressing in the kitchen.

"Reckon Uncle Jonas ain't got his stuff from the island."

"Really? What island?"

"They gits sent to him from these islands. Uncle

Jonas gits 'em in Georgia an' he boxes 'em an' sends 'em to me. You better write him a letter."

"I will, but you don't need to burn any more for me."

"How you figure that? I thought that Mista Farrar was shippin' off and, with Johnsy working in Philadelphia, you gonna be left by yerself."

I tried to explain to her Stephen wasn't going away. I remembered his exact words. "Not this summer, Sunshine. I'm too happy here." And again, later, "I couldn't leave you and Junior. Maybe next summer I'll go and take you with me. Right now, I'm too happy to move. Drives to beaches and mountains is about all I want." I, too. The beautiful drives and walks we three took together last weekend were almost too full of wonders, with every sight and touch fresh and new. "Let the nervous, unhappy people travel," said Stephen. "People who have to run around looking for the lost thing. I've found it."

He smiled at me, that crazy, sleepy smile of his, looking at me through half-closed eyes. I said, "Have you?" and he answered "Ummhmm." And now with Johnsy working at a genuine job in Philadelphia, making nearly sixty dollars a week, with weekends off beginning Saturday at noon, and with us spending every possible hour together doing practically anything we wanted, going everywhere I'd always wanted to go, who could need any plant burning?

Rose listened as she buttoned on her flowered street dress. "They're most always reasons for burning th' plants. If they ain't right away, they's gonna be soon."

"Not now. Not for a long time, as far as I'm concerned. I've been accepted at Barnard, and my summer's just what I want."

She didn't answer for a while. When she finally spoke, I wondered if she'd heard me. "I hates like to mischief run out of my stuff from the island. You better write a letter to Uncle Jonas this very day, you hear?" I reassured her I would, even though plant burning with incantations seemed obsolete to a sophisticate aged sixteen, going on seventeen, and into a whole new kind of life. "You write it off, mail it for me today, you hear, Mercy?"

I said, "Yes, Rose, today," and she went on home to her ironing. I had a busy day ahead of me, going over all my papers, arranging which ones I would pack to take to New York, writing in my diary, buying clothes and then dressing for the night ahead.

The next hour comes to mind. It comes as a sound in my ears, the second movement of the Beethoven Fifth, complete with colors reflecting visually on the eyes, from the persistence of the sound pounding away down there in the old anxiety furnace.

I remembered having the diary downstairs and writing, *I'm sitting in the parlor looking through the window at Stephen's house, waiting for the extra thrill of seeing his Stutz Bearcat drive up, then watching him go up the steps. Sometimes he is with a young boy student he has to push through an exam. I watch till my eyes are tired and the gray stone house begins to fade.*

This was what I'd written then and I had put no items in the diary for days now, not since the experience in the basement which I'd written out fully, partly in code. S.K.M.A. means, Stephen kissed me again. L.O.M.D. is not the name of a foreign doctor. It means, *Long one, must describe.*

Planning to write some more, I ran upstairs, unlocked the desk drawer and reached into the secret place. The diary was not there! I pulled out the drawer and looked again. Still no diary! I took out all the drawers, looked between the slats, moved out all papers, searched again, in the other drawers, too. The diary was not in the desk! I remembered I had sometimes put it under a broken slat at the bottom of the wardrobe. It wasn't there! Back to the desk, I took out all the drawers, searched again, then to my bureau, then again to the wardrobe, all without success and with rising panic. There was one more place, under the mattress, which I now threw off the bad. The diary wasn't there!

It is gone! Someone must have taken it! But who?

No one in my immediate family. No one came into my room but Rose and she couldn't read. I thought of Ruth. I had hardly seen her since the day after the Burton party when her efforts to break up my "going with" an older man had failed, Mamma having expressed only pride in the entire matter. Still, Ruth was the only one *likely* to steal a person's private possessions. She'd done it before, hadn't she? I kept on searching mechanically, as the panic rose. Finally I gave up and ran downstairs.

In a flash I was out the back gate, flying down the alley to Riggs Avenue where I turned into Rose's alley, stepping over the usual dead cats, fishheads, discarded junk and weeds, as the diary pages with their devastating revelations jumped up and down in my head. A few steps and I was at Rose's shanty with its one window boarded up with rotting wood, old lace curtains supplied from Mamma's leftovers and the familiar smell of fried fish and sweet burning tobacco. Rose was standing in her bare feet ironing clothes.

"What's you doing here?"

"She's got my book!" I announced, flopping down in her old Morris chair with the broken springs.

"Who got any book?"

"Ruth, of course."

"What book you talking about?"

"My diary! I guess you wouldn't know. It's highly personal."

"I knows what diaries is. They's things peoples gets up in court."

"Well, then you know. I've got to get it back!"

"How do you know Ruth got it?"

"Who else would want it?"

Rose ironed on. "What you got in there worrying you so?"

"Everything!"

She chuckled. Clouds of smoke, gray and purple, came from inside the bedroom where Rose's mother and her young nephew, Clip, were smoking corncob pipes.

265

"What you gonna do if you can't get it back?" asked Clip, coming out from the bedroom.

"Maybe I'll kill her!"

Clip laughed. "How're you aiming to do that, Mercy?"

"With a knife."

"What kind?"

"A carving knife. Or a penknife. Sharp."

"You gotta tie her up first."

"I know."

"Well, how you gonna tie up a woman mean and fast as that one?"

"Creep up from behind with the rope."

He chuckled, as he settled on the floor. "What's this here diary look like?"

"It's green with a steel thing on the front that locks."

"You mean it's got a key sticking out?"

"Ummhmm."

"How big is this book?" I showed him with my hands. "Where she live?"

"Twelve Calvert."

"Them Stumps, huh?" he asked Rose.

"That's right. I'm ironing that ole Dale Stump's drawers right now."

Clip's voice softened to a whisper. "That place got an upstairs porch?"

"Yes, it has."

"And she goes out mornings right after him?"

"Usually, yes."

"She go out nights a lot, too. I seen her downtown walking around nights, and he goes off hunting, Klan meetings, stuff like that." I thought it over and nodded. I'd heard that Dale added to his income recruiting members for the Ku Klux Klan. The person bringing in the new member was allowed to keep most of the dues money, the Klan receiving only a small token portion. "Goes out on rides with 'em, too." Clip smiled his heavy, sad smile. He was about to ask me more questions about Ruth's house. I could almost see his clever brain working behind his bloodshot eyes, when Rose said, "None of that now, boy."

"None of what?"

"You know what. You still on probation. You ain't stealing nothing from nobody."

"You gotta take that woman her laundry, ain't you?"

"Yes, I have. But that ain't got a thing to do with you."

"I can come along and carry it like I did last time?"

"Maybe."

"Well, then, if I see this here green book belonging to Mercy I can just pick it up and bring it back to her, cain't I?"

"*I* can. *You* cain't."

"You won't see it fast as I can see it."

"Well, you can come with me, but I picks it up, see."

"You're too slow. She might see you."

"That's a chance we're gonna have to take." After a while they went out with the laundry. I said I'd wait. It was warm and comfortable being there in Rose's shanty. It seemed like hours, but I had comforting thoughts as I sat eating chocolate layer cake and drinking coffee. I had friends, true friends, and I was true friends with them, a situation hard to come by. Even Rose's mother, sick and half dead, but smoking her way into the other world, was a friend of mine. Hadn't she taken time off from her visions to call Rose and wheeze, "Give Mercy some chocolate cake." I heard her, and it seemed infinitely knowing. I felt renewed, refreshed, having partaken once again of the precious gifts that come complete with *giver*.

I must have fallen asleep and, when I woke up, terrible imaginings took over. Who was reading those pages I had written in blood? Was it Smile? Right now she might be reading out loud to her pimple-faced husband. Maybe she had taken the diary to his office. "Listen to this, Dale, '*Iway ovelay Ephenstay.*' " *I love Stephen.* From there on she would read the whole thing, while Dale sat there listening with his queer little mind. All the themes, plans, titles of books I would write, characters, people, *including them,* Smile and husband.

My secret self was this minute being devoured by vultures! And my dreams, Al-Balkhi, Dr. Gardiner, everybody. The places I put my hands nights when I first accepted Al-B, Stephen and Johnsy into myself. Those hideous leering people, those Stumps, had me pinned down, helpless as a patient, legs up, undergoing a medical examination. Those dirty eyes were staring up my vagina! Oh, God, no!

Maybe it was even worse than that. Maybe Clip had found it and was handing it to Rose just as Ruth came in and caught him. "That's not your property, you thief!" she'd yell, it'd be just like her and by now she'd have called the police and poor Clip would be in the clink. Or worse, maybe my diary was already in the hands of the police!

A whole hour came and went. I sat under Rose's shed, walked around her yard in the rain, petting Larky, an old half-blind raccoon Rose had taken in when Mamma wanted to put it to sleep. At five past one Rose and Clip came on in. I was standing near the doorway when I saw them. From the way Clip looked I could tell nothing, but the minute he entered the door he held the green diary high over his head. "This here book belong to you?"

"Oh, Clip!" I hugged him, wildly joyous. "Oh, God, what can I ever do for you?"

"Gimme some cigarette," he said.

I gave him the package of Melachrinos I had crushed in my pocket, but it was like giving him a shadow when I wanted to give him my heart. "What happened? Tell me everything!"

"I looked my head off, that's what happened," said Clip. "Tearing up everything she had but I couldn't find it. Where do you think it was?"

"God! I don't know where. Tell me quick."

"In her suitcase, locked up."

"No-o-o. How'd you get it?"

"I just picked the lock is all I done."

268

"But how did you ever know it was in there?"

"It had to be there. I'd been everywhere else in that place. It had to be there."

Every feeling, thought, sight, taste was different with me these days, almost as if I had been born all over again. I was aware of Johnsy, for instance, as an actual male. I saw the newly awakening man. Walking between him and Stephen, whenever Stephen touched my arm or held my hand, his touch was delicate, restrained, as a person eating a meal slowly, waiting between bites for the full flavor to seep in, a tidy, careful touch, whereas whenever Johnsy shoved into me, he was all awkward, full-hearted male thrust. Often as not they both had hold of me as we hurried along streets, and then I would feel on one side of my body the subtle, knowing touch of the god, while on the other the eager jab of the plain, warm human being. How happy I am, I'd think as we went along, oh, what a lucky girl and oh, how fulfilled.

We did whatever we wanted. We would walk around town together, and suddenly the maddening odor of an oyster cellar would hit us all three at once. "Hey, I smell oysters frying in butter!" Stephen would say. And we'd hurry to the corner, fly down the steps, settle at one of the white enamel tables and start eating the crackers with butter and horseradish while we waited for the dozen oysters frying in fresh butter.

We'd sit there eating oysters and crabcakes, drinking coffee served in mugs, watching legs and feet of strangers walking by in the street up there above the cellar. Talking away, guessing who *they* were from their shoes and stockings, trouser legs or skirt hems. Everything we said sounded just right, witty or absurd or plain obvious, it was just right. Then up and out, stomachs full, faces grinning. "Let's go down to the wharves."

And off we'd go on a three, four mile walk through parks and side streets where graceful, long-faced brownstones on narrow brick pavements curbed to set them off from the wide-paved thoroughfares where cars stayed parked for hours and even days on end. Downtown, the tangy smell of the wharves—salty, oily. Breathing in the soft, sweet, sticky air from the harbor, with the smell of fish and brine and fruit from the boats.

I can see and smell it all at this minute. Basketsful of peaches and cantaloupes and watermelons, bushels of corn with golden husks shining in the sun. Stephen buying a bag of peaches which we all eat as we walk. We sit on the sunny wharves, watching the boats come and go. The excursion boat pulls out, taking a crowd of Sunday school picnickers to Tolchester, its whistle blast shattering to the ears.

Stephen had ushered into my system of thought, into my very being, a whole new idea of men. Men were alive in the world, on streets and in schools, in houses and offices, in movie houses and in orchestras and balconies of live theaters, at soda fountains and in restaurants. Everywhere a person looked or moved were men, hundreds, thousands, millions. Enough to last you as long as you lived. There were men now and the men to come later. Johnsy, why Johnsy was no longer a part of me. He was separate and distinct from me as another world. A whole and entire man. Remembering Stephen saying, "Johnsy's a natural—just raw life! That boy has it!" I now saw Johnsy with fresh new eyes, I kindled to him with the newly-awakened life inside myself. Sometimes I was dimly aware of wanting him.

Stephen was a god, and in him I had the ultimate, but all the other men in the world, they were kind of interesting, too. I'd watch the heads and backs of the men as they moved bathtubs, toilets and sinks from the warehouses of Lane and Co. into the dark interiors of trucks, finding something fiercely beautiful in the workings of the muscles in their shoulders under the sweaty shirts. And if we accidentally caught one another's eyes we would break out into smiles, even giggles of joy.

This was one mood, feeling myself a powerful female being in a world of men ready to love; a flying mood, and it was great fun because I stood on top of the world smiling down and ready to fly, but then would come the other mood. If I met Stephen at his house I'd notice the silver tray in the Farrar foyer spilling over with mail all addressed to him, and it would come over me, the sense that he was the one on top, with access to all the women in the world, and men and boys, some of the handwriting had masculine characteristics, and I was one of a crowd. The favorite maybe, but not the only one.

There was another cloud on my horizon. I was coming home from my strictly-for-money summer job at Lane and Co. one afternoon, on my way to take the streetcar that let me off at the corner nearest home. I was hurrying along in one of the fast-darkening downtown streets where the sun hits only the tops of the tall buildings, leaving city blocks a dull, shadowy gray, when I heard someone walking behind me, a man's footsteps keeping pace with mine, hurrying as I hurried, slowing down as I slowed down. I turned my head when I knew he had nearly caught up with me. I faced Dale Stump.

"Well, young lady, what's the hurry?"

"I've got to get home." My voice went soft. I was somehow afraid of Dale. We were at the corner where I had to cross to get to the streetcar, but he blocked my passage by standing in front of me.

"Whyn't you come on down t'see your Cousin Ruth?"

I didn't answer at first, not knowing what to say. I got as far as, "Well, I've been busy." We stood there staring at each other. He'd grown thinner. His clothes looked loose, giving him more than ever the appearance of having his arms, legs and head attached to his body by wires. His pimples were worse, too, with the tarry stuff on his cheeks running down to his mouth. But his eyes stopped me; those cold, cold eyes with no expression, not joy or sadness, not even any curiosity or interest. Dead as the open eyes of a dead animal and therefore deadly. His mouth hung open, and he breathed heavily in my face. I'd occasionally seen him at his desk in his office at Lane and Co. and each time he had his mouth open, giving his lower lip a dry, crusty appearance where air poured in and out drying up the saliva.

"You better come on over and see her. We want to talk to you."

"I'll try."

"Aw, you've got to do better'n that, if you know what's good for you."

I thought he was referring to my job, for which he had recommended me. He might be threatening to have me fired. But I didn't care. Then something else came to mind. It might be about the diary. "Come on inside here a minute, come on now." He started pushing me toward the entrance hall of an office building. His hands felt rough, abrasive against my thin voile dress. "Go on in there like I say." At that very minute a couple came by, dressed to go out, and noticing them glance curiously at us, I pulled out from under Dale's hands and ran across the street.

The streetcar was a few blocks away. I had to wait, but meantime the man and woman were crossing over in my direction. Dale must have seen them and decided not to follow me. When I glanced back he'd turned and was going into a soda shop two doors down from the building. The woman smiled at me. I barely had time to smile back before the car stopped and I got on.

Daylight again. And Sunday. An oblong of sunlight was already on my bed pushing across my feet, pushing yellow diamonds so bright I couldn't make out the hands of the clock. It must be late I knew, but I was not yet ready to sit up and face the day. I'd just lie still a few minutes more, wallow in the warmth, waiting for the beat to start up, the beat from the drummer not far off. Love and fear, beat-beat, beat-beat, nearer and nearer. In the room, on the bed, in the clock. Everywhere.

Quarter to eleven. I went to the window and listened to the sounds of the city. Church bells pealing, opening hymns already starting up in the nearby alleys. "We shall come re-joi-cing, Bring-ing in the sheaves." I

272

glanced down into the Dowses' backyard. The pathway leading to the basement door, where Johnsy used to bounce his ball, was strewn with torn flowers and leaves from last night's storm. Petunias looking torn and old, morning glory buds, pieces of green mint and honeysuckle. I kept staring, almost as if I expected Johnsy to appear, as if I didn't know he had already left for Philadelphia where he said he'd soon be making "good money" and would telephone me long-distance Monday night. Johnsy making money, telephoning long-distance, buying clothes. Johnsy, a man.

Sounds from the street seeped in as I ate the breakfast Rose had left for me on the dining room table, familiar sounds, but today not comforting but disquieting. Through honking horns, whistles, the chatter and screams, through voices on radio shows and Victrola records and brakes screeching, I kept hearing someone playing "Memories" on the piano and singing, and somehow this irritated me most of all.

After breakfast—canteloupe, muffin and coffee, I sat listening to the empty house. My parents were away, down to Uncle Clifford's on the Chesapeake. Rose, who had the day off after ten o'clock, was probably busy in her alley, or perhaps by now driving out to see her cousins in Chip's borrowed car.

I thought of Stephen. I knew he was visiting his dying grandfather, going over accounts, he said. That was when the beat started up, remembering Stephen and then Johnsy. Love and apprehension, beat-beat, apprehension and love, beat-beat-beat. How much did people know? And what people? Did I really see a face last week at the window in our house? Had we all three actually heard someone running through the grass when we went outside to look? Or did we imagine it? If there had been someone, he or she must have been fleet of foot, for no one was there when we went to see. No one at all.

I got up from the table and stood looking through the door to the street. I knew immediately what to do. I must go to see Marian Swoboda. I had a good excuse, too. Marian's husband Boonie Thompson, whom she had married a good year ago, had been killed most tragically in an automobile accident and, while I had written her a note expressing sympathy, I hadn't yet paid her the expected condolence call. Meantime, I'd heard Marian was "going out" with Boonie's brother, that he indeed seemed to be living at the Swoboda residence.

Had I or hadn't I heard that she'd married again? I couldn't remember. It seemed impossible on the face of it but, knowing Marian, I knew that nothing was impossible there in that bright darkness where she lived. No, nothing was impossible where nothing was either *bad* or *good*.

I knew my parents' resentment of Marian went deeper than her obvious "faults." She was not afraid, and this was what was most disturbing to them. Marian went on living her "evil" life and laughing, laughing, as if she had in one wink the complete approval of the Great Being they were forever flattering.

Marian never telephoned me, but whenever I called she welcomed me. I jumped to the telephone and called her. "Hello, Marian."

"Hi, Skeets." Ah, she was home. "Watcha doin'?"

I said, "Not much," which was true enough.

"Then come over quick, you hear?"

We both hung up without another word and inside of a minute I was walking down the side streets where Negroes were living in every other house, with the white steps black with children of all shapes and sizes, the whites staying mostly inside their houses looking out through the windows, living their lives in parlors, dining rooms, and bedrooms, kitchens, basements and backyards till they could find a suitable house in the suburbs and a way of financing the move.

It was said to be dangerous to walk in these half 'n' half streets; tales of terror went the rounds as black families poured in from farms and plantations, four to five families to a house, and whites drew themselves up in shame and fear, but none of these stories were proven. The only one we knew to have happened came from the deVaughn child down the street who, coming up to one of the half 'n' half streets to deliver a note to her mamma's washerwoman, had stopped to exchange greetings with a little black girl sitting on the steps, only to be surprised by the girl's mother watching from the parlor window, screaming, "Come on in here, Liza, 'fore that white dog licks the 'lasses off your bread!"

The Swoboda house, a four-story red brick with gingerbread trimmings on the upper and lower porches, looked as inviting as ever. I rang, and Marian opened the door.

"Howya, Skeets?"

"Hi, Marian."

She looked almost pretty, much cleaner and fresher than ever before. She had a new dress of some expensive-looking, gray material, with a smart white organdy bow at the neck. "Folks gone to the country, all except Aunt Lisha," she informed, as she escorted me through the hall and empty dining room straight into the familiar old Swoboda kitchen.

I began to feel better the minute I saw the big, cheerful black stove with the red-hot front plates, the blue enamel coffeepot bubbling at the back and still further off to the side the four man-sized pies, a pan of muffins and a huge round cake with fruits and raisins showing at the top. All this gave off such a delicious aroma I hardly noticed Marian's Aunt Alicia, who was sitting in a rocker beside the screen door reading the Sunday papers. She said, "Good morning, Mercy," and then I saw her loving, plain face with the steel-rimmed spectacles and the contented smile.

I greeted her while Marian turned on the fancy green glass overhead light which, mingling with the sunlight from outside, turned the big room into a wonderland with streams of silver pouring over the old red and yellow linoleum floor. "My, it's a nice day." Aunt Alicia leaned over and rubbed her legs. She was the smallest of Marian's four aunts with the plumpest legs, encased in those black cotton stockings all except the very youngest of the Polish women wore.

275

"They're almost cooled off, huh, Aunt Lisha?" asked Marian who was holding her outstretched palms over the pies.

"I expect they are, but they're good hot, too. 'Specially the peach pies with ice cream."

Aunt Alicia was a cook in a beautiful house, an "estate" as she called it, in Roland Park, riding an hour and a half on a streetcar morning and night six days a week, a task she had performed for a dozen years without complaint.

It hit me hard then, the essential characteristic, the very *Zeitgeist* of these people in their time and place. Marian and every member of her family had it. Poles, here a bare century or so, they all had this plain, sweet way of living. It came to me in a word. *Strong.* As if they had roots going down to the bottom of the earth. Marian's pappa was a greengrocer who wore a derby hat with his Sunday suit; her mamma and her aunts wore plain, dark dresses with white collars, even in summer. They had no help, were forever baking and boiling, washing and ironing, dressing up to go to mass, coming home and playing cards and, yet, they were extraordinarily polite, good-natured and generous. Yes, *strong,* that was it. By contrast my own family, here since 1648, with their theological rhetoric, Bach chorals and Chopin études and sense of shame, were incomplete and shadowy, and at last, unknown.

"Want me to cut you a piece of pie?" Marian was asking Aunt Alicia, but her aunt shook her head, no, and rose to leave.

"Well, I guess you girls want to visit," she said and promptly went up the back stairs.

The minute she was out of sight I started my condolence speech. "Marian, I'm awfully sorry about your husband."

She was just opening the door to the icebox to take out a bottle of milk. She turned and stared at me, her mouth wide open. "What!"

"Sorry to've heard about your husband."

"Whatsa matter with him?" She put down the milk and started to cut the pie. "He's fine."

"I meant Boonie."

"Oh, him!" She sliced the pie and lifted out the first piece. "He's dead." By now she had placed the pie on the two plates, poured the coffee and sat down in the nearest chair. "Buried him in Hagerstown. Must be six, seven months ago. Forget how long." She spoke of Boonie as of some object she had dropped in a wastebasket. "It's nice out there. Real pretty."

"Hagerstown?"

"Yeah, 'specially the graveyard. Nice and shady. Had to stick him in there. That's where he's from." She ate pie and sipped coffee. "Whole thing cost sixty bucks. Can you imagine them funeral skunks?"

"It must have been terrible."

"Yeah, they're real mean, them burying bastards."

"I mean about Boonie's dying."

"Oh, that. Truck come smack over his head. A neck as thick as that you'd have thought he'd of lasted for years," she laughed, "but the damned fool went out like a light."

"Oh, how awful!"

"Yeah. You shoulda seen him. Jesus, that one. Mashed up like a pumpkin. The undertakers had to stick his head on his body with plaster Paris which is why it went so high. We shoulda had him cooked."

"What?"

"Burned. You know, cremated. Only his religion's against it. It's cheaper, though. Coulda been for fifty, whole business. Down to Romando's, with the coffin and burying and all. Anybody knows *plaster Paris* don't cost nothing. Ever need a funeral, Skeets, you try Romando's. He's good and cheap, only you better die in Hagerstown."

"You must miss him." Marian looked at me. "I mean, poor Boonie gone and after all that loving you told us about."

She burst out laughing. "I got his brother, Silly. Jumps is better'n Boonie ever was. Drives better, too. And he

277

can cook and wash dishes. He, he's *organized*." The word had cost her some thought. I knew Jumps drove a truck but I wasn't quite sure what she meant. "Stands to reason a man can do all that got to be good at screwn."

"What?"

"Screwn. You know what I mean, Skeets." She roared. "I liked him better first anyway, only Jumps had a girl in trouble and he couldn't do nothing with me, so I fell in love with Boonie."

"I'm so sorry, Marian. I really am."

She said, "Yeah," as she continued eating and giving me the details of Boonie's end exactly as if she were talking about some stranger in an accident she happened to witness on the road. "Couldn't of been helped. Sonofabitch drove like a bat out of hell. Just couldn't of been helped. Don't matter, though. Never knew what happened. Went out like a light."

It wasn't sad at all; it was wrong of me to feel sad. Inappropriate. The way it all came out through Marian's earthy speech was as if it had happened years ago.

"Jumps dresses great," said Marian, the proud wife. "Boonie used to sit around in his underclothes. My daddy used to say men sits around in their drawers are no good. He told Boonie, too, he'd come to a bad end. He sure was right."

I started arranging my own thoughts on how to begin to tell her about Stephen and Johnsy and me when a young man came in and stood in the kitchen doorway.

"Howya, Babe?"

"Howya, Jumps?"

I looked up and found myself watching a handsome young man with merry blue eyes picking his teeth with a toothpick.

"That's Mercy, hon." Marian grinned up at him.

"Howya, Mercy?"

"How do you do."

He was indeed neater than Boonie. He was actually wearing a good sports shirt and tie; he wore neat trousers, too, shoes and proper socks, whereas Boonie had often been seen sitting on the front steps barefoot and

278

half clothed. I'd barely acknowledged Jumps' greeting when he said, "Well, you girls go on visiting," turned and went straight into the dining room where we could hear him flicking a deck of cards.

"Let's go inside. Table's bigger." Marian swept in with our two coffee mugs on her fingers, the remains of the peach pie on dishes along her arm. Once inside the dining room, coffee and pie settled on the table and her new husband, his name was actually William Jones, but I never heard him called anything but Jumps, laid out his game of solitaire, I wondered impatiently if I would ever get to tell my story and receive the help I so sorely needed.

"This damned deck's crazy." Jumps threw the cards up and down, shuffling them with remarkable dexterity. He was blonder and generally larger than his brother. He had the same blue eyes but with a different expression, at once more alert and more mature, as if he understood everything at a glance, but was less human than Boonie. When Jumps glanced at you, it was more the look of a wary animal sparring for time, whereas Boonie's expression had been that of a baby feeling his way to you on untried feet.

"Go on tell me what's on your mind, Skeets," Marian began. "Jumps won't care. He don't even hear nothing when he plays solitaire." She waited, but I found it difficult to start. "I know it's about that Stephen Farrar. Go on and scream."

"Well, he's been tutoring me," I began. "Tutoring is important, especially in math."

Marian giggled. "I heard it called a lot of things, but calling it tutoring. I swear to God, I mean I'm laid out."

She laughed more than my words warranted, I thought. Jumps glanced up from his cards as if to tell her to stop, and I felt embarrassed. A false note had been struck and I doubted I could speak now about such a personal and sacred matter.

"Aw, go on and talk, Skeets," she said softly. "I won't giggle no more."

"Maybe some other time."

"Aw, come on, hon. Jumps won't say a word. He can't talk much even when he wants to."

"Why not?" I asked, seizing at any subject to divert the conversation from me.

"I don't know. He just can't," she whispered. "Look, I'll show you." After a brief silence, "Hey, Jumps, Skeet's has got a case on Stephen Farrar."

"Eumm," said Jumps, not taking his eyes from the cards which he was now studying with deep intensity.

"What do you think of that, Jumps, huh?"

"Euch-eumm," said Jumps.

"Dead gone on that Farrar hound," she shouted it this time. "The rich fellow down to the big gray house."

"Euch . . . eumm . . . eumm," said Jumps, wrenched from his concentration into a guttural sound in triplicate.

"What d'you say, Jumps?"

"Eumm," said Jumps, the throaty grunt now low but conclusive, as he slowly moved a card from one line to another.

"Go ahead. Pour your heart out, Merce. He won't know the difference."

I believed her, but it was difficult to speak now, rather like dancing with a corpse in the room.

Marian lit a cigarette and offered me one which I refused. "I had a case on him once myself."

"On who?"

"Rich man Farrar is who." I heard what she said, somehow I knew it was true but I managed to push it aside with the *"Down, down"* you say to obstreperous animals. "That Stephen is something. I can tell you that for a fact."

"You know him?"

"Yeah, sure." This time I took the offered cigarette. "He was real nice. Generous. Took me to the movies and for walks, stuff like that. 'Course I had a lot of fellas then, and he always took them along. Pay for ten, twelve kids going to movies, eating supper and all. I didn't have no nice clothes then and neither did the boys, but he took us all out just the same. What's the matter, Skeets?"

"Nothing. You two, well, it just seems funny, you and Stephen!"

"Me and Stephen ain't so funny. Besides it wasn't never me and Stephen. It was me and a crowd of bum old kids and Stephen. I mean, him so high-class and us such punks."

The entire room with its big table, heavy high chairs and ancient cupboard, together with Jumps and his large face and the cards, and Marian laughing hilariously, all must have undergone some change as I listened. I remember thinking, as I stared, the entire place seemed larger and nearer, closer to my eyes. It must be true, what Marian was saying. Oh, it was true as steel, and now it was coming even nearer with the big furniture crowding me. Marian and Stephen and all those boys.

Why, I even remembered Stephen mentioning Marian. "That little troll," he'd said. He wasn't critical of her, rather the opposite, he was amused and delighted as he was at anything fresh or unusual. "The way she speaks, her words, everything. Oh, that priceless little troll."

"Used to ask me the craziest questions," Marian went on.

"What questions? Can you remember?"

"Like what I thought about things. Only I didn't think nothing much about what he was asking me about, anyway."

"You must remember more than that."

"No, I can't, Merce. I remember some funny things about that Stephen, that rich old horse, but not them questions."

"What else?"

"He used to give me books to read. I tried one once and I asked him, I says, do people really read stuff like that? Or do they just say they do? And he said they did."

"What was this book you couldn't read?"

"Well, it said short pieces but, Jeez, they was long, awful long. Somebody named Pushman or somebody. Some French or Russian fella."

"Pushkin?"

281

"Yeah. That was him. Long-winded sonofabitch. And that Stephen, he was long-winded, too. Specially on questions. He was always trying to get me to talk and tell him things about myself. I didn't know the answers, I guess, or I'd remember better so's to help you out."

Jumps had started up a kind of chuckle of his own. It sounded like chek-huh, as if air was hitting the top of his mouth and escaping through his lips, and then, to my amazement, he spoke actual words. He asked her what time it was, and she didn't know the answer. He hadn't taken his eyes off the cards, but he began chuckling, *chek-huh, chek-huh,* and Marian laughed along with him.

I began to feel left out in the presence of the mirthful couple and thought of leaving—after all, I hadn't got what I came for—when Marian stopped giggling and began speaking quite softly, just as Jumps moved a new card. "Don't bother nothing about what people talk, Skeets. You got him dead to rights, and everybody's after him and they're mad as hornets."

"What?"

"You got him dead to rights."

"How do you know?"

"I know like I know I'm eating pie. You got him, Skeets."

The words liberated me. I felt no longer isolated from the bubbling laughter going on at Marian's house. I said good-bye to Jumps, and he said, "Hurry back now, you hear?"

Marian and I fell on each other's necks at the door. "Don't you worry none no matter what that crazy-horse richboy does. I heard tell you got him tied up with ropes. And don't worry none about that mean old dead Stump!"

"Who?"

"Pardon me, Mrs. Dale Stump. I know she's burned as cat's bacon."

I said, "I know she hates me, but I didn't realize . . ."

"That one! She's hot after richboy herself. Like to

have threw herself on toppa him one day right on the street. I seen it. He didn't pay her no mind. Burned her up. But don't you worry none. She can't do nothing."

I walked a block, then turned off down the alley, threading my way again past dead birds, wet paper bags, old orange peels, soaking-wet baseballs and jungles of weeds, some up to my shoulders. But I didn't mind any of it. Marian had delivered me once again.

We three, Stephen, Johnsy and I, very much at home now in the old Farrar place, had begun to think together. One of us would say something and, bang, the other two would chime in with another facet of the same idea. One afternoon, sitting in our kitchen eating strawberry shortcake and drinking coffee, I said, more-or-less to myself, "I don't think I can eat any more."

Stephen had already stopped eating.

"Ain't that what that poor Mr. Corona's eating?" came from Johnsy. "He's getting electrocuted today and . . ."

Stephen said, "My God! We were all three thinking the same thing."

It wasn't any wonder. The story of Tom Corona's murder of his wife, trial, sentencing and final hours had been filling front pages for weeks, and yesterday's paper had contained details of his last dinner, with strawberry shortcake for dessert. Stephen started cleaning up the dishes, talking, trying to cheer us up. His conversation took rather a macabre form, I decided, but maybe it was better than changing the subject, the way most people do. "A doctor gives the condemned man a shot before the current goes on, and then he's unconscious as soon as the current hits."

Johnsy said, "I can't think of nothing, I mean anything, much worse." And Stephen said, "I can. Dying slowly." I don't know what else was said.

Johnsy hated to leave but had to work at cleaning rooms. He kissed me good-bye. "Four o'clock," Stephen reminded.

"Yeah, four," Johnsy made the signal, arms crossed overhead, and hurried out, his soft shoes squishing on the damp grass. Stephen and I stayed on quite a while talking. Then we were kissing, and the rest went into murmurs, but I heard his words. "We're so alike. It's kind of terrible, being so like somebody else."

We'd started putting out the lights when he mentioned he had something to show me. "A letter came in the mail this morning. I don't want you to worry about it."

"Why? What letter?"

"It's obviously from some crank, but I just might be seeing a lawyer." He opened the envelope, handed me a piece of cheap stationery, and I read a typed letter. My face grew hot, my heart beat wildly as I read,

```
You've been seen doing certain things
to an innocent young girl. You better
stop if you want to keep your balls.
```

When I looked up from the letter, Stephen was watching me and he was smiling. He looked as if nothing unusual was happening, as if the note was in fact a joke.

"Came from some nut, of course. This town's got plenty of them, all right." He spoke lightly, as if he were above the sordid, brutal threat in the letter. He looked remote, even from me, way up there in the world of the rich who lived in the great stone houses and were immune to assault. But I lived in a red brick house and I felt the knife cutting through the cheap paper straight into my entrails and I was speechless.

Later, as I was closing up the Victrola, I noticed him pacing back and forth across the living room. He began talking, rather abruptly, as if addressing himself.

"An announcement!"

"What?"

"An announcement. That's the idea, of course. Right away."

"Announcement?"

"In all three papers." He ran his hand over his cheek.

284

"Legitimize the situation, that's it. A formal announcement would do it."

"Announcement of what?"

"Of our engagement. Oil on troubled waters. Quiet the bastards. It's the only thing that'd work. Give us time to think and plan. Agree, Sunshine?" I nodded.

It wasn't until we got into his car, which was parked at the corner, and had started to drive off, that the full impact of the letter hit me. Stephen was being threatened with mutilation; the threat had been written out in a letter and sent through the mail. Other disturbing ideas came to my mind. Stephen's change of tone as he spoke of this "announcement." Why, his whole attitude was suddenly different, cool, thoughtful, almost crafty. I'd had a vague hope of receiving the answer to some deep, sweet dream, even—was it possible?—a proposal of marriage. He was beloved, and eligible as all hell, and now this sudden talk of an announcement in newspapers!

The idea of the printed words turned over and over in my head. He had said "engagement," but no kiss, no talk about the future, not even a repeat of the vague plans he'd mentioned in the past about the three of us living together.

He was driving much faster than usual. Nothing was the same as it had been up till now. It hit me hard when we reached our street, and I got out of the car to go home. Stephen kissed me once on the lips. "Don't worry, Sunshine," he said. "Now, this is important, don't look or act frightened or guilty. Don't change your usual, well, your usual procedure in any way."

"I won't. But why?"

"Just in case we're being followed. That would only encourage our nut friend. Tomorrow at the usual time. And Johnsy will be there, too."

Yes, tomorrow, I told myself. Tomorrow will be different, tomorrow things will be all right again. But, oh, that cool voice and the way he hurried off from the house. The sound and the image stayed with me as I

285

came through the dark hall. The small light was still on in the parlor over the picture of Martha Washington, but I hurried by, not daring to look at her.

I had read a tract somewhere about the Tarascan Indians; these people have an Oriental streak in them and do not lie awake nights worrying about whether a slide of boulders will destroy acres worked by hand. They don't concern themselves with anything "between the immediate and the eternal." I remember the author writing, "They are Catholic fatalists." She said further that while their lives were materially insecure, "they were no more so than most lives," and "the worst of insecurity may indeed be apprehension."

During the next two weeks, I came to understand appprehension. How its presence, and it is very much like a presence, can change the taste of the most delicious food, the pleasant feel of the warmest sunshine and the sound of the longed-for words.

"You must learn to turn off all thoughts of the past," said Uncle George, who knew I was worried about something. "The past is nothing, and there is no future. You must turn off all thoughts."

"There is no future?" I asked.

"No. Try thinking about it and see. The future will drive you crazy. There's only now, this minute."

Mamma explained that this philosophy had helped him with his drinking, so I tried to do it. I told Uncle George when I saw him again, "I've tried but I can't do it."

"Wait a minute, not at all? You can't do it at all?"

"Well, yes, sometimes, for a while. But then it starts again and I'm scared again."

"But you can do it for a while. How long?"

"I don't know. Ten minutes, fifteen minutes, maybe half an hour."

"You've started. It will get longer. One day you'll have it."

286

"It must be quite a trick."

"It is. I can't always do it myself, and then I fall."

Four days after seeing Stephen, the Saturday he showed me the note, an announcement did indeed appear in the newspapers, all three of them, as he had mentioned.

Mr. and Mrs. Harrington Thomas Bassford

announce the engagement of their daughter

Mercy Blaise Bassford

to Stephen Farrar III

son of the late Stephen Farrar II

and

Mrs. Stephen Farrar

of 1428 Hollins.

The events came faster and were different than any I'd ever dared to contemplate—Stephen calling on Mamma and Daddy. Him, sitting in the parlor; the visit from the knight with the horse and the shield asking for the maiden's hand. Them coming out and kissing me, smiling as they hadn't smiled in a long time. Them looking at me with new eyes, as at somebody they had never seen before. The party Mamma gave, the house echoing with Daddy's growling about the money we were spending.

The visit from Cousin Ruth. I heard her, early one morning before I went to work, in Mamma's bedroom where Mamma was having her coffee. Ruth's voice raised in anger, Mamma cold and imperious. I couldn't make out what they were saying, but just once, as I stopped near the door to listen, I heard Mamma say, "I don't even want to discuss it!" Ruth must have said something terrible, because I heard Mamma say, "That's quite enough!" The three words she uses only when driven to the wall.

Rose saw me listening at the door and spoke her piece when I came downstairs. "I wouldn't do nothin' like that no more if I was you."

"Why not? I know what they're fighting about."

"What's that?"

"Me. That's what. Ruth saw the story in the paper and she's mad."

"If you knows so much, why you hafta listen?"

"She's jealous of me and Stephen and now she's trying to stop it before . . ." But I didn't finish. I didn't believe what was happening, or what seemed to be happening. I believed the Ruth part, of course, but the voices floating down from upstairs had a queer, tinny sound, as if all that going on up there was part of a drama being played in a theater off somewhere in the distance. When I came away from the door and went back to my breakfast, I found I couldn't eat.

"Whatsa matter with you?"

"Why do people hate each other? Why does she hate me so?" I said this aloud to Rose, who was standing in the doorway taking a cleaning rag out of her apron pocket, but I was actually asking myself.

"You goes off in crowds, that's why. You'se having a good time!"

"Am I?"

" 'Course y'are. You'se got two fellas."

"You mean she sees me with Stephen and Johnsy?"

"Ummhmm. Two men."

"One and a half." I tried to make a joke. "That's not exactly a crowd. Besides, she can go anywhere she wants. Dale has a car."

"I dunno." Rose wasn't helping me this morning. Why, she hadn't even mentioned the engagement, the announcment in the papers, the party, since it all happened. And Mrs. Farrar was going to give another party.

"Now, of course, Ruth knows about the engagement."
I tried to keep Rose talking.

"Yes, she do. She sure do know about that."

"Well, she's married. She's got her own man."

"He ain't no man, Mercy chile."

"What do you mean?" We heard the upstairs door bang. Then Ruth came down the stairs, stood in the dining room doorway and stared at me. Rose went back into the kitchen. Ruth's face was flushed bright pink, her green eyes were shining and all her teeth were showing in the old hard smile. I was about to say something, but no words came, and in a flash she was gone. I knew she was gone because I heard the front door close. For some reason I felt scared and called to Rose, who appeared with a basket of fresh muffins.

"She gone?"

"I guess so."

"What happened?"

"Nothing. She came to the door smiling. She didn't say a word." Rose offered me no help besides the muffins. I tried to cheer myself up. "Oh, well, she'll soon be having a baby, and that'll keep her busy."

Rose had started for the kitchen but she stopped at my words. "She ain't going to have no baby. She going to have dogs and that's all." She chuckled to herself. "Even them dogs ain't going to have no puppies."

Shortly after her marriage, Ruth had acquired two small, yapping terriers, Morris and Wilder, both of whom she had promptly had castrated.

"Why do you say she's not going to have children?" Doing the Stump's laundry and some of their extra work gave Rose inside knowledge of the household.

"Because she ain't, that's all."

"How do you know?"

"Way she talks about her husband, that's how I knows. Peoples talks that ways about their husbands most generally don't have no children."

"What does she say?"

"Reckon she don't think too much of him. Sez he
289

don't sleep good and he has nasty feets. His feets is cold and wet, and he pees all night like an old man."

The yard gate clicked open and shut. I heard Clip's voice in the kitchen and called to him. "Hey, Clip."

He came to the dining room door. "Hey, Mercy. How you?"

"Bad."

"Me, too."

"Come on in and have some coffee."

Rose closed the dining room door. Clip sat down opposite me and ate muffins with peach jam and drank coffee, while Rose went about straightening up the room. "What troubles you got, Mercy? You're going to college and you're getting married or engaged or something, ain't you?"

"Maybe, maybe not."

"And you got a job."

"It's an awful boring job. You wouldn't want it."

"I couldn't get it if I did want it."

"You got plenty good a job, Clipper Singman," Rose cut in sharply.

"Yeah, I guess so."

"What are you doing, Clip?"

"Frying fish, mostly."

"He's getting near twenty bucks a week." Rose sounded proud and pleased.

"That ain't no money for what I do."

"You children's never satisfied."

"I'm satisfied, Aunt Rose. The hours are pretty long's only trouble."

"What are the hours?"

"Nine till two, sometimes."

"Two in the morning?"

"Sure. Whenever the place closes up."

"He don't start till late. Nine o'clock is late."

"Maybe so. But I had to give up my night course."

"Never mind, Clip. If I get money I'll send you to college, I swear I will."

"Thanks, Mercy."

"His Uncle Joshua'd send him to school if he'd go on back to Mississippi."

"I think I'd rather fry fish than file papers about bathtubs. And they both pay practically the same," I said.

"Is that all you gets, twenty bucks?"

"Nineteen fifty. And I might get fired."

"What's you talking about, chile? Getting fired?"

"Dale Stump looks at me awful funny."

"That's account of *her*."

"Well, I guess so. All I know is I run when I see him on the street."

"My friend Buck Hendriks don't like him none," said Clip. Rose opened her eyes very wide and sucked in her underlip. "He says Miss Myrtle seen him up around the Hendrik's place the time they tarred and feathered Hardy."

"Hush up that talk, Clip. You don't know nothing about that!"

"You mean they killed Hardy?"

"No, they didn't kill him." Clip watched his aunt, afraid to go on.

"Tarring and feathering don't kill peoples, Mercy," Rose explained. "It's mean and sinful, but peoples don't die."

"Well, where is Hardy now?"

"He's all right. He's working in Chicago."

"I wish those Stumps would move to Chicago. They're saying Dale might be transferred to the Chicago office. I wish they were both dead and in hell!"

"You quit talking that ways, Mercy Bassford. That ain't no fittin' talk, time like this."

Clip looked at me, and I looked back. A signal passed between us, and we were silent. Rose straightened up from her cleaning the telephone table and crossed the room. "Listen here, chile. Them peoples worry you anymore, I'll fix up the blue water." Clip pushed away his plate of unfinished muffins, as his eyes fixed on his Aunt Rose who was standing still near the window. The light coming from outside made her face inscrutable.

"What's the blue water?" I asked.

"Something fixes the devil in peoples so they burns to a crisp."

"How do you use it?"

"I makes up a little vial."

"A vial?"

"Little bottle."

"What do you put in the vial?"

"B'ilings from roots. Don't need no more than a drop. Puts it on anything they uses. You better not touch no blue water till somebody does something real bad. Ain't time yet. Ain't nothing real bad happened." She picked up her can of wax, pushed her flannel rag into it and began rubbing the arms of the Morris chair. Clip and I looked at each other. We didn't think much of plant burning or blue-water dropping. Clip moved his chair, and I moved mine, and we both got up to go.

These days I had a deepening sense of unreality. A whirl was going on around me. I was the central figure, in this whirl, but not at the center, and therefore couldn't see into it. It looked good, it sounded good. The top was pure gold—engaged girl moves toward castle—but the other part was black as an old crow and more than a bit confusing. I took side glances and caught both sides in the periphery of my vision. Gold and darkness, fairy tales and daylight reality, life and death. I saw them all, never quite knowing what they were, and kept going.

The party at Mrs. Farrar's. All those upper-class people who speak with such charm and goodwill, a continuous soft chatter, and yet you somehow know that if you were found dead an hour later the chatter would continue, uninterrupted. The ring arriving in the purple velvet box. My father opens it first, takes it to the window and, sitting down in his Morris chair, examines it with a magnifying glass before I have seen it. Mamma is seated in her small telephone chair, sitting sidewise, watching him with impatient interest, biting her lower lip. "Well, what is it, Tom, *for goodness sake?*"

My father speaks slowly. "Don't know yet, deah. I reckon it's about three carats."

"Well, what is it? What is the stone?"

"It's a diamond, with small emeralds. Very neat. Comes from D. P. Paul Company. They don't handle cheap merchandise."

Mamma rushes from her chair and stands staring down at the ring. "Well, so it is. Goodness! She shouldn't wear it, then. She's so careless."

I sit watching them, wondering how soon I can leave home. And is this stone the opening wedge? Or is it just some peculiar phenomenon? I say nothing, resenting the way they have appropriated the package. Imagine! It was already opened, the paper wrappings out on the table when I came in.

"He wants her to wear it. That's what the note says." They both call Stephen *he* and me *she* as if we are two strange animals who have somehow produced a diamond. Mamma reaches for it and puts it on her finger. "It's a beauty!" she says. "It's a real beauty. Well, I never!"

"Do you mind if I see it. After all, it's mine."

Mamma places it back in the box and hands it over complete with wrappings and tiny card. "To be worn," it reads. "Love, Stephen." I put it on my finger.

"That's your *right* hand. *Tsk-tsk*. Don't you even know what finger to put it on?" Mamma is irritated until I take the ring off and put it on my left hand. I feel like a character in a comic strip. I have no emotion about the ring. I'm only mildly resentful when I hear Daddy say, "Take it off now. Here, give it to me." I hand it over, and he puts it back in the box.

"Aren't you going to let me wear it? After all, *he* said I was to wear it." I am imitating them, but they don't get it. They never know when you're making fun of them.

"You can't wear a ring like that until it's been *appraised* and insured. You children don't know a thing about money." He wraps up the box in its original paper and puts it in his vest pocket. I find I don't really care very much. I might have enjoyed looking it over in private, but it doesn't really matter now. Anyway, it is returned to me in a few days with instructions to wear it only in the evening "on visits," and to put it back in the box and either give it to Mamma or put it in her jewelry case which has a lock and key.

The minute I got it back I wore it across the street and showed it to my Cousin Honey, who took advantage of the occasion to whisper, "Come up to the bathroom with me, Mercy darling. Oh, I've missed you so."

Once again I traipsed up the dark stairs behind her, with Screamer trotting on ahead. I was aware of this change in my world, this elusive but not pleasant shadow. In fact, this new plateau upon which I'd been pushed was so unpleasant I was glad to be back potsitting with Honey, grateful to touch home base and be once again in a familiar human situation.

Honey locked the bathroom door and made for the toilet, as I settled on my old white wooden chair. "Lemme see it, darling," she grunted. It was still an object of unreality to me, but now, seeing for the first time how the stone sparkled in the light, sending out small, brilliant rays as I held up my hand, I began to think more highly of it. "I declare, it's beautiful!" Honey pronounced, staring at it as she completed her task. She was still staring at it as she pulled the chain and let down her skirts, and she turned back to it the minute she finished washing her hands. "May I?" She reached for it delicately.

"Oh, yes, certainly. I'd like to see it on somebody else."

She put it on and walked around the room, arm outstretched, watching the diamond glittering on her finger, then lifted her hand to her hair, modeling the ring. "Imagine, Stephen Farrar giving a girl an engagement ring!"

"What's so unimaginable about it, Honey?"

Honey tried to smile but she couldn't make it. She had said more than she meant to say. She leaned down and began petting Screamer, a sure sign she was trying to keep from talking. Then she must have realized the new diamond was still on the hand stroking Screamer's unkempt neck hairs, and, with his damp nose and salivating, open mouth nuzzling against it, he might somehow damage the expensive object. She moved quickly away, starting for the bedroom dressing table. I kept after her. "What were you going to say, Honey? What's so *unimaginable* about Stephen giving a girl an engagement ring?"

"Why, nothing much, darling. I'm just glad to have you back, I guess . . ." Her voice trailed off.

"You were going to say something, Honey."

"What was it?"

"So *unusual,* something like that."

"Ummhmm. It is unusual. A first time for him."

"Yes, go on, Honey."

"Well, he's not a young man. He's older than you. More near your daddy's age."

"Daddy's thirty-nine."

"Well, Stephen is thirty. Maybe more. Everybody over thirty's practically the same age."

Stephen thirty! It did seem old, but age had never been discussed between us. In the golden haze of these months the very mention of anything as mundane as anybody's age would have been like dropping mud into champagne. Inappropriate, immaterial and inexcusable.

"I know he looks awfully young," she went on. "You two will look wonderful together. Nobody'll ever see any difference in your ages. I just wonder."

"What about?"

"I want you to be happy. I know it sounds marvelous. Every girl in town's been after him."

"Who, for instance?"

"Everybody and everybody's daughters. That Mrs. Whitridge's daughter, with racehorses and money flowing around like water. She's tried hard, and now you come along, and, bang, you're engaged. It just seems unbelievable. I guess that's what I mean, darling."

"I feel the same way, Honey. Unbelievable."

"You do? Then you know what I mean." She got up

295

from the makeup table and threw her soft, plump arms around me, and I threw mine around her. We stood like that, not saying anything. And there for a minute the trouble stopped. In fact, as I sniffed the Yardley toilet water mixed with talcum powder and soap and the faint, acrid odor of those awful creams she was forever using to make female things come out or go in, I began to think I was back in the world again.

"I guess you won't be coming to live with Clarence and me, then, will you, Mercy?" she asked when we finally separated.

"I might. Maybe I will."

"You can't if you're married."

"I'm a long way from being married." She looked so sad, I asked, "What's the matter? You'll be married, too."

"I reckon I will. Only it's so lonesome being married. It's just so lonesome. Now if you came to live with me, it wouldn't be so lonesome."

"I'll come to see you. And I'll write to you."

"You're going to college and then get married, isn't that the idea?"

"I guess so." I hated to say I didn't know. We'd had announcements and parties and rings, but no actual discussion of anything. Come to think of it, we'd had much less openness among the three of us, Stephen, Johnsy and me, since the newspaper announcement. We'd all three met at the house just the same, we'd gone for drives and to the theater. Everything was the same, *too much the same!* A door had shut somewhere, closing off the winds of growth and change. Like when the needle gets stuck in the Victrola and goes back and forth over the same groove in the record. It was still love, or a faithful facsimile of love, but it was the same, the selfsame mood all the time, whereas love jumps and whines, love runs and comes back, now wild and now tame.

Stephen was cheerful and generous as ever. Was it us, Johnsy and I, who were hesitating in the face of all this munificence? I showed Johnsy the ring, and he said, "Yeah, I saw it the last time." I *saw* it, not I *seen* it, a certain sign he was serious. He looked at me with his big, male-child eyes, questioning. "I guess you like it a lot, huh?"

I said, "Oh, it's a nice ring, but I don't know. Sometimes I feel funny wearing it."

"Yeah?"

"Mostly, Mamma keeps it locked up. It doesn't feel like it's really mine."

"I got a raise last week," was his inadvertent comment.

"Congratulations."

"Sure." I knew he wanted to say more, but what he said was, "I'm coming back early next weekend. They're giving me a half day off for working late nights. Soon I'll be making a lot of money, Mercy."

Thursday noon. Middle of August, a wonderful time of year. And of life, at least my life. Did I not find myself triumphantly flipping the Lane & Co. invoices into their cubicles in the giant-sized files as carelessly as last week's flypaper? Which indeed they were to me. Two hundred blue enamel toilets to Sizemore & Co., Davenport, Iowa. Hadn't they all been shipped and were by now delivered and hence dead? And so would this damnable job be dead, come next Friday.

As the office emptied out for the evening, I seized a phone and called Thel.

"Hey!"

"Hi."

"Congratulations!"

"What for! I haven't seen you since the party." I realized she meant Mrs. Farrar's engagement party. "You looked marvelous! And that ring! Everybody's going on like crazy about you, Merce. You're the talk of the town. A regular Barbara Fritchie."

"I'm on an office phone, hon. Call you later."

Why on earth did the mention of the party trouble me? My parents and relatives were all pleased as Punch, but as for me, there was apprehension in the very air I breathed. I picked up the phone again and called Marian Swoboda, this time to make sure Jumps wasn't home.

My worry increased as the phone rang on. How did I know but what Marian might be leaving for one of those boardinghouses her family went to in the summer. The phone rang five times without an answer. On the sixth, I hung up, deciding to go anyway and started up the alley where the weeds, garbage and dead things suited my mood better than the staring eyes of strangers in the streets.

Marian was in the backyard feeding her animals, a dog and three cats, and saw me through the fence as I came toward her house. "Hey, Merce," she unlocked the gate. "Come on in and have supper. Jumps ain't home. He's working tonight, everybody's gone to the country, whole kit and kaboodle." She was clean and fresh, her teeth flashing out from the pixie grin and the eager look of welcome on her face, as if she had been expecting me. Her hair was shiny and soft, hanging in long curls. As we walked into the dining room I saw she was wearing the self-same white dress with the soft black bow I'd admired in a window downtown this very day, but had thought too expensive to buy.

"Combed cotton," she explained, quick to notice my admiring glance. "It's from Paris, France, I swear to God." I said it was beautiful as we sat down in her empty dining room facing on the yard, she in one straight-back, cane-seated chair and I in another. "What's the matter, hon? That richboy skunk ain't done nothing mean, has he?" I said, "No," and she replied, "Well, you better have coffee before you eat," as if that would solve the problem like medicine. She disappeared into the kitchen, returning with two mugs of coffee with fresh cream and sugar which tasted delicious.

"You had screwn, huh? You didn't get hurt too much, did you?"

"You make it sound like a traffic accident."

"First time sonofabitch hurts like a bastard."

"Yes."

"Now you're scared you're gonna have a kid?"

This was not exactly what I was afraid of, come to think of it, and I was just readying my reply when I saw from the way she continued that her comment required no answer. "Well, don't fool yourself, Merce," she began. "Don't believe them books going on about that. You don't get no kid every time you do it. If you did, I'd have a thousand."

She slapped me on the knee, laughing as if having all those small Joneses was a cheering thought. As for me, the very picture of Marian surrounded by that many duplicates of Jumps was more like a rain of bullets. Between Jump's conversational vacuum and Marian's illiteracy, they could easily set the South back into the Indian and buffalo era.

Oh well, there was something both comic and scary in Marian's attitude toward every situation, hypnotically appealing to me. I felt myself recharged and began to feel better.

"Didja take a hot bath?"

"No."

"Shoulda taken a hot bath. Kills a kid better'n arsenic. Lissen, I'll lay you ten to one you won't have no baby for five years."

"You mean for what I did six weeks ago?"

She burst out laughing again. "You didn't use no injection bag?"

"What's that?"

She looked up to the ceiling, addressing God. "You hearn that! She don't even know wash'n." Then to me, "Enema bag."

"Oh, no, I didn't."

"And he didn't use no rubber?"

Again I shook my head, feeling helpless and inadequate before the hideous mechanics of love. Thus far my lessons had gone no further than the teachings of movie queens. I knew how to look, talk and kiss. Now the glimpse of this new world of strange devices reared its ugly head.

"Chances are you won't get caught, Skeets. If you do, why, just go horseback riding and you'll pass it."

"Where, on the horse?"

"No, in the toilet, silly. There's bushels of babies in toilets."

"There are?"

"Sure. Look, I'll go horseback riding with you and then you come on over here and stay all night and we'll pass it sure as shooting."

"We will?"

"Aw, sure."

No matter what nauseating images leapt through Marian's laughing mouth, they arrived fully dressed in everyday clothes. There was something tranquilizing for me in just entering her big, dirty world filled with dark daymares such as passing babies into toilet bowls, seeing her accepting these horrors as natural by-products of living. Thus relaxed, I began to consider how much I really wanted to tell.

"Don't worry, Skeets, old kid," she kept saying as she began putting down plates for dinner, laying out platters of thick sausages and delicate brown doughy objects from which apples, nuts and raisins were protruding. "Like I say, hurts first coupla times. Sonsofbitches blast into girls like they was rocks. But just waita month, you'll starta yell for it, I swear to God. And I'll help you out dumping a kid."

I decided to leap before eating. "There are other things, besides having a baby."

"Yeah? What other things?"

"Well, there were three of us."

"Who was that?"

"Well, there was Stephen and Johnsy and . . ."

"*You . . . ?* There had to be *you!*" I nodded. "You mean you all three done it together?" I nodded again, and she burst out laughing. "Hey, Skeets, that's good. Jesus Christ, that's really something. That's one for Hollins Street. I always said there ain't nobody like you, Skeets." Her face opened wide, showing all her pretty, cleaned-up teeth. "I wish I'da been there. I'd give a nickle in a cup t'a seen that." I tried to stop her by mentioning how serious the entire matter was. "Yeah,

yeah, sure. I'll bet it's s-s-s-sacred. Excuse me, Skeets, I'll s-s-s-stop in a minute."

I went on talking. I was having more difficulty explaining than I had anticipated, with all her laughter going on. But slowly, I heard myself spilling out the whole thing. The part about the letter came out more easily.

"What did it say?"

I told her. I even quoted the end part, *if you want to keep your balls,* and she became serious for the first time. "You know anybody in the Klu Klux Klan?" I said I thought some people I knew were connected with it. "Aw, they're always sending them letters. They're always after peoples' balls. I tellya the way them nightshirts go after balls you'd think they was potatoes. Them turds cuts 'em off, too. They git blacks and they git whites, far as I can figure, just for screwn."

"But if people are *engaged?*"

"Aw, that don't do no good. You gotta be married and depressed about it, man wants t'keep his ass. They liketa think people can't do screwn no more, that's what they're after, them shits. Have some more sausage, hon." She filled up my plate with sausage and those marvelous apple things before she continued.

"My Uncle Sigismund down to the farm, Port Creek, got 'em figured out. They was after him with one of them letters threatening to cut the lemons off him. My aunt's been dead ten years, and he knocked up one of the fruit pickers, a girl named Thyrza something. He said for her to go ahead and have the kid and he'd marry her, but he's a forgetful sonofabitch and he kept putting it off till he got one of those balls-off letters. He just tore it up, he was so sore. Well, one night his son, my cousin Stanislaus, come in his bedroom with a gun and tells him, 'Pa, get the hell up on the roof.' There was twelve cars coming down his private road real slow. Only my Cousin Stan was awake and he seen them white nightshirts and hoods in the moonlight.

"Well, Uncle Sig locked up the place and him and his son got up on the roof. Then when them cars pulled up in line and them Halloween turds started toward the house, him and my cousin started picking them off with their guns. They got the ass off the first four, and when the others seen what was happening they turned and hightailed it back in their cars, running like mad dogs."

"I see. Well . . ."

"Of course your richboy's too high-class t'sleep with shotguns by his bed like Uncle Sig."

During the conversation I had gone up and down like a person riding a carousel.

Weeks passed, and my apprehension slowed down. How could a person remain in a state of unreality, meeting Thelma and Marian Swoboda at Tobin's of a bright summer's afternoon, wearing my new blue linen dress *and* my ring? Thel was first. "Let me try it on! It's beautiful, Mercy." I noticed she kept it on her finger the whole time we ate our platefuls of pistachio and chocolate ice cream. "How'd you ever do it, Hon?"

"Yeah," said Marian. "Come awn—near as you can to the truth."

"I don't know," I said. "Maybe I have the thing, the magnet."

"You must have something. I mean you must have something over on him."

"Years," said Marian, "she's years younger."

"You're not pregnant?" asked Thel.

"I don't think so."

"Didja get your sickness?"

"Umm*hmm*."

"When?"

"Last week."

"Then you're not caught. You did it, didn't you?"

"No," I lied to Thelma. "We're only engaged."

Thel went right on as if she hadn't heard me, and Marian kept my secret like the good friend she was. "In that case we've got to give you a party of our own, with presents and all." I said it wasn't time for that, but I went away feeling relieved and happier, especially after the way they both kissed me. I felt claimed, back in the world, where nothing was strange and shadowy such as existed behind the polite and empty chatter of the wealthy.

By now, I had begun to accept the situation. Stephen, too, went back to his former ways, and he and Johnsy and I actually talked about living together, with Stephen always dominating the conversation. But lately, Johnsy was questioning, "Aw, I don't know about me living with you two after you're married." He seemed disturbed by the entire idea.

"It won't be for a long time," I said.

Stephen spoke up, "Meanwhile, let's just be happy." And we were.

Every day was special, as it is to everyone at some time who wakes up to the special haze of love. The fresh discovery, *This is it.* The end of the old world, the beginning of the new. Awakening to an unseasonably cool day, I'd sigh with joy at the thought of Stephen and Johnsy in our house waiting for me, with Johnsy lighting a log to crackle in the fireplace and Stephen opening those big packages he was always bringing, putting out jars and boxes of delicious food, new records to listen to and dance to.

I'd think of the conversations we'd had, ideas left unfinished, perhaps to be finished today. More and more clearly it came to me, I was the heroine in a moving picture that was being projected on a living screen; I was speaking, feeling, loving in a role I was playing, and I was the audience at the same time.

I could hardly wait for the day to begin; then, once it had, for the hours to pass, bringing on the night, and *them.* The emotion I felt for Stephen engulfed me like a tidal wave, but having Johnsy in his new dimension, a grown man, I now had something even more precious, a sense of union, of family. I'd never felt at home with my own family, never known who they were behind the masks. To get any sense of being connected, I'd had to turn to the soft, soiled people on the bottom of the world, to Rose and Clip and Marian Swoboda, to Thelma and Honey and beat-up old Uncle George. And now, I knew who Stephen and Johnsy were, and they knew me.

The slow falling through space gone at last, I was into life and ready. Came one flood tide of a day with rain and fate coming down together, a day I'll get to on my own steam, for steam is required to bring it all up out of the cauldron, and it must come clean and true, e'er you misprize us three, the stars in the drama, and those other members of the cast, forsworn, or doomed to play out their roles.

So be with me this Saturday. It is raining. And I have a date with Stephen and Johnsy awaiting me at six o'clock. The pink and white China clock on the mantle tells me it's five past nine. Less than nine hours, count 'em. I peep into the evening, see the room there waiting, with them in it. "Let's not plan anything for the weekend, what d'you say?" Stephen asked us. "I have to pick up the car from the garage at five-thirty. Hope to heaven that damned mechanic's done his job. If he has, I'll be right over."

We agreed we would float, as we often did, let the spirit move us. We could drive out to the country for dinner, go to the White House Club, where they had to know you before they'd let you in. Or we could stay at home or go somewhere else, whichever we felt like at the time. We could go anywhere we wanted. We were flexible, happy and free.

Promptly at five o'clock I began to dress. I must have taken longer than I thought trying things on, and it was well past six before I left. I'd decided to wear the new rain clothes, the blue dress and coat ensemble I'd planned to save for college. Catching sight of my full figure in the upstairs mirror just before I went downstairs to the basement, I was so pleased I decided the ensemble was good enough to wear even on a bright day and was happy at the extravagance.

Johnsy was already there, sitting alone on the small sofa with the window behind him. He got up as I opened the door and came toward me. I noticed he had on a new, expensive-looking suit and, if I was not mistaken, a new shirt and tie and, for once, his shoes were shined.

"My, my, look at that!"

"Just some new clothes." He shrugged it off as if new clothes were hardly worth mentioning.

"Philadelphia?"

"Yeah. Buy everything there. They got good stores."

"Stephen here yet?"

"Yeah. Went upstairs looking for those papers his grandpa wants. He'll be down soon as he finds 'em." Johnsy helped me off with my coat, as Stephen usually did, and hung it up in the closet. "Come on, sit down, Mercy, you're wet." I came over and sat down in the chair opposite him. I noticed he wasn't grinning the way he usually was whenever he saw me. Instead he was sitting with his hands on the sides of the chair. I smiled across at him, but he stared at me without smiling back. He was in some kind of a new mood, quite serious. The way they worked him on that job! and then more work when he came home. That must be it. He was tired. He had never had a vacation in his life. It had grown dark outside, with rain pouring steadily.

"It's gloomy in here. Let's turn on some lights."

"Sure." Johnsy got up and turned on the lamps, one beside my chair and one beside the sofa. "How about a drink?" I wasn't used to drinking this early, just one cocktail with Stephen and Johnsy before dinner and sometimes wine. But what was this? Johnsy pulled a nickle-plated flask from his hip pocket. He went to get glasses, ice and soda, came back and began to pour the drinks exactly as Stephen had done so many times.

"I didn't know you had a flask."

"Philadelphia. Wasn't expensive. Three bucks." We lifted our glasses. "Here's to us, Mercy, you and me." He was deadly serious.

"Here's to us, you and me," I repeated after him. Something was going on with him, I decided, as I wondered what was coming next. But whatever it was, he wasn't about to tell me at this time. The clock struck one chime. Seven-thirty. "I guess we'll be driving out to dinner," I said, just to say something. "I'd like to go to the White House Club, I like it better than the place on the shore."

"Yeah. It was raining the last time we went. You can go there if you want."

"What do you mean, I can if I want? You're coming, too."

"Maybe, maybe not."

"Why not?"

"I don't want Stephen buying my dinners. I can buy my own dinners." He leaned toward me. "Yours, too, Mercy. I can buy your dinners, too. I can take you to the White House Club."

I was so startled by this sudden change in Johnsy's conversation, the serious tone, the correct grammar, I wondered if I'd heard right. "But what—?" I stopped, and he continued.

"I can buy your dinners, too. That's what I said." Dear God, Johnsy Dowse, well-dressed and handsome. He had learned to speak correctly. Was it possible? Or just some strange new mood?

"Let's have another drink," I said.

He got up, poured us each a fresh drink from his flask, splashed soda into the glasses, added ice and went back to the sofa. His red hair, lighted by the table lamp, stood out sharply against the darkness of the yard outside. "Here's to *you* and *me again.*"

"You and me again." We drank.

Johnsy looked down at his feet. "I told you, I've had a raise, Mercy. I'll be making good money real soon."

"That's wonderful, Johnsy."

"I'm never going to live with you and Stephen, like he said."

"Well, that's in the future. But why not?"

"It's wrong, that kind of thing is wrong. There's something funny about it."

"But Stephen loves you."

"Yeah, maybe so. But I don't love him." He was still looking down at his shiny shoes, but now he looked up.

"I guess you know who I love." He lifted his glass. "Come on, let's finish this one and then we'll talk."

We had just lifted our glasses when I noticed a movement in the bushes outside the window behind Johnsy's head. I couldn't see anything much, just branches separating and leaves moving this way and that as if someone were out there moving them about. Stephen must have come down and gone outside, I concluded. I wondered why he would do such a thing in all that downpour. But just then I heard Stephen come clumping down the inside stairway and felt relieved that he was going to join us.

"I've got a lot to say, and I want your answer," Johnsy was continuing.

Suddenly there was a bright flash from the window, and at the same time I heard a sound like a loud, sharp crrrr-ack. Something whizzed by me with a vicious buzz. I kept staring but I didn't believe what I saw. I was looking at Johnsy, as a hole appeared in the very face I was watching, a hole about the size of my fist. The glass I was holding must have fallen from my hand. I have a vague memory of hearing glass shatter. I kept staring at the thing I saw. The face below the crown of red curls, Johnsy's face—his nose and part of his cheek was missing. A piece of his face was gone! His body jerked as if he were going to get up from the sofa—*it is not happening, he's going to get up,* but then it slumped forward, and again I heard the sound of glass crashing. I saw and heard all this with a cool clarity, as if a camera had snapped in my head. Johnsy, Johnsy Dowse is in the picture, falling apart. Piece by piece, this bright young being falling, falling away.

Someone was in the room, pushing me hard. "Get down!" I recognized Stephen's voice. "That was a rifle! Down flat on the floor. That's it, under the chair. Stay there."

"But Johnsy!" I screamed. Stephen said "Hush!" but I couldn't stop; in fact my voice was up so high the words coming out were unintelligible. "*Johnsy, look!*"

"Keep down flat! Don't move!"

But I did move. I crawled under the chair to where I could see him rushing across the room to Johnsy. He lifted him up in his arms and laid him on the sofa. He called out loud, "Johnsy! Johnsy!" But I didn't hear any answer. Stephen leaned over, listening for the heartbeat, then trying to detect a pulse. I saw all that, but just then he began talking out loud. I thought he said, "Bullet. Hit him in the back of his head—came out in front."

I heard myself saying something as I started to get up. I don't know what I said. I knew everything, and there was nothing to say.

"Don't look at this, Mercy. Do as I say now. Go upstairs and wait—I'll call the police. Hurry now! Don't look, dear." He picked me up and pushed me toward the stairs; but I saw it all in the glance I caught as I went up the steps. Johnsy's hair, that bright red hair, but just beneath his forehead, where those merry, serious blue eyes had been, gray stuff was oozing out.

That is the last image I had. The rest of that day is of strange forms moving in a black fog. I remember sitting in the empty upstairs dining room wondering if I were going to be sick and, if so, where the upstairs bathroom was. This worried me so much it occupied my entire attention. I know that when the police came, one of them said, "We're speaking to you, miss. Where is he?" I said, "Downstairs," and pointed to the steps, and they went on down. Shortly afterwards, a doctor came in and asked the same question, and I gave him the same answer. Then one of the men was asking for my name, address and telephone number, and I gave them the information.

It seemed like a long time before Stephen came up. Somebody asked, "Is he dead?" And somebody answered, "Yes." Then Stephen was near me, speaking clearly, and I heard what he said. "I'll take you home and then come back. Try not to think now. Just try to close off your mind and wait for me." But I didn't have to try to close off my mind. It was already closed off from everything but the face, or what had so recently been the face, I'd seen downstairs, with gray stuff where those blue eyes had just been looking into mine.

The street is almost empty. At least, that's how it looks, I'm not sure. I keep on walking in a straight line beside Thelma over and over the old octagonal stones of the pavement leading to my house. Thelma keeps on talking. So many families are away, in the mountains or at the seashore, she says, taking with them their screaming children, their noisy automobiles and motorcycles. Even the hum of strangers spouting endless street talk is down. "People are away," she keeps saying, or maybe she says it just once. "Isn't it quiet?"

There are cars parked at intervals at the curbs, others are coming in to park between them, but the drivers must be driving more carefully than usual, parking more quietly, and the people walking the block speak more softly, some even in hushed tones, or that is how it sounds. The blocks of red brick houses with the high white marble steps are endless. Small squares of green with pots of ivy and geraniums on and on, all the same, all splashed with pale blue light from the sky where a bright full moon is just rising.

The scene has changed, it has moved further off, looks more like a street in some huge old painting, and even the painting is seen through water. The picture trembles, so pieces of steps and houses move up and down, up and down, this way and that in the icy water.

"What's the matter, Merce? You tired or something?"

"No, I'm fine."

That's definitely Thelma walking beside me, comfortable Thelma, thick and bland as a thick soup, with her greenish light hair and her beige skin. *That is Thelma's voice,* oh yes, and mine, my voice answering hers. Both voices sound strained and heavy, as if being pushed out by some unnatural force. Maybe it's because the voices are coming up through this icy water.

"We said we weren't going to walk on this side of the street, Merce."

"Why not?"

"You mean you don't know?"

"Oh yes, I know." I remember we made some plan or other, but I've forgotten what it was. I try to remember, and at that very moment, we're passing the deVaughn house, eight doors down the street from my house. I see the white crêpe, oh, those foolish white satin ribbons with a bouquet of phony white lilies of the valley, a single phony orchid at the center. A satin ribbon lifts up in the summer's wind and floats through the icy water like a hand calling for help.

"You better come on over to my house." That's Thelma speaking. "Norman's got some great new records. You can't even get them here. They're from New York."

"From New York, are they really?"

We're at my steps. I look at Thelma, at her face and her dress, and listen to her saying, "All right then, I'll call you right after supper, and you come on over, you hear?" She really does look queer. But then, so does my vestibule, the three steps leading up to the front door have moved back, a bulky mass of marble, hard to reach. The parlor and the picture, that woman, whoever it is, stuck up there over the mantle. She looks queer, is dark as a cave. It feels so cold. I hurry past.

There's no one in the dining room. A lamp is lit, the after-dinner cloth is on the table. The people who live here have eaten and gone their way. There's a place set for one, so one person has still to eat. The clock ticks on the mantle. The hands point to quarter to nine, I am not quite sure what day it is or what time of day, morning or evening. Then, I decide it's evening because there is moonlight over the peach tree in the backyard.

I sit down at the telephone table but have no one to call and that's when I see light coming from the kitchen and hear sounds, awful, continuous, sharp sounds. I get up and stand at the kitchen door. Rose is sitting at the kitchen table, her back turned to me, her black cotton head bent over as she cuts biscuits from thick white dough with a round biscuit cutter. She keeps banging down through the dough to the wooden breadboard.

"That you come back, I know."

I look at her hands holding the biscuit cutter, the fat, black fingers with pink undersides. They tremble at first, moving crazily through this peculiar wall of water, but then, slowly, they settle into plain old hands. I hear a sharp voice, "Stop that cutting!" and know it is my own.

"What's the matter with you?"

"Nothing's the matter with me. It's you, making that awful *noise!*"

"This here cutter ain't making no awful noise."

"It *is.*"

"It cain't. It only goin' through dough." She stops for a minute, and it is remarkable how quiet it is without the banging. "You gotta calm down. You gotta start eatin' your meals and going to bed when it's bedtime."

"Why do I have to do that?"

"You can't pack up clothes and get offta no collitch looking beat-up and wore out like you do. Them peoples up there gonna think they seen a ghost."

"What're you making all those biscuits for?"

"For the wake."

"What wake?"

She turned full around to look at me with those big red, white and black eyes and went on talking, half to herself. "Johnsy's mamma's got relations pouring in from all over. I'm figurin' to take a mess of biscuits over and cook 'em soon's peoples starts sitting tonight."

"I don't believe all that about any wake."

"Round eleven or so, peoples sitting up at wakes eats a peck of food, I can tell you. They's already twenty peoples in there and they's still coming. I hearn cars stoppin' out in the street. And just look at what's hanging over there on that there porch."

"Where?"

"You knows where. Just look through the window over the sink to the Dowses' porch."

I went and stood where she was pointing and there I saw what she meant. Dead birds and animals hanging from hooks everywhere, ducks and pheasants and quail, rabbits and chickens and turkeys, dead eyes and dropped heads, burlap bags next to baskets of rosy apples.

"I kept your vituals heating on the back of the stove. You go on sit now and eat your supper."

"Eat. *Eat!* Everybody's always eating."

"Course they do. You eats your supper."

"I've already had supper."

"Where at?"

"Thelma and I ate downtown."

"You ain't et nothing, I betcha a nickle. I could cut you a piece of sweet potato pie. You always likes that with coffee."

I wasn't quite sure now what she was saying. All those dead bodies hanging over there in full view began to move. Rose pushed me down into a chair at the table. I sat looking down at a slice of sweet potato pie and a cup filled with coffee and milk, as she went on.

"Time my Cousin Albert died, down to Virginia, house got so full up with foods they had to set the eggs for breakfast out under the shed in the backyard. When we all come to get 'em to cook up the breakfast, they was setting in the sun so long half of 'em was rotten. Had to make do with ham and sausages and that kind of truck, but the menfolk wanted their fried eggs. Last minute, I went out and made 'em fried tomatoes dipped into egg batter and fried up in butter nice and brown. Stuck 'em next to the ham and the sausages on top of the pancakes and them men didn't know the differences, they was talking so hard."

I got so tired of her heavy, singsong voice I cut in, "What were they talking about?"

"Talking about politics and how hard it's gittin' to put food in the mouth and peoples dying off without no notice. 'Course I knew when I went'n seen that cheese-cloth draped over my cousin's bed and that there doctor giving him ox-gins he was fixin' to go. My Aunt Anna sez to go on and speak to him, but when I went up to his bed I knew he couldn't hear nothing nobody was saying. Peoples can be breathing for hours but all the time they's on their way, and you cain't git 'em back with no talk. They's already over there gettin' settled, that's where they are."

I began to hear her very clearly now and I wished she'd be quiet.

"Peoples think it's hard to go, but Cousin Albert didn't have no trouble. He gits into a coma. Just starts goin' and he kept right on goin' the way he started." She began cutting biscuits harder than ever.

"Stop!" I screamed. *"Stop that cutting!"*

"You quit grabbing my hands. I'll tell your mamma on you, that's what I'll do. You been acting real funny, goin' crazy."

"Maybe I *am* crazy."

"You hasn't done nothin' bad, child. Your mamma told me you was a real little lady talkin' to them policemen. Your Uncle George settin' on one side of you and your daddy and Mister Farrar on the other. They sez you was somebody to be proud of."

"What was there to be proud of?"

"Way you upped and told 'em about the letter and all."

"They knew 'bout it, anyway. Stephen turned over the letter."

"Your mamma read me that there piece from the paper, all about finding them footprints. A whole baker's dozen men out to kill one young man just startin' life. They's awful mean, them killin' peoples. And them making a mistake, getting the young one. I know how you feels, but you've got to pick up."

"Why? Why?"

"Because that's the onliest way there is, that's why."

The whole terrible scene came back to me. Uncle George, his face paler than the dough Rose was cutting, put his arm around me as we sat at the coroner's inquest. My newspaperman uncle was hit harder than my parents. But at least he actually answered me when I asked him, "Why?"

313

"A whole lot of people don't like lovers, Mercy," he said, when we were out of hearing. "You find that out working on newspapers. A whole lot of people don't like to see love anywhere. Makes them uncomfortable."

"It does? Love makes people uncomfortable?"

"They especially don't like an older man and a young girl. Don't ask me why. It's plug-ugly. I know that much. You try to forget it all now. Take it easy and try to forget."

Stephen, remote, speaking in his low, controlled voice. Papers to sign, papers and more papers. Then walking out. Daddy and Mamma going off as if nothing much was happening.

"Stop that noise! Please. Just for a while."

"I cain't. I promised t'git these things over there and I'm aimin' t'do it. What you think all them peoples goin' t'eat, I listen to you?"

"They don't have to eat."

"They're goin' t'eat just the same. What you think peoples do at them wakes? Starve theirselves?"

She jerked her hands out from under mine. I hadn't realized I had been holding her until she wrenched free. She took a package of tobacco from her apron pocket, wet her thumb to pick up a cigarette paper from her tin box and began rolling a cigarette. "Peoples got to get hold of theirselves. Folks dies when their time comes."

"How do you know when their time comes?"

"I know when they time comes 'cause that's when they goes." She lighted the cigarette and began puffing, blowing the smoke toward the window. "You quiets down real nice, and I'll tell you something."

"What? What can you tell anybody?"

"Somethin' I got in the mail this morning."

"What did you get?"

"Them plants come from Uncle Joshua. I'm aimin' to burn 'em all during the wake."

"Those plants, huh? What good will they do me now?"

"They's done you plenty good, times past. Fixed up

314

your nasty old measles and them mumps doctors said was doin' you in. But these ain't for you. Not this time."

"Who are they for?"

"They's for my Johnsy, that's who. He's on his way over there and he needs help. He's gone from here."

"He has not gone! Nobody goes that quick! Why, just last week I got this present from Philadelphia." I felt for the thin gold chain with the locket and found it still around my neck. "And he said, he said . . ."

"Don't do no good talkin' about last week and what all he said, child. You got to help him now, and I'm goin' to help him."

"Help him do what, stupid?"

"Help him get out of his shock feeling and git on his way." I wanted to hit her big, black cotton head and I must have grabbed her again. "Mercy, you let go of my hands this minute, you hear me?"

I let go. In a second the pink and brown hands were flying up and down, the terrible banging sound started up again, faster and louder than before. She looked as if she was sitting in a tank of water. Her head and hands were floating, together with the biscuit dough and the cutter and, looking through the window, I saw all those dead bodies hanging on the porch next door, but now mercifully separated by water, and I drew back from this crazy piece of the world stuck under the sea.

The funeral comes back as a blob stuck somewhere in my mind. I remember the disturbing noises, starting Wednesday morning before daybreak. A great clatter in the street, trucks arriving, brakes screeching, horns honking, followed by what sounded like an army of men carrying loads of wood and dumping them down in the house next door.

From my bedroom window, I could see men standing in the Dowses' yard, talking loudly and placing straight-backed chairs on the porch, then leaving the surplus chairs in rows in the yard. When I came downstairs Rose was wearing her black serge Sunday dress with the white collar. The conversations were still going on in the Dowses' backyard, the men talking together in groups, laughing aloud. The coffee smelled so funny I wondered if it were coming from somebody else's kitchen, until I saw Rose right there, pouring it from the blue pot into cups on the table. She kept talking to me, giving me a lecture, something about the funeral, something about the funeral starting at ten o'clock and there I was at five past nine still in my nightgown. The fact is I might just as well not have gone to that funeral. The main impression I have is of the sickening odors of massed flowers and men's breaths, Uncle George's, for instance, who was sitting just behind me in the hall, at the very point where the sharp smells of applejack and whiskey met with the floating heaviness of carnations and lilies. The place was overcrowded and hot, with people sitting in the hall all the way through the dining room and kitchen stretching into the backyard.

I thought I saw Stephen and his mother somewhere in the back. I couldn't be sure because just then the minister began to speak. He droned on and on, reading from the Bible. I don't remember a word he said till he got to that part about how the Lord giveth and the Lord taketh away. I heard that part, especially about how the Lord taketh away. He does it suddenly, I thought, sneaking up behind you when you're least expecting Him. In the presence of Love, He permits hate to win. Something was said about life being "snuffed out like a candle." I thought, *snuff*, then of Rose's *snuff*, and I must have made some sound because Mamma tapped me on the shoulder to be quiet. She needn't have, there were plenty of other sounds going the rounds, loud drunken breathing, feet moving, the preacher's voice droning on, then the prayers and the screech of chairs and the tramping of feet trying to find their way out into the street where the cars waited to carry us all to the cemetery, where, after a long time and more reading from the Bible, a white coffin was lowered into the damp, dark earth. Someone touched me, and I realized I must have been still standing there waiting after the crowd had gone.

The Old Town Boys' School, where Stephen taught English Lit, was having its first football game of the season. I didn't much want to watch a boys' football game, or to visit a school and have tea with the headmaster. But I did enjoy riding in the open car with Stephen, breathing the heady September air and substituting miles of country roads for the old familiar streets.

"You mustn't act that way toward me, Sunshine," Stephen said as we drove along. "You must not, you hear?" I had heard him, all right. I now not only heard what anyone said but I was able to answer back without thinking twice as I had in the past. Something was new, some element had been removed from day-to-day, minute-to-minute living. Some threat had come and gone. Before this it had been important to think twice before speaking. Now it wasn't even necessary to think once. Just speak and be damned.

"Which way?" I asked.

"As if I'm something *important*."

"You mean some kind of a god, Thor or Jesus or Eros?"

"Something like that."

"I don't think you're a god. Are you?"

"Then stop being so goddamned polite," he said.

"Was I being polite?"

"What do you really think of my mother?"

I thought that over a second or two. "She's not too different from my mother, except that she has more money, and that makes her calmer."

"Great. Perfect. Go on."

"She has what's called a charming personality. She's gracious, easy to talk *at*. You immediately strike up a deal with her. She says nothing, you say nothing back. It could go on for years."

"Marvelous. Suppose you *said* something."

"Well, if I came over and told your mother, 'Mrs.

317

Farrar, I just killed my father.' I think she'd say. 'How interesting. Did you see our autumn flowers? We have the purplest asters this year we've ever had.' "

"Oho, that's exactly right. She doesn't hear you. Go on."

"But she confers *favors* with all that noncommittal conversation. She's constantly conferring favors. Mamma's more scared. She placates and conciliates and lies. Neither of them really sees you, but I don't think your mother'd forget your name."

"That's because there's only one of me, *and* I'm a man." We did imitations of our respective mothers, their speaking voices. I knew he was coming to something, didn't especially care what it was and wasn't surprised when he asked, "How'd you like living with her?"

"It wouldn't be too bad, if you have to live with adults." I tried to explain what I thought it would be like. No change in anything, no place for the enlargement of anything, but, then, no thumps or screeching brakes either, no trouble and no drama. Like living in a large jar of dried rose petals.

"Or under an enormous wool blanket. It's so easy, so inevitable, just to accept not breathing." He put his arm around me. We were just coming upon the school buildings, entering the tree-lined driveway. "Only I won't. I can't." he was saying.

"Can't what?"

"Can't not breathe, I just can't go without air, Sunshine. I have to breathe, you know, and somehow you help me." He said this as we stopped in front of the school. I'd never been inside the place, but I recognized it from the times we'd driven by, and the old brick, ivy-covered buildings looked exactly as they did in the photograph Mrs. Farrar kept in her living room, where they served as a background of Stephen as a young boy sitting on a horse, looking bored and skeptical and sad.

I can't tell you much about the game. Two groups of boys, hulking huge in padded clothes, rushed at each other on the field, landing in tangled heaps. The long, wooden, tiered seats for the spectators, students and some of their families and the masters and teachers, with or without wives, were filled to capacity, a couple of hundred on each side of the field. I remember the heads turning, the great buzz of conversation, the singing, the screaming and the cheering. I always go down a flight of steps inside my head whenever games start up, baseball, football, tennis, and watch it all from there, and come up at the end of it.

We sat down front. There was a cheerleader named Dan, tall, young, blond, with troubled blue eyes, a big pink mouth and dimples, who sat beside us. Stephen kept talking to him, trying to draw him out. "Tell Miss Bassford here the funny thing Mr. Reagan said about the other team."

"Well, you know," said Dan, "this team we're playing comes from a Catholic school called St. Ignatius. They're all Catholics, of course, and they come from this coal mine town in Pennsylvania. We call them the Muckers, and they're all pretty tough. Last year one of them bit one of our team, a deep bite on the neck. So Mr. Reagan said maybe we should change the playing date from Saturday to Friday. See? They couldn't bite people on a Friday, only fish they could bite. It's a joke, kinda." He blushed. "Oh, I hope you're not a harp, I mean, a Catholic, Miss Bassford."

I said, "No," and Dan blushed again and ran out on the field to lead a cheer. He put tremendous energy into his gyrations and stirred the hundreds of watchers into throwing their total lung power into songs and cheers to encourage and inspire the team.

"You listen good to this one, Miss Bassford," he instructed me as he got up during one of the intermissions. "Tell you why later," so I listened to a great cacophony in which I was able to make out certain words of a song, which, for some reason, stays in my mind.

Old Town Boys' School
Plays today.

Our cheers ring out,
  RAH! RAH! HOORAY!
We'll play to win
  With all our might!
  So . . .
There'll be a good time
  In the old town
  tonight!
  OLD TOWN! OLD TOWN!
  RAH! RAH! RAH!

I can't recall too much of the tea party in the headmaster's study. I know the headmaster's name was Mr.
Masterman, because Stephen and Dan referred to him as
Mr. Slaveman. He had silver hair, but his face was so
young, young and pink and glowing, and, with his silver
mustache he resembled the colored cartoons of cats in
the Sunday papers, smiling and well-fed.

Mr. Masterman had a smooth, conciliatory voice. I
have a vague memory of exchanging a few words with
him. I know at one point he said, "Football is a boy's
best friend." But whether he let me have that priceless
aphorism or passed it to one of the older ladies standing
nearby I can't say. We stood about in a long, high-
ceilinged room with a mission table at either end and on
one of which were two large, china teapots, silver plates
with small sandwiches and cake. Ladders led to bookshelves lining the walls between the windows on both
sides of the room. There were soft dark leather chairs,
a fireplace, an Oriental rug underfoot and paintings of
men looking either dignified and depressed or determinedly cheerful and ready for the worst. I told Stephen,
"I've seen this room before," and he said, "I'm sure you
have. In the movies, maybe. Mr. Goldwyn must have a
room just like this on his lot, for lawyers or judges, or
murderers, that sort of thing."

I hadn't expected to see Dan the cheerleader at this
tea, but there he was. It seems his mother and father
were among the visiting parents, so he was included.
The minute they left, he found me and placed himself

at my side like a bodyguard, waiting till he could whisper in my ear, "How'd you like the football song?"

"Why, fine," I said, recalling the corny jingle. "Why?"

"I wrote it." He was grinning, showing his dimples, proud of his variation. "Didn't take me long. I like to write. You think it was good, huh?"

I said, "Yes, very good."

Stephen had asked him to have dinner with us, and he had refused at the time, but now to my surprise he asked, "Where was that place you and Stephen were going for dinner?" Stephen, who was talking to Mr. Masterman, leaned away from the headmaster long enough to tell Dan the name of the place and how to get to it.

It got to me that this innocent, blond boy was attracted to me, and a faint nagging sadness started up inside me. He left immediately after hearing the name of the place, no doubt heading back to the dormitory. I found myself wishing he'd forget about it or not be able to find it. A nice, good-natured boy, but I didn't want to see him ever again.

Stephen did, though. Later that afternoon we were walking by the stream running behind the school grounds, talking on and on about nothing. He had already asked me, "How'd you like Dan?" and I had answered evasively, "Oh, just fine." When he asked me again, "Dan is beautiful, isn't he?"

I knew what he meant. "Yes," I said.

"A pure soul, you might say. Unsullied, not cynical, not wise. I hope he doesn't bore you."

"No, he didn't have time. And I see what you mean about him being unsullied."

He took my hand. "You know, Sunshine, I was thinking."

"Yes, Stephen?"

"Maybe we shouldn't keep away from our old place. If we just went on back there, maybe tonight, we might feel better."

"Do you think so?"

"Yes, I do. It's wrong to hide from anything. I

thought maybe after dinner we could go back there with Dan. He's so genuine, a real boy, a masculine boy. This staying away from things is self-defeating." He put his arms around me and began pulling me towards him. "We've got to affirm. You can help me affirm my life. I know it sounds serious and kind of ridiculous even, but you might, you know, just help me to make it!"

He kissed me, then went on talking. "Say yes, and then I'll become more sophisticated immediately." We were standing still. I wanted to say yes, just to be polite. I knew he was feeling troubled, I could sense some fear he had. But I couldn't speak just then. In coming close to Stephen, I had felt nothing, not anything, that is, but the rough texture of a tweed coat. The mouth pressed on mine might have been made of rubber. And then I knew very clearly, for the first time, that some warm life force had been withdrawn. It was gone, sucked up into nowhere, gone out of our bodies, out of the world. *Johnsy,* I felt like calling out, but I didn't, not loud. *Johnsy come back!*

"You're not reacting, Sunshine, dear." He stroked my hair, and I tried again to speak but I couldn't. It came to me in a terrible crash, like some important organ breaking up inside, say your lung or your heart, never to be mended! Johnsy has gone! Johnsy is dead!

I stood completely still, I couldn't move, but only for a moment, and then we walked down the path that ran beside the stream. I began to see the place more clearly, the red brick buildings now a burnished pink in the fading sun, the darkening shadows moving here and there like long, black hands, the grass just turning, the beds of scarlet sage, impatience and ivy. I saw it all. Johnsy is gone, and all this crazy life goes bursting on, and here, in the midst of it, two people who are no longer connected. When Johnsy was with us, he made the connection and we were flooded with light.

"We might, you know, Mercy. You ought to think about it. You might just fix the whole thing. You could help me. It might be quite good." He smiled.

I didn't answer. For no reason I began seeing and

hearing Dr. Gardiner. Hilary moaned, whereas Stephen spoke calmly in a faintly British voice. Educated Americans. But they both wanted me to, well—to—fix them. I was hit with a terrible sense of people wanting to be helped, to be fixed. Some work done on them, some new life poured into them. Why, they were like streams that were dammed up, gone sluggish. People who had everything, the Hilary Gardiners and the Stephen Farrars and how many more? Oh, God! Maybe, was it possible? I was entering a whole world of people wanting to be fixed. A whole world of people looking for the connection.

I thought of running fast. If I could run away now I'd go down the alley, over the dead cats and the wilted lettuce and rotten apples—to Rose or Marian Swoboda. I'd even go across the street to pot-sit again with Honey or talk with Thelma or, yes, him, Johnsy. There he had been in his long, dirty overcoat; *he* had had it!

Why was it only the people on the bottom were in the clear? Only those at the bottom were connected. And me, what about me? I had it too, at least sometimes I did. It came on Tuesdays but by Wednesday or Thursday, sometimes, it was gone.

"You're not answering me, dear," said Stephen. "Well, then it can wait." But, of course, nothing can wait. It never does.

The red brick houses with the white marble steps, strips of green lawn with the pink geraniums and green ivy and lavender-blooming frog plants bursting over their iron pots, tremble as I walk, as at the beginning of an earthquake. I can see them change into streets in old, old paintings, so old the canvases are giving way. How trivial and poorly constructed this whole place is; streets turning this way and that, parks with trees and fountains and benches, gaunt gray stone houses, even six stories high, falling, *falling*. The stone castles fall, they are no more substantial than the brick with gingerbread trimmings. A city thrown together by a big hurrying child eager for the quick Christmas effects.

The afternoon I go down my street to take my street-car for the last time to Lane and Co., to collect the things left in my desk and the overtime money due, it is all still, silent and so terrifying. The Dowses' parlor windows are closed up tight. Two great black eyes in the sunny street, they stretch and lengthen as I hurry by, but I know they see me. What was the nightmare I had last night, or was it this morning? A sound came clump-thugging into my sleep, clump-thug . . . clump-thug . . . growing louder and nearer till it woke me up. It was still thug-thugging as I opened my eyes. It was coming down a long black corridor in a cave, disappearing slow-ly, an accordion pulled in by unseen hands. The whole cave receding, drawing up into itself, the last of the thug-thugs sounding even more ominous in the daylight. I closed my eyes, crept back under the covers, but the dream had shaken me wide awake. Now, passing the Dowses' windows, the sound comes rushing back into my mind and I know where I heard those thug-thug sounds. And who made them.

Without thinking much about it I'd been putting off this visit to Lane and Co. for fear of running into Dale. Now Lane's is a big place, with warehouses, garages for trucks, shipping rooms and three floors of office space. The personnel office was on the third floor, the account-ing department on the second, so there was only the slightest chance of my running into him. Nevertheless, I had timed my arrival at five past one which I knew to be his time out for lunch. Arriving at eight past, I quick-ly collected my envelope of overtime from the cashier and the package I'd left in the desk, signed the voucher and was just going down the elevator, congratulating myself on having avoided Dale, when I ran smack into his assistant, a plump middle-aged blond man named Schmidt who, I thought later, went out of his way to stop me.

"Why, hello, Mercy. Glad to see you back at Lane."

"I'm not back at Lane, Mr. Schmidt." I moved as if to start walking away, but he put his fat fingers on my

324

bare arm. The fingers felt damp and cool, or maybe they were damp, and I felt cool. Anyway, I shook them off with a quick movement of my arm, but to my amazement they landed right back as if attached by rubber strings like a yo-yo.

"Not so quick now, please, young lady. I haven't had a chance to speak to you. Say, why don't you come on up to my office and have a chat?"

"What about, Mr. Schmidt?"

"Why, your future. I hear you'll soon be leaving these parts. You're going to that awful city, New York, where you take your life in your hands every time you walk out in the streets."

I said my life was in my hands anyway. I was stalling for time, not wanting to be completely rude but finding those fingers on my arm more repulsive by the second, especially as his grasp increased in dampness and intensity, a mean combination. Finally seeing my arm jolt up again, he had to make time now or never, so old Schmidt started talking fast. "I thought you might just want to talk about your cousin."

"Which one?"

"Why Dale, of course."

"My cousin-in-law. What about him?"

"He's gone, you know."

"No? I didn't know."

"Oh, yes. Flew de coop."

"I'd heard he might be switched to Chicago."

"Yep. We thought so, too. Only he's not there."

"No? Where is he?"

"Nobody knows. He's disappeared! Police have been around here asking questions. You mean you really didn't *know*?"

I shook my head as he went on but I barely heard what he was saying. I didn't care where Dale Stump was. I hope's he's dead, I thought, only the word "dead" gave me a chill. I moved away. "Well, good-bye, Mr. Schmidt."

He made one last stand, like Custer, coming back with the fat old paws. *If you must have nasty, damp fingers, then don't be passionate about it. I mean, stick them in your pocket or somewhere but not on other people.* "They'll be calling on you, my dear. I was only trying to warn you."

I said, "Yes, thanks. Good-bye. I've really got to go now."

"They've been bothering his wife, too. The poor girl must be distracted. Your Cousin Ruth was here last week, her eyes all red, poor little thing."

I had a clear vision of Smile collecting Dale's salary; it's funny how evil falls hard and clean through the worst fogs; the picture must have strengthened me as I stepped back quickly and left Mr. Schmidt standing there reclaiming his paw, staring after me with those pale, watery blue eyes.

Sitting at the dining room table, counting out my money, over twenty-eight dollars, Rose came in on her way to the kitchen, carrying bags of groceries. "You wants to keep mos' of that money," she muttered, standing at the door. "You adds that to your bankers account. They's so many busses and trains and things in New York City you need lots 'n' lots of money just getting around."

"Dale's disappeared. I bet you didn't know that."

"You bettin' wrong. I just come from fixing up over there to the Stumps' place. Your Cousin Ruth's got things going."

This news surprised me. "You mean she's still keeping a servant, with her husband gone?" Rose chuckled as I came into the kitchen. She had put down the groceries and was just rolling a cigarette. "Why, it's almost like a, like a death. A man running away, disappearing!"

"That ain't the way she taken it."

I poured two cups of coffee and settled at the table. Lately I had taken to sitting at the far side where I couldn't see the Dowses' shed. I hated what I sensed was going on at Cousin Ruth's. Her very name reminded me of Dale, and Dale reminded me of policemen questioning me about the murder, and then the pictures would come reeling back, harder and brighter and faster the more I tried to push them down, as the whole chain of events would begin all over again. Starting with the happiness in the basement, moving on to the letter Stephen received with its ugly threat, and then on to Johnsy—"I can buy your dinner now, Mercy," and "I guess you know who I love," and "I can take you to the White House." And then the sound out there beyond the window in the bushes, and then, dear God, the piece of a face.

"She's getting fixed up like for a wedding," Rose was saying as she sat smoking away. "Got herself some new clothes, real nice, and music records and a set of new dishes, real pretty. Gimme a whole dollar extra for ironing all her underthings. Fix 'em like she's going somewhere or having a party or things like that."

"She can't be having a party. Not with him gone. It's not human!" Rose laughed aloud, went on smoking. "Do you think she knows where he is?"

"You don't know nothing for sure with that one. All you know 'bout that one's what you see. Changes from minute to minute."

"Well, what did you see?"

"She's mighty pleased about something. Got flowers coming from people in a big box. And, Lordy me, a skirt dress, shiny red satin. She taken it outa a box and make me put some extra stitches in the hem with red silk."

"I don't understand," I said. "The house must be lonesome with him gone and her not even knowing where he is. You wouldn't understand, but a police inquiry is still going on."

"I knows about police peoples."

"Her marriage interrupted—"

"They's types of marriages that're interrupted more when they're going then when they stopped."

"You going to keep on working for her?"

"I don't know. Nobody don't know what that one's up to. But I can tell you one thing."

"What?"

"She ain't standing still. She's jumping."

I went shopping with Thelma, to movies and theater, to buy luggage, to last, weeping pot-sits with Honey, where I spent precious half hours advising her on her wedding clothes while listening to tearful conversations.

Honey had finally agreed to marry Raymond sometime in the future. He was taking her to visit a wealthy aunt who lived in Kent in England, but instead of looking forward to crossing the ocean she sounded as if she was crossing over the River Styx. "If I go to live in New York, you'd come live with me, wouldn't you, Mercy?"

"Yes, Honey, I most certainly would. Only it might be inconvenient for Raymond."

"What would?"

"Well, moving his business to New York."

"They have banks in New York."

"Well, having me living in his house."

"He wouldn't care. He'd love it. And I . . ." She started to cry.

"You *what?*"

"With you and Screamer and all, I'd feel more like myself." She cried, and I hugged her till she got to the inevitable. "You promise," and I said, "I promise," as I realized I was part of this world where people required each other in order to feel complete. Happy at last, or at least temporarily relieved, Honey began to bubble.

"Did you get the invitation from Cousin Ruth?"

"What!"

"Mrs. Dale Stump is giving a supper, m'dear. A musicale with supper."

"No-o? Who's going to play, with Dale gone? A ghost?"

"Maybe."

"You going, Honey?"

"I don't think so. I want to, but Mamma won't let me. Mamma and Daddy both say Cousin Ruth has been

328

seen walking out nights, picking up people in restaurants and speakeasies." She sighed. "How about you?"

"I haven't been invited, thank heaven," I said, thinking, that's one problem I don't have. Smile could become the Whore of Babylon and sink in her own red skirt, for all I cared. I was going away in two weeks. I was already away.

Coming home the very next day from a shopping trip I found Rose setting the table for dinner and, seeing her making a *shhhhh* sound I knew something was up. "What's the matter?"

"I said, *shhhhh*. That means quiet down."

"What for?"

"Your mamma's upstairs with her." I knew immediately who she meant, but asked, just the same, and Rose replied, "You knows who. Been up there over an hour. They having one of them long teas. Your mamma be took up with it, too. She ain't come down to answer the phone."

I found out at dinner from Mamma herself. "Your Cousin Ruth is giving a musicale, Mercy." I didn't reply. "She's inviting you. It's this Friday, and she's most anxious to have you come." I could tell from Daddy's silence and Mamma's choice of words it was they who were anxious, Ruth who was eager. "I promised her you'd be there."

"You ought not to have done that."

"Now Mercy, Cousin Ruth is worried these days. Not knowing where her own husband is. Takes courage to keep face and offer her hospitality to the family."

Daddy cut in, "We'd be very pleased if you'd go, dear."

Mamma picked up after him. "You go along now, and let bygones be bygones. Cousin Ruth says Stephen already accepted." A sense of evil waiting in the wings hit me as Mamma went on, "The invitation came yesterday, and I said we'd all be there."

There was something about the idea of the musicale that bothered me no end. Ruth's visit to Mamma, the long upstairs whispering, my parents' suppressed anxiety when they asked me to go; but since everything about Smile was unpredictable and I would soon be out of reach, as it were, forever, I didn't think too much about it. And that Friday evening found me sitting in the Stumps' parlor at nine o'clock as promised.

There were twelve persons there, not one of whom had any relationship to any of the other persons, besides being alive, yet there they were sipping sherry from sparkling glasses and talking animatedly to one another.

There was Mamma, for instance, talking passionately to Mrs. Farrar about, first, the life and death of house plants. As Mamma's tall tale of the philodendron that was pushing us all out of our own dining room finished in a lovely laugh, Mrs. Farrar came on with the one about the birds the Farrars' servants kept in their rooms, notably a parrot named Horace who had found out Mrs. Farrar's christened name, Beryl Anne. "Nobody calls me that but Horace," she confided, "so I can only conclude that bird has found my birth certificate and keeps calling out, 'Hurry now, Beryl Anne, there's trouble down here!'"

Daddy was giving Stephen his opinion on world affairs. Stephen listened, polite but restrained, watching me as he nodded and answered Daddy as required. Once, as he came over and sat beside me on Cousin Ruth's love seat, and I heard him whisper, "How are you, Sunshine?", and felt him beside me, I felt an awful pang of emptiness, remembering how any contact with him had once set up a thrilling vibration inside me, warming my skin from face to feet. Gone, leaving nothing but this emptiness, cool, echoing emptiness—which makes for mechanical poise but is without life or vitality, "Why, I'm fine, Stephen, and you?"

Dr. and Mrs. Burton talked animatedly with Mrs. Farrar and Mamma, and Edythe—she had never forgiven me the fib about Miss Gaither's death—was left to Stephen and me. The Gaither fib, why that was thousands of years ago. I imagined old Miss Gaither, now in her nineties, still alive and teaching drawing to the new juniors at Wesleyan, with the life force rising and falling back just like a wave washing up on shore. And, oh God, there came Johnsy, bursting with life, telling me about flowers he'd delivered to her house. "Come over and meet Mr. Rinaldo, Mercy dear." My Cousin Ruth was speaking to me. Ruth looked taller than ever—maybe it was her high heels—and quite majestic in her red satin skirt and embroidered white silk blouse. She's beautiful, I thought, noticing her shining green eyes, her long black hair done up high on her head, the perfect long teeth over delicately painted lips; only the steady, fixed smile was still there and the big, cold hands that grasped mine pressed too hard. She was playing the gracious hostess—it seemed odd and inappropriate—but the thing inside her that was running her was still in power.

I recognized Mr. Rinaldo, a middle-aged Italian who ran a speakeasy downtown, from the time Stephen had taken me to dinner there. This Mr. Rinaldo had brought two young musicians named Albert Something and William Something, a duo-piano team, who were going to play on the two pianos the Stumps had placed back to back on the far side of the room. There was an elderly man with a long, pale face who did something at the museum. I can't remember his name, only his sharp black eyes as Elderly watched Cousin Ruth's every move, along with some lady who resembled him, they both had long yellow faces, so I concluded she was probably his sister. A waiter from the catering service downtown passed trays of tiny appetizers and provided lace napkins and sherry, until at long last the two young men settled at the twin pianos. Conversation stopped like a finished Victrola record and, relieved, the unlikely group sat back, leaving the responsibility up to the eager young men who fell to with a vengeance. They played and played, receiving applause and praise and then playing on. The first movement of the *Eroica,* the second movement of the Haydn *Surprise,* a Brahms sextette, Beethoven and Bruckner. The two were congratulated and received into the group. Daddy, who listened intently to Dr. Burton's cataloguing the wonders of bronchial tubes and gallbladders, was claiming the human body was poorly made and should be reconstructed, adding, "Any dunce can see that."

Once Stephen whispered, "What the hell is this all about?" and I replied, "God knows."

Thin roast beef, chicken and lobster salads, devil's food cake and jellies of all kinds were served, but nobody seemed very hungry, except Daddy who ate food upon sight of it. Then, quite suddenly, everyone was standing and saying good-byes and thank-yous; the Burtons left in a group with my parents and the Farrars, then Rinaldo left with the two musicians.

I got up to go with Mamma, but she whispered, "You can't go yet, Mercy. Cousin Ruth wants to say good-bye to you."

So I said, "All right, you wait, I'll tell her good-bye."

But Mamma said, "No. She wants to visit with you. It's her last chance."

The doors closed, leaving only the elderly man—his sister had gone with the group—the waiter, now busily removing the dishes, and Cousin Ruth and me.

Voices of the departing guests were echoing in the street outside as I witnessed a transformation in Cousin Ruth. The over-friendly look dropped from her face and she turned to Elderly, he of the sharp black eyes, who seemed to be waiting. "You'd better go along now, Jack." Her voice came out cold and flat as she stared at him across the table.

"But I thought I was invited to . . ."

"You were. Go along now."

"But why?"

"I want to talk to my cousin. She's going away soon."

"But I thought . . ." He didn't finish as Ruth passed by him into the hall, returning with his hat and walking stick. And Smile.

"It was nice of you to come."

"Well, I *see*." He bowed to me, muttered, "Good-night then," and hurried out. Cousin Ruth slammed the

332

door behind him; it made such a racket in the hall it shook the folding doors.

I waited uneasily on the love seat, staring into the fireplace, now filled with pots of summer greenery, rubber plants and ivy struggling with crysanthemums and fading geraniums. I heard her saying to the waiter, "Just stack and rinse the dishes." Then, "Yes, that's all. You needn't stay any longer."

It seemed to me I waited on the love seat a long time, but logic tells me it was likely no more than ten minutes. I thought of leaving. I could tell Mamma I'd said good-bye; I'd just make a dash for the door. Only as I turned to see where she was, I found her staring in my direction as if she were reading my mind. As our eyes met, I knew I had missed my chance and that the waiter had gone. Cousin Ruth came into the parlor and pulled down the blinds. When she came toward me, furious, I was afraid.

She sat down on the love seat opposite holding a glass in her hand. "What were you and Stephen whispering about?"

"Nothing much. Why?"

"I didn't invite her."

"Who?"

"His mother. But he had to bring her along. They broke up the party. Is that what he was saying, they were going to leave soon and . . . ?"

"No."

"Then what was it?"

"Mamma said you wanted to say good-bye to me. I've got a lot to do. I'd better be going."

"What was it Stephen said, Mercy? You'd better tell me."

"Why?"

"You'll be sorry if you don't."

I blurted out, "He asked me, 'What the hell is this all about?' "

A pink flush crept up her cheeks to her forehead as she stared across at me. She didn't say anything, though. Then she lifted her glass and drank all the brown stuff,

I supposed it was whiskey, and when she put it down the smile stretched slowly back over her long lips.

"Well now, Miss Engaged, he still whispers to you, doesn't he?" I didn't answer. "I reckon you think you're still engaged." No answer. "And I see you're still wearing his ring."

Mamma said for me to wear it. "It goes so well with your yellow wool," and I did. But Cousin Ruth couldn't see it now, as I had my left hand at my side where I kept it all during the conversation, so she must have noticed it before.

"Hold up your hand, stupid. Let me see! Let me see!"

I should have bolted, but it was too late now, and seeing her face harden into the old cement smile, I held up my hand and let her see the ring. I watched her stare at it. Then the smile vanished. Her mouth fell open as she stared and stared, and a stone turned over in my chest as she got up from her chair and strode across the room. In a second, she was standing over me. She reached for my hand and before I could stop her she had torn the ring off my finger and was trying it on. I watched, fascinated, as she stood there, pressing and pressing until it finally went down over the fourth finger of her left hand as she pirouetted around the room in a wild dance step, her eyes riveted to the ring, her hand outstretched.

"It's pretty." Her voice went soft, as if she were speaking to a lover. "It's really pretty." And then, exactly as if it had been given to her, "Oh, I like it, I really do! It's just what I would have chosen for myself." She sounded as if she were speaking to someone there with her in the room, and I remembered Virginia Anne's early pig Latin when she came to live with us. *Eshay's azycray.*

"You'd better give it back now, please, Cousin Ruth. I've really got to be going. We've said good-bye."

"Oh, no, we haven't said anything." She hurried across the room. I could hear her moving glasses around. I got up, deciding to just run on out and get the ring the next day, but she saw me stand up because she

334

ran back across the room and stood at the end of the love seat.

"You're not going anywhere. You're staying right here. I know how you got this ring. I know all about you and Stephen and that boy. I watched you and I told on you."

"You told? Who did you tell?"

"Never mind." She moved sideways. She looked sly and coy and cruel all at once. "I knew who to tell. I know how to make things happen." Watching her, I remembered Martha Washington, the Mother of our Country, looking down at me, whispering, "You'll never make it. Not you." Ruth was prancing around, holding out her hand at an angle to see the ring to best advantage. Smiling again now, she seemed to be addressing an audience, speaking the playwright's lines in her very best voice, preening, "I told on you, and there's nothing you can do about it. They all thought it would work out different."

"Who thought it would work out different?"

"Never mind. I'm not going to tell you. Only if you want to know, that's why your old Johnsy's dead. He'd be living right now if you weren't so bad."

A stone turned over inside me. "You're crazy," I whispered. *Crazy* was a cruel sacred word, never to be said aloud, but to be passed from one person to another in pig Latin, or whispered behind peoples' backs. After that word was uttered about someone, he could never come back fully into the world, or so we thought. Yet here I had gone and let it out. Cousin Ruth didn't seem to mind. I wondered, had she, perhaps, heard it spoken in those big old buildings she had stayed in, where young girls looked out through barred windows at green trees on a lawn and automobiles passed on the roads of a Sunday, filled with free, laughing people? "Anyway, nobody would believe you," I finished off.

"No? Maybe not. That's why I took pictures."

"You what?"

"Took pictures. Oh yes, with a camera. You all oughtn't to've had those windows open." I stared at her, only half believing but remembering we had thought we had seen faces at the windows. "You want to see them, Mercy? I hid them down in the basement, where nobody'd steal them. Come on down, I'll show them to you. Hurry up now."

I followed her down the dark steps into her basement, but the minute I heard the upstairs door click behind us my heart began beating wildly. It was pitch black. I could hear Cousin Ruth moving around; she ran down ahead of me, but I couldn't see her. I stood still on the bottom step, wondering whether or not to run back up and try to open the door. I could creep up the stairs without her hearing me and make a run for it. There was still time, but then, slowly, I made out her figure in the red skirt as she lighted the wick on a kerosene lamp. She pressed down the glass chimney over the wick and the light came up full. "Well, where are the pictures?" I demanded, staying near the bottom step as I began to understand she was in no hurry to get them out. If the pictures didn't materialize, or if anything else happened, I could still run back up, I thought; but suppose I couldn't unlock the door up there, it had a catch lock and . . .

"Give me the ring and I'll show you the pictures."

"You've got the ring on your finger."

"I mean for keeps. Give it to me, and I'll show you what I promised."

I thought that over. "Show me the pictures first." She shook her head. I was beginning to feel pretty scared but I knew enough not to show it. "All right," I said, deciding Daddy would get it back, if she hadn't already done something with it. This last idea bothered me somewhat, but it was too late to change. "Now show me the pictures."

"All right. Come on over here in the light."

She reached down. I thought she was opening a drawer in the table, but as I approached she was just straightening up and I saw she had nothing in her hands.

"Well, where are the famous pictures?"

336

"Somebody must have stolen them. I put them down here and . . ."

"I don't believe you."

"Well, I took pictures in my mind. You come over here and I'll show them to you."

"How?"

"You'll see how. I'll demonstrate. I'll do to you just what Stephen and Johnsy did. Come on back, and then you'll know what I told them about you."

She was getting taller by the minute, as she came toward me in those long strides, and she had to duck her head when she got to the stairs, but I was already at the top step, feeling with my fingers for the knob. I pushed hard against the door. She was already on the step behind me, her arms around my waist, pulling me back down. I found the latch and tore away from her, stumbling through the open door and falling into her living room, with Ruth fast behind me. She started to pull me back by the hand but I shook loose from her and tore across the room and held on to the love seat. I was so frightened I couldn't tell what was happening. Then I realized someone was pressing on the bell so that it rang continuously. I started for the door, intending to run past her, but she stood in my way, pushing me back on the love seat. She walked out and soon I heard Stephen's voice, and in the next minute there he was in the room, and Cousin Ruth was smiling exactly as she had been when the party was going on, speaking in the selfsame actressy voice, "What a nice surprise. Sit down there with Mercy, and we'll all have coffee."

Stephen looked at me but he remained standing. "Can't now, thanks. Well, I guess you've said good-bye now and . . ." I got up and he said, "Good-night" as we hurried out, but she followed us to the door, got there before us, and was turning the knob when I spoke up. "The ring, please," was all I said. She threw open the door and pushed us out; then she stood on the top steps, where she seemed to be twisting the ring off her finger and having trouble getting if off. I wanted to wait and get it back, but Stephen didn't seem to understand what was happening. He had hold of my arm and was hurrying me down the steps and into the street. I heard her call after us. I thought she said, "There!" and turned to see her as she threw something into the street. It fell near the maple tree next door, hit the trunk of the tree and fell back on the earth just behind the wrought-iron protector where it caught the light from the lamppost at the corner and sent out small silver and gold signals.

It's empty in the house. An afternoon, sunny, sunny September day. The only close sounds are from Rose downstairs in the yard mumbling on to her sister Dahlia who is paying Rose a visit. Dahlia thinks it is all right, even fashionable, to wear her new pink dress in the street, with burlap tied around her feet, provided there are satin bows tied around the burlap. Rose insists on shoes, but Dahlia claims shoes hurt people's feet and are only for wintertime. I'd like to talk to somebody, but Rose is too busy trying to tame Dahlia. I might go visit Marian Swoboda, or better still, Clip. Only he goes off somewhere in the daylight hours, nobody knows where.

Where I am going, people will all have lives and purposes of their own and won't have to go spying on a young person. It must be awful to have no life force of your own so you have to go looking to warm your hands at other people's little bonfires. I knew because I hadn't any bonfire going myself.

Once I had these bonfires going, all right. Once I had Al-Balkhi at nights, he of the sword and the white horse. Where are you gone now, Al? What in hell kind of a thing are you, that one person's leaving me can make you vanish? Left me with no character. I am not Sister Carrie, Hurstwood's mistress. That was when I had Hilary and Al-B. And I'm not the heroine of a great new drama, fully alive, many bonfires, that was when I had Stephen and Johnsy—oh, fully alive.

Now I am in between. A person separate, and separated, wounded. I'm not sure if I'm in a dream or waking state. I am in a street where the houses and the people walking can't be seen because of the fog; there are blocks and blocks of this gray street with no crossings, no particular color. I imagine as I go on, the only way for me to get out of this street is for someone to come and claim me but, as I walk on, I begin to think the person who will claim me may not know who I am because I, too, am gray like the street, without distinguishing marks, *and so is the claimer*.

I thought I heard the clump-thug again in the Dowses' yard, so I get up and look out the window. Nobody down there, of course, only that awful, ugly wooden shed, the dart board still on the outhouse with the last dart sticking out. The thug-thug is coming from somewhere over in Riggs Alley. There are certain things I'd like to speak about, questions to ask, the kind even if you knew a person a thousand years you wouldn't ever tell, and that's when I feel this separation. I can still hear a voice calling "Ex-ter papar!", hear him breathing beside me in the dark movie theater where we watch Lon Chaney climbing the steeple. I experience him as mine, belonging to me. He didn't have to understand what I said; he listened with this animal secret he had that made him contented with his lot, gave answers in that sweet animal silence. Johnsy!

Someone is knocking at the door. I hear Rose. "Whatsa matter, you up there by yourself?"

I say, "I'm writing."

She's inside my bedroom carrying a parcel wrapped in brown paper. "Why'n you come down help me get shoes on Dahlia? She's walking out tonight and she won't put on no shoes." I promise I'll come down and help, seeing the shoes have become a problem.

"What's that in your hand?" I ask.

"It ain't nothing but a package Mrs. Dowse left for you." I take it, and she goes out, mumbling directions. "Cleared up day like this and you sittin' up there by yourself. You gotta be gettin' ready college clothes 'n' papers an' things. You come on downstairs, you hear?"

I open the brown paper parcel addressed to me from

Philadelphia and find a large photograph of Johnsy, about ten by twelve. In a gilt frame and covered with glass. He must have had it taken in Philadelphia. There's a letter attached, addressed to me, and, forgetting to mail it, he brought it along on his last visit home. It is not a good likeness; it's a color photograph, his cheeks are too pink, his eyes too blue and his head of curls more violet than red, but his big lips with the grin are there, his dimples showing, and he looks as if about to burst out laughing at something.

"Dear Mercy," the letter reads, in his awful scrawl, "I got a lot to tell you when I come home and it's all good. Don't you worry about a thing, you hear. With love, Johnsy."

I start to cry and I cry so hard I have to lock the door. Every now and then I stop crying and I think of all the dead people I know. My grandpa is dead, but he died wheezing away of double pneumonia. He is really dead, I know. Aunt Grace had an operation and came back all white and quiet and waiting. She is so dead she can come back and haunt people and scare them half out of their wits. Miss Mamie Callendar down the street is dead all right. Here are two big dead people, Grandpa and Miss Callendar, who went off in black coffins and had black crêpe on their doors. And Aunt Grace in a gray coffin with gray crêpe on her door. And Rose's Mammy—my, is she dead! And the time it took her. Stiff dead, you might say, like the dead birds and cats in the alleys, given a good chance for a long, last look, why, they practically faded off like a long day. Not Johnsy. He's more like hiding somewhere, say, behind the piano. His eyes are bright and, my God, I can see the line of dirt in his fingernails.

It's getting hot in my room. I'd better wash my face and help Rose with Dahlia's shoes. And put away that crazy letter and forget the entire contents, especially that line telling me not to worry about a thing.

The clock on the mantle in my bedroom tells me it's five to six. For some reason, this clock is friendly tonight. Maybe it just looks that way because I'm leaving it. I'm already dressed in the very same navy blue dress with white silk braid and pleated skirt I'll wear on the train the next day. The cape to go with it is hanging on the door, together with my bag bursting with extra paper, notes in a small notebook, notes torn from a large notebook, letters, lists of things to do, plots for novels, poems, prefaces.

The front doorbell has already rung twice, and from downstairs booms the big, convivial voice which can belong only to Uncle George, a man who, even at this early hour of the morning, sounds not only content with life but capable of great courage and brave deeds. I hear Daddy and Mamma answering him in controlled, conciliatory voices, but there's laughter here and I conclude Uncle George has barely arrived at his first stage.

I was not in the best of humor toward my parents who have, as I consider it, betrayed me utterly and in the most shameful fashion imaginable. It's not their first betrayal, it is one in a series of betrayals common to all *as-if* people—the people who act *as if* they're going to do something for you, perhaps even love you, and instead take something away from you, nor is it their last betrayal. But there is something majestic about this one, a regular Alps in the mountains of their former thrusts.

In the course of "breaking" my "engagement" to Stephen I had to act, that is, to do something concrete to end things in a friendly but proper way. With this in mind, I discussed it with my parents, starting with Mamma.

"I'll have to let Stephen know and, of course, return the ring," I said at some point in the conversation.

I remember Mamma moved forward as if about to leap. "Oh, yes." She sounded as if she'd been waiting for just these words, "You must write a letter," she began. I don't know what else she said, but later on in the course of the day Daddy took up the subject and

341

reiterated her words as if they'd rehearsed it all before-hand.

"You write your letter, dear, and we'll have Rose deliver it," Daddy concluded.

Stephen was away visiting his grandfather at the moment, so this seemed as good a time to write the letter. The minute I finished and sealed the envelope, I went into Mamma's bedroom to get the diamond from her jewelry case, but it was locked, as usual, the drawers and closet doors kept locked in that house, hinting of secret fears, of gnawing anxieties far beyond the actual value of the objects locked inside. So, deciding the letter would have to wait till Mamma returned and gave me the ring in its pretty velvet box, I came downstairs and left the letter on the buffet.

When I came home late that afternoon I found the letter was gone. Daddy, in his Morris chair reading the newspaper, told me Rose had "taken care of everything." Since this was a matter of concern to me, I wanted to hear more about it. Who, for instance, had received the ring and the letter? Was Stephen home? Or was his mother at home? Daddy didn't know. Rose wasn't in the kitchen, she was off for the afternoon and we were going to dine out that evening. So I had to restrain my burning curiosity.

Late the following day I had a letter from Stephen waiting for me on the table in the hall:

Of course I understand, dear, but please keep the ring. I want so much to think of it on your finger. Don't deprive me of the one small thrill left. Love, Stephen.

There was a P.S.

The ring didn't arrive with the letter. Hope it wasn't mislaid. But if it was I'm sure you'll find it. S.

My face felt hot, my hands damp. I read the P.S. again. *The ring didn't arrive with the letter. Hope it wasn't mislaid.* The ring had not been mislaid, I knew that much immediately, but Rose just might have forgotten it. I tore into the kitchen where she was calmly shelling peas and asked her straight off, "Did you deliver the ring to the Farrars' yesterday?"

She looked up at me, her big eyes staring through circles of blue velvet smoke. "What ring?"

"Did you deliver a package?"

"I ain't seen no package. Your daddy gimme a letter an' I taken it over."

When I found out what had happened I felt another plug being pulled out of my gut. Daddy had sold the ring! And for a pretty good price, I gathered. Mamma was the first to tell me. "What would a young girl like you want with a diamond ring in New York City? Why, you might be murdered, for pity's sake!"

Daddy came in shortly afterwards. "Jewels don't bring in dividends laying around in cases," he explained. "Sending girls to college costs a fortune today. Time to put all the money we can get into stocks." He tried to explain how *we* were buying stocks on margin, making it sound as if *we* were not only smart but somehow heroic, having committed an act requiring brains, strategy and courage. We'd soon be moving out of this neighborhood into a bigger house in the suburbs.

This is a family dinner, I remind myself, the kind people take pictures of, paste into albums and show for years to come. I am sitting at the dining room table, wearing the navy blue dress. I *was* going to wear the blue rain ensemble, the one I had on the day I went to meet Johnsy and Stephen, but I felt so funny every time I saw it, I shoved it into a paper bag, and seeing how crushed and stained it was, Mamma had it cleaned and gave it to the House of the Good Shepherd.

Uncle George is sitting near the buffet where he can reach the decanter of bootleg whiskey; four bottles arrived this very day from Daddy's drugstore downtown. Aunt Jenny is laughing at Uncle George's jokes, the special kind of provocative remarks he makes when he is in his first stage. Jenny is settled into one of those recognizable lifelong arrangements in which she can safely give good warm food instead of the more personal benefits of marriage. Aunt Margaret, the other old maid, is growing larger and plainer by the minute, but nobody notices, or, if they do, they like it. She loves everybody, would give you anything, and this gives her a long, sweet glow.

Honey tells Mamma she's marrying Raymond sometime in the spring or summer, as if these seasons were two different hours. She confides to me she might just change her mind and marry Clarence, who is more impetuous and pushes her harder to name the day. "I'm going to do it, Mercy, I swear I am. Only it's so scary. You go off and get married and after that you just can't *move*. It's like getting hit by a big old truck." Once married, she'll let her behind "grow itself to death" and her bosoms "shrink down to the bone."

They speak of my going to college at Barnard, the female part of Columbia University, as if it is a place where girls go to learn and die, where all the odds favor being raped or murdered or meeting up with men of unknown "background"—financial standing—perhaps the very worst form of death. And when I say, "This is Nineteen Twenty-nine!" or "Girls know how to take care of themselves!" nobody believes me, not even Honey.

The dinner has a dual purpose, to let the relatives see me as I am for the last time, a culture virgin, before the horrors of education and career take their slow, inexorable toll, to see me with my face still fresh before the drop by drop of the Chinese torture marks its lines, and second, to give Uncle George the opportunity to tell me a few things, wise me up about life in the big city.

Some time after dinner, around ten or so, I find myself sitting in the parlor with only Uncle George for company. The other guests have gone, Mamma and Daddy to drive the aunts home and have their visit at Grandma's. Raymond has called for Honey, unlocking her hot arms from around my neck where in a trembling voice she whispers, "Nothing will ever be the same." Raymond looms big beside Honey, he looks so big and capable, she looks little and soft as she goes off.

Uncle George sits staring at the empty demitasse cups. I ask if I can pour him more coffee, but he shakes his head. Mamma has left one of those half bottles of champagne in a small ice bucket, with two glasses— "just enough for each of you to have one glass, and that's all"—thinking he might drink champagne and forget the whiskey, but I can see it's going to be the other way round. He pours himself a drink from the whiskey decanter, drinks it down, clears his throat, so I know the talk is coming. My newspaperman uncle will now tell me about New York, how to get around on subways and buses from where I'll be staying at the home of my Cousin Clara who lives near some place called Gramercy Park to where I'll be studying much further uptown.

"Things are going to be different, Mercy," he says. Adults always start talking about "things." "Yessiree, things are going to be different, if you believe what old man Babson in Wellesley Hills is saying." I listen politely, waiting for the real talk to begin. And meanwhile it's not too clear to me what Uncle George is talking about. "People're getting too greedy," he says. "Easy money. It's got to have an end."

"I thought you were going to tell me about New York."

"Oh yes, of course I will, dear." But he pours himself another drink and, when he starts up again, what he says makes even less sense to me, something or other about "hard times." He keeps saying, "But you won't feel it too much. You've got that crazy thing, that youth."

He reaches for the decanter again, but this time I stop him. "Mamma left us champagne," I say. "Aren't you going to give me my glass?"

"Oh yes, of course I am. I'll uncork it right away." He does, too, and most efficiently, and we click glasses.

I try to sip mine slowly but next thing I know I've drunk it all, and am just wishing I had some more, when I see my uncle crossing to me and refilling my glass from his own. I start sipping my second large glassful of delicious cold champagne and, as I do, I begin to feel kind of excited. I see Uncle George reaching for the decanter. "Never cared too much for the bubbly," he says. I notice his voice is getting fuzzy. I hope he won't fall on the steps when he leaves and begin singing "Stand up and cheer," because if he does I'll have to go and get Elvin way off there in the alley down near Grandma's.

Meantime, he goes on talking, but I don't seem to hear him very well. Maybe that's because his voice is getting thick, or maybe it's because of the wine. Or then again, maybe it's because of what I am *seeing*. I try not to look, I try to think. *I'll be leaving here to-morrow. I won't be sitting in this parlor any more watching for Stephen's window to light up. I won't feel the horsehair sofa against my legs or listen to the street sounds as I peer through the shutters. Maybe I'll never feel the horsehair sofa again. They'll get new furniture when they move to the suburbs.*

The red roses stand out on the grass-green Brussels carpet. The petals open as I look, the yellow centers widening, moving, as if they're coming alive and getting ready to speak. The streetlight falls in the same familiar oblongs through the shutters, gold over green, green under gold. But the gold part is lifting up, or is it that the green part is pushing it up? I close my eyes and take a big sip from the glass.

For no real reason I think of old Jesus. And then of Dr. Gardiner and Stephen, and it's like a dream. Maybe it is a dream. Why, Al-Balkhi on his horse is more real than Dr. Gardiner and Stephen, stronger, too. And then there is Johnsy, he is real, Johnsy the backward one, alive and loving, and that is why . . . but that is the nightmare part of the dream, where the horses with flying manes and foaming mouths carry the dreamer home and set him down hard.

Uncle George is saying something. He's going to tell me about New York. He's going to—oh, no—but he is—singing, "Stand up and cheer for old Columbia."

If you're inclined to believe there really is something peculiar and almost unworldly about all this business of being alive, and damned mysterious and unintelligible, why, it's like the secret code is in the mind of someone who happens to be a mute! If you have a hunch like that, well, then you know how strong it can hit you riding in a train. You've suddenly left the regular, noisy world and entered a world that moves at its own pace, a soft, cushioned cone of a place in which remarkable new people move down carpeted aisles speaking in soft voices. Everything extra fresh and interesting, the plush seat of the chair, the gray-haired black porter with his easy smile, the long-legged stranger in the chair next to mine who is just now stretching his torso as he glances sidewise at me.

I look through the window to where fields of brush and goldenrod are just beginning to sweep by. In the bright sunlight the sudden sparkle of rivers and lakes light up here and there like huge diamonds. There are big houses in the distance half hidden by the trees, and ugly flats and tenements up front near the tracks with small windows cold as angry eyes. Right now, I feel as if I'm being carried back into the world after being picked up by a powerful wind. It's already noon now, the first bell for luncheon has just rung. People are getting up to go in, singly or in groups. I decide to wait for the second bell and listen to my unknown friends whispering to one another as they walk down the carpeted aisles. A man with dark gray eyes and a discrete smile looks at me as he passes. Who is he? I wonder, and what does he know that grants him the bemused expression?

The old dream is ending. Remember what I told you about the bonfires, about Johnsy and Al-Balkhi, well, now I feel it breaking down, being sucked back into the past. And I'm glad, I feel more comfortable with them gone. What a cast! All those people—all that has happened, I feel over a hundred and fifty thousand hours coming and going in one moment.

What am I taking with me? Nothing, if you want to know the truth. You can't take anything from a dream—except maybe a message—*if that*. But wait now, Daddy took something out of this one: the money he got for the ring. You remember my Daddy's talk about the stock market. What's the name of that man in Chicago —Sam something? Well, Daddy's putting all his money into securities with this Mr. Sam . . .

What about me? What am I getting? A new dream. I'm entering it right now on this train. I can feel it, too. You can't take too much out of these dreams, but, Jesus, it's fun to feel the new one starting up. Maybe this one will be good. Rose told me the plants liked to burn their heads off, and that makes a bright thought, crazy as it is.

But what my Daddy got is definite. These securities he's got from this Mr. Sam—oh, Insull, that's his last name, Mr. Sam Insull, well, at least, Daddy's going to be rich.